ne

You're not dying

Poet and novelist Kathrin Schmidt was born in 1958 in Gotha in the former German Democratic Republic and lives in Berlin. She trained as a psychologist and later worked as an editor and a social scientist before writing full time. Her first poetry pamphlet was published in the famous 'Poesiealbum' series by the GDR publisher, Verlag Neues Leben, of which Christa Wolf had in earlier years been editor-in-chief. Two further collections were published in the GDR. In the process of Germany's reunification Schmidt represented the anti-reunification United Left, the most left-wing of several newly-formed groups in the GDR, at Berlin city's round-table discussions. Schmidt's to-date eight poetry volumes and five novels have garnered a host of residencies and awards, notably the Leonce-und-Lena Poetry Prize in 1993, and in 2009 she was awarded both the annual prize of the reputed Südwestfunk Radio Best List and the German Book Prize for *You're not dying (Du Stirbst Nicht)*, beating a shortlist that included Nobel Prize winner Herta Müller. The novel has since been translated into thirteen languages. Schmidt's short story collection *It's over. Don't go there (Finito. Schwamm drüber)* translated by Sue Vickerman will be published in 2021.

Also by Kathrin Schmidt

Poetry
Poesiealbum (Lyrikreihe), 179. Ausgabe, 1982
Ein Engel fliegt durch die Tapetenfabrik. Neues Leben, 1987
Flußbild mit Engel. Suhrkamp, Frankfurt am Main, 1995
Go-In der Belladonnen. Kiepenheuer & Witsch, 2000
Totentänze. Mit Karl-Georg Hirsch, 2001.
Blinde Bienen. Kiepenheuer & Witsch, 2010
waschplatz der kühlen dinge. Kiepenheuer & Witsch, 2018
sommerschaums ernte Kiepenheuer & Witsch, 2020

Novels
Die Gunnar-Lennefsen-Expedition. Kiepenheuer & Witsch, 1998
Koenigs Kinder. Kiepenheuer & Witsch, 2002
Seebachs schwarze Katzen. Kiepenheuer & Witsch, 2005
Du stirbst nicht. Kiepenheuer & Witsch, 2009
Kapoks Schwestern. Kiepenheuer & Witsch, 2016

Stories
Sticky ends. (science fiction novella) Eichborn, 2000
Drei Karpfen blau. Berliner Handpresse, 2000
Finito. Schwamm drüber. Erzählungen. (short story collection)
Kiepenheuer & Witsch, 2011
Tiefer Schafsee und andere Erzählungen. (short story collection)
Leipziger Bibliophilen-Abend, 2016

You're not dying

Kathrin Schmidt

Translated by *Christina Les*

Naked Eye Publishing

First published in the German language as
"Du stirbst nicht" by Kathrin Schmidt

© 2009, Verlag Kiepenheuer & Witsch GmbH & Co. KG,
Cologne/ Germany

© 2009, Kathrin Schmidt

First published in English translation
by Naked Eye Publishing 2021

English translation © 2021, Christina Les

ISBN: 9781910981139

Book design, typesetting and front cover by Naked Eye.

Cover photograph © 2021, Mike Kilyon

nakedeyepublishing.co.uk

Translator's acknowledgements

Many thanks to Kathrin Schmidt for such detailed answers to all my questions. Thanks also to Sue Vickerman, Jutta Heinen, Mike Kilyon and David Gordon for their support, suggestions and generous hospitality. Finally, thank you to my family, particularly Bill and George, for cheering me on.

This translation is dedicated to all my German teachers over the years, but especially Frau Heinen.

Christina Les

I

In the blink of an eye

THERE'S A CLATTERING ALL AROUND HER. When her sister got married, their mother had put all the silver cutlery in a metal bowl lined with foil. Then poured in hot salty water. After a while the clean cutlery was taken out of the bowl and dried, and it had clattered just like this. Who's getting married then? She tries to open her eyes. Nothing doing. She doesn't attempt anything else. Enough for now. But she can very clearly hear her mother's voice. Aha, so it *is* the cutlery! What's her mother saying?

'The right hand's a lot colder than the left, though,' she's saying, 'and the right foot's the same.'

Why is her mother's right hand cold? she wonders. And can't help smiling, imagining her checking the temperature of her feet.

'She's laughing!' says her mother.

'It's just her face twitching.'

Did her father say that? Yes, that was definitely her father's voice! Now she really does want to open her eyes. What's she doing in her parents' kitchen, where they're clattering cutlery and checking the temperature of their hands and feet, and she can't open her eyes?

'Oh, where do you come from? From London?'

She said that to her daughter in English. Didn't she? She's able to open one eye, and does so. Her girl is fourteen, and set off on a language exchange to England today. Why is she back already? She's crying. For some reason she's crying. That must be why she'd wanted to speak English, to cheer her daughter up. It doesn't seem to be working. Something's upsetting the girl. But what? Who can she ask? Her gaze wanders. There! Next to her daughter is her husband. '*My husband*,' she says in English. Hopefully that'll make them all laugh...

Nothing.

At least the man is smiling. The more she looks at him, the stranger his smile looks, hanging there as if tethered between his cheekbones like a *Salzgurke*.

'*Salt cucumber*,' she says.

Does that even exist in English?

'...date of birth is 3/12/1972, lives in Hückelhoven...'

Stop! That's not her! Why can't she shout it out loud like she wants to? She has to, damn it!

'All right, don't get yourself in a tizzy, we'll be with you in a minute!'

Who said that? That young man there? She thinks she might be able to open both eyes at the same time. It's a bit of a struggle – there seems to be something on her eyelids. The young man smiles, but that's hardly reassuring.

That's not her, though! She's fourteen years older, and doesn't live in Hückelhoven!

'*I don't... I don't...*'

Why can't she get any further with the sentence? Now the young man is telling the other men in blue coats that since she's been waking up again on and off, it's almost as if she's trying to speak English. The men laugh. She looks for a woman. There's one standing behind the men, but she seems to be busy with something.

One of the men leans over her.

'Can you hear me?'

She's not going to tell him whether she can hear him or not. He can bellow away as much he wants.

Eyes tight shut.

She knows that voice. It's Inga. She seems to have brought someone with her. 'Come on in!' says a deep voice, but then there's the sound of falling over, followed by a gloating laugh. Why can't she just open her eyes! She has to work out what just happened. Her friend Inga wanted to visit her and was encouraged to come in, but there must be a deep pit on the other side of the door. They've fallen into it. She becomes agitated. Is she in fact lying down? Why? She tries in vain to lift her arms, legs or head. That's making her even more agitated now, she realises. What's happened to her friend, whose voice she heard so clearly? Ah, there she is again, unsurprisingly upset. It can't have been easy getting out of the pit, then? 'Come on in!' says the deep voice.

After a while, though, she starts to wonder: where has Inga got to? Surely she can't have fallen into the pit again?

She's moving! She's going forward like the *kleine Häwelmann*. Or rather *kleine Häwelfrau*. It's nice. She could do it forever.

Except the light's dazzling. She should have known, really, that the moon would be this bright up close. She had just never thought about it before.

She's moving.

She's moving!

Once again, she can only open one eye. She's in luck, a woman! The woman is smiling and seems to be riding along next to her, though the woman's upper body, unlike hers, is upright. She wants to suggest that the woman lies down too, it's lovely to ride along like this. She's got something in her mouth. She can't close her mouth at all. She wants to ask the woman what she can see stuck in her mouth, but the woman takes her arm and connects it to a tube. Some kind of network? So they can control her remotely? Heavens, that's scary. She wants to defend herself, but the eye snaps shut.

The top of her skull is being taken off. A robot carefully removes a blood-red piece of flesh. Something needs to replace it. So the robot is going to insert a wonderful, light-blue piece of stone. What was the stone called again? It won't come to her. Her daughter has a bit of stone like it, and has declared it a fake because of the colour. Aha, this must be something different, then: the robot won't be wanting to stuff anything fake into her head! When the piece of stone is in, everything that's been unpleasantly bright up to now gets darker again. A brief moment of twilight. She can just see a long, thin, flexible plastic tube above her. Where's it going, and where does it come from? Shame she can't move her head and follow it along. Dark browny-red liquid is moving along inside it like rolling teardrops.

For some time now, a noisy young woman has been busying herself around her, talking incessantly. Who's she got so much to say to? Is there someone else there? She can't turn her head, but yes, there is… Now she really needs to open her eyes because something is changing, she's being brought upright, lifted, sat down. She starts to feel sick. It must be something funny she's eaten.

The torrent of words from the woman comes closer and closer.

'… Can you hear me, Helene? Not easy to say so, I suppose, is it? Anyway, soon we'll have to start getting you upright more often. Today was the first attempt, okay? Okay? I think she can hear me…'

Was that addressed to her? She doesn't know. Wants to sleep. Knackered.

Funnily enough, she can believe her name is Helene.

What's the man got in his hand there? Looks like a pacemaker. Actually, he's holding the pacemaker in front of her nose, and saying that they've finally found it and taken it out. Why've they removed her pacemaker? She can't get the question out. The man laughs slyly, laughing behind his hand – a hand that has her and her heartbeat in it. She has to defend herself, anything but fall asleep. They must have the heating on at night here – last night it was so hot she thought the place was on fire. That must be why they've taken her pacemaker out, because she's the only one still alive and they can't believe it!

If you've got one of these pacemakers your heart just beats and beats, even when your body's had it. They all smile at you in such a friendly way here, and yet it's a murderers' club: they want to kill you just as they do all the others. She absolutely must tell her husband. Hopefully he'll come again before night-time. Where is she, anyway? She's managed to keep her eyes open for a good while now, but she just can't work out where she is.

Her parents are back! She wants to sit up and ask who's got married. Why've you got a cold right hand, Mum? She can't do it. Can't sit up, can't ask.

Pulling herself together.

Pressing her lips together. Opening her eyes.

It really is her parents! Her father looks exactly like he did that time her sister went down the Geissenberg on her scooter. How long ago is that? She works it out. Is it 2002? Her sister was born in 1961 and was about six when it happened. So, 1967. That makes it thirty-five years. So long ago! Why has she remembered the look on her father's face? Daddy, don't be sad! she'd whispered at the time, and he'd hugged her and cried with joy when the doctor brought her sister home again. No, they didn't want to keep her in hospital.

In hospital? The house she was staying in now could also actually be…

Her mother interrupts. Asking the woman next to her when she can start having something to eat again. Typical, always thinking about eating. She's not hungry, though!

'That won't be for a little while yet,' the woman says. 'She's being tube-fed for now, you see.'

Tube-fed, see. Satisfied, she closes her eyes.

A young man on the left, one on the right. They're looking at her, and they seem familiar, but she doesn't want to look them in the eye.

Actually, she would like to know who they are. They're smiling and talking quietly to each other over her head. She has a think. Wants to ask the one on the left to pull the ... a bit lower, so that it's more in the small of her back, but she can't think of the damn word – what on earth is it called? She makes signs to both the boys for what she wants, namely that they pull the ... a bit lower for her. They don't seem to understand.

What did she even use to make these signs? Her hands? The left hand is fastened down, with a tube in it. Is she still hooked up to the network, still being controlled remotely? She wants to signal her fear to them with her right hand, but it just lies there and won't move. Strange. Why can't she move her hand? They must be using the network to control all her movements.

And the boys? Are they network operators? She has a closer look at them now. Relief: she knows them. They're her sons. Their names won't come to her, but that doesn't matter right now. She thinks she's laughing. Her sons! Why didn't she look at them sooner? Then she'd have been happy for even longer! One of them is at university. Where's he studying again? In Weimar. Oboe. Yes, oboe. The oboe son holds a CD under her nose that he's burned himself – there's something written on it but she can't make it out. He puts the CD into a little gadget and the headphones into her ears. Ahhh, that does her good, what lovely music. Oboe. She must surely look blissfully happy, she thinks.

So now she starts to think about what she looks like. What *does* she look like? She has no idea, she can't picture herself at all. They've pinched the picture of her! It's like being in limbo, which comes before Hell proper, and proper Hell comes at night, when it's dark. Somehow her sons have got to be made aware of this – they can't just leave her here and go away again! Are you two listening? Hello, where are you? She looks up, exhausted: the boys have gone. Completely unaware of the danger.

A blonde woman comes up and busies herself with something next to her. She tries to turn her head at least a little bit. The blonde gives her a dirty look, but she manages to do it, and sees a whole load of monitors all piled up on top of each other. The blonde holds a pouch of mud-coloured mush in her hand. She hangs the mush on a hook and fastens a tube to it. 'Lunch,' she says, and laughs.

No, she doesn't like the blonde woman. And the blonde woman doesn't like her. She likes the young girl who never stops talking. She has dark hair. When *she* comes, the fear goes away. With the blonde woman, it comes back. Coming and going. Between the blonde woman and the dark-haired girl there's also a man. A moment ago he was wiping up her poo. That was embarrassing. She has no idea what's going on down there. What exactly is going down there? Ah, here comes the man again. He pulls the bedcovers to one side and her legs apart. Stop, you can't do that! Stop! But he smiles, like they all smile here, these criminals. Is he washing her? He's washing her. It's pleasant actually, she should stop resisting. He hasn't noticed her resistance anyway, has he? So she lets herself be washed. Why they don't let her do it herself, she'd rather not know in too much detail. No doubt they want clean corpses for the coming night. Not shitty blood dolls like her. She's bleeding, you see. Her nappies were full of blood. Nothing hurts, though. It can't be that bad. What's the date anyway? No idea. Her daughter has recently gone off on her language trip, though. That was the tenth of July. And yet she was back again on the same day! When she thinks it over, she can't understand it. Are we on the fifteenth or sixteenth of July? Yes, probably. Or thereabouts.

Could it be her period? She's going round in circles. When was her last period? She can remember how her father looked thirty-five years ago, but not when she had her last period.

Now the man's putting a new nappy on her.

She wants to sleep.

More hustle and bustle in the night, above and below: beds creaking, trolleys trolleying – they must really have been struggling to deal with the removal of all the bodies. She now knows just what they do with people: they extract all the moisture from them with unimaginable heat while simultaneously driving an electric current through their bodies, so they're left with a dry, wrinkled little block. She's seen blocks like that before, someone had built a wall out of them somewhere. Maybe they even build houses out of them! Has she resigned herself to her fate? She was tense when she herself was lying in the dryer. The man operating it said she seemed to be too fat, it wouldn't work, so he turned it off and brought her back.

She's definitely scared, but it isn't making her sad. That surprises her. It's just the way of things, that you become aware of almost everything when you're nearing the end. Something still wells up inside her but it's getting less and less. Last night she'd been hopeful of clearing off out of here. The young bum-wiper had sat next to her. Somehow he'd understood that she doesn't want to die. He gave her to believe that during the night he'd hide her in a store cupboard, and in the morning, when he'd finished his shift, he'd take her out with him. She was happy.

Of course, nothing came of it. Instead he came in the morning and said goodbye. Only with a slight wink did he let her know the attempt had failed.

To hell with it. He can hardly risk his job and his life to get her out of here.

When the blonde woman approaches, she gets agitated. The

blonde woman's always fiddling about with the monitors and is definitely one of the ones controlling her. She falls asleep whenever the blonde hangs those bags on the hook above her head. She doesn't want to sleep, but that's what happens. The blonde hangs so many of them above her, one after the other.

Sometimes, when she's awake, the troop of men comes by. Every time, at least one of them asks whether she can hear him. And each time she's too stubborn to answer. After all, she wasn't born in 1972 and doesn't live in Hückelhoven. If they hadn't mixed her up with someone else then she might've had the chance to get out of here sooner. There's no point opening her mouth and making the effort: they wouldn't believe it anyway.

'A-fa-sia.'

She knows the word, of course. But what does it mean? Why won't it come to her? She knows it from somewhere. When the man in the blue coat said it, she recognised it straight away. After 6pm, she wants to say out loud. Yes, afasia could be their way of saying after 6pm! Night-time starts here around six. No doubt they'll all be herded together and arranged in a spiral, once they've been knocked unconscious by the bag full of liquid. They watch from outside through a glass screen to see who dies. She's become so calm about it. If she's to die tonight, then fine, she won't resist it. Why would she? She's already discovered their secret plan anyway: they make little blocks out of people and stick them in the landscape.

 After six o'clock, then.

 She says her goodbyes. Her time has come.

Hang on – is she still alive, then? It's dark. In summer it's only dark during the night, not in the morning or evening. So it's night-time. Why is she not lying in the big spiral with the others? Maybe she's unexpectedly been the only one to survive again? If the campaign started at six it could have been over around nine, and now they've brought her back.

 Something is itching like mad on her head and she wants to scratch it. Does her right hand want to scratch it too? No, it doesn't. It lies on the bedcover as if strapped down. So she has to try with her left. She yanks it up against all possible resistance and can actually touch her hair. But where it itches, she doesn't have any hair. What's happened to her hair? That's why they've pinched the picture of her! Ha, she'll win it back, and that's a promise. With all her strength she starts to run her fingers over her scalp. They don't get far. There are little metal anti-tank obstacles stuck in her skull and she tries to prise out two or three. Suddenly she feels fluid on her fingers. She tastes it. It's blood! Where did they get the right to ram these anti-tank obstacles into her skull? She starts to shout and throw herself around in the bed – and it's definitely a bed she's in.

 Someone is coming. The blonde woman? Yes, as it happens. She looks down at her moodily.

 'Oh, for goodness' sake, really? I'll have to wash and change you again now. I'm going to strap you down and take your cover away, to teach you a lesson. Who knows what you'll get up to otherwise!'

The woman keeps grumbling as she cleans up around her, putting back the anti-tank obstacles and cleaning the blood from under her fingernails. When she's finished, she binds her left arm and left leg firmly to the edge of the bed with a piece of white material. The bed seems round to her.

There, she's hanging yet another bag on the hook!

She's freezing when she wakes up. Absolutely freezing. It's cold here – so the blonde really did take her cover away. Now she's making her report to another woman who's also in a blue coat. They're both standing a little way from her bed.

'Frau Kiering, Yvonne,' says the blonde. 'Punctured lung after a road accident.'

Here we go again. They're still mixing her up with other people. The blonde says Yvonne Kiering has slept peacefully through the night. They never once look at her while spreading such lies about, of course.

Or are they perhaps not talking about her at all? She tries, slowly, to follow their gaze, arriving at another bed, with another woman in it. She seems to be unconscious. She's got tubes in her mouth and nose, in her arm and in her groin.

Where did she come from, all of a sudden? Could it be she's not the only one to have survived the night?

Questions upon questions.

Questions upon questions. There's a rattling in her head when she's awake. She seems to be awake for longer now. Which means the rattling goes on for longer, too.

Yvonne Kiering! Born in 1972 and resident in Hückelhoven! Now she gets it! She laughs loudly, pleased she's worked it out. She wants to tell the dark-haired girl, who's currently doing contortions with Yvonne Kiering. But Yvonne is unconscious! Since when can you do contortions with people who are unconscious? Oh, it's so stupid that she can't say anything. Why is it she can't say anything? After all, what she wants to say takes shape in her head. It just doesn't come out of her mouth. She lifts her left hand, with the tube in, to her mouth. And her nose. What, has she got tubes there too, just like Yvonne Kiering? Right, that's it. Determined, she pulls them. It doesn't hurt. She pulls and pulls. The dark-haired girl calls out. Comes over to her bed. Asks in an aggrieved tone whether she wasn't enjoying her food.

'Were you not enjoying your food, then?'

But she's smiling a bit, too.

There's a knock at the door.

'Your husband's here, Frau Wesendahl.'

Wesendahl… Her husband is here. Is he called Wesendahl too? Before she can think about it, her husband takes a step towards the sink. He pulls a plaster off and removes a dressing from his right eye. Gosh, what's wrong with him? She'd so like to ask him, really she would. When he comes to the bed, he's crying. Has she had a baby perhaps? The last time she saw him cry was when their youngest daughter was born. That was five years ago, and he'd stood at her bed exactly as he's doing now. She has a quick look, just in case there's a bundle of baby on her chest.

No.

Just checking, obviously.

Is there something wrong with his eyes? That would explain the crying.

Why, in the time she's been here, has she not once thought about her five-year-old daughter? And – she has another one! And another! Five, fourteen, eighteen, twenty, twenty-three – yes, she actually has five children! Astonishing, the stuff that just pops into your head.

Three hundred and twenty-seven minus eight times seventeen. The minus eight in brackets. That makes three hundred and nineteen times seventeen. Three hundred and twenty times seventeen is… five thousand, four hundred and forty. Take off another seventeen, and that makes five thousand, four hundred and twenty-three.

A little bit beyond her feet, in the corner of the room, is a table. Two pots of yoghurt on it. Paperwork. And a picture. Curious, she cranes to try and see it. But that's me! That's the picture of her they stole! Didn't she say she'd get it back? She can quite clearly see medium-length dark hair, a narrow face, full lips. Eye colour? The picture is black and white, you can't tell. Weren't her eyes blue? She tries to picture the colour of her eyes. Blue. With a watery tinge when the sun shines, shot through with dark speckles in dull weather. She's glad to have the picture back.

What do you say to that, Lissy?

Wouldn't it be lovely if she could ask her!

Because Lissy is there. She has come with Natascha. Lissy is her eighteen-year-old daughter, and Natascha is her husband's. Yes, she believes her husband was married before, before they got together. She's almost as fond of Natascha as she is of Lissy. Or has she got it the wrong way round?

The two of them have brought a wheelchair, and want to take her home in it. Surely they want to take her home. But why can she only see the wheelchair when she closes her eyes? She doesn't know. When she opens her eyes again, it's gone. Oh, Lissy and Natascha have gone now, too! Shame…

She cranes to see the picture of her again, but it's not there any more, either.

She thinks it might've had a black ribbon on it.

She gets yoghurt to eat.

'She pulled her feeding tube out?!'

The blonde woman had asked the dark-haired girl this, incredulous.

Now she has to be fed.

She smirks.

'What are you smirking for?'

She knows exactly why she's smirking.

She's not going to tell her, though!

The black-ribboned picture is in a long white tent, on a table right at the front. Rows of chairs behind. Where is she looking from? She thinks she's floating under the roof of the tent.

The rows start to fill up. Her parents right at the front. Oh, her in-laws are there too! Good to see you both. Her children. His. She and her husband have three together, and they both have another two. Uncle Willi comes in, he's over eighty now. His wife Urte. Aunt Stössel, Cousin Tabea, Aunt Usch – but hasn't she been dead for years? She's surprised. Uncle Karl. Aunt Karla. Kira and Kaja, their daughters. There's Max, the father of her second son, whose name she can remember now: Bill! Ah, Billy, little Bill … Both Ritas, Pietro, Elke, Carmen, Yvonne, Ingo – so many people, it's getting pretty full! What's the occasion?

She looks expectantly at the doorway, but nothing happens. Everyone goes quiet, not talking to each other. If anything, they all look rather sad.

Someone is pulling at her legs. She looks round. Ah, her husband. He wants to pull her out through a flap in the front bit of the tent, but there's no need. She slips out of the tent herself. Her husband hugs her. He says that the people are waiting for her funeral, but they've got it all wrong because it's not going to happen.

Look who I've brought with me!

She turns around and is struck motionless with joy. It's Sulagna! She got to know Sulagna last year in India. Sulagna is five or six years old, nobody knows exactly, because she'd been found in the street with neck wounds full of maggots. Hadn't they wanted to adopt Sulagna? Oh Sulagna, seeing you here now…

She wants to hug her, but Sulagna makes a firm gesture: both hands raised, to keep her at a distance, then a finger on her lips. What's this, how can Sulagna direct her like that? Now Sulagna lies her flat on the floor, lifts her right foot up a bit with both hands and holds it tight. Sulagna waits. Her husband sits a little to the side, looking tense. Suddenly she can feel a current wanting to pull her back into the tent. Only a flap in a piece of fabric separates her from her own funeral. She laughs. The current gets stronger and stronger, but Sulagna sits quietly and holds on to her leg. What strength the girl has! The current can't make any headway against this little one. She's actually not bothered how it's going turn out.

How long *is* it going to go on for, though? Shouldn't she get some sleep first?

Sulagna seems to have managed it. She's still alive, isn't she?

Matthes will surely have taken Sulagna home with him. So now they have a sixth child.

Matthes? His name is Matthes!

'Mads.'

She opens her eyes and looks into the face of the dark-haired girl.

'There you go, that's your first word said – now the rest will follow.'

'Mads? Mads! Mads, Mads, Mads, Mads…'

Was it her saying that? Her voice sounds brittle. No 'e' to be heard, and the 's' just a buzzing sound after a 'd', instead of clicking its heels after the 'e'.

Matthes comes more often now.

Or is he coming as often as before, only then she was always asleep? Not a pleasant thought.

Every time he visits, Matthes takes a dressing off his right eye before he comes over to her bed.

She'd really like to ask him how she ended up here, because she just can't remember. But she can't say complicated things like that.

She says:

'Hey, Mads!'

or

''lo, Mads!'

He understands. He understands! It sparks her ambition.

'You Eulen?' she asks him. He looks at her. Is he thinking about it?

Calls out suddenly, 'Yes, I'm Eulen! Yes, yes!'

She wouldn't be able to say 'Jandl', she thinks. Or 'Mayröcker'.

She got lucky there. 'You Eulen?' had slipped out quite easily.

Yvonne Kiering isn't there any more. She's alone again.

Again?

◆ ◆ ◆

The bum-wiper de-tubed her today.

A tube out of her bladder.

The tube from her hand. ('The Venflon's staying in, though!')

She has the feeling something's being removed from her groin area, too.

He gives her a machine she has to breathe into. The balls inside have to be moved to the next level up as she does it. She tries. Fails miserably.

As well as that, there's a little board with four springs on it. She has to hold it and press the springs, one with each finger. She wants to reach for it with her right hand but doesn't manage it.

'Can't do it.'

'Why can't you do it?'

'Right hand can't.'

'Use the left hand then!'

'Why?'

Has he understood the question? Will he give her an answer? Why can't she move her right hand?

He doesn't give an answer. Instead, smiling, he takes her left hand and presses the springs. With her fingers.

What is a Venflon, anyway?

The troops arrive.

'You're being transferred today.'

Transferred? What does transferred mean? Are they going to pretend afterwards that they can't remember where they disposed of her? Her fear – here it is again.

Hello, Fear.

Nice of you to drop by.

The fear doesn't listen to the friendly greeting. It gets straight to the point. Stands in the corner of the room with a sledgehammer, ready to strike.

'You're going to Ward 21, we need your bed.'

Relief. Of course, transfer doesn't mean just dumping her somewhere and forgetting about her, but moving from one place to another. Not out of choice, though, right?

The bum-wiper comes with a wheelchair. She's put in it, and wheeled out of the room. The sudden warmth takes her by surprise. Why is it so cold on the other side, when outside it's glorious summer?

The bum-wiper carts her up and down two corridors so she can see the ward one last time, and does a loop to the staffroom.

Farewell.

She tries to look cheerful, but oddly the thought of saying goodbye brings tears to her eyes.

'Now then, Frau Wesendahl, just be glad you've done it! Three weeks in intensive care is more than enough!'

Intensive care?

Once again, she can hear almost a rattling in her head. She ponders why she might've been here, but gets nowhere.

II

Shadow Shapes,
Silhouettes

SHE HAS SLEPT WELL. It's nice without the tubes. But twice she forgot to call for the nurse, even though the button was on the edge of the bed, right by her left hand. So the bed got wet. To start with she found it pleasantly warm. She'd better be careful now, though, or they might put the tube back into her bladder.

The wheelchair stands next to her bed. If she wants to go to the toilet, someone has to take her. A nurse comes, sits her in the chair, wheels her there, sits her on the toilet seat, waits, wipes her bum, pulls her knickers up and her nightie down, and wheels her back.

Sometimes she feels sick when they sit her up.

Sometimes, when she's on the toilet, nothing comes. That happens when a male nurse is standing next to her. She just can't wee or poo in front of a man. The urge just vanishes. She wonders if her body soaks it up. Absorbs it.

The moment she thinks of the Latin word 'absorb', the fog lifts from another foreign word: aphasia! Without speech!

She has to laugh, remembering that she translated it as 'after 6pm'.

Eight hundred and nineteen minus four hundred and fifty-two? Three hundred and sixty-seven. Is that right? Yes.

◆ ◆ ◆

She's lying in a room with three beds. Alone.

Although now there's a rumbling in the doorway. A woman is wheeled in. She gets the bed by the window. She'd have really liked that one herself. She gives the woman a friendly nod. The woman smiles.

But doesn't stop smiling.

Her smile looks like it's fixed in place with fishing line as fine as a cobweb. She looks for holes in the corners of the woman's mouth where a double line might have been threaded through, and looped behind her ears. Helene finally notices that she doesn't have her glasses on.

'Gasses,' she says aloud, 'gasses.'

Still no 'L'.

'Gassesgassesgassesgassesgassesgassesgasses.'

It wasn't her saying that, it was the woman.

The nurse comes to introduce herself to the woman.

'Hello, Frau Schröder!'

'Frauschröderfrauschröderfrauschröder!'

Why is the woman repeating what other people are saying? Is it something to do with echolalia?

She's delighted that she sometimes has foreign words at her command.

It's also just occurred to her what it was she wanted to ask her sons to put behind her back, when they were there: the pillow, of course.

She grabs the pillow with her left hand and plumps it into a fat ball.

Goodnight.

Of course *goodnight* was inappropriate. It's only lunchtime. She's wrenched from sleep and fed. Still with mush, but it doesn't look as beige as it did when it used to come through a tube. Today it's mashed potato. She turns her head away when the nurse dips the spoon in gravy. Socialist gravy, they used to call it. Only on the third go does the nurse realise she doesn't want gravy.

Why didn't she just tell her?

'Not gravy!'

'I've already gathered that!' she laughs.

Already?

She doesn't get the big, light-blue pill in her little bowl any more. She's pleased about that. They can keep it up. Since that pill hasn't been there, she's been staying awake for longer. Today they took the anti-tank obstacles out of her skull. She didn't feel anything. They weren't actually anti-tank obstacles at all, but metal clips. It seems her head has been operated on. Why? No idea. When she's taken to the toilet, she's eager to have a look in the big mirror. She hasn't noticed it until now! That surprises her.

So *this* is what she looks like. Can't argue with that. On the left half of her skull, she hasn't got any hair. No, that's not quite true: there's two or three millimetres of new hair sticking out. A fine red line runs in a high curve from the hairline on her forehead, down to her ear. On either side of the line, which is about fifteen centimetres long, she can see fat red dots. They were made by the clips and remind her of an avenue of felled trees, the stumps of which are only just poking out of the ground. One stump is inflamed and it hurts.

Interesting, she has to say.

Broca's aphasia, she thinks suddenly.

When Matthes comes, she tries it. She tries to tell him that she'd like some reading material on types of aphasia. Matthes doesn't respond. Has he not understood her? It's probably incomprehensible.

Matthes hasn't got a dressing on his eye any more. He looks so young! He's brought the newspaper with him and she wants to snatch it eagerly out of his hands. The tenth of August! She's already been here more than a month. She just can't comprehend it.

Should she be puzzled that she can do sums pretty well, and keeps setting herself exercises? Practising sums in her head? Whatever. She decides she'd rather not let it puzzle her.

Instead, she waits. Waits for something to happen. Nothing happens here. Nobody comes to do contortions with her. In intensive care the dark-haired girl used to get her moving. Or rather, would attempt to get her moving. But here? 'This is your third day now on the general ward,' Matthes had said earlier, 'and you shouldn't be here at all.' He's obviously trying to get her moved somewhere else. She hasn't understood where to. The door opens. A young woman comes in and introduces herself as a physiotherapist. Finally! A minute ago the word "physiotherapist" wouldn't have come to her, but the moment the woman says it, it's at her disposal again. She wants to hear words. Instead the physiotherapist bundles her into the wheelchair, and wheels her out and down, across the way, and into another building. They arrive at a big exercise room.

'You should definitely be moved over here!' the physiotherapist says.

'What's here?' she asks. Ooh, it's working!

'Stroak yoonit,' says the woman.

'What's that?'

Before the woman can answer, it comes to her. Of course, the Stroke Unit – for patients who've had a stroke! What would she be doing in with the stroke patients? She looks at the physiotherapist doubtfully.

The physio says she's been called over at the behest of her husband, to exercise her. And that would be much easier at the Stroke Unit because you don't have to factor in the journey over, and she'd be able to look in on her from time to time as well. Plus the Stroke Unit has speech therapy and occupational therapy, which she could make very good use of as well. On the general ward she'd just be left lying around.

That's true.

She's starting to speak. She still can't believe it. She can't say much, and what she does say is often clearly wrong. Matthes was here again today and asked her what she'd had to eat. Sand. When he asked again, she said sand again. He repeated it, and then of course she realised: sand was totally wrong. She'd wanted to say quark. Quark with potatoes. They had a good laugh about it.

Matthes said that her move to the Stroke Unit was a done deal. When does he manage to do it all? Could it be that he's in the hospital longer than she supposes?

The lady in the bed by the window often has visitors. Her husband and son come. The son is about twelve. Frau Schröder seems to understand very little. You can't communicate with her. The husband and son laugh a lot. They already seem to be familiar with her in this state – it comes as no surprise to them that she doesn't understand them.

Today she asks Matthes what happened.

'What happen?'

'You had a brain haemorrhage,' he says. 'A ruptured aneurysm.' She's gobsmacked. She hadn't expected that. She has a vague memory of reading a lot about aneurysms not too long ago. Why was that?

'You've been operated on. Twice. The first time they clipped the aneurysm, and the second time they moved the drainage tube from one ventricle to another.'

She's heard everything. She'll just have to take her time over understanding it.

Aneurysm comes from the Greek word *aneurysma*. Aneurysma sounds nice, she thinks. A girl's name. "Aneurysma Wesendahl". She wallows for a while in the thought of being called Aneurysma.

The male nurse comes into the room, all vim and vigour, the usual jokes at the ready.

'Now then, Helene love, did we sleep all right?'

'Nah, not really, Hartmut love.'

He laughs. Actually, last night she'd had another panic attack. She'd imagined a big fire all around her. In a state, she'd called for the nurse. The one who came was the nicest one here. She had stroked her hair and put the light on. She remembers saying something. What it was won't come to her. The nice nurse had told her that nothing and nobody can threaten her here. Helene had realised she was starting to believe her. It was the first time since she'd been here that she'd come anywhere near believing something the staff said. As if the nice nurse had straightened up the facts again, just when she was starting to get used to them being lopsided.

'Old Hartmut's taking you over now, to the Stroke Unit!'

At last.

She's allowed to go to the toilet by herself, until she calls the nurse to come and get her. She gets taken to a common room, and gets proper food. She gets exercised. She gets visits.

Natascha is there again today, her husband's daughter. Natascha is already twenty-seven.

Matthes has put Helene in the wheelchair and taken her down to the hospital café, where she has an ice cream.

Natascha has brought her a flat mussel shell from the Atlantic. She's been to France.

In a flash she has a memory: Helene is reading to Natascha, who's four. As a friend of Matthes's first family, Helene has stayed overnight at theirs, and Natascha has come into her room early in the morning to wake her and fetch her for breakfast. She's wearing a little short-sleeved vest and washed-out grey pants. She wants a story. Her brother Mischa is two.

Just as suddenly she remembers that, three years ago, Mischa stepped in front of a high-speed train.

The Natascha visit ends in tears.

She's unable to say why.

Ward rounds.

The nurse is relating how Helene had called out for her in the night, crying, because she'd pooed herself. Strangely, she hadn't been able to say anything about it, and just pushed the covers to one side and showed her the place... It stank, and was already starting to sting, to burn, like she remembered it doing. (So how old had she been when she last pooed herself?)

'If she's depressed to this extent, we'll have to increase her dose.'

But no, she's absolutely not depressed! Are you not allowed to cry when something's embarrassing?

'No, ... don't.... want... attidepresses!'

'Really? You ought to, though, because things aren't easy for you now.'

Not easy?

She's astonished. That she feels no grief at all.

'What medicine... for sadness?'

The nurse looks at her questioningly.

'For – sadness, for – crying!'

Damn it, just when she wants to say the word antidepressant, it's gone. It comes back: another try. Again it disappears the moment she starts to speak.

This aggravates her so much she starts to lose her temper.

She snorts.

'Oi, less of that temper – just doing me job!'

'Anti... anti... de-presses.' It comes out a bit mangled.

'Oh, right!' The nurse laughs, and points to a little tablet in her bowl. Strange that such tiny pills are supposed to take away immense sadness.

She takes the tablet out of the bowl and puts it to one side. She swallows the others. One of them is an antibiotic for water infections. She doesn't really need it, because she's had asymptomatic bacteriuria all her adult life.

But she's not able to say that.

She's still getting the antidepressant in her bowl. She makes no secret of the fact that she's not taking it, but nobody notices. So she's got a nice little collection of pills in her drawer already. She wonders who she could give them to. The only person she can think of is Raphael. Raphael wants to come and visit, today or tomorrow. Raphael has depression, but refuses to take antidepressants because he's scared of getting addicted. She can't give him the pills, then. Besides, he's mostly okay as long as he has someone to fuss over. She'd never have thought that the Someone might soon be her.

She sighs.

The occupational therapist comes in the mornings. She practises getting dressed with her, without much success. Cleaning her teeth with her left hand goes well. Squeeze toothpaste on to the brush, run water into the cup – a one-handed adventure. She can get the flannel wet, but there's not enough strength in her left hand to wring it out so she can get through face-washing without mishap. Afterwards she looks like a drowned rat. Luckily it's a warm day, and her underwear will soon be dry again. After her morning wash, the occupational therapist takes her to breakfast in the common room. She's given a little board with spikes sticking out of it and suction cups underneath. It gets fixed to the table. She pushes a bread bun down on to the spikes, and tries to cut it up with her left hand. The sweat is dripping off her. She spreads butter and jam on it and gets stuck in. As of yesterday, she no longer gets a cup with a spout. Some of her drink runs down her chin, it doesn't all reach her mouth. The right side of her face is paralysed. She laughs when she pictures herself laughing with only half her face.

Her sisters are there. When the door opens and they step into the room, she's so surprised that she wets herself in her excitement. Luckily neither seems to notice. Marika is three years younger than her and Ellen six. One lives in Dresden and the other in Thuringia, where they all come from. Helene is touched that they've come all the way to Berlin just for the afternoon, so they can visit their big sister.

Why are they looking so awkward? She's so pleased to see them! Ah, now she can see why: fat, one-legged Frau Bandner in the bed opposite has flung off her flimsy nightclothes again. She's tube-fed – a tube goes directly into her stomach. When she flings her clothes off it means she's pooed herself. Yep, it stinks in here. They have to call the nurse. Ellen and Marika are sent out of the room. They want to take Helene with them. But she's wet from the wee, so tries to stall for time and signal to the nurse without them seeing. Unfortunately the toilet is right at the end of the long corridor, so she can't get there unnoticed. She gives up and shows her sisters the mess she's in. Now they look even more awkward, and Ellen is red as a beetroot. Helene tries to say that she'll come out once she's been changed. They head off for the time being. Hopefully only as far as the corridor? It's a while before the nurse can see to her. She washes her quickly in the bed, then strips it afterwards.

Next to Frau Bandner there's an old woman who was showing signs of dehydration when she was brought in. She's always seeing gunmen in the big tree outside the window, all aiming at her. That's why she's holding the lid of the chamber pot tremblingly in front of her face, too scared to move. Ellen and Marika must have seen her, too. If neither has any idea of Helene's condition, but see her in a room with two mad old women, then they'll come to their own conclusions. She'll have to convince them the opposite is true. But how?

When she's all cleaned up and wheeled out in the wheelchair, she sees that Marika has been crying. She acts as if she hasn't noticed, but it's too late for talking. Mornings are better. She guides Ellen and Marika to the cafeteria. Exhausted, Helene has a cup of tea, but then she just wants them to go.

The weeks leading up to her aneurysm have been wiped out. There's nothing left. Sometimes a fragment of a memory surfaces, but before she can grasp it, it's gone. All of a sudden, she wonders why her little girl hasn't been to see her yet. Why does she hardly ever think about her little Lottchen? After all, she's only five. When Helene closes her eyes, she sees a small face with almond-shaped eyes and an impish grin. Does she love that face? Of course she does! It's really tugging at her heart now. She absolutely must ask Matthes, *must must must* not forget.

She should come up with some sort of memory thread that she can pull herself along. It's bound to be arduous, but how else is she going to get those lost weeks back? It could even be months. Matthes says she was in an induced coma for two weeks. Do you have dreams in that time? She *feels* as if she did, but the transition from dream to experience is a fluid thing. At any rate, when it comes to this film she's piecing together, those two weeks can be edited out straight away.

Does she love Matthes?

There's no tug. And there used to be. She knows that much.

A visit.

'Where's my little Lottchen?'

Great delight that she's remembered to ask about her. She hasn't forgotten her. Her youngest child. Matthes explains that she's with Helene's parents. Hopefully their little one will be having fun there... Her father will take her on the summer toboggan run at Inselsberg, or to the leisure pool in Tabarz. She's happy for her daughter, even if she won't get to see her for the time being.

Bengt has taken a term off from university, says Matthes, and Bill is spending a lot of time at the house in Karlshorst, even though he'd actually moved in with his girlfriend in the spring.

That's right, they have a house. They built it in 1998, just under four years ago. Suddenly the layout comes to her: the big alder-wood kitchen with the bay window; the long living room with a fireplace. The downstairs bedroom, Lottchen's room. Upstairs Lissy's and Mareile's rooms, her husband's study and – her study! Of course, she's a writer! She really hadn't been prepared for that recollection. She recalls books that she's written. Hadn't she been working on a new book? No working title pops into her head. It might not have had one yet, of course.

'Laptop!' she says.

'Got it right here,' says Matthes, and gets it out of his rucksack straight away. Now that's service for you.

Yes, now there's a bit of a tug.

What's 'before'?

She's piecing her forty-third birthday back together. She can recall so many people... Everyone came, even Carla from the Moselle. She had brought a man with her who Helene really took to. A stonemason from Rostock. She remembers: he touched Carla almost casually, which sent tingles down Helene's spine. Why can she not remember whether Matthes touched her that day?

He'd organised a quiz. *Who knows Helene Wesendahl best?* There, a question's coming back to her: *What does she touch first thing in the morning and last thing at night?* The correct answer: her alarm clock. And there, another one! *Which politician's spots would Helene really like to squeeze?* Every time she saw Gerhard Schröder on TV, her fingers used to itch. Amazingly, it was the stonemason – who'd only seen her for the first time that day –who got all the questions right and won the quiz. By contrast, she can barely remember her forty-fourth birthday six months ago. Maybe she hadn't wanted to celebrate it.

She wants to read Agatha Christie. Not Martha Grimes, whose early Richard Jury novels she'd really liked. She's afraid she probably won't understand Martha Grimes. So she'd rather have Agatha Christie. She'd read her as a very young girl, so maybe the familiarity would help.

Naturally she can say what she wants much more easily

using her laptop. She's put together a long list of things she'd like to do. Write with her left hand, for example. She'll need a pen and paper for that.

Matthes says she should try writing some poems. He's got a pen and paper with him.

Poems? How would that work? She just can't imagine it at all.

There's a gaping hole between Helene Wesendahl and any potential poem. A vast black one.

The fourth person has moved into their four-person room. An old lady who's had a stroke. She has the same humorous take on life as Helene. She says lemon for tissue, and litter bin for lunch. Mentally, she's perfectly sharp, and wants to go home to her flat. She just needs to be sorted out with her medication – blood thinners – so she doesn't have another stroke any time soon. She's small and dainty, and looks fit. They take turns keeping watch for Frau Bandner's pooing incidents. If they don't, it really stinks the place out. Helene talks to her first thing in the morning, when her speech is best. The lady gives good advice, and is totally understanding, because of course she's in much the same boat. When she says lemon or litter bin, she doesn't notice what she's done. If you repeat it, then she does.

Helene still doesn't have any reading material on aphasia. Maybe that's for the best. She's had her first appointment for it with the speech therapist, who did a whole series of tests with her. Stuff that. She can do a better job herself.

As soon as Matthes comes she feels calm and at peace. As if he has a magnet in his pocket that draws all of her confusion out of her. She watches Matthes, to see if his trouser pocket is swelling up because her anxiety is being drawn into it. Maybe the magnet's not in his trouser pocket at all, but in his jacket or his shirt! He takes his jacket off and lays it over the chair. She touches Matthes with her left hand: his hands, his head. His lumps and bumps. Yes, her hand recognises them, and moves over them as it would over familiar terrain. His skull makes her think of a military training ground with trenches, pits and hills. His hair, still very dark, is long. You can't see the lumps and bumps, and would think you were looking at a normal, rounded skull.

Her hand moves over his back as he hugs her. His shirt is wet – it's really warm outside. When he wants to let go, she puts her hand in his shirt pocket, too. No magnet. Now there's only the jacket left. She shoots furtive glances at it.

'What's up with my jacket?' Matthes asks.

'Magnolia,' she says.

Magnolia. A flower. Spoken aloud, as if she'd been daydreaming about it.

What does she actually dream about?

Helene can't tell the difference between daydreams, night dreams, coma dreams and anaesthetic dreams. One particular dream which really affects her has to be classed as an actual experience, because that's how she remembers it. She's on a prefab housing estate, sitting in a pub beer garden, and it's windy. In front of her there's a huge courtyard, with half-grown poplars, shrubbery, and a small pond at the lowest point in the hilly terrain. It's really blowy, the wind's whistling, and the nip in it makes her ears hurt. A crowd of thugs rocks up – repulsive, shaven-headed creatures – and she feels pity and disgust in equal measure. Pity and disgust. Pity and disgust. Between these two feelings there's no room left for her: she needs to make herself small, and somehow clear off out of there – but they've already spotted her. Cracking jokes, they come nearer. She sips her cappuccino in a bored way and looks towards the lake, when suddenly she sees them: toads, olms, salamanders, frogs in wonderful earthy tones, but with Indian faces. They're human-sized, smiling broadly, and slowly coming closer. Their warty-skinned cheeks and foreheads are olive brown, their eyes are dark, and they all have long, black hair. When the leader of the thugs follows her intent gaze, he's frightened, and cries out. His mates turn round in surprise, and when they see the Indo-amphibians calmly striding towards them, they scarper. The amphibians move through the pub garden in a leisurely way, apart from one toad-woman, who sits down at Helene's table and looks at her in a friendly way. Her tongue darts out to catch a fly, and she smiles at her. She reminds Helene of Jayashree. She'd had the Jayashree experience last year in Calcutta. She was a teacher, and German learner, who harboured illusions that she'd one day be able to emigrate, and her well-meaning clinginess wasn't at all easy to cope with. Helene wants to talk to her, but fears the usual questions: can she give Jayashree money for a flight to Germany, get her this or that Christa Wolf book, send her a box of coffee. Thankfully she remembers that this isn't Jayashree at all, and merely a toad with Jayashree's features. She asks its name in a friendly way. There follows a very loud, belching 'Quaaaaak', a slight bow, and it sets off after the others, leaping to catch them up. Helene sees them all go round the corner of the flats opposite, and is glad that they'd kept the thugs at bay.

At breakfast in the common room, Helene mostly sits opposite a young man whose spasticity means he can't eat by himself. Even so, he goes to great efforts to keep his bread roll on the spikes of his board, dragging the butter knife across it with his other hand, though it's down to pure luck whether the knife makes contact or not. Usually someone helps him, which he always grumbles about. Saliva drips out of his misshapen mouth. His shaved skull is disfigured by large scars. Somebody said they knew him from before – apparently, until recently, he'd delivered Meals on Wheels between Kaulsdorf and Köpenick. She's disgusted at the idea of having a meal delivered by someone with strings of spit hanging out of his mouth. Apart from that, he'd barely be able to hold the plates. As she's thinking about this, she sees herself in the wardrobe mirror. Oh yes, she can't hold anything in her right hand any more, either! She'll no longer be able to play the piano, or sew or knit, and her face looks different too, even from a month ago. She looks strange: fuzzy hair is starting to grow back where it was shaved, high up on the left side of her head, and look! – she's dribbling, too.

◆ ◆ ◆

Today she tries to write an email. It takes a while for her left hand to get her fingers in the right places. It's an email to reassure Carla. Matthes says she'd been planning to visit Carla the day after her aneurysm. Taking Lottchen on the train... After five sentences she's exhausted, but happy. She tries to envision the process of copying the emails on to a floppy disk, which she can then give to Matthes. That takes a while too. At home he'll be able to send them from his computer. She leans back, feeling quite cheerful, and suddenly an image of the cork board in their kitchen in Karlshorst appears before her. Yes, the tickets for the trip to see Carla were pinned up on it, she remembers. She reconstructs it: next to the tickets is a long list of important phone numbers; two little wooden jumping-jacks; a business card for Mr Nagarajan from Bangalore, who'd been wanting to send her an article for over a year. She laughs. And underneath – the list of things she meant to take away with her.

She's not laughing any more.

She'd been planning to move out.

Now the memory has come into her head, the left side of her body also goes stiff and numb. A gingerbread woman. When gingerbread gets wet, it goes soft. She immediately starts sweating, producing her own water to soften herself.

'What's the matter? Have you got a temperature?'

The nurse. In her state of shock, Helene hadn't heard her coming. After checking her temperature with her hand, the nurse wipes her face with a cool, damp flannel.

She feels sick. Going to f..., she thinks, as she comes to herself again. She lets the a-i-n-t out by itself, in an audible sigh.

The thought of leaving Matthes eats away at her windpipe from the inside. Separating...

Yes, Matthes had been living upstairs in his room, while she was sleeping downstairs in what used to be their bed. Everything had been arranged so she could move out for a few months. Months during which they wanted to work out whether anything still tugged at them? She'd been unable to even think about her forty-fourth birthday, so it got cancelled. When they were together, their sullen silence broke the top off each day, so that no single one stood taller than the others and they had to take care not to be crushed by the uniformity of it all. After all, they still had two of the children living at home. They hadn't said anything to Lottchen yet, but Mareile must have guessed what was going on. They'd blamed different sleeping patterns and Matthes's snoring for them being in separate rooms. The snoring really was very loud, but it'd never bothered her. Suddenly she's bothered that she can't hear it here: she wants to hear it now, right away! Although he's definitely been looking youthful recently, in reality he's aged. The muscles in his face look slacker than they did five years ago. His back is becoming increasingly hunched, and his stomach – once all gleaming sinews – now bulges slightly, bringing with it the beginnings of little flabby rolls around his hips. The buttons on his trousers with the 46-inch waist tear the buttonholes, and she fixes them on her sewing machine. Or used to fix them. He'll have to learn to sew, or else buy his trousers in the next size up.

It annoys her that she cares.

How is she going to face him, now that this knowledge has

returned and lodged itself in her throat?

There's just no time to sort things out on her laptop. Every word's a real sand-stuffed cabbage roll. When she was a little girl, Helene would play by herself in the sandpit for hours making 'cabbage rolls': wrapping wet sand up in maple leaves and poking the stalk through at the end so they didn't fall apart. In time she mastered the perfect rolling technique. She would gaze at her rolls in wonder, and arrange them according to their prettiness. When she went to bed at night and closed her eyes she'd see great piles of them. She feels the same pride with every word that leaks on to the screen from her cut-up-and-stapled-back-together brain. But that hardly ever happens. Occupational, physio, speech, psycho – the different parts of her rehabilitation are only ever referred to by their first names, but everyone knows they're all called therapy and they all rob her of time. She plucks time out of the darkness when her three neighbours are asleep, or during the day she'll go down into the grounds in her wheelchair, her laptop clamped to her side. Unfortunately it's old and not very powerful, and the battery only plays along for a while. But she knows by now that she can't keep going for any longer than the battery, anyway.

Helene sits in the shade of the lime trees, glad that no one's visiting. Lunch is finished. It was meatballs – Königsberger Klopse. The caper sauce always left a furry feeling on your tongue, something she's familiar with from years of eating in canteens – rat tongue, she used to call it. The rat tongue hangs around for a good while and isn't easy to get rid of. Hang on, though, Matthes brought her some chewing gum when he came yesterday. She roots around in the pocket of her tracksuit bottoms, and sure enough, there it is. Unwrapping it is tricky. Her left hand fiddles with it awkwardly, although the feeling is one of dexterity. Weird...

She sits and chews. The pungent peppermint flavour cleans out her mouth. The laptop stays snapped shut in her bag. Hadn't she wanted to get things in order? She can do it without her laptop. She wants to draw up a list in her drilled-into, sawn-open and spliced-back-together head, and it seems at first to be a completely normal, textbook list. Keywords on the left, and what she understands by them on the right. She finds it difficult to understand anything right off the bat, so she'll need a lot more time to understand the right-hand column than the left one. On the left she puts in the word Love. And on the right, the names of men? No, she laughs, on the right should be everything she remembers when the word love takes shape in her mouth – though her mouth isn't really making any shapes at all at the moment, inside or out. Everything's happening elsewhere. She tries to imagine the regions of the brain. Unfortunately she doesn't even know yet where the aneurysm happened. But it'd definitely happened, that much is certain.

Where had she got to on the list? Love. A feeling. It sees to it that your blood circulates faster. When she thinks of the word love, she thinks of being all hot and flushed. Of how addicted to Matthes she'd been. Where has that gone, where is it now? It's got to be somewhere! She's annoyed she can't find it in her head, that she can't get hold of it. It moves around in her brain behind white sheets, which flutter in her brain as if in the wind. What kind of wind could there be in your brain? Brain wind? Headwind? Prevailing headwinds? Such a din then prevails in her windy head that everything comprehensible suddenly becomes incomprehensible. She starts to despair, and wants to hurl the laptop away, but she's so worked up that she can't even get it out of its case. She doesn't know why she even wants to get it out of its case, when she can just as easily chuck the whole thing away as it is – away, be gone, into the nearby drainage ditch.

Someone shouts 'Mummy'. The voice seems familiar, and immediately makes her feel something like love, only she doesn't go all hot and red. So there must be another kind of love. How can she have just forgotten that? Why is it hidden away, until someone shouts Mummy and yanks her out of her list-writing – which is only a vague plan, an intention, anyway, and where even the first entry is secured by seven seals.

A little girl shouting 'Mummy', and holding a man's hand, comes running along the concrete path. They both stop, and the girl looks her expectantly in the eye. Curious, Helene looks back. Slowly it dawns on her that she knows who it is. Her little Lottchen.

Lottchen sits on her knee in the wheelchair as they all go back to the ward.

'Where do you live, then?'

Lottchen wants to know where she lives. Her absence seems

so long to her that she thinks Mummy has moved house. Moved out. Which she'd wanted to do, of course. If it comes to it that she has to stay here, would she then be closer to that intention, or further away? Yet another thought she can't get hold of when the question arises. Helene's (inwardly declared) uncertainty fights off any kind of answer, ensuring confusion reigns inside her head. Blethering about separation would be totally out of place in this situation. She makes a forcible effort to keep calm, and shuts her eyes, which is fine because Matthes is pushing her.

'Ow!' Lottchen shrieks, giggling. 'You're pinching me!'

'And how's it been in Reinhardsbrunn? Have you had a good time with your grandma and grandad?'

A trump card. Lottchen tells her everything Grandad's been doing with her. Looking for raspberries and bilberries in the woods. Telling her the proper names of birds, butterflies and plants. She's turned into a real butterfly expert, Matthes says.

'And look, Mummy, that one there's just a cabbage white, there are lots of those, but a peacock is much prettier and rarer, and you *really* have to hunt for a marbled white or a red admiral!'

Her own childhood had revolved around butterflies, plants and birds, which her father had watched with her devotedly. She's touched that he's now doing the same with her daughter, while her mother is at home cooking and baking, just like she used to. She doesn't even need to ask if that's the case: their behaviour is on a continuous loop. Suddenly there's something very calming about their history repeating itself. Her indignation that her mother stays at home to do her womanly duty, while her father shows Lottchen the world, has disappeared. When they came home, the laundry would be washed and hung out to dry, the potatoes would be steaming in the bowl, and there'd be fried black pudding and sauerkraut – she can smell it already. She'd never have thought, beneath her feminist outer layer, that there could be anything like indulgence towards her parents' self-assigned roles. Indulgence? No, if anything, it's gratitude that's spreading through her. Suddenly she sees her father, how he kisses her mother with a look of pride when he comes in. Why had she not been able to see that before, though she'd seen things clearly enough later on when her father came home from the same trips with her little sisters, and she'd been old enough to rebel against her own supposed destiny... Her mother had always worked – as a teacher she'd taught hordes of schoolchildren, day in, day out, to read and write. Had that not been enough for Helene? Had she been unable to see the division of tasks in her parents' actions? Hadn't it been so much calmer and less chaotic in their household than in Helene's own, with the five children, and wasn't that because it was clear who did what? Each person doing what they did best?

Strange how firmly-established opinions can suddenly pounce on each other, and show themselves in completely different contexts. How they can cancel each other out with little more than a single sentence, spoken by a child.

She gazed endlessly after Matthes out of the window when he left. It's a long time since she last did that. It was when they were still students, he studying Maths and she Psychology, and he'd been running to the tram from an ice cream shop on

Marktplatz in Leipzig. She can still see the way he ran. Long hair blowing, head swinging from side to side, flailing arms and a dangling stride which made his knees knock together constantly. The tram would get him home. His home was a flat in Wiederitzsch with a wife and two children. Born two years apart, one in his first year of university and one in his third. They were now in their fifth year.

He loved her.

She hadn't loved him.

Until they did that play together, student theatre, and she'd seen his awkward, bony shoulders while they were getting changed. She'd immediately wished herself into these awkward, bony shoulders and, astonished, watched her own transformation. She hadn't been able to imagine *going steady* with a man. When they slept together for the first time, he called her Little Blue Eyes, and talked the yellow cherries red on the tree outside the window of her student room. He'd smelt of fear but did it anyway. Her son Bengt was having his lunchtime nap in the room next door. She and Bengt actually lived together in a room twelve metres square, but her neighbour was away for a week and had left Helene her key. It was Bengt in the end who called her away from those shoulders. Matthes had got dressed fast. So fast, in fact, that he was sitting at the table like he always did when she came back in with Bengt.

She'd loved Matthes.

She'd watched him for a long time when he ran for that tram in Wiederitzsch. Her tears had been tears of hopelessness – the hopelessness which seemed to hang over their relationship.

If it's hopelessness she's supposed to be feeling now, it's not causing her any tears.

'You could leave the ward for a few hours without us knowing exactly where you are,' says the nurse, and winks at her.

What's that supposed to mean? Naturally up to now Helene has always signed herself out to go the cafeteria, or into the spacious hospital grounds, but never for longer than an hour or so. They wouldn't want to know where she was? Helene passes this on to Matthes when he next visits, and he raises the prospect of a little getaway at the weekend. Aha, she thinks, and is proud to have conveyed the information to Matthes without any further prompting. Unfortunately he still doesn't drive. Though she can't either, of course! Not any more! She hadn't thought of that until now.

'We'll have to sell the car,' she says.

'Let's wait and see,' he says.

He always says 'wait and see'. There's nothing to wait and see about. Any fool could see she won't be able to drive any more. She's angry.

Who's going to come and take her home for a few hours? It'll just have to be a surprise.

'See you tomorrow.'

There aren't many staff in on Saturdays. A nurse for the early shift, one for the late shift and one overnight, plus two young helpers doing their national service in the community. Those two are definitely glad to see the back of her.

It's just before two.

The lady in the bed next-door has her boyfriend visiting. A

really jolly pair, and both on the wrong side of seventy! He was supposed to bring her some knickers but couldn't find any at her house, so he's gone out and bought some. They're tangas. She rolls her eyes at him. Helene can see her looking very fetching in a tanga, with her petite and slender figure.

Frau Bandner, the one-legged lady, is dressed and grinning madly as usual in her wheelchair. She's waiting for the volunteer from the Catholic church who's supposed to be coming to visit her.

The shrivelled old woman is trembling with fear with her bedpan over her head.

Whether Helene goes or stays leaves her strangely cold.

At ten past two, a huge bunch of wildflowers steps into the room. Instead of a card hanging from them, there's Jürgen, dragging Ernestine into the room behind him. Top marks for the surprise factor, because they live a long way away, in Lübeck. They've been friends with Matthes for a few years. They put the flowers in water, bundle Helene into the wheelchair, and let the nurse know they want to take her down into the grounds – the weather's too nice not to. And once they're out, they wheel her slowly down the long concrete path to the overflow carpark. Hardly anyone knows about this place, but most importantly, it's free. Helene is amazed at how quickly they've found something like that out, not being local. Getting her into the car turns out to be quite a performance – Jürgen lifts her top half, the left leg she gets in herself, and Ernestine takes tight hold of her right leg, shoving it in after her with great effort. Folding up the wheelchair is a scene worthy of the stage. Finally, they set off.

Short sentences. Subject, verb, object. 'I saw you coming. I'm looking forward to home. You both look good. You're wearing a nice shirt. Your hair has gone grey. You've shrunk.'

You've shrunk? She doesn't know why she said that, or to whom, but Ernestine in the driver's seat hasn't heard, and it's Jürgen who queries it.

'Eh? What am I? Drunk?'

No no no: Jürgen's been through alcohol rehab, and a long period of therapy, and has been sober now for years. 'Chunky' comes to mind – she looks down and Jürgen is in fact wearing chunky sandals with his shorts.

'Chunky! Chunky sandals!' she repeats urgently, and Jürgen is off, rattling way. He talks so fast that by the time she's trawled through the sentence in her head looking for the subject, the object and the verb are lost forever. 'Socks-shirt-heat-athletesfoot-hands-feet-scholls.' Slim pickings. She shrugs her shoulders when Jürgen looks at her enquiringly, and goes red.

'That was too quick for me,' she says slowly.

'Then I'll talk slowly,' says Jürgen, quickly.

Everyone is standing at the garden gate waiting for her. Even the Farber family, from next door, and the Suschkes, who live on the plot in front. Many hands come and jiggle her right one; Frau Suschke is the only one who actually offers Helene her left. Former matron at the university hospital, so no surprise there.

Helene sees her children, all five of them, and just can't get her head round the idea that she once had enough room inside her for all that flesh. She sees herself blowing up like a balloon but Matthes quickly lets the air out, not wanting to let go of her again. She remembers wanting to make herself smaller, so she could slip under his wing whenever she had to face something unpleasant. Her finals. Various job interviews. But she was always so big and fat, which she was doubly conscious of when facing these unpleasant things. Firstly, because her size made it impossible for her to seek refuge under his wing, but secondly because it always put her at a disadvantage: examiners and employers maybe weren't interested in big, fat people. So she regularly turned up at appointed places with her shoulders hunched, and wearing loose, fluttery dresses. Hiding her extra padding was *in*. But she suddenly realises her black trousers have got quite a bit looser in the past few weeks...

In the house there's cheesecake: Matthes has been baking. Helene loves eating his cakes, loves the way he bakes them, but only manages to get half a piece down. Matthes reacts strangely, sending the assembled crew off for a walk – 'Just an hour or so!' – and takes her to bed. Before she knows it, he's on top of her, ripping off her clothes. She's not in the mood, she feels like an *invalid* – she's stammering, wanting to tell him, but physically doesn't have anything to counter him with. She thinks of all the weeks he has had to manage *without it*. She lies there in disbelief, unable to say a single word. Slowly something rises in the intact left half of her body, something she thinks she recognises: resistance. She doesn't dare deploy it. Matthes kisses her lavishly.

She's crying.

No doubt he thinks she's happy.

She thinks.

Matthes heads towards the others, pushing her in the wheelchair. The pushchair they'd had for their youngest daughter had a seat that swivelled, so they could either have her facing them as they went along, or let her look out at the world. Matthes usually chose to have eye contact with their youngest, and Helene would have her facing outwards. Now she's glad you don't have that choice with a wheelchair. Matthes would probably still be bent on eye contact.

Her tears have left behind salty crusts which she tries to wipe away. It's not enough. She scrapes the salt from her skin with her nails. Did that really just happen, or was it one of her indefinable dreams? She immediately despairs because she can't decide which it is. Her face is twisted into an ugly grimace in an attempt to stop herself from blubbering again. She can't close her mouth. She looks down, seeing her legs in their baggy trousers. There are beads of sunlight strung together with saliva. The strings extend until they come to a stop on the black fabric of her trousers, in even blacker blotches. She wants to break them up and wipe them away, but she hasn't reckoned on one thing: without a tissue, there's nothing in the world she can do about it. Like towlines they loop round her hands, which are lying, saliva-bound, in her lap. She musn't let Matthes see them.

Matthes sees them.

He acts as if he hasn't seen anything, of course, and pulls a pack of tissues out of his trouser pocket. He unfolds one and lets it sail over her head, on to her hands.

Helene still can't close her mouth.

Later they're all sitting in the kitchen together. Ernestine has brought berries from her garden, wonderful raspberries and blackcurrants. Helene feasts on them with abandon. When a berry falls off her spoon, it feels as if her right arm jerks towards it a little bit, as if to catch it. She cries out softly, and they all look at her in alarm.

'There! My right hand!'

She'd clearly felt the movement impulse, even if her arm probably didn't move a millimetre. Can nerves grow back? Were these phantom impulses? Were there connections trying to be made again?

Jürgen was the first to react.

'Wow, that's great! Everything's going to be okay again!'

Straight away he realises the thoughtless stupidity of what he's said. They giggle awkwardly. Jürgen because he hopes she hasn't heard his exclamation. Helene because she has heard it, and hopes it wasn't Jürgen who'd come out with it. Wordlessly they resolve to let it enter the netherworld of Things Spoken and Ignored. Lottchen treads on the fallen berries when she comes in from the garden.

It's nearly five. She's getting fidgety. Wants to go back to the hospital but doesn't dare say so. She longs for her bed and the peace she gets there once she's pulled the covers over her head. Of all the many people around her – there are eight still there – she can only make out silhouettes. She doesn't hear what they're saying. Little Lottchen's losing patience, Mareile's messing about. Bill's baiting, Bengt's berating. Lissy's loving. Jürgen's yacking. Ernestine assessing: there's nine of them, with Helene. Two too many for the seven-seater.

Matthes marshals.

She shrugs.

It's after ten. She'd fallen asleep as soon as she got back. It's by no means fate that she's awake now: the light came on for the shift change and they did ward rounds. Although everyone's been asleep for ages. Helene sighs. She goes over the day.

Did Matthes really sleep with her?

Her fingers reach into her pants, and when she pulls them back out, she smells them.

Fish.

It's true. It's true!

Even a few hours ago, she'd have preferred to say that she dreamed it. It's wonderful that things are now straightening themselves out, and she can compartmentalise dream and reality into different drawers. She's so pleased about this that at first she doesn't notice Fright waiting in the wings. When it suddenly looms over her threateningly, all her joy disappears.

She looks at the clock. It's ten past twelve.

She's having an intelligence test done. She's presented with rows of patterns and geometric shapes, and has to pick the odd one out within a given amount of time. Once she's been doing it for a while, it's ok. Then there are number sequences to complete. 121, 100, 81, 64 – what comes next? 64, 16, 4, 1, ¼ – what comes next? Easy. Admittedly, things look a lot different when it comes to speech-related tasks. She just about manages to find the odd one out in rows of animals or fruits, but reciting as many kinds of fruit and vegetable as possible in a short time, without repeating the root of any compound words, is infinitely difficult. Rearranging rows of letters into meaningful words brings just as little success. In the short-term memory tests, she's totally lost – even the shortest scenarios, just read out, are irretrievable within seconds, and don't come back even after several minutes. She's noticed that before now: she'll be wanting to do something – go and fetch something, or say something to someone – and in a second she's suddenly forgotten what she wanted to fetch or say. Then she'll roll back in her wheelchair two or three metres, and sometimes it'll come back. Mostly it doesn't, though. The tests show her to be of only just average intelligence.

Just how stupid has she become?

Uncertainty grabs at her.

Today she's got the afternoon off. That makes it sound like she's been labouring under some huge workload. As if. For her it means an afternoon free of *family*. Free of *visits*. She doesn't like to admit it, but she's glad. The grounds here used to be dominated by an enormous psychiatric hospital, which she knew well. They've now built an ultramodern trauma centre. The old buildings are still standing, scattered about. Two of them houseda private eye hospital. Helene starts the afternoon with a reconnaissance mission.

First, off in her wheelchair to the zoo. Fifteen years ago, for Bengt's eighth birthday, they'd come on a big trip here with the kids. They'd set off with a horde of eight or nine little rascals along the Wuhle, a tributary of the Spree, which stank back then and only flowed reluctantly in a few places. Lissy's pushchair was close to collapsing under the weight of all the goodies they'd brought: potato salad, little sausages and meatballs, three or four kinds of cake, and punch for the kids transported in the stock pot that had a lockable lid and a tap. Prizes for the party games of course. She and Matthes had really had to lean on each other at the time, what with Matthes drowning in tears because he wasn't allowed to see his children, and her scared stiff because she'd decided to declare Bill's paternity, contrary to the agreement she'd made with his father. Matthes had to pay maintenance for both his children, and it suddenly seemed absurd to go without money that Bill – not she – was entitled to. Six years without a father... Now he had to re-emerge from wherever he'd been.

A time of waiting.

Matthes was waiting for the authorities to convince his ex-wife of his existence. Helene was waiting for the authorities to turn a man into a father.

They clung on with all their might. She was in the better position, because no one could accuse her of anything. She sang louder than Matthes with the children, too, though he usually had better ideas for games. On that day they romped about, clambering over tree trunks and on climbing frames – she was still light on her feet. Suddenly two of the boys had disappeared. Her heart started thumping, panic spreading through her. At least they were in the grounds of a sprawling psychiatric hospital. Matthes was calm and in control as always; she was barking at him from the sidelines out of panic. He thought for a moment, then ran to the river and climbed into a sluice on the bank, emerging before too long with the muck-smeared little boys. Grinning, the two got themselves into a frenzy through all the excitement they'd caused. Helene and Matthes joined in – what choice did they have? – with their Red Indian howling, and persuaded the whole gang to come and have something to eat. While she's thinking about all this, the smell of meatballs wafts into her nostrils from deep inside her. Suddenly she sees Matthes: head slightly drawn down, back hunched, he's standing at the cooker, all tensed up. He has put two frying pans on it, and wants to light the gas so he can fry the meatballs. The gas flows, and she waits for him to light a match, but he does nothing – just looks down at the hand holding the gas knob, lost in thought. Now he looks up and across at her. His ancient eyes look right through her: somewhere far behind her there must be a much worthier object of his gaze. As she closes her eyes there must be an explosion, because when she opens them again she can see his skinless skull rolling towards her.

'Now then, Helene love, asleep again are we?'

Yes, she was asleep. The national service volunteer has caught her in the act – he's on his way home, and greets her in a semi-friendly way. Half an hour has passed since she left her room. Can't take the pace, was what she'd have said before. If she said it today, the irony would come crawling up behind her on all fours to wipe the smile off her face.

Didn't she want to see what she recognises? One thing she doesn't recognise is thrusting itself rather out of the tall trees: the hospital church. A ruin before, now it's a venue for services and concerts. She rolls inside, and all is deep blue: a simple little sky with stars curves over the altar.

She and Matthes never stood at the altar. They got married in Henrichshorst. Right where Matthes had pinned a bulletin up at the town hall shortly before, making public their "exit visa application" for China. It was 1984, and no one wanted to give them a flat. The socialist powers that be wanted to outmanoeuvre the adulterer and the slut with her benefit bastards. They were living in two little hostel rooms, each one twelve square metres. Five-year-old Bengt and Billy in one, Helene and Matthes in the other – she with a big Lissy-bump. Shared kitchen, shared bathroom in the basement, shared toilet. The bed in their room was a single. They longed for night-time, when they could forget about what was happening during the day. Matthes travelled into central Berlin to his job as a cost accountant at a power station – a job he was completely overqualified for, but which he'd had no option but to take after leaving his wife. Three kilometres by bike, six kilometres on the tram, thirty kilometres on the train, two kilometres by bus. It could take him up to two hours each way. In the meantime, she took Bengt to nursery at six, went three kilometres by bike to take Billy to the childminder, then six kilometres on the tram and twenty on the train before getting another tram in the city centre. This got her to the Berlin hospital where she was doing a six-month placement, which she had to complete in order to be ready for paediatric neurology and psychiatry at the hospital in Henrichshorst. She could only stay until two o'clock, because the childminder finished at four. The Berlin hospital notified Henrichshorst about this and so she only got a fraction of her salary, even though the full amount had been agreed to for the duration of the placement. They all got cold. At seven o'clock she always had both boys ready for bed and sitting on the edge of the couch, where she'd then try to read a bit to Bengt while rocking Billy in her arms. Mostly they fell sleep just as Matthes, after his long day, appeared on the doorstep they didn't have. Time to pass the baton. He'd take both boys to the other room and then lie down with her on the couch – on their sides, with her bottom tucked right into him, so there was room for them both.

One weekend – which didn't even come close to offering them anything like respite – was spent cutting and sticking. They stuck their faces on to a demonstration of Chinese workers. China's population had just passed one billion. They let it be known that they had the prospect of a flat there, which is why they wanted to expedite their departure. If, for reasons of political interest, their leaving for China wasn't agreeable, they wrote, they would go to Kazakhstan. There could definitely be no objections there, because Kazakhstan was a union republic within the great Soviet empire. There were fifteen of these the Soviet Union supposedly wanted to tempt them with – they counted them out with fifteen fingers on three hands. The bulletin was up for less than half an hour.

In exchange they got a message from Matthes's firm two days later, saying they were prepared to give them a flat provided they got married.

She'd never wanted to get married.

They were married as soon as Matthes's divorce came through.

In their bedroom in Karlshorst is a bed that's over six feet wide. A simple little sky with stars curves above it.

As she rolls out of the church she sees Pastor Wittusch. He's coming slowly along the avenue on foot. His sleeves flap like batwings, and he seems to be mulling over something. He doesn't recognise her, of course. Where does she know him from? Ah yes: he came to visit shortly after they'd moved into their first flat; it was nine months after the wedding and Lissy was already six months old. He was on the lookout for any members of the church who'd settled in the prefab housing estates, which had practically sprung up overnight. They invited him in for tea and a chat, which was a big deal at the time for someone turned away on most doorsteps. It occurred to her that she'd been christened, because her Christian grandparents had still been alive at the time and no one was allowed to upset them. This fact ran like a silent ribbon around her and Wittusch, while Matthes clearly emphasized the atheist cut of his cloth. Despite that, she seems to remember the men having plenty to say to each other. She can see Wittusch sitting at the table in the hall, laughing. When he left that day, he was glad to have found someone who'd still let him in.

'God... can you hear me?'

Oh God, what's happened to the alcoholics' unit... *The house stands empty and silent,/ and out of the window rises/ the white birch, splendidly* – Helene's aphasia modifies the lines of the old poem by Claudius. Involuntarily her mouth twists into an embarrassed smile which she can't explain to anybody.

Because there's no one there to see it.

She's on the long concrete road to the overflow carpark, looking over the field towards the old alcohol withdrawal ward. She'd seen it from the inside a few times when she'd worked as a voluntary carer for a young local woman. The woman's two children had been put into a home because she drank. She was an intelligent chemical lab assistant who'd done her A Levels. Helene can't have thought about her at all in ten years. Would she recognise the woman if she bumped into her? When she tries to remember her, she sees a jaded, leathery face, aging all the time. And only in her early twenties! Helene had wanted to somehow force her into rehab, even though she'd known it wasn't working. For a few days she'd visited her on the ward every day, then the girl with the old face had scarpered. Now the great hulk over there is standing empty. The building was typical of children's homes and care homes in the GDR - there are others like it all over the eastern part of the city, many now empty. There was one in Marzahn, used as a children's home. Gerhard pops into her head: between 1989 and '91 he'd made a film about the residents of this home, and their release on reaching adulthood – he followed them for two years. The girls became very young mothers and the boys very young fathers. Some just couldn't get away from a life of crime. It turned out not to be a depressing film, but one which plainly did away with any illusions – you certainly no longer had any once you'd watched it. There'd been something pleasing about that.

Gerhard lives around here! She's just not quite sure how she'd manage the kerbs in the wheelchair. Plus, she should ring beforehand, otherwise she might have to turn right back round again if he wasn't in.

Shame, no phone book.

◆ ◆ ◆

Done. She's done in. And she's done *it*. Managed to spend the afternoon outside on her own. All the things she's remembered! She shuts her eyes, overwrought, but the highly-charged images remain, changing in rapid succession. Matthes again and again, his current face superimposed on to the old days, although he'd actually looked different then.

She had, too.

The occupational therapist comes to give Helene her evening wash. Her hands are both floppy tonight, even the left one which has been pushing the wheelchair. Carola takes her to the bathroom, and with her help Helene gets undressed. Really it's Carola doing it all, if she's honest. She pushes Helene on a shower chair into the stream of warm water. She can see out of the window while she's being washed, slowly and with unwavering calm. Matthes has given her an expensive-looking body wash and it smells lovely. She stops looking out of the window and closes her eyes instead, imagining it's Matthes washing her. When he used to do it, she'd wash him, too, until they became entangled in each other in the shower all over again.

A long time ago.

She's blushing when she opens her eyes. No stirrings, luckily.

When she's been wheeled back, and is about to be ferried from her wheelchair into bed, she feels as though – for a second – she could stand.

◆ ◆ ◆

Matthes' sister Jutka comes to see her. Helene immediately starts crying. In a way she's relieved that she's able to cry now. She wanders sceptically away from her feelings. She's not actually sad at all – so why the tears? But equally she can't stop crying. She sticks a laugh on underneath. Her mouth is laughing down below, the tears are flowing up above. What's her voice doing? Holding back. Jutka is grinning.

Helene remembers: a few years ago, Jutka had told her how she and Matthes couldn't stop grinning when they buried Granny Hilda. With giggly faces, the ten-year-old boy and seven-year-old girl had walked to the chapel holding their parents' hands, sat down between them, and got really cross with themselves, because of course they'd felt like crying but just couldn't stop grinning, which was completely beyond their parents.

Helene can't be dead, or else she wouldn't be able to see Jutka grinning. Surely?

◆ ◆ ◆

Flood.

High water.

She doesn't understand what's meant at first when the newsreader on TV is talking about floods – the news is only still on in the common room because the 'good' films don't start until quarter past eight. The images that follow make it clear. They show Dresden flooded – water in the Semper Opera House and Zwinger Palace. Tharandt and Freital have been utterly inundated too. Two dams have burst, Malter and

Klingenberg. At-risk premature babies are being brought to Berlin, because they don't know whether the Dresden hospitals will have to be evacuated. Power and phone lines are down. It's a similar story in the upper reaches of the Danube, around Passau and Regensburg. The newsreader says it's the worst damage caused by any disaster since the Second World War.

She's looking at the screen and eating a yoghurt. It doesn't get through to her – a thick layer of gelatine hangs between her and the TV. The sight of the water triggers something she's afraid of, but can't put a name to.

Helene's heart skips a beat.

Helene's heart keeps skipping a beat until it gets things under control.

With her heartbeat under control, she rolls back to her room. The Bandner woman is grinning broadly, and Helene's immediate neighbour is already asleep. What's she actually called, the woman she has most in common with here? Can it be true that she doesn't even know her name? As she wheels past, Helene reads the little bit of paper slotted into the clear plastic case at the foot of the bed: *Mittelner, Renja*. So, Renja Mittelner. She's astonished that this hadn't interested her before now.

She gets her laptop out of the bedside cabinet. Her heart has only just started to get its beating under control, and still gallops away from her in brief bursts if she's not paying attention. It's got something to do with the water. She opens the word processor and searches in this year's files for the word 'water'. Success: watersoup.doc, waterypopawtery.doc, heavywater.doc. Opening one, she has a memory: heavywater.doc was one of the last texts...

You want to go swimming,

The sea roars, as if it longs for you, and yet I can hear the sand crunching beneath your beautiful big feet, now climbing over the seaweed and the wood and the stones washed ashore; you stop, take your right foot in your left hand, have a look at the sole, have you cut yourself? Then you put it back down and hesitantly take the last few steps to the water, suddenly breaking into a run and throwing yourself with wild enthusiasm into the waves; you disappear between them, re-surface, wave at me and I wave back; I lay my head on my knees and the smile on my face somehow isn't right, I want to retract it but it stays there as if you've nailed it down – have you nailed it down? I don't want to smile. You probably can't see it from out there but you can make me out: how I'm sitting here, bottom in the sand, knees pulled up to my chin, my hands now tightly clutching my legs which would otherwise want to stretch out again; yet you always like me, with my wide dark-red mouth and blue eyes – Little Blue Eyes you called me, over twenty years ago. I saw your chest, with its sparse covering of hair, and was lost for several minutes while you bided your time, and turned me over; now you've turned over yourself and are lying stretched out on your back, the salt water rocking you. I'd rather you didn't like me – how am I going to make that happen? Nothing comes to mind, and I want to lie down and be buried in the sand so you can't find me when you come back – although it would be better for you if you didn't look for me at all, just stopped thinking about me altogether, and the fact I even existed; better if I was erased from your thoughts both small and great, which still break over me stormily, morning noon and night, since I chew over my own affairs, and yours are so alien to me; because I wear the same breasts under my shirt as I did back then, and so find it strange that your touch no longer sparks what was once inalienable: my passion, my obsessive lust. Now, instead, your touch demands something I don't want to part with, something trapped in my sealed mouth, and behind my locked-and-bolted eyes; in this dungeon crouch passion and desire, wizened little gnomes whose blood has gone astray over the years. You've turned over again now. Your honey hair has fallen in dark matted clumps over your eyes, so you sweep them to one side; you're looking up at the sky - a squadron of fighter planes leaves white streaks; you too have sometimes left white streaks on my back with your nails, which would quickly turn red – you used to push the blood to one side with your fingers first, then it would rush back even redder than before, and sometimes I'd end up with bloody spirals. There! You disappear again among the waves. I want to close my eyes to prolong this moment in which you don't exist, where you're simply out of the picture, and the curtains are closed; though it would be nice to have a view – it's always the view I look for when I'm in an unfamiliar town, when I pull back the curtains in the hotel and look out; best of all, I like wide vistas on the edge of a town – over housing estates and fields, and away to the distant horizon with its lips pressed together. I usually notice, then, that my lips are pressed together, too, and if I'm not careful tears start rolling towards the view I was looking for, so that it's blocked to me again. Why can't I cry when you're around? You'd finally realise there was something wrong with my smile, and with the cheery blue of my irises – you'd see that that cheery blue drowned long ago; but if I don't cry, you'll probably never notice, and the only thing I could do then would be to stop eating until I disappear completely. Of course, giving up eating just like that also means slowly but surely giving up my metabolic connection with world, which I don't want to keep fuelling when for so long I haven't felt a metabolic connection with you. So long that my hair has gone grey over it, while yours has kept its colour – the colour of wild honey; once upon a time it even seemed to taste like honey, when its waves brushed my mouth – as sometimes used to happen when I passed you one of the children, and you quickly turned your head because another child was shouting for you, and the third had probably just fallen over, and was now sitting and howling on the stairs. Your lovely long hair would billow past my lips, electrifying me, and I struggled then to get back as quickly as possible to the children, who'd be waiting for us all to play, eat or go off somewhere together. Each one had very quickly passed the baton to the next; they came and went; moved away a long time ago; and have no idea we're up here on the coast, for a summer week – they don't see you, their father grown old, ankles shimmering with bluish-red spider veins, while my varicose veins strangle my calves. I rock back and forth on my feet to counteract it when I walk or stand – toes up, heel down, heel up, toes down; you see? My existence is a continual rocking; even here on the beach, I'm raising and lowering my feet incessantly, feet which want to run away but aren't capable of carrying me in a direction I haven't disclosed to you, which is completely unknown to you, and which you're not even able to look in because you only see me, only ever me; and so when you're looking at me, I feel like I'm in the field of fire, constantly anticipating the fine, hook-ended arrows you never shoot, because of course you're such a good 'un – man, friend, lover – who'd never do anything to harm anyone, whether me or you or the big wide world beyond the newspaper you read every morning, just as you think you can read me but don't notice that I'm not at home in your gaze. I'd rather say that you only get out of me what you put in, but you don't want to hear it, and instead grasp my head in your hands and nail down that smile, examining your handiwork with satisfaction before going off to *chop wood, or dig, or swim. Why can you just not foresee what's in store for us, what's on the horizon for us if we don't step out of each other's way – because where we're standing now has long been too narrow for two, and where we are tomorrow might be right at the end of the path. And now you're so far out in the water that I almost don't have to see you any more; I put both hands up to my cheekbones and tear out the tacks so that my smile collapses. It's only a small world that comes tumbling down with it, a cosmos in miniature – a moment ago I was sitting at its centre, and now I'm rising up out of it, amazed at how quietly the coordinates can become a little more skewed; no longer perpendicular to each other, but arranged at an oblique angle instead. This gives me the foothold I need to not be a burden to you later, when you come ashore – when I'll patter and rock back and forth, and not be able to tell you what's just happened.*

Did she write that? Of course. If Matthes were to ask what she's just read then she wouldn't be able to say. It's definitely good not to have to read anything about aphasia, she thinks suddenly. Then comes a feeling which brings her closer to the time when this text came into being. Can a feeling even do that? What she's thinking bobs about as if on water. She can hardly hold on to it, and clutches at the railing: Pietro had celebrated his birthday on the sixth of June at his little house near Anklam, and the day after they'd gone over to Usedom, an island off the Baltic coast, with Lottchen in tow. There'd been a kind of torment in the air – even the memory of it torments her. Whenever they went anywhere as a couple she always put on a smile so as not to unthinkingly pull down what Matthes had so painstakingly constructed. When he'd finally moved away from her a bit to go into the sea, it collapsed.

Her smile.

She's slept very deeply. When the student nurse came at around four to take her pulse and temperature, Helene was off with her, annoyed at being disturbed. The girl didn't notice.

Now she's lying there and thinking.

What is Thinking?

Thinking should be something like inwardly moving through the wilderness of perception, attached to a long safety line. By looking at the line every now and then, you shield yourself from too many impressions. Then your Thinking doesn't get tangled up so easily.

Where's her safety line?

She can't see it. Instead, one thought flees from the next, entering as the pursuer from the left, before leaving the scene as the pursued on the right. Leaving no trace.

What's she thinking about, then?

That she's trying to think.

Never think that you've thought, because thinking about thoughts is thoughtless thinking. When you're thinking, you think – so you think – that you're thinking, yet you're never actually thinking.

That saying was always on her father's lips. She's known it off by heart since she was little, so even now it's still there.

I've got the key to the garden gate, where three lovely maidens wait. The first is called Binka, the second Bibbledibinka, the third Zicknicknacknobbledibobbledibibbledibinka.

Her father's sayings seem to be coming thick and fast. Here's the next one already:

She sells seashells on the seashore.

And before she can do anything about it, another one comes – to mind?

Peter Piper picked a peck of pickled pepper. A peck of pickled pepper Peter Piper picked!

Yes, they must have come to *mind*. But things only come to mind that appeal to the senses. 'Out of sight, out of mind!' as her great-grandmother would always say, whether she'd lost something and couldn't find it, or whether she meant her brother Walther who so rarely replied to her long letters. These were written in Sütterlin, the old German handwriting. Helene should have a book in Sütterlin brought in, to see whether she can still read it. She used to be able to write in Sütterlin, though she hasn't tried it for a long time. But – she can't write anything at all when she picks up a pen with her right hand! Not the Latin alphabet or Sütterlin... She'll have to have a go with her left. After all, she's still going to have to do a signature every now and then. That's going to look different to before: she used to just break the H down into two jaunty arcs, one on the left and one on the right, with the E, L and E the same shape but three different sizes, then the N and E petering out into a line. The W of her surname would be large and clear while the other letters, up to the final L, just came out as a line. When had she taken to doing it like that? The period after the wedding comes to mind: she can see herself sitting at the desk in their flat at the time and practising. It was a while before she took the name Wesendahl. My Wesendahling, as her then-boss used to call her, not without smug emphasis on the fact that he saw her marriage as irrelevant, and, privately, she'd continue to be a convenient object of his lust. She can see his face before her: early forties;

really long sideburns, even though they were no longer fashionable in the early eighties; starting to go bald. He always had his white doctor's coat on, even getting out of the car first thing in the morning. His wife was a nurse on the General ward, and had her own car. Very unusual for an East German relationship. She was insanely jealous, and made scenes only those who worked with him could understand: she had a way of glaring at him – silent but flashing with anger – that was so loud it made your head pound. Hadn't a trainee doctor started a placement in the Outpatients department at the time? Her face is coming back to Helene now... This girl reckoned she was madly in love with the boss, but strangely he avoided her like the plague. Normally he'd never pass up anything in a skirt. Verena? Yes, Verena was definitely her name. She had a little girl and wanted to be a gynaecologist like her sister, whose clinics Helene went to when she was pregnant with Lissy. Lissy eventually came into the world looking like a big blue sausage and weighing nine and a half pounds, a week after a scan had predicted low birth weight and Helene had been rather impertinently accused of smoking. Ooh, she'd love a cigarette right now...

She returns to her senses because cigarette smoke is drifting into the room through the open window. The torrent of thoughts subsides, retreats, when she smells the aroma. Someone's smoking Gauloises! But she doesn't have the energy to heave herself into her wheelchair and go over to the window. She lets herself be lulled by the scent. Befuddled.

Matthes parts the fog. He's come earlier than usual today.

Helene gets anxious straight away, and doesn't like being in bed when he comes, but of course she's safe here... Isn't she?

The anxiety doesn't go away. Matthes is looking at her and smiling. Is his smile different to hers? Hers is probably more often in the process of collapsing, while his turns into an enormous big grin just when you think it's about to disappear.

Women and men.

Don't go together.

But now she can't help smiling a real smile, one that isn't going to collapse. She takes his hand and feels good. Her anxiety seems to have sunk behind the smiling – it's gone as suddenly as it appeared.

Matthes is pleased Helene is holding on to his right hand with her left and stroking it. When did she last do that? She'd rather not have to think about it.

They look steadily into each other's eyes. His dark-brown irises give nothing away. Nevertheless she notices how her senses completely desert her when she immerses herself in this colour. Just like before. And a long time before, when there was no thought of separation and they'd spend their evenings whispering sweet nothings to each other. The days existed purely for them to build up their desire for each other. When he came home it was she, often enough, who'd pounce on him and lock the door. She who'd tear the clothes from his body, while out in the playground the children lost track of time just as much as they did.

His dark irises had been her underwater place, down where the light hardly reached. When he lay there, gazing at the ceiling, she couldn't help but climb on to him and look into his eyes, and sooner or later she'd sink into them.

A once-familiar feeling reaches for her.

She closes her eyes, because the emotion is going to make her cry. She realizes this and is cross she can't just let Matthes share in these tears.

'Women and men really don't go together,' she says, slowly and quietly.

A scornful saying, which always used to accompany their differences of opinion. Now it crawls out from the embarrassment caused by her blubbing, and throws itself, like a cowering dog, at Matthes' feet.

'You're right there,' he says. He doesn't kick it. Or chase it off.

He laughs.

A little while later he's got Helene into the wheelchair, and they're off along the ward. The room next to hers has a quarantine notice – this is the first time she's seen it. She wonders why on earth infections would bother with the Stroke Unit. A nurse with gloves and a mask comes out of it, but before Helene can get a look inside the door has closed again. She has such a burning curiosity that she can very precisely feel where her face and neck is going red.

Matthes has been watching her, and smirks. She wants to scream. Is she now a little child whose longing, curiosity and bungling are there for all to see? She's so angry that she tries to kick him with her left leg, and he jumps aside in alarm. This mix of anger and shame has knocked all the speech out of her. She can't summon any at all. Language, that sleeping beast... She has to search out every word, and say it quietly to herself before she says it out loud. But now it's all gone and there's only confusion in her head, with the sleeping language-beast nowhere to be found. Her heart races, and she gets the feeling that the clip in her head is starting to clatter like a typewriter;

and when she puts her head in her hand – really she wanted to put it in both hands – she notices the strings of spit hanging out of her mouth, right, left and centre. They cling to her hand, which gets wetter and wetter. Now she's really howling, and Matthes is pushing her, as she wanted, right to the end of the kalidor.

Kalidor? As in the Hindu goddess Kali?

This would never have happened to her in Calcutta.

Why not, though? Because India's gurus would have shielded and protected her with their slender, long-fingered hands? She's certainly sweating now like she did every day she was travelling in India! The fact she's just thought of Calcutta while wanting to be pushed to the end of the corridor turns her tears to laughter. Or is she laughing through her tears? In her head at least, language seems to be working better. It's as if the building plans for speech fall apart just before its translation into the spoken word, rendering it impossible, and meaning she no longer has any idea what she was supposed to be talking about. As soon as even a little bit of excitement chips in, the whole house of word-cards collapses. And so, while she's laughing through her tears, she sees herself in the Ramakrishna temple in Belur Math. Squatting down, she's seized by a whisper of belief in her unbelief: might he be able to save her? Make her walk again? Write, even? She keeps her eyes closed so she doesn't have to see what's going on around her. She can tune everything out as well as she ever could. All of a sudden, it feels lovely: seclusion, peace and quiet. She's immersed: not in belief, but in memories, and a kind of gratitude spreads through her that she managed to get to India before her aneurysm. No one would be asking her in her current state whether she might like to fly out there for six weeks and have a look around, doing the odd reading from her books and soaking up the culture. But then she remembers waiting for her driver at Varanasi Airport, and seeing the way some passengers in wheelchairs were manhandled out of the plane. They were Israelis, setting out for India's holiest city. What a slog, she'd thought at the time, in awe.

Now she's one of them.

Helene feels a hand on her forehead. It belongs to Matthes, which she realises even before she's opened her eyes. Matthes doesn't look angry. He's been angry a lot in the last two years. The very sight of her was enough to put him in a rage. But is that actually true? Quietly, like just-hatched snakes, uncertainty starts to flicker its tongue. What had seemed like a memory just a moment ago now appears to be a sudden, abrupt and ultimately groundless suspicion. Has the present taken her hostage, so the past can be set free? But who would there be to blackmail with a thing like that... She can't think of anyone. Uncertainty licks the skin on her forearms, making the little hairs stand on end. She shivers. Now the sight of Matthes is enough to drive *her* into a rage: how sympathetically he looks at her, how wisely! A father through and through, who wants to comfort and soothe his awkward little child, but with just that faint whiff of scorn on his lips which is the final straw. The child struggles, kicks, lashes out. The father smiles, and holds on to the child firmly.

She can't express what she's thinking.

It's terrible, but she's the one who's struggling. Who's

lashing out.

Emotional turmoil is new to her. As are thoughts that keep getting tangled up with each other, and whose beginnings and ends she isn't even aware of: they're just suddenly there, and then gone again. Whenever she forces herself to pursue one of them, it inevitably ends in tears because she can't do it. It's horrible that she's not capable of expressing any of this – not that there'd be anyone out there to receive such a message. Is that worse?

Helene is glad that Doctor Know-All has gone back home. Today, all she could make out in his face was understanding, and now she feels thoroughly made a fool of. He doesn't know anything! He doesn't understand any of it! What is there to understand anyway? She tries to make sense of her anger. She'd gone ballistic. Because she couldn't fake it any more, could no longer hide like she used to, and because all her curiosity was right there on her face for all to see. She'd felt caught out, robbed of all caution. No, there wasn't even the option of being cautious. It's a terrible feeling, to be smiling dumbly (and above all openly), and at the mercy of others. Only now does she feel she's noticing her excessive smiling: the smallest joy immediately pulls her mouth wide, and at some point she realises she's dribbling. And the joy doesn't stop there. She's like a comedy frog. She looks for her face in the mirror by the sink. Nope, no goggly eyes yet, and her fingers haven't turned into clubbed fingers, still less her toes. She does look a bit green, though. Do you see, Helene: green with rage. She smiles, and there it is, coming over her again – a frenzied, roaring rage. Helplessness goes dismally round in her head, faster and faster, and as she starts to sob, fat old Bandner rudely starts laughing. It's lucky she's there. Her laughter makes Helene catch herself. Not with the long rope, but the short one. She goes over to the other woman's bed and, howling, laughs along. It's good when the pain subsides, she thinks. Though the fact that it's still crouching inside her, with only a flimsy covering, is something she knows only too well.

Doctor Know-All doesn't say anything. About the situation, anyway. Helene is pretty sure they'd been living apart, but when she tries to remember those last weeks, she fails pretty miserably. Maybe they'd decided to call off the separation... Maybe they'd had a brief happy period before her aneurysm... That would explain Matthes's face when he slept with her. Blissful is how he looked. When he was in a state of passion, his eyes would swell almost shut, and on making a great effort to open them, so he could look at her, his irises would be cut off, top and bottom. In those moments he reminded her of a sleeping lion, who'd just raised an eyelid because a fly had landed on its nose: he'd look drowsy and contented, and yet be trembling with arousal. She'd learnt to come to terms with this contrast, even if it had thrown her at first. At the same time, it was never the case that he was waiting, behind his fevered expression, in a state of great calm. His agitated constitution matched the agitation in his eyes.

The Doctor Know-All in the fairy tale doesn't really know anything, but in his ineptitude he always says the right thing. Matthes actually knows a lot. But his particular ineptitude means there are times when you'd never be able to tell.

III

Lessons

HELENE GOES THROUGH THE YEARS, practising remembering.

She takes as a given anything that comes up spontaneously out of the dark vat it's been mouldering in. If it then stands before her, glowing – in the colour of a jacket she wore twenty-five years ago, for example – then she's happy. Needless to say, her mouth is pulled into a broad smile. At all times. Now and again, Renja Mittelner asks what Helene's just been thinking about. Renja's probably pleased that she's smiling. Helene isn't.

But when she practises remembering, she's in suspense. Feeling tense? Yes, that too.

Today she's taken on the year 1988. She was pregnant – Mareile was born in the June. The largest new housing development in East Berlin had a polyclinic, where she'd been working since late 1987. Departments such as the local Children's Neuropsychiatry team and Youth Health Protection had been moved out of the main building, meaning that Helene and her colleagues worked in normal, modern flats some way away. She didn't have her own consulting room to start with – four of them had to share the three rooms of the flat. In the biggest one, which would have been the living room, a corner had been partitioned off to make a windowless kitchen, where records were being stored temporarily and where they could make themselves tea and coffee. There was a table. The unlucky fourth person – whoever was currently roomless, and therefore didn't have any young patients booked – would withdraw into this kitchen. This meant that any conversations going on between colleague and patient could be overheard through the hatch – an opening in the wall, about half a square metre in size, which had glass panes. In the beginning, whenever she was the unlucky fourth person, she'd make an effort to be extra quiet so the patient wouldn't register her presence. But she soon lodged a forceful complaint about this untenable situation. The only man in their team of four was a Party Group Organiser, committed to suppressing anything potentially rebellious. So, one day, she'd stood in the partitioned kitchen doorway as he was coming into the room with his patients, and said she wouldn't be able to help overhearing their conversation. Would they therefore be willing to go ahead with the consultation, under the circumstances? He'd ummed and ahed, turned pale and hadn't a clue what to do. He knew he should really report her conduct, but feared creating a bad atmosphere among his colleagues. In the end, they agreed – along with their boss in the building next door – to practise a version of collectively turning a blind eye. They all knew that one of them would now leave the flat rather than squeeze into the aforementioned kitchen. That seemed to work. Month by month, her bump grew bigger.

Helene draws up a list of the normal-for-the-time maternity clothes she had in her wardrobe. A long cotton pinafore dress in turquoise, her favourite thing. Two pairs of trousers, one black and one in a grey tweedy fabric, which had big elastic panels at the waist and had to be worn with maternity blouses. She had three of these blouses. One was in a shiny synthetic material with little flowers on, and the only good thing about it was that it dried quickly and didn't need ironing. The second was a pink blouse with grey embroidery on the collar, and just as ugly as the first. The only one she liked wearing was made of black polka-dot cord. Wasn't it called babycord? Probably. Unfortunately, it wasn't long enough, and she had to wear her trousers with braces so that the elastic panels didn't peep out. She's really pleased – she hadn't even thought about these clothes since passing them on. That was shortly after Mareile was born, when she reckoned she was finished with so-called family-building. They hadn't planned on having another baby at all – four was enough. And now she can pull all these funny old clothes out of her memory chest, at the drop of a hat!

But now she's ambushed by another memory.

Why had she got pregnant?

Out of spite.

Yes, she remembers: before Mareile, she and Matthes only had Lissy, along with Helene's two sons. Then there were two children from Matthes's first marriage. Helene wanted at least two with Matthes herself, so she'd be on equal footing with his first wife. Now and then, Matthes would call Billy Mischa, the name of his second child, and attached qualities to him that were Mischa's, too – not exactly difficult, because Billy was a beauty, as was Mischa. But Billy wasn't Matthes's son. She was tormented by a strange pain whenever he likened Billy to Mischa. So she took Matthes out to a lakeside wine bar, and got herself drunk. Brave from the drink, she came out with her desire to have a fourth child. She didn't give a reason. Matthes laughed, clearly not thinking she was serious. When she realised she was, he went pale, and said with steely calm that he'd then have to have another child with his first wife, otherwise the number of children would be too unequal. He'd said it so emphatically, she thought she'd never be able to speak a word to him again. She'd run out and started screaming. After that there's just a blank, and to this day she still has no idea how she got home. She'd immediately stopped taking the pill. Matthes acted as if nothing had happened, and at some point she did too. Nine weeks later she was pregnant.

Mareile is fourteen, and going on language exchanges.

Main kya karoon...

Another strip of tarpaulin is rolled back from the picture: she'd started learning Hindi! In the last few weeks before her aneurysm she was spending her evenings on the balcony, wrapped up in blankets. It stayed light for long enough. Her Hindi textbook was a copy of an English edition, and all the other students on the course had much better English than she did, so she'd wanted to brush up on her English too. Was that why she'd tried to speak English in those first few days after coming out of the coma? And another thing: no one will have cancelled the course, or let them know she can't come any more. Matthes did know she was doing a Hindi course, but not where or who with. She tosses and turns anxiously in the bed. Someone needs to sort it out! When the nurse comes, and looks at her questioningly on account of the anxiety, Helene momentarily gives up rather than attempt the long run-up needed to explain what's bothering her. Though she always knows in advance what she wants to say, when it comes to actually saying it her physical capabilities and the chaos in her head are pretty much neck and neck in the race to stop it happening. Plus the nurse doesn't exactly look like she has the time for it right now, either. Not for long-drawn-out explanations about Hindi courses that she wouldn't be remotely interested in. *Main kya karoon* – what am I to do... That had been a favourite phrase of the teacher, whose small and withered left arm stayed hidden under the dupatta of her salwar kameez. Whenever she wore a sari, she'd draped it over her shoulder in such a way that the arm disappeared. She'd done it so skilfully that Helene hadn't noticed it the first three or four times. She can't recall anything other than that phrase, though. Only the "hai" at the end of a sentence, the "is", which has so little in common with the rules of German syntax that literal translations are often ridiculous. But she can't think of an example, and the letters she'd drawn so often and with such dedication – until D-Day – had fallen through the cracks. Shame. In any case she wouldn't be able to write anything like that now. With her left hand she can barely manage to write in German – it comes out as a scrawl, with pointy bits and exaggerated curves. She can forget about the unfamiliar Hindi script, that's gone for good.

Dejected, she flops back on to her pillows.

Slowly there stirs in her a desire to lurk. She's never had that before. When Helene was a child, her great-grandmother had had a cushion on the kitchen windowsill to put her in just the right position for watching the people crawling up and down the street. Traffic was rare, so you could hear what people were saying as they went by. During pauses between these overheard sentences, Great-Grandma would very energetically add her own. Such delicate webs were spun at this kitchen-window rumour-mill: they swirled into the house next door, where they picked up further stuffed-in sentences, and ultimately hung over the small town in a dense cloud. Sometimes pricking it with a simple fact was enough to make it quickly disappear. Blue sky again. But if there was no simple fact to hand, and you had the uneasiness of a rumour instead, it could stay hanging there for days or even weeks – especially when people denied themselves the contact that might clear things up, and instead stayed within their four or eight walls, beneath their cloak of suspicion. Helene hated cloaks of suspicion as much as she hated the desire to lurk, and used to go after simple facts like the devil after souls. Now she's virtually forced to remain within these walls, and the desire to lurk is stirring. She wants to be the first to know who's on shift today, and who's being visited by whom. Who's eating what and who's smoking in the toilets. Who's on speaking terms and who isn't. Helene leaves the door open a crack when she wheels herself into the room. This doesn't prove very successful, because far too often someone comes into the room and shuts it again. So she's starting to spend her time out in the corridor. Opposite the room next door there's a lovely, deep bay window. The bay itself is nicer than the view from it, of the old coal yard. She positions her wheelchair so that half of it is behind the heavy, dusky pink velvet curtains, sometimes on the left, sometimes on the right. That way there's always one side from which she can't be seen until someone is right alongside the window. She has a book in her lap, but doesn't read it. Over the last few days she's had a go, and can actually do it. At any rate, she can read whole pages aloud – faltering and stumbling, particularly over sibilants, but with excellent intonation – and yet afterwards she has no idea what any of it was about. Yesterday she'd got to work on individual sentences, with the same result. By the time she reached the full stop she'd forgotten how the sentence had even started.

For goodness' sake, no one's going to notice, she thinks, dismayed at the thought of having to read from her own books, and answer questions afterwards on what she's just read. Surely no one there will twig that she can't do it! She imagines her pauses for breath, and the audience in darkness. The whole business is so embarrassing that she has to wipe away the threads of saliva which, thanks to her agitation, have abseiled down from her mouth once again.

It's good. It's enough.

It has crippled one of her arms and one of her legs, and has caused a right ruckus in the Broca area of her brain. *It* doesn't budge when she wants to think about *It*, but stays hidden. *It* has probably piled up all her lost words into a huge heap and hidden underneath. Masterfully *It* pulls her face into all kinds of grimaces and ensures a free flow of spit. In doing so, *It* occupies her entire mind, playing with her thoughts the way the black widow spider plays with her diminutive mates: every time they touch *It, It* gobbles them up. It can take a while for her thoughts to reappear, and by then, of course, the page is blank again...

It has taken a seat. *It* didn't ask her if she wanted to offer *It* a chair, or at least a little stool – *It* just plonked *It*self down. *It*'s sitting there now, but slips into her blind spot whenever she wants to look right at *It*. She can't really explain it any other way, that *It* won't properly reveal *It*self. She decides to resign herself to the fact that she doesn't really know what *It* is.

Today the word Heidemühlen comes up for the first time. When she hears it, she sees a wide landscape of windmills, and dark heather showing off its purple blooms. As far as the eye can see. How far can the eye actually see?

Yesterday the consultant had questioned her intently about double vision. She hasn't experienced any. A perimetric test of her field of vision showed no reduction in it whatsoever. A sort of pride could be seen in the doctor's face.

'We exposed your optic nerve, you see. It's rare for that not to cause double vision.'

So just how far can the eye see?

We'll have to see.

Matthes has chosen Heidemühlen.

Helene has complete trust in him.

Heidemühlen isn't far from Berlin. In fact, it's close to Henrichshorst, where they'd lived and got married... Something about that doesn't sound right. Marrying is part of living, thinks Helene. So you can't say 'lived *and* married' because phrasing it like that makes it sound like the marrying happens outside of life – doesn't it?

She's not sure.

Heidemühlen is supposed to make her surer.

'I'm giving you another six weeks in the wheelchair,' the physiotherapist says.

And then?

She's alarmed, wondering whether they're still expecting her to die from whatever *It* is that's slumbering somewhere inside her.

The physio means that's when she'll start walking again.

Helene lets out a guffaw when she hears that. Of course she'll never be able to walk again, how's she supposed to manage that? The strength on her right side is just enough to let her pause for a split second when transferring from her wheelchair to the toilet.

The physio nods and shrugs. Today they're going to try to get her right foot moving together with her left. A tiny bit, at least? She gives a loud shout when she notices she's got her right leg maybe twenty centimetres up into the air.

'Right, let's do that one again right away!'

Summer perks everyone up. Helene's in a good mood. She's had an iced coffee in the hospital cafeteria, and is now enjoying herself with Inga. If she had to say what this enjoyment consists of, she wouldn't be able to right off the bat. Inga is wearing a short black dress. Maybe it's the way her pointy knees are poking out from under it?

Inga's always a good one for surprises. She has a new hairdo. If you look at her from the left, you'd think her hair is pretty short. From the right, though, it's almost down to her shoulders. Inga looks at Helene, and asks if it wouldn't be a good style for her, too. She's had it done to test it out for her.

Helene could keep more than half her hair, and still look well-coiffed. Laughing, Helene shakes her head.

Yes, that's where the enjoyment is.

Another iced coffee? Inga would rather have a glass of chilled, dry white wine and asks the waitress, who responds with a pained smile. Sorry, this *is* a hospital, you know! Ok, then she'll just have another iced coffee, but no cream. And Helene? Helene hasn't stopped laughing. Inga seems to be fine with that, or at least doesn't ask the reason. A – green – tea – please. Halting and stumbling, the words crawl out from under her laughter – which she stifles, not wanting to let it fully escape. But Inga confidently draws the words out and translates for the waitress.

When the waitress comes back with their order, Helene has composed herself again.

On the Sunday evening a bewitching calm descends, like a swarm of silent mosquitoes. Renja Mittelner is at home for the weekend, not back until tomorrow. Old Frau Bandner is asleep, while the dried-out old biddy has gone out with her family. No, not mosquitoes – the calm is like aspic which has crept over her, slurping noisily. Right now, she'd have a job lifting an arm, or a leg. Strange that stillness can materialise like that. The stuff weighs so heavily on her that Helene doesn't even want to lift her eyelids. She knows she could tear through it with a single determined lurch of her whole body, but she doesn't want to. She lies still under the aspic, and tries to think. She's already noticed that remembering goes well when she casts a line. It hooks on to something in the darkness and she can then pull herself along it. Today she plans to tackle Matthes's infidelity.

Infidelity?

Exceptional circumstances.

The phrase comes faster than she'd like, because what it brings with it immediately rumbles around her insides. At the time she could barely keep anything down, mostly puking it straight back up, while the little that did stay down made a liquid break for the back door.

Sixteen years ago, after spending what to her had been a lovely evening together, Matthes had got the tarps he'd used when he moved in with her down from the attic. Everything he owned had been bundled up in them. On that evening sixteen years ago, which to him had been agonising, he'd told her after a last game of scrabble that he was leaving her. He couldn't say any more about it, everything else he'd explain in writing. He said his piece, packed up his stuff, loaded it on to his bike and left. At first she'd thought it was one of his so-called surprises, which he could still pull off. Yes, she'd been trembling as he'd packed his things, but hadn't known whether that was through fear or anticipation. She'd then lain awake in bed for a long time, wondering whether she'd dreamt the whole thing, or whether it had actually just happened. He wasn't there in the morning either, when she woke up and reached over to the other side of the bed. She'd woken the children then slowly fallen into a kind of stupor, which made the kids fall silent and lent the usual morning routine a sense of sleepwalking automation. She didn't even come round once the children had disappeared off to school and nursery, and she'd had the youngest to the doctor with an ear infection. She expected Matthes to come back at any moment, and in doing so burdened each moment with a weight she could never have borne in a fully conscious state. The next day had brought a letter in the post from Matthes, in which he expressed thanks for their *lovely time together*. To Helene it read like an obituary, and made her sorry she hadn't died a long time ago. Then she'd suddenly screamed so loud that Lissy had come staggering out of her room, and their next door neighbour had rung the doorbell continuously. Lissy opened the door to her. From then on, Helene had started to throw up whenever even the smell of food reached her nostrils. Her friend Heidrun was the Chosen One who now had the privilege of sleeping with Matthes, and of taking up all his lean-on-me offers. In her mind, Helene could see her lying under him next to him over him on top of him and fucking him teasing him cooing whispering. She couldn't comprehend it, and scoured the clear skies of the day before yesterday over and over again for signs of doom, leaving sentimentality out of it. She failed to find any hint of a grievance towards him or her, and simply felt *maimed*. The significance of the word suddenly became clear to her on reaching the end of the letter, when she felt the hellish pain repeatedly laying into her. When Bill got in from school, he'd rung her mother-in-law, who had a go at her son the very same day with harsh, angry words, and who then took the helm. ('Get the job done properly. Put your money where your mouth is. He's not in his right mind. But we'll take him to task. We'll squeeze him til it hurts, then squeeze some more.' The sayings had poured forth from her mouth at random, into the rooms of the new-build flat.) Helene doesn't dare imagine what would've happened if her mother-in-law hadn't taken the wheel. And now is hardly the time to be imagining it, either, when the very thought of it all comes with a rumbling in her bowels. The thing to do now is to leave that rumbling in her bowels alone, and remember: sixteen years later she's lying in hospital in the bewitching calm of a Sunday afternoon, and can't get to the toilet as easily as she could then.

When she wakes up, it's still dark outside. She thinks she's slept deeply and didn't dream. She rolls on to her other side. Covers off. Covers back on – it's a bit too chilly after all. Head up, head back down. So it's still just her and old Bandner? When she lifts her head again to check, she bursts out laughing: the old biddy is staring at the moon as it shines down on her, a blissful smile on her face. No, it's not the moon – that would be shining in at the window closest to Helene's bed. It's a streetlight on the path that goes to the free carpark. It's shining directly on to old Bandner's face, which someone must have put cream on because her porky jowls are really glistening! A godly sight. Helene's hardly ever seen the old woman smiling. She smirks when she shits herself, she smirks when she spits yoghurt – which she's allowed alongside her tube feeding – in the nurse's face. Supercilious. Funny word, Helene thinks. To think it's come to her now! It doesn't actually have anything to do with *silliness.* She remembers that for several years she'd thought it did: a foolish sense of superiority. Until she'd looked it up in the dictionary.

Now she's lying quietly, and her thoughts wrestle their way back to yesterday evening. Matthes's *affair*. His *mistress*. Her *love rival*. His *other woman*. She recalls the rumbling in her bowels, and trying to calm it so as to avoid the slow ride to the toilet with the nurse. She'd nodded off thinking about it. The more quietly she lies there, the louder the images become. Heidrun's daughters holding Matthes's hand. Her heart had started pounding fit to burst when she saw him with them in the supermarket – she'd leapt behind some shelves and looked at her mother-in-law, who was with her, like a bewildered child. Then her mother-in-law had spotted Matthes, too, and made a beeline for him, giving him a right *pasting, slapping, pummelling, trouncing* (Helene honestly doesn't know what she can feel more clearly: her former frenzied state, or her current delight at all these words coming at her.) Matthes had stalked away without a word, holding both girls by the hand and with one side of his face completely red. Yes, stalked is indeed the right word: he'd walked out with exaggerated slowness, *just like a stork*, simply abandoning his full basket. She hadn't been able to watch him go. The house Heidrun lived in was only just around the corner, and she'd been constantly afraid of running into Matthes. Their holiday was coming up: they'd booked to go to the Harz mountains with the children. Her mother-in-law now wanted to come instead, in his place – it was nice of her, but would've been virtually unbearable for Helene.

One evening the doorbell rang, and it was Matthes standing there. He asked Helene to go for a walk with him, and her mother-in-law approved the request. The great trembling came over her again, but she put on her coat and bravely went down – where Matthes explained to her that he saw it as his duty to go with them on holiday.

...?

Her heart had stopped for a moment, then remembered

itself and started beating again. She didn't say anything. Couldn't say anything. It had *left her speechless*. Matthes had looked at her, grinning sheepishly, and asked when exactly they were due to leave. Two days later, they all met at the station. What had Heidrun had to say about it? Another sheepish grin. At times on the journey, they must have looked like shy young teenagers in love. Whenever she touched him accidentally, that part of her skin got hot, as if it was dissolving. She'd wondered if she was the only one afflicted by this prickly heat. They'd got two rooms at the workers' holiday camp for themselves and the three children they had at the time. At first Helene had wanted to be left alone. She hadn't struck up any conversations. The children were the same as always, loving and trusting – Lissy a real Daddy's girl; the boys keeping their distance. The very first night she'd reached for him, and got him. What about Heidrun? she'd wanted to ask, but Heidrun wasn't here – wasn't involved, fortunately (for them, not Heidrun). Then in the morning there was distance again, not excessive, but definitely there – as if he'd remembered his other *duty*, to Heidrun. As if fulfilling his *duties* was what drove him, conquering his will so that it never even had a chance. As if he wanted to be beyond reproach: someone tossed between *duties*, of whom you could never say that he'd neglected his *duty*, not the *duty* to his family nor the *duty* to his other woman. But she'd known he was deceiving himself, with zeal and earnestness and inner turmoil, and when she'd first perceived signs of this inner turmoil she'd been tempted to drive it further away, to drive Heidrun out of him and Matthes out of herself. Let him see for himself where this obsession with *duty* would leave him, this demanding hunger for her which was perhaps merely his hunger for

Heidrun. Maybe it was Heidrun he saw before his closed eyes when he slept with Helene; maybe – being sufficiently conscious of his *duty* – he mistook her body for Heidrun's (Helene had got thinner in the weeks before, after all). In a great outburst of rage, she'd wished a court-appointed *duty* lawyer on him, in case she died choking on his *duty* maintenance payments – because he'd be to blame for her death, that much was clear... She'd been taking a Spanish course at the adult education college at the time, and had taken a dictionary with her on holiday. She always carried it about with her, in her handbag or her rucksack – it had been his, she'd bought him it. Helene can see it before her, and can see herself hitting him with it, then getting hold of her shoes and laying into him like the pain had laid into her for all those weeks, while he does nothing – just sits there and takes it all, keeping his eyes shut, and no doubt believing it's his *duty* to endure it. When she lets up on him, one of the shoes has lost its heel.

The light's gone out and old Frau Bandner isn't staring any more.

Instead, dawn is breaking.

Beyond the dawn is a hot, sunny day, as tempting as a warm bath with scented oils. But first of all, a shower, with Carola. Afterwards Carola wheels her to the breakfast room, but her appetite's been spoiled. The memories of Matthes's affair have cost her strength she didn't know she possessed. Now she's lost that strength and, weakened, passes on food *like she had back then*.

The TV is on. There's still flooding in Germany. Sixteen years ago, she thinks suddenly, there was her and Matthes and three of her five children, and Matthes's two other kids, and Heidrun and her two daughters, and Matthes's ex-wife and the fathers of Helene's own sons – but this entity now calling itself Germany didn't exist. A place where East and West mix together very directly, and are thus supposed to form an East-West hybrid buffer between the true East, and the actual West. Peculiar. Since she regained consciousness it's been neither here nor there, even last night when feelings from back then – from a whole other country – were bubbling up, as if they'd just come into being in this one. Anyway: before her aneurysm, before her blackout, hadn't the experience of disappearing, but without being erased from the map, hovered over everything – like a buzzard ready at any moment to snatch at its prey? The subliminal, lightning-quick weighing-up (haircoatshoes...) whether someone was from *here* or *over there*. Then instinctively turning it around: if the other person really *did* come from over there, then that Over There was their Here. (She was thinking whether he was thinking that she was thinking that he ...) Only her blackout could've erased that, surely? Now she thought about it, she could see herself shopping last summer: she'd found some new chocolate in familiar packaging and pounced on it eagerly, hoping to relive a childhood pleasure as she spread the bars out on the kitchen table at home. When Helene was five years old she'd taken three marks and eighty pfennigs from her mother's purse – the only time she'd ever done so – and bought herself a bar of Red Star milk chocolate, tearing it open as she went and eating it piece by piece: it was the most intense taste experience she could remember. And now she'd brought home a bar for each of the children, pressing it on them in great anticipation. Mareile tried a bit, but instead of taking the rest to her room she let it disappear into the family treat cupboard, in the hope that someone else would like it. Lissy had insisted on dark chocolate, citing a stomach bug, and Lottchen had decided she didn't like ordinary milk chocolate, only Kinder Chocolate. Later, when she was alone, Helene had taken Mareile's bar out of the cupboard and, with her eyes closed, put a little bit of it on the tip of her tongue. She'd pressed it against her gums, and by moving her tongue in slow circles got it to melt. No, this chocolate didn't have the slightly sandy consistency she'd expected... Helene wipes away the threads of drool hanging down into her coffee cup. Carola asks her again whether she wouldn't at least like a yoghurt. Yoghurt? That's it, the end of the affair: one morning, after seven weeks with Heidrun – five before their holiday together, two after – Matthes stood at her door with a bag of yoghurts, little quarter-litre jars with a layer of dark red fruit under the metal lid. She used to love that yoghurt.

In the end he'd eaten it out of the hollow of her stomach.

Matthes comes two hours later – he's been signed off sick from work now, too. Why? No answer. That makes her angry. She pulls the covers down and her nightie up. Slowly she opens the pot of yoghurt she's brought back from breakfast, and lets it all splodge on to her stomach. There's no hollow there any more, like there was sixteen years ago, so it runs off down both sides, left and right, on to the sheets. A little heap of it covers her belly button. And her expression? It demands nothing; it has closed itself off. On the other hand she can't just say *closed for a private function*, because Renja Mittelner is looking on uncomprehendlingly, which Helene doesn't see, and one of the national service volunteers is just coming in. Helene stubbornly holds the spoon up twenty centimetres from Matthes face and waits. He bloody well can eat it off her stomach! Not quite the same as eating out of the palm of someone's hand, is it? She can't really put a name to her anger at all. It's as if all the rage in the world has caught a cold inside her – of all people – and is suddenly shoving its way out in a massive coughing fit. The yoghurt jumps around to the rhythm of her stomach contracting and spreads out even further, and Matthes now throws the covers over her and then himself on top, telling her she needs to calm down. Calm down. The fact that he's lying on top of her makes her even angrier at first, and she screams her disability out heartily, from deep in her bowels: that it needn't lie so heavily on her stomach and kidneys any more, it can stay outside for all she cares, because deep down she's still the same Helene as before! The volunteer comes to Matthes's aid, and they hold her down together, amazed at how much strength there is in this body that can't stand or walk. Just as she's giving herself an A for rebelling, her lovely courage starts to collapse, leaving behind a little heap. Not of misery, just of the splintered remains of her revolt, which could still all turn to ash if she's not careful. She doesn't want to place herself under strain, and have the remnants burn away to nothing. She's slowing her breathing down. There we go, now. There we go.

In the afternoon Matthes comes for the second time that day. Helene is lying in bed, her head turned towards the window. Once he's sat himself in the chair, not saying a word, she suddenly asks him whether they'd had a *political* relationship before. Of course he thought they'd had a *positive* relationship – how could it have lasted so long otherwise... Her head is still turned towards the window, so he can't see her mouth.

'No, *political*!'

She's annoyed with him for misunderstanding, blaming herself, then him, in quick succession.

He doesn't say anything.

Does he think it's a stupid question? She goes red. It is, in fact, a stupid question. Political relationships are what you have between nations – bilateral or multilateral, of course – but she can't think of a way to describe what she means.

'I loved you from the moment I first saw you.' As he says it, his eyes move to the window – perhaps their gazes will meet out there somewhere.

She knows that, though. He's often said it to her. No doubt he's repeating it because he thinks she's forgotten, that it's been erased by the deluge of blood in her stupid skull. But *that* doesn't have to be programmed in again, no: it's in there, and it'll stay in there. Did he say it in the past tense, though? Now she turns her head towards him.

'What?'

'I loved you from the moment I first saw you.'

His gaze is still wandering around out of the window. It doesn't seem to have encountered hers.

Yes, definitely the past tense. And in the present tense – would it still apply? Does he still love her? How's she going to find that out... She starts to get agitated. Her left hand moves over the outline of her voicebox, and investigates her bratwurst-like double chin. (Still there.) It moves up to her stubbly hair and fingers the scabby stumps. (Unchanged.) Yes, she's ugly – where would love come into it. It's quite simple really, she doesn't know what she's supposed to think.

Are there any other words for love?

She can't think of any.

What does he think he's doing, starting on about Heidemühlen. It's too much for her: she's on a completely different track now, with a lump in her throat, her leg in irons and her arse nowhere near a loo! All at once she's laughing, because the words have come into her head all by themselves, and what's more, they're accurate: she's fighting back tears (lump in her throat), her paralysed side is her ball and chain (leg irons) and now she's getting pretty strong toilet urges – she can't say so, but pulls the wheelchair fiercely towards her, directing Matthes to get her into it, then she's off. Matthes is hesitant, but follows her into the corridor. She beckons him closer: he's going to have to come in with her and get her on the toilet – she can't do it herself, and by the time a nurse came it'd almost certainly be too late! She spurs him on with hissed sequences of letters which, through sheer agitation, she genuinely can't put in order. With expressions ranging from grandeur to shame. With timid tugs at his sleeve, and in the end a weak poke with her foot, he's finally understood. He pulls down her pants and sits her on the toilet seat, then turns away and goes over to the window. The noises are torture for her – there are splashes in the toilet bowl – but she can't hold them in and ask him to leave. Never before has she felt so wretched in front of him. But it passes, and he comes over to pull her pants back up. They've never pooed together before, she has to say.

But whether things will stay that way, after everything going on here, she just has no idea.

He takes her back, but when they get to the bay window with the curtain, she slams her left foot on the floor and insists they don't go any further. He can certainly go and get himself a chair – there are two just a bit further on, either side of a pot plant. When he sits down, it comes again: 'Well, were we *political*?'

He's not smiling at all – the expression on his face is soft, tender even; serene. He brushes back his hair with his right hand, then the hand comes to rest on his neck, or rather grabs hold of it – his own hand! That looks funny. The tenderness slips now, and a grotesque face emerges from the mush: C-a-n y-o-u r-e-m-e-m-b-e-r, i-n t-h-e e-i-g-h-t-i-e-s...?

He's said it in a fake, quavery old man's voice while rocking back and forth, and she suddenly remembers that this question had often slipped out of his mouth when he wanted to recall something. She responds with the same expression and gestures, but no words. Now he gets it.

In the mid-eighties...

In the mid-eighties they moved from Henrichshorst to Berlin, and it was the first time they'd needed more than just a certain number of children to be eligible for their flat. (Marriage? Marriage!) She was unemployed for a while after that, even though the concept didn't officially exist in the GDR at the time. She'd got to know Raphael, and Sibylle, who'd been banged up for their fondness for criticising the government by repeating the same arguments, over and over. For a while she'd felt like their silent reflection: they opened their mouths to speak, and Helene stared in open-mouthed wonder. When she thinks about it now, she feels like an animal rights activist who's had fur chucked at her, and who half-fearfully, half-angrily just wants to be rid of it. Is she going to fight back? She's going to fight back. Something is disagreeable to her. Hadn't she sat there far too quietly in the boat, year after year, just drifting through thirty-one of the forty years granted to the East? Instances of rebelliousness which seemed quite bold at the time had, in retrospect, turned into ludicrous little anecdotes. An example? In the mid-eighties, her eldest started school. For the first parents' meeting Helene had prepared a presentation – the teacher, fresh out of teacher training college, had requested it of her. 'How can I help provide a focussed and happy start to my child's schooling?' This and that, plus a bit of TV. On the back wall of the classroom there was a picture of Samson, one of the characters from the German-language version of Sesame Street. She was a bit suspicious of television, but if she had to allow it, then The Programme with the Mouse and Sesame Street were fine and perfectly watchable. She'd said it without thinking, because Samson was smiling at her. Which ripple came first? The ripple of laughter among the assembled parents. But when Helene brought Bengt to school the next morning, the picture of Samson had gone from the back wall, and an invitation to a discussion with the school's party executive committee lay on the fledgling teacher's desk instead. The party secretary had a daughter in Bengt's class, and felt herself called upon to trigger the second ripple – no laughing matter, by this point, but a laughable one. It had the same effect on Helene, even now: she found it entertaining. But it had a dark undercurrent. That suck-up of a secretary had torn down the picture of Samson the very same evening – the teacher had hissed this to Helene in passing from behind her hand. It was an incident without consequence – this narrow-mindedness wasn't really the teacher's problem, but she was too green to stick up for herself. She reckoned she had no idea who the picture was even of.

'Yes, how exactly do *you* know, Madam Party Secretary?'

A silent, slow-witted expression, then the redness of shame or anger (it wasn't exactly clear which), because no answer was an answer in itself. From then on, this *comrade* had brushed the matter under the table, and taken the credit for the act of mercy she claimed to have brought about. The teacher felt a good bit of obligation towards Helene after that but Helene had simply brushed it to one side, and it had never cast a shadow over her son. (Two years later, in his Marx-and-Engels lesson – probably Local History – Bengt asked in all seriousness why the working class revered a factory-owner, which of course Engels had unquestionably been, and therefore a capitalist. Apparently this meant that even capitalists could be good people.)

Another example? In the mid-eighties they'd suddenly got a telephone. Matthes's idea that the *Security* could chime in at any moment had seemed paranoid to her, until the day she'd taken the phone off the hook early in the morning – Lissy needed sleep to rid her bruised little body of a bout of glandular fever – and gone over to her neighbour's for a coffee. When Helene came back, the very same phone was back in its cradle – where it belonged, but where she swore she hadn't left it. She'd gone over the start of the day again and again, but could only ever see herself lifting the receiver, not putting it back. She never did establish whether, in an unthinking moment, her love of order hadn't perhaps got the better of her. But the security seed had been sown, growing and growing until it put Matthes off using the phone completely, but providing more and more fun for Helene: 'Apparatchiks, note this down,' she'd say loudly and clearly, whenever she was arranging times or places to meet friends. It was a creeping transition towards courage which gradually became a habit. In the mid-eighties, the von Trotta film about Rosa Luxemburg was also shown on their side of the Wall. The foothold she found in it lent her own voice a touch of hardness, at least, when allowing herself the odd outburst at the narrow-minded idiocy she encountered day in, day out. She can't piece back together how everything used to work in those days. A film as a foothold, a book as a balustrade... Although it was a long time ago, she'd been profoundly shaped by the idea that *life* happened between the lines, and couldn't be understood by just anyone. Today, even after long and thorough questioning, books from back then didn't tell her what it was that turned her into a grown-up, and into the railing of the ship from which people could look out to other places. *Everything is relative*, she thinks now. Everything is contained in its historic little patch of garden, and when you're no longer in a position to cultivate it, you have to move over and make room.

Move over and make room.

In an instant she feels cold.

Matthes fetches a jacket and puts it round her shoulders.

Oh, Matthes.

Matthes has gone again, postponing Heidemühlen until tomorrow. She went out with him up to the main gate – the raising and lowering of the barrier there gives her a not-nice feeling. As if the air was being continually cut off, and only released in gusts into the hospital grounds. A hasty goodbye – she even pushes Matthes away with her left arm so she can turn round quickly, and not have to look at the barrier any more. What time is it? Five o'clock, she thinks, after a glance at the sun. Matthes's way of estimating the time has stuck in her mind over the years, although she doesn't understand it at all. He's always very nearly right, give or take half an hour. Even points of the compass are no problem: he lines the hand of his watch up with the sun, and halfway between the hand and the twelve is South. He hadn't needed to tell her that a church's steeple is often at its west end, and the altar usually at the east, but he had shown her that trees in the open mostly lean to the east, because the wind blows most often from the west. And that the rings on a lone tree stump are wider apart on the south side, while moss on trees exposed to wind and weather grows on the northwest side. Snapshots of the boy's life he once led. Her feet in their dark blue sandals want to jump like boys' feet: over the ditch next to the main entrance; over the benches – using her right arm for support, and leaping over with both legs in one move; over the lines between the concrete slabs on the path to the carpark; or over the fence surrounding a long-empty building in the grounds, like a belt fastened at three-metre intervals. Her feet are itching – she wants to, she's going to: she engages the brake on her wheelchair and pulls herself up using one of the cafeteria tables.

When she comes round, she's being carried into her room on

a stretcher. Carola is pulling the wheelchair along behind her.

'Now then, Helen love, what've you done this time, eh?'

Ah, Hartmut... What's *he* doing over here in the Stroke Unit? And what's she doing on this stretcher anyway? A niggling memory, little pieces coming together only slowly – she'd tried to stand up. Hadn't she even wanted to jump?

That's a boy's life for you.

They've done another CT scan of her skull after the fall. She's told about it the following morning during ward rounds – they want to rule out further bleeding as the cause of her loss of consciousness. Apparently it's not yet clear to the doctors whether it was an epileptic seizure.

Epileptic seizure?

She wants to fly into a rage.

'A boy's life!'

With that cry, her breath does a runner, leaving her completely empty of air: she wants to breathe in deeply, but gasps and chokes and doesn't have the necessary strength to cough it up. Air! Air! Her body crumples into the pillow, when it would rather fill out with a warm current of breath, and fear comes from behind her, from the back of her neck, surrounding her throat with a firm grip and closing her airway completely. She gurgles, catches her breath in fits and starts; the word oxygen comes into her head, oxygen's the name of the stuff she's starting to run out of – oxygen with an "x" as in box, detox, paradox, exotoxic; breathe, breathe... Something moves, clears its throat; something clears the way – her airway – cautiously, bit by bit, making the fear loosen its grip, tighten again, then loosen once more. That's it, now; and slowly, very slowly, she can now draw breath (or try to). It comes to her from far away, via secret and circuitous routes; past the uvula and through the voicebox, whose flap should be able to shut better than it did a moment ago, when she was choking so violently on nothing – no, not on nothing but on saliva, which she's now bringing up with great effort. Has she done it? The team doing the round are staring at her, wide-eyed. A junior doctor has shoved an arm under her and sat her up, while a nurse looks on in alarm and the senior consultant looks thoughtful.

Well, she's done it.

'That's going to happen more often now,' says the senior consultant. A consequence of the paralysis.

'But epileptic seizure?'

She asks aloud, addressing everyone there, and launches into an explanation of how she'd wanted to jump in her blue sandals, and her feet had twitched as if they could do it – she'd wanted to try, just stand up and go for it, make a leap for it. So she'd put her left foot in front of the right, and that was the last thing she could remember. At that moment she becomes aware of the headache – she has a huge bump on the back of her head. A little horn, as her father would say.

'Crikey, now I understand.'

Luckily there are witnesses who saw what happened. The waitress in the cafeteria. Two women sitting at the next table. The conclusion is reached that it probably wasn't a seizure.

Do they really believe her?

Before she can answer the question, a 'Wanted' poster goes up for abnormal brain activity: EEG, as a precaution.

Again and again she puts the past back together in reverse, using the pieces she comes up with, both big and small. Something like that, anyway. But is that right? Never has she spent so much time practising how to remember. It's not going too badly, she finds – it's just the last few weeks and months before the event, which ultimately turned everything inside out, that she can only access in fragments. Her putative decision to move out stands alone and unconnected to anything else, such as whether she'd intended taking Lottchen with her. Had they maybe even been planning to sell the house? Or had the decision become redundant? Did her aneurysm intervene dramatically, or had they already come to some agreement beforehand? An agreement which, from today's perspective, would either ruin or brighten the rest of her life: a life she *didn't* want to have to justify to anyone, *simple as that*? How had they left it – what had been their final position? Why was Matthes not saying anything about it? Uncertainty makes her gaze lose focus. She has no idea whether she'd be able to summon up the concentration and the energy to ask him about it.

And what if she's a *disabled person* now?

Yes, for the time being she couldn't possibly live by herself. In the same moment it's as if she can see before her the little flat she's just rented: two rooms, a balcony, kitchen, bathroom; she can see herself in it – sitting at the desk, cooking, welcoming Matthes as he delivers Lottchen. But then the relief: no, that was where she'd lived when she was on her scholarship. Where was it again? And when?

Nothing.

Nothing at first...

But then it gets clearer: she'd spent half the writing-up period with Lottchen and half without, enjoying the time with her as a holiday just for the two of them, and not worrying about the manuscript on her laptop – which had increasingly distanced itself from her – until she let it out again at home and let everything carry on again. She questions herself strongly: the Lottchen she remembers isn't that much different from the Lottchen she's seen in the last few days, so it can't be very long ago. Winter, then – the trees bare, and the flat countryside congealing in grey oil. They'd sometimes hung around in a big discount store where, yes, they'd bought Christmas presents. They'd ridden out to the industrial estate to get to it, Lottchen on her little bike and Helene on her big bike, then they'd locked up their bikes and whiled away their time in the shop. They'd biked back to the old manor house laden with bags, in the end packing up two big parcels to be collected by the postman before they got the train home themselves. They'd taken a rucksack full of dried fruit with them, as an unorthodox way of sweetening Christmas for the others at home – the idea was to have a celebration without chocolate, but then chocolate of course barged right in, to rousing cheers. Meanwhile the fruit, completely ignored, carved out a lonely existence in the family treat cupboard, in a shoebox sacrificed from Matthes's inexhaustible supply. That was it: last Christmas had been the midpoint in her scholarship period. Before that, she'd spent three weeks in Nottuln, and the same after New Year, in – Münsterland, wasn't it? Yes, now she can see Münster Station, and the kiosks outside which smelt of old fat for frying fish, chips and burgers. She's carrying her red suitcase – no, pulling it along behind her with one hand, and Lottchen with the other, and she has her red bag on her front for her money and cards, which she's worried about in this crush of people. She has to wait for the bus, which will appear at some point in the endless stream of buses – never when the timetable says it will, always unpredictable. She has no inkling of this the first time she stands there, looking at the timetable she'd printed off at home, but finally the right one comes and they get on. There's a young girl sitting opposite them, whose suitcase is standing next to theirs. It falls over when the bus sets off and the girl jumps up, knocking over Helene's case in the process; they laugh. The girl eventually sits back down and seems to want to say something; Helene does too; but neither them does, and so the girl reads and Helene looks out of the window, and at Lottchen dozing. Yes, the flat countryside in grey oil – you couldn't really describe it any other way. They travel for a while on the motorway and then turn off. By this point they've moved the cases from standing to lying down, so at least they can't fall over any more; they can't slide anywhere either, because there's a lady with a pushchair standing right in front of Helene's case. The bus stops and goes, and goes and stops, finally stopping in Nottuln, and the girl gets off with Helene and Lottchen, the only ones to do so here. They look at each other. Helene is hesitant, unsure which way to turn, as is the girl. When the girl finally asks a passer-by how to get to such-and-such an address, Helene says that's exactly where they're headed too, so they can walk together. It's maybe about another quarter of a mile further on...

She's so pleased that last Christmas and the events leading up to it have come back to her. After Nottuln, the girl – Marlene – also wanted to move to Berlin. She was a graduate of the German Institute for Literature in Leipzig, and had just made her highly-regarded debut. Helene had said she could live with them in Karlshorst to start with, until she found a suitable and affordable flat. Marlene was staying a month longer in S. than Helene, so in the meantime Matthes repainted one of the rooms they hadn't been using much since the boys moved out. They'd put the bed, a table and a cupboard back in, but left everything else in the cellar. Then, at the end of January, when Marlene was finally due to come, she'd sent them a rejection letter: she'd fallen in love, and was moving in with her girlfriend. Helene thinks of how she'd had to pause between reading the two announcements: that Marlene had fallen in love, and that she'd be moving in with her girlfriend.

Patricia comes to mind, from her student halls all those years ago; she was studying medicine. Helene had been dumbfounded when this married woman with two children had invited her over for dinner, and confessed her love for her. The husband wasn't there. Helene had listened and given Patty a kiss on the forehead without saying a word. Then she'd left, leaving Patty sat there, equally silent and her eyes brimming with tears. From then on Helene had avoided her, giving her a wide berth – always timid, and at pains to make herself thinner than she was, if she did happen to see her; and twenty years later Patricia had suddenly turned up at Helene's door with her wife, more than a little proud and with a dignity that was quite something. Yes, it was four years ago: they'd just moved into the new house and were in the middle of unpacking crates and boxes. The cellar was flooded, and they were having to put up with a whole load of stress getting the contractor to sort it out – they couldn't store anything down there and were worried the damp would spread to the rest of the house. In the midst of this glorious chaos Patricia had come knocking, having got the address from an old fellow student Helene was still in touch with. Had she come all the way from Eisenhüttenstadt just to see Helene again? Not quite. Two more children had come along to join the first two – twin boys, who had retinal damage as a result of very low birth weight, and who'd started at the school for the visually impaired in Berlin the previous week. Patricia had just brought them back after a weekend at home, and used the opportunity to call in on Helene. (She can't remember the boys' names, but who knows whether she'd have been able to under other circumstances either.) Patty's wife was an electrician. Patty had simply referred to her as 'my wife', although a lesbian wedding still wasn't possible at the time – maybe they'd been to the Netherlands or Denmark to get married, if you could even do that? – and Helene had been able to look the wiry blonde very squarely in the eye and find her attractive. They'd left two hours later and Helene had watched them: crossing the road in front of the house, hand in hand, to their car parked on the other side, and, after a none-too-brief kiss, getting in. And she'd wondered (or so she believes now) what she and Matthes looked like when they left friends' flats after going to see them, and ambled back to their car. They didn't kiss, and of course she'd be rummaging around in her bag for the key, rather than holding Matthes's hand. She'd yank open the door, flop down on to the driver's seat, and then wonder impatiently what was taking Matthes so long – if it was dark, guaranteed he'd be off somewhere having a piss against a tree. Like an old married couple, she thinks, though Matthes was a mere boy next to his peers: still unpredictable, acting on a whim – someone who brazenly subverted any expectations he blundered into, and would suddenly appear on the opposite side to the one expected. His grin was infectious, his smile wasn't; but his perceived age, which was better than his real age by miles, of course has nothing to do with the length of their marriage – they've been officially committed to each other for almost twenty years now. A murmur rises from her bowels, and the fact that she *thinks* she knows him deep down – but on the other hand finds his behaviour imponderable – suddenly presents her with a conundrum.

Imponderable.

The Latin word arrives like the urge to make a mockery of it all. Completely and utterly.

Exhausted, she has slept – remembering takes it out of you (but where to?). Then she gets woken up because it's time for the EEG, which is supposed to shed light on the fugitive brain lesion. She has to get dressed, which takes a while; the nurse, a new one she doesn't know, has to help her pull her tracksuit bottoms up, and get her yellow jumper over her head. They're in too much of a hurry to think about shoes, but think about them she does, and insists that she has them. Insists, too, that she combs her hair, and puts her face cream on. All to the nurse's displeasure. When she's finally in her chair, she wonders whether being proud of her memory might seem strange to other people – but then it occurs to her that other people don't know anything about it. The nurse pushes her to the lift, and they go down, then it's back up in the main building to Neurology. There the nurse hands over the great sheaf of papers of which Helene's merely an appendage, then leaves without saying a word, or even looking at her. Silly cow. She could've done all that by herself. She sits and waits. In front of her there's a *damaged* man – could you call him that? There's a big piece missing from the top of his skull, on the left. His skull looks bashed in, and something is pulsating violently under the pink skin, but she doesn't feel any disgust – she'd actually like to ask him what had happened. She can see he's missing an arm there, and also – the icing on the cake – a lower leg; have they sewn his foot on at the knee, or something? Now she does actually feel sick, but the damaged man can't see it – he's dozing, his eyes are only open a crack, and the glint she can see behind them is white. When she looks at the half of his head that's still intact, she comes to the conclusion that he must be young and good-looking. Or must have *been*.

They've really cobbled him together any old how.

She's ashamed of herself straight away. Luckily someone comes to get the boy, a beefy nurse with a gentle face – she can even see something almost like pity welling there, and she's never noticed that here before. How are they going to attach the EEG electrodes to a skull like his? She was probably lucky with what happened to her. Things could have been worse. Things could always have been worse: everything is relative, once you look beyond your own frame of reference. That must illuminate things for her, surely – is there a light on in there?

There is.

The beefy nurse comes to get her, now. No pity. Just as well. Pity eats into you like napalm, she thinks; even if you could run, you wouldn't be able to escape it once it's got its teeth into your skin. She looks at him again cautiously, but there's no trace of it in his face. He wheels her into a long white room, with a window at the far end that's not letting in much light. A kind of partition wall in the middle of the room turns the long, thin space almost into two long, thin spaces. In the one furthest back, where she is, it's pretty dark. She sits there. This is taking a while. It gets darker. Outside it starts to rain, beating on and dribbling down the window panes; this makes her sleepy, and she half-dozes off, waking again with a start when a butch-looking dragon sticks her head through the door. The dragon looks in, pulls her head back again, and then shoves her wiry dragon-body through in its place; her head comes last, nodding slightly. Her head and body seem to move in opposite directions – she turns her top half to the right, then the bottom half to the left. And vice versa. Only her feet, bizarrely, are standing firmly on the floor. Helene watches them in disbelief, how they gather momentum and distribute it in the muscles and tendons; she can clearly see them flexing, thanks to the woman's loose Birkenstocks. She's wearing a short little work coat over her Capri pants. Because of her muscly calves, the trousers are a bit shorter than they're supposed to be. On both the middle and ring fingers of her left hand, she's wearing a gold ring; they're practically identical, with a ruby nestling in gold petals.

'Right then, let's make a start!'

Her voice reminds Helene of the teacher she had for the first four years of primary school – a rasping voice that does the occasional gurgling somersault. More onerous, however, is that she's talking incessantly, and in a jerky, bouncy way that's hard to stomach: her sentences ebbs away towards the end, but she has to get the necessary airflow going again before she can start a new one. She's not old, thirty-five maybe? She puts a frame, with straps attached, on Helene's head, and rubs some kind of stuff on her scalp where the electrodes are going to go. She's still talking incessantly. Helene hardly understands any of it, except *pairs of shoes*, *braces*, *daughters* and *homeopath*. The sentences where the sound ebbs away have no real connection to each other – Helene attempts to follow, but gives up in the end, letting herself slump into the chair. She'd learnt as a student that an EEG only gives meaningful results when the patient is fully calm and relaxed, so she closes her eyes and gets comfy. She's surprised at how well she manages it, because in the last few weeks she doesn't think she's been very supple at all. Her spine is curved to fit the chair perfectly; her hands are resting on the end of the arm rests, fingers lightly curled; and it's nice just keeping her eyes closed and knowing she's being looked after – by someone she doesn't know, but who doesn't mean her any harm (unlike the intensive care staff a few weeks ago, and the evil intentions she'd ascribed to them – possibly while half-asleep). It's also nice to know that life has caught up with her again, and hasn't dismissed her for poor attendance. On the contrary, life has taken her poor attendance as an opportunity to remind her of its existence, quite literally; and while she's reclining in the EEG chair, the hands of a strange woman busy about her head, Helene can suddenly *feel* how this woman's existence basically depends on bad things happening to people like her. On people like her needing a frame with straps attached put on their heads, in order to search for a lesion. The doctors owe their existence to that of damaged people, towards whom they sometimes seem to feel more derision and malice than respect. Conversely, the respect shown to doctors *by* those damaged people can degenerate into awe or blind obedience. Strange how the world is set up. A twisting of the facts, she'd say, if anyone were to ask. But no one will, here. Not about that, anyway.

The butch dragon gives instructions. Now, if you could close your eyes. Open them when you hear the bleep. Close them again when you hear the next bleep. It's dim in this tunnel-like bit of the room, and it's an effort for Helene to keep her mind on the bleeping; sleep is crawling over her skin, like a dark slug-like creature. But the next instructions are already coming – keep your eyes open now, please – and a sequence of flickering lights, intended to provoke, disturbs the slug-like creature, which withdraws faster than she'd have expected for a slug. One more time. And again.

In between, there are checks to make sure the electrodes are sitting securely. Now if you could breathe quickly and deeply! For several minutes. Helene remembers as a child blowing up the airbed on a camping trip to the Baltic, while her parents were putting up the tent, and how sick that made her feel. She waits for nausea to set in now, but nothing happens.

Twenty minutes have passed.

Twenty minutes *of life*.

Today, nothing comes into her head whatsoever: it's all a complete blank. Everything she sees before her looks grey and has a metallic gleam, as if it's been polished – a downward-sloping track, on which every thought immediately rolls away. She's already had two or three days like this since she's been here, but doesn't know if she also had them *before*. There's nothing tangible between her synapses, she thinks, and is amazed she can even think that, when she thought she'd just observed that she's incapable of thinking anything. She's getting impressions here and there from somewhere, then, but before any of them can develop into brain work, they've already rolled off and away. They're not always gone for good, because sometimes they come back as insinuation, and buzz and flap about; but she can't get hold of them in this animated, agitated state, and so they're quickly gone again. Now she's afraid they really are gone for ever, and her heart rate starts to exceed the rate of her pacemaker. She's pleased when her heart beats faster than sixty beats a minute all by itself. Joy and fear balance each other out for a moment – then the latter wins out, and her heartbeat is swallowed up in the fearful tangle of manic thought fragments. She wants to force herself into a state of calm and composure. And to be allowed to hang on to just a single tiny thought fragment for a moment longer! Forceps try to get at the fragments, but it's futile, and really she knows that. With an effort, she closes her eyes. Her eyeballs are darting about behind her eyelids, and so restlessly that she has to use her left hand to cling to the bed frame. In the end her fingertips go white from keeping her hand clasped tightly round the bars. Finally the force making her eyeballs dart about starts to dwindle – only gradually, but it's happening. And as she slowly releases her hand it's as if she's recently run the 4000 metres, but has already started to recover – the agreeable trembling in her legs still tells of their previous exertion, but her breaths are already coming more steadily. She stays lying like that for a while, then puts the top part of the bed almost vertical and reaches for yesterday's newspaper, brought in by Matthes. Since the fall of the

Taliban, she reads, enforcing the ban on poppy cultivation for the manufacture of opium has become practically impossible. The UN's agricultural agency is expecting a yield of just under three thousand tonnes of opium, which is enough for three hundred tonnes of heroin. What does that mean? Hadn't the Taliban, as radical Islamists, tried to prohibit poppy cultivation? The ban must have existed before last October, when the USA and its allies began their bizarre anti-terror campaign. Ah yes, it also says here that the ban was put in place by Mullah Omar, the leader of the Taliban, and that it had been a great success because only eighty tonnes of raw opium had been produced in the previous year. So that was *one* good thing at least to happen under Taliban rule (she purses her lips scornfully) – the drastic reduction in opium growing. But hadn't one of the pretexts for this war been the claim that both the Islamist Taliban and al-Qaida were supplying themselves with money and weapons from the opium trade? Something doesn't add up there – she can clearly sense it, but not formulate it properly. She remembers seeing in a film that poppy production can easily be exposed by satellite; that it's not possible to conceal it. It's true it had been drastically curbed by the Taliban. What wasn't adding up here had to do with the Americans, and their claim to want to breathe down the opium growers' necks. Since the occupation of Afghanistan, production had been in full swing once again, with the Americans showing no signs of taking decisive action against it. So yet another reason for war has proved spurious. Or has it? Her uncertainty starts deep inside her, where she should be thinking about why the Americans and their allies had invaded Afghanistan in the first place. The cliché "on false grounds" is there in her head, but she's incapable of nailing it down in concrete terms. Apart from opium production, of course, but that was never the primary reason for war.

Damn and blast, why was it again that the Yanks had gone to war?

There it is: the image of the collapsing towers... When was that? September, just under a year ago, an event which, together with its consequences, had kept her in perpetual suspense and anxiety ever since! Until God had raised merry hell inside her head, and blocked off everything coming in from the outside...

Are there not the tips of cautious young shoots coming out of her? All at once she notices the glass ball surrounding her. In one place, only a tiny spot, a powerful tendril has managed to shatter the glass, and it was through this hole that she'd been able to see the collapsing towers. Yes, that's the only way: she has to get this blasted ivy (or whatever the stuff is) to smash the ball! A shower of glass shards is not without its risks, but the thicker she can get it to twine around the ball, the less likely it is that the glass will fall back on to her. She can't comprehend that *the world* is out there. Until today, she'd attempted to dig channels into the past, but only ever her own past – she'd tried to reconstruct the film in which *she's* still the heroine. In doing so, she simply hadn't seen how shielded she was here – what a sanctuary it was! She'd looked up at the clouds as if looking up into a bell, stretching over her and ending at the horizon; and the cats that'd crossed her path in the hospital grounds since then remained unconnected to the wild ones living in the woods, which she always used to think about; and the oats in the muesli had simply fallen out of the packet, along with the laptop from the sky, and the pen from the pencil case. It was all so simple that there hadn't been room for doubles or multiples, and her eyes had been full and yet empty at the same time – she's noticing it now that what she's seen is starting to dwindle, and what she's remembered suddenly arrives, still hesitant, still stumbling. It gives every object a halo, and every word a big leather speech bubble, which overlaps with other bubbles around other words; then the intersections themselves take shape, and new words emerge within them... On and on.

And always determinedly headstrong, even if that head now has two fresh holes in the skull and a visible join on the forehead, and might be more delicate than she thought.

The EEG yielded the discovery of the lesion, of course, but no increase in excitability, so the doctors now seem to assume that Helene's story – her desire to jump – is true; the murmurs during ward rounds point in that direction, anyway. So no medication, but she's to be monitored more closely. She'd have refused medication for epilepsy, anyway – she knows how she fell over. Heidemühlen is postponed for a few days. Anger wants to come to the boil, but before it can get itself frothed up, Helene is able to turn it down. Got lucky there.

She's sitting in bed – the top part of it raised again, her left knee drawn up. The right one can move too, but not enough, so she grabs hold of her trousers and pulls, until it's bent up next to her left. She hastily grips her right hand with her left, so both arms are now slung round her knees. She stays still. Probably looks relaxed. She'd like a cigarette. Though she wouldn't be able to pick up even a cup or a book in this position – her right leg would inevitably slide back down the mattress. Before, she'd have been able to do it. Before, meaning: six weeks ago.

Back then, though, she never sat like this in bed, because the bed at home wasn't adjustable. As she's thinking this, it seems to her as if someone is leaning against her back. Someone with sharp vertebrae. She can even feel the person's head, and long hair now falling over her shoulders. The hair is already going a bit grey, so the someone isn't exactly young any more – it's not the henna-red hair of one of her daughters, or the black-brown hair of another, so that rules both of them out, though their vertebrae are probably sharp enough. The someone is reaching over their heads now and putting a hand on Helene's forehead, so that she trembles at the soft touch: she can feel the gentle pressure so clearly, even on the sections of skull where she has no sensation because of the operation, and slowly leans back further, loosening her tightly-clasped hands. Her right leg falls weakly on to the mattress. The left slides down slowly, too. She sits like that for several minutes.

She knows who the someone is.

Who *she* is, to be precise.

Her name is Viola.

IV

Venation

VIOLA HAS DESCENDED ON HER SO SUDDENLY that she's left incapable of speech for the rest of the day. It's too exhausting hunting for words to answer the questions she's being asked. Is she actually being asked questions? Probably. The two nurses look at her for a long time. Their mouths are moving. Carola is even holding her hand, and her face comes so close that the ends of her blonde hair tease Helene. Why is she aware of this, but unable to hear anything? She doesn't really want to think about it. Exhausting. Eyes shut.

Viola clearly hasn't lost her shape in Helene's head, but that shape's been stashed away somewhere – did the scalpel cut it off? Now her form rises up: tall and masculine, even from a distance, with an oval-shaped skull, very slender nose, eyes that are easily annoyed and a disparaging, downturned mouth. Then the jutting chin, badly-pruned fringe, thin hair twisted into a little knot, long fingers, large feet, and breasts merging with her paunch. Shabby trousers, a knitted beige jumper, and an army-green parka on top.

Something about Viola had confused Helene when she saw her for the first time, though she couldn't have said what it was. But when Viola introduced herself, it sliced like a guillotine through the words on the tip of Helene's tongue. What did you say your name was? Would you believe it, I thought I heard Viola! That's what she'd wanted to say, but in the same moment shut her already-open mouth: Viola had spoken in a man's voice. She'd actually taken Viola to be a man – it wouldn't have occurred to her to see anything other than her eyes were making her believe. She only just managed to stop those same eyes looking for Viola's breasts, so she could verify everything that had just taken place in her head at lightning speed. She went red on the spot, and submitted to Viola's brittle, condescending smile with almost servile meekness. Guilt. The feeling arrived as unexpectedly as the sun which suddenly shone down on their grey early-November encounter. Really the sun coming out was perfectly fitting for the park at Sanssouci, where the incident took place, but up to that point the day had only made Helene think of the water in her mop bucket after a full and thorough clean of their Karlshorst house, before she tipped it down the toilet: leaden and viscous. And so Helene, crestfallen, had stood there in the surprise sunshine, shoulders hunched, while Viola's face slowly lost its acquired haughtiness and something like emotion started to show round her mouth. Later on, neither could say exactly how long the moment lasted, though Viola's estimate was decidedly longer than Helene's. When the slow-motion scene faded, they shook hands and went their separate ways.

Anyway, at the time they reckoned it was only a few moments before they both turned back towards each other, and Helene smacked a hand to her forehead: of course, their encounter hadn't just dropped out of the now-blue sky! Viola hadn't wanted to tell Helene her name via letter. They'd met at Sanssouci because Viola lived in Potsdam, and Helene was the one wanting something from her. That's why Viola hadn't come to Berlin, because she hadn't actually wanted anything from Helene. They'd arranged that Helene would carry her raspberry-red leather satchel, so Viola could identify her – to this day, Helene's sure you wouldn't find another bag like it. And the reason for their meeting...

Matthes arrives. Interrupts.

No, she doesn't want to do any more talking today.

She can see Matthes isn't worried about her. Maybe he thinks her silence is just her up to her usual antics; she frequently used to stop in the middle of talking, even if only for a short time – half an hour, an hour – then the words would come tumbling out of her mouth again completely of their own accord, like strange naked lemmings. He probably even takes it as a good sign – that the bouts of silence he's learnt to interpret as a protest are coming back. A protest against his stupid way of twisting the lemmings before they were even out of her mouth, so that once they were they went round in wild swarms, spreading unrest. Admittedly it's never occurred to him to do it since she's been in hospital – on the contrary, he's thoughtful, and tries to interpret her wishes without her having to say anything – but he certainly hasn't forgotten about it. She's happy to see him talk. A natural-seeming border has been drawn between Matthes and Viola and runs right through the middle of her. When she closes her eyes, it hurts all the way along it.

She doesn't challenge him.

She leaves him for several minutes so she can watch the sun disappearing behind the ruins of the old boiler house. Is that the time already – what about supper today? She can't remember, then suddenly sees the prepared sandwiches, half a boiled egg garnished with chives and an apple juice on the bedside cabinet. Carola's probably brought her it, thinking Helene was asleep. She grabs the egg now and goes to stuff it in her mouth. Matthes intervenes, grabbing her hand as the first half of the half disappears down the hatch. Ok, fine – she'll just bite a bit off, she won't just shove the whole lot in – it probably wouldn't have gone down well anyway, given she's so prone to choking at the moment. She chews slowly, then her hand goes back and puts the second half of the half back on the plate. No, she doesn't want to eat anything after all. Matthes bends over her, puts his arm round her, lays his cheek against hers. Is he saying goodbye? Yes, as it happens – but she didn't hear that either.

She's pleased about that, and falls asleep.

'Legs up! Both of them!

Helene's lying on the mat. Her left leg gets to ninety degrees, her right leg manages maybe thirty. Not bad, she thinks. She knows her right arm won't manage anything, though – she can't direct a single finger even a tiny bit. And here comes the command already.

'Arms out in front, and up!'

The left one goes up.

'And what about the right one?'

The physio knows the answer to that, so can't she just get off her case?

Now the woman shoves her fist under Helene's shoulder and stimulates the shoulder blade with her knuckles – she can clearly feel it, but it's hardly painful. The physio guides Helene's right arm up and turns it slightly outwards. As she's holding it outstretched and up in the air, she challenges Helene to brace herself against her hand, at short intervals. They don't get anywhere with that, so the physio does minute elbow bends and stretches with her. Finally, she has to keep her hand up in the air – for as long as possible! – when the physio lets go. It only stays up seconds before her arm falls back down. But still. The physio starts stabilising her shoulder girdle, keeping her shoulders forward. They repeat this little game five times. Then it's time to try turning over. Helene lies on her back. The physio stands at her head and pulls her right arm, rotating it slightly and gripping underneath her right shoulder. Helene feels the impulse to move her pelvis and so initiate the turning over. The whole of her right side is extended, lengthened, stretched; it's a blissful feeling, and she realises how much she's missed it up to now. When she's finally lying on her front, the physio also wants her to prop herself up on her hands and knees. Somehow she just can't get her balance. She can definitely imagine giving clear preference to her strong, left side and managing to support herself like that, but it doesn't happen. The physio intervenes, but it still comes to a pitiful end.

Tears. Just briefly.

And her reason for meeting Viola?

She was doing research for an article for some women's magazine, about couples who'd divorced and were prepared to talk candidly about their relationships. She was doing it purely for the money. The letter Viola sent her – in response to the ad placed in various newspapers – was not untruthfully signed 'V.' Viktor, Volker, Volkmar. Helene had got Matthes to scan the letter and transfer it to her laptop, and she now looks feverishly for the file in question. *I divorced my wife in*

1994. We were forced into it. I don't know, however, whether my ex-wife would still want to talk about us now. V. There it was. It was the forced break-up that had piqued Helene's curiosity. She'd arranged to meet V. in the gardens at Sanssouci, at the foot of the famous steps, and had there encountered Viola for the first time – who of course was expecting Helene's confusion. The fact that Viola had also carried on walking after they'd made their introductions was something *she* later put down to her own confusion on seeing Helene. For some reason, their respective confusions hadn't yet finished with each other, and had made them both turn their heads to look back at the same moment. Helene couldn't help laughing then, with guilt breathing down her neck, and after a few embarrassed twitches even Viola broke into a broad grin. Helene didn't know what else to do apart from offer 'a thousand apologies', at which point Viola started to look somewhat more gracious, and they decided to go and find a café. On the way Helene went to great lengths to outline the proposed article, and emphasize her interest in Viola's version of the forced break-up. But Viola had gone quiet. Once they'd found somewhere small and quiet, she began laboriously peeling off her parka. By then Helene thought she could detect uncertainty behind the condescending manner, so she grabbed hold of the parka by the collar and it came off more easily. The thing was clearly a very snug fit.

Viola ordered two small glasses of herb schnapps for herself along with a large beer, while Helene lingered over a white coffee, stirring time into it like milk. Time she should have had with her youngest – she'd left Lottchen with a friend that afternoon. It seemed pointless to ask any questions, so she waited – as Viola was presumably waiting too – for the schnapps to take effect. The bloke in Viola fascinated her, which made her feel ashamed, just as earlier she'd felt guilty. Shame and guilt: two such closely-related feelings, and she couldn't locate the cause for hers. She had to force herself to keep her expression cheerful, though now her face was going red in random blotches. She could feel exactly where the redness was crawling upwards from her neck, as if she'd been drinking wine. Her hand pulled the roll-neck of her jumper further up, over her chin, and she buried herself in it, hoping Viola might be looking out of the window.

Viola was looking out of the window.

It looked like she suffered from rosacea. Around her mouth there were little pus-filled spots the size of pinheads, residing on the swollen, angry skin as if they knew they couldn't be got at easily. If things got stressful here it would likely make her skin reaction worse. Sympathy joined company with shame and guilt, and Helene wanted to slip away unnoticed so she wouldn't get involved in their three-way fight. An unpleasant set of circumstances. Viola carried her chin high so her eyes actually looked down on the dull people around them. The way nothing escaped those eyes seemed to Helene to be a laboriously-learnt skill. Those Viola eyes darted. Swerved. Flitted. Whirred. Scurried. Lunged. Struck. Helene, too, received one of these strikes when, despite herself, her gaze fell on Viola's breasts. They weren't big but they were definitely there, and from behind you could even see the outline of a bra. If Viola constantly had to put up with instinctive staring like this, then you could hardly wonder at the rosacea and defiant chin. Helene could've kicked herself.

Time swirled in her coffee as she stirred it, on and on.

After twenty-five minutes – Helene could see the clock

above the cake cabinet, ticking away – Viola started to talk about her children, who she hadn't seen for five years. The two boys lived not all that far from her, in a little village in Teltow-Fläming. Sometimes Viola had gone out there and spent an hour or two walking round the village, just waiting to bump into them. Forlorn attempts. Her wife didn't want to any more. Or couldn't? Helene was tempted to retort, but thankfully kept it to herself; after all, she didn't know her. Viola used to be a Viktor, who'd become increasingly less able to deal with his role as a man. At the same time, he was growing his beard thicker and thicker, and having his hair cut shorter and shorter. Until one day, when he'd put on a loose, turquoise empire-line dress – his wife's favourite – and shaved off his beard and hair and put on makeup; and then, with a silk scarf wrapped around his bald head, waited for his wife and kids to get back from doing the shopping. Helene had instantly pictured Matthes in her dark-red velvet maternity dress. Was Viola crying? Her eyes were swimming, anyway, but luckily their faraway gaze was directed at the floral decoration on the half-wall around their table. Helene had brushed away the image of Matthes in crushed velvet, but it was a stubborn one, crawling back out of the woodwork four or five times between two of Viola's sentences, ready to make Helene laugh. That was something she'd wanted to avoid at all costs...

What she experienced that afternoon was like something from another world. Like snow in summer, it fell and settled, which undoubtedly made it all the more surprising.

Viola's story had played out close to home.

As a child, Helene had once heard her mother telling a colleague on the quiet that the father of one of her pupils,

Helga Rant, also used to be her mother. Helene had puzzled over this sentence for a long time. The sense that she couldn't just get to the bottom of it hung in the very air in which the sentence had been uttered. She'd never forgotten it, and when, four years later, she saw Helga Rant hand in hand with her father, now fourteen and on her way to her coming-of-age ceremony at the local community centre, Helene had suddenly realised what it meant.

Oh, Viola.

The first afternoon with her wasn't something Helene wanted to waste on a women's magazine, however sophisticated it might be. "Sophisticated" was all too relative.

The medical team has decided to authorise Heidemühlen now. She's booked in there for the day after tomorrow. The psychologist is quickly asked to do new performance diagnostics, but Helene is equally quick to refuse. The speech therapist's assessment turns out to be remarkably banal – Helene had just stopped playing along. The woman only wanted her to do things she could do – what she couldn't do was left *unspoken* – so they clashed and parted on bad terms. She proved to be a 'non-cooperative patient', which she's pleased about. The physiotherapist's report, on the other hand, says 'very cooperative'. True, she can't yet stand, as the physio had predicted, but she's well on the way to doing so. Helene almost believes it herself…

The next morning she again wakes up with a very clear sense of being as strong and flexible as she was before. It always takes a while for her to get down off her high horse, and regain a sense of reality. Still, it's a nice way to wake up. The fact that it's not true, and it's only her sleep-drunk state making her believe it, doesn't wrangle much more than a smile from her in the meantime.

Today is Tuesday. The tenth of September. The schools have already been back for three weeks, as Lissy told her the last time she was here. Strange how everything carries on without her. Sourcing textbooks and exercise books for the children was always her job. She can't imagine Matthes now making it his. He's much more likely to have sent the children themselves out on the trail. Matthes is different to her. What he doesn't know can't hurt him. Whereas Helene must've gone the other way at some point: if you want something done properly, do it yourself. She prefers to buy the children's stuff so they don't forget half of it, for starters. She doesn't love herself for doing it, but she doesn't exactly love Matthes for handling it differently, either.

Why *does* she love him?

She just doesn't know any more.

It doesn't matter now, though, she thinks.

It doesn't half hurt, though, she thinks.

Something flashes in her head. If she's got a nice little titanium clip in there now, it can flash away as much as it likes, surely? Yes, something's flashing. And shadows? Shadows in between. Slowly they do themselves the honour, exchanging images with each other – images that take shape slowly at first, then increasingly thick and fast. Without having to close her eyes? She's amazed at it all flaring up. Amazed that it's frozen snapshots she's seeing, over and over again. No moving sequences. And over and over again – Viola! Viola in a vest, covering up her private parts in embarrassment. Viola in the woods, sitting on tree stumps. Viola birdwatching, striding out, singing, whistling, at the butcher's, at the computer, reading a book, reading a magazine. Drinking wine (not schnapps, not even the one she'd drunk on the day they first met). Mending some trousers, mending a blouse. Viola in the dark, sleeping. If Helene has seen Viola sleeping, then they must've been in a room together at night. Her memories drag themselves along, slowly and deliberately dragging what used to be along with them.

At the same time, her stomach flips.

She had loved Viola.

Helene is in her wheelchair, on her way to the ambulance taking her to Heidemühlen. She had a good day yesterday, or as good as it could've been with the matter of Viola in her head. She'd really like to know where exactly the Viola matter is. Whether it was cut off, literally, and has now come in round the back. Via different channels? The matter of Viola is incomplete. Viola isn't here, and hasn't once been to visit. Helene ransacks her drilled-into, sawn-open skull. She presses her hand down tightly over the distinct holes, as if she's afraid that fragments of the Viola matter will sneak off elsewhere if she's not careful. And she might never catch up with them again.

Even the day before yesterday, lacking in any *political correctness*, she'd probably have laughed at the idea of her loving a woman. How quickly everything staggers away, again and again.

But then something staggers back over to her again: as she crosses Outpatient Admissions in her wheelchair, she's suddenly reminded of her arrival at the hospital. It's all coming back! Is it really all coming back? She's getting nervous, her left hand is trembling. The way it's lying on her thigh makes it look like a plucked chicken in fear of its life. Weeks ago, she'd been wheeled in here on a stretcher – she traces her journey now, with her eyes closed. First, she was in the corridor, for what now seems like an infinitely long time, with the crippling pain in her head buckled on like a helmet. Later she'd been wheeled into one of the treatment rooms. When a doctor came at last, he'd looked serious and at the same time unreadable – nothing could be coaxed out of him regarding her condition. He'd asked her to give her name, the date, the day of the week, her date of birth. Then he'd tested her reflexes with his hands and a little hammer, and left the room without a word. She'd zoned out. Or fallen asleep? In any case, when she came to, she was lying in a tube with her head tightly clamped. When she was out again, a nurse had started fiddling about with her. Getting her undressed. Helene had asked what she was doing there, and the nurse had said with a deliberately calm expression that 'a little bit of blood' had 'escaped'. The words *subarachnoid haemorrhage* were never uttered, as if things should always be made nice and simple for the patient. As if no patient would ever have a clue about things like that. The nurse was shortly going to give Helene something to let her have 'a nice sleep', and when she woke up again the worst would definitely be over. Then she'd smiled, but to Helene the smile had seemed forced. That was the last thing she could remember. After that there was nothing.

'Eyes open, please – can you hear me?'

The ambulance chap is a lanky young man. The superiority emanating from him is painful to her. She'll have to get used to it. Her wheelchair is bundled into the vehicle and strapped down. The windows are two-thirds frosted glass, and when the door is closed you have to crane your neck to see anything. As she's having a look around, she sees Matthes sitting there. Must've got in before her. She's not surprised. Or is she? Today's his birthday. She hasn't got a present for him. She stretches her left arm out to him, and hopes she can say with her eyes that she wishes him all the best. Better than using her mouth. Matthes takes her hand and squeezes it. His hand is warm, and his grasp so familiar, that she doesn't want to let go, but wants to keep clinging on to it tightly for the whole journey. It's not far to Heidemühlen, maybe about three-quarters of an hour by car. Matthes says nothing and looks out of the window, her hand bound in both of his. Two old soldiers who don't need to say any more.

So they don't.

Looking out of the window she can see tree trunks, and beyond them fields. The odd village in between. She recognises Tasdorf from the hacked-off render of a derelict house on the cross-country B1. The windows on the first floor are the only ones she can see as they pass by. The render has been in the same state for ten, even fifteen years. Astonishing, really, that the house has survived. A few new ones have been built nearby, and others have at least been patched up. It's a rough deal for anyone living here, but a tiny handful will get lots of money for their bit of land by the main road, so they no doubt just accept that they're staying put. The old folks at least. She remembers an assistant at the neuropsychiatry clinics whose parents lived on the B1 in the early eighties, in a dilapidated house with an outside toilet. You only got hot water by firing up the boiler in the washhouse across the yard. Luckily they were 'only' renting, so sometime after the Wall came down they were able to clear off out of there, and spend their old age in a well-equipped flat in a better location.

Helene sighs.

Matthes looks at her enquiringly, but she still doesn't say anything.

She's surprised at the people popping into her head. She'd never met the parents of this clinic assistant. They'd just blundered through the breakfast discussion at work one morning, like absent-minded old ghosts. This discussion always took place at half past nine, in the outer office linking the three consulting rooms. The psychologist from adult neuropsychiatry would come up from her basement room in the hospital in Henrichshorst, as would Helene herself, from the far-off cubbyhole – down a corridor near the document store – where she held court as a child psychologist. At the time she could still fit into her striped skirt, as well as her checked one, both of which were now in a suitcase in the loft waiting for her to slim down again. It wasn't easy for her to part with clothes. Her daughters, on the other hand, regularly cleared out their cupboards to make room for new things. It was never a question of something being too big or too small: fashion alone came out on top. What for Helene had been *precious items* naturally meant nothing to her daughters. Her great-grandmother might've had it exactly the same with her. The way she'd unravelled machine-knit old clothes, well into old age, to turn them into socks and gloves! Helene had never been able to part with these mountains of wool, either. They were still languishing in the cellar in an enormous box, and in the first year of their marriage had led to repeated enquiries from Matthes, who'd wanted to throw them out. Clearly at some point he'd given up. As she's wondering what her daughters might be into now, she feels so far away from them that it makes her dizzy.

'Right, ladies and gents, time to disembark!'

The words hit home, but she doesn't let it show. She's lifted out of the ambulance in her wheelchair. Matthes pushes her into the rehabilitation clinic, to Admissions. The driver gets impatient – no doubt he'd rather pull the wheelchair right out from under her arse so he can bugger off. Now it's her turn to feel superior.

'Room 324. One of my colleagues will be along to do your admission. Feel free to go up and have a look around!'

She steers her wheelchair slowly towards the lift. Matthes is waiting for some paperwork, but then quickly jumps in too. As the doors close she takes pleasure in seeing the annoyed face of the driver, who's outside the door lighting a cigarette.

The first thing she sees as she leaves the lift on the third floor is a large, inviting dining area. Not all the people sitting there having lunch can eat by themselves. Some are being fed, others are trying to guide spoons to mouths with shaky hands. She feels sick.

She wheels purposefully towards her room. More purposefully than Matthes, who in situations like this needs time to get his bearings. Aha, nothing has changed there, then. She feels pride, then in the same moment finds that pride ridiculous. And Matthes? She turns round – he hasn't noticed anything. Instead he's at the nurses' station asking for the person who's going to do her admission. The woman comes and opens up the room, which is very nice. There's a hospital bed with all the fancy technical gear, accessible from both sides. A television. An armchair. A cupboard. From the window there are sweeping views down to the lake, which nestles into the hills only a short distance away. It's going to be harder than before to get to her without a car – Matthes doesn't drive, though he's been thinking about having lessons for years now. Despite that, the thought of being here is soothing.

A male nurse brings her a wheelchair belonging to the clinic, and takes the other one back downstairs. It's been quarter of an hour since they left the driver down there.

She's satisfied.

The first afternoon in Heidemühlen.

Matthes has gone home. They haven't talked any more about his birthday. He'll have a visit from his parents and his aunt. Maybe from Raphael? He at least will insist on giving his heartiest congratulations. Matthes won't have had the time or the leisure to bake a cake, so she imagines there'll be berries and ice cream. A hint of vanilla momentarily passes over her taste buds: a phantom flavour. She's been getting them more often recently.

She's lying on the bed, in a tracksuit Matthes has given *her* for the occasion. She wants to force herself into a state of calm where she might be able to pursue a thought, instead of seeing so many of them shatter into pieces.

Viola's surname... Damn, what was her last name again? Is that possible – that the name just won't come to her? She's skipping around in semi-darkness, having pulled the curtains closed around Viola, but it remains so: there's no surname for this Viola person, whose existence Helene is certain of but whose whereabouts is a mystery. Uncertainty spreads and starts to threaten her, swimming as she is in her blind spot with nowhere to stop, rest and catch her breath. Helene wants to get into her wheelchair and get away from it, so she can pull herself together, but her hand is too jittery to pull the chair next to the bed. And just at the point where she wants to bawl and scream about it all, it moves in: the memory. It advances with drummers and trumpeters, who are intoning marches inside an open concrete seashell; she recognises Radetzky, and Count Zeppelin. Then she's holding her hands over her ears, and pressing down firmly and repeatedly with both index fingers on the gristly bit at the start of the ear canal, to a fast beat. The ear must have a flicker fusion threshold too, she thinks now, because what she's hearing stays beyond it – it's just a quick sequence of individual notes which yield no arc, no melody. She has to laugh, and turns round – to Viola: who has her head on one side, and who reaches for Helene's hands and slowly pushes them down. Helene closes her eyes, smiling, as Viola kisses her. For the first time. The kiss seems so natural to her that the music from the seashell becomes a protective cloak around them, and stillness reigns beneath it. No sound disrupts the moment, which spreads out like her uncertainty did before, and when they break away from each other, Helene is quietly and completely captivated.

No, she doesn't want any supper tonight.

The nurse goes off with a shrug.

Helene nestles into her memories, and is lying in bed like a crooked old thing when the nurse comes back to help her get ready for bed.

'Viola, Malyutka...'

The nurse looks questioningly at Helene, whose eyes are suddenly wide open – 'Sorry, what was that?'

'Malyutka.'

Someone small.

Someone young?

A fifty-year-old wo...

Of course. Her last name is Malysch.

Viola Malysch doesn't come to Helene slowly, but at a run. Coming *back* to her? She doesn't think about that.

The kiss had happened in the Baltic resort of Zinnowitz. Winter of last year, a few days before Christmas. Helene had just got home from Münsterland. She hadn't said goodbye to her family, just left a note on the table: Back on Christmas Eve.

On her way to Berlin East station she couldn't help acting as if it was the last time she'd see the city for a long while. The steam mushrooming from Rummelsburg power station thrust whitely into the sky. Before the switch from coal to gas, in 1988, it had looked grey. She remembers this because for many years she'd spent a good deal of time at the Lichtenberg music school every week with the children, before and after the Wall came down. Small children, who couldn't yet make the journey by themselves, kept growing back on her like hair or fingernails. For the first few years they'd gone there on the train. Then, the year after the Wall came down, she'd gone back to the driving lessons she started in 1988. She'd packed them in after doing her theory and initial practical training – at the 'idiot' zone in Schönefeld, in a jeep-like Trabant Kübel – because she reckoned she'd never be able to afford a car she didn't even have on order: yet another consideration which, after 1989, became meaningless. She took the test. Her first car was a Wartburg. It got them to the music school faster, despite the constant roadworks on the B1. Only years after the Wall came down did Helene realise that the grey mushroom from the power station had been choking the city – along with the smoke which used to hang over the old residential areas, from their many coal fires – because suddenly it was possible to breathe. The place had been *cleaned up*. So white were the magnificent curls now on that innocent steam-lamb. She saw it, and something inside her contracted.

Only when she was coming back days later did she realise what it must have been: she'd sensed she was going on a journey to the loss of her innocence. That thing in some inaccessible corner of her mind that she took to be her innocence, anyway, even if she'd have laughed loudly at the idea and denied it, had anybody asked.

The crumbling backdrop of Ostkreuz Station had always conjured up feelings of familiarity for Helene. She ignored the platform, with its kiosks and counters, and saw only the rearing presence of the "Penis" – the Ostkreuz water tower, threatening to go limp at any moment – and the ruins on the side turned away from the platform. Then she felt at home: in a state of ruin. Two more stops to Berlin East, and the train juddered on through an equally ruined cutting. She thought she should even commit the pointed bricks to memory, and kept closing her eyes for a few moments at a time. When the train stopped at Warschauer Strasse it was the missing paving stones on the platform that held her hostage, so that when she got off at Berlin East she heaved a sigh of relief: remembering was harder here. Things had been tidied up here. Perception is a funny thing, she'd been thinking, just as the train from Potsdam came in. Viola got out, red in the face, and stumbled clumsily towards Helene. Her face seemed grimly set, but couldn't deny itself the odd moment of release. These occurred in particular whenever Helene tried to look her steadily in the eye.

'Bewitch me, Malyutka, Malysch, talk to me sweetly.'

Quite suddenly, those eight words were on the point of simply uncoiling out of her mouth. She just managed to hold them back, but her look had already changed into one of infatuation. Viola saw it, and for a moment her face did the same.

They didn't touch, if you didn't count shaking hands – something that'd still always give you away as an East German, Viola reckoned. Helene speculated that non-East Germans would've kissed each other on the cheek, left then right. That wouldn't have seemed any more intimate to her, though. They spoke little throughout the journey, avoiding each other's glances over and over again: not least because Helene couldn't grasp what was happening to her – she was on the verge of falling hopelessly in love! – and because Viola, who'd already fallen hopelessly in love, was feeling less and less sure of herself. They had hardly any luggage – just underwear, a jumper and a toilet bag each. Pasewalk. Anklam. Helene kept her eyes open and stared into the distance. She was on a journey in her own imagining of Viola's face, which she couldn't see. She nearly left her rucksack on the train when she was suddenly urged to get off in Züssow – the connecting train was waiting. Arriving into Zinnowitz in the early evening, it was getting dark, and as they made their way to the Catholic community centre, where Viola had booked them a room – for two female friends, she'd specified, when asked – the march was ringing out from the seashell bandstand.

Suddenly, silence. The kiss.

And then: the night.

So the nurse on night shift wants to wash her. Helene wants to do it by herself. She doesn't manage to get from her wheelchair into the shower, however. The nurse grabs hold of her. Grabbing hold of *Malyutka Malysch* – suddenly she doesn't know whether that would be better. A relief? Something stands in Helene's way whenever she pictures Viola at her house. Then a thought comes into her head: Viola speaks excellent Russian. Helene speaks decent Russian, but it's not excellent. No: she *used* to speak decent Russian, but would rather not find herself in the awkward position of having to test it out. *Malysch*? In Russian it means a little boy, a nipper. Men use it with each other too – a bit disparagingly, perhaps? – when they're asking about each other's circumstances: 'Now then, young nipper, how're things?' Viola's surname meant "little boy" but she preferred to be *Malyutka*, little girl. Malyussenkaya no less, littlest one, but there's no word in German that even gets near to expressing the tenderness of the Russian one. In the end Helene left it at *Malyutka Malysch*. It was ambiguous, just as Viola seemed to her in real life – part man, part woman; depending on the circumstances, according to taste, as and when desired. And what had Helene desired?

She doesn't know.

But she does know that she hadn't come away from that first night empty-handed, however little attention she'd paid to herself. Instead she'd crept under Malyutka Malysch's skin, eventually, and hadn't needed to ask herself what she was doing there.

Thinking about it makes something swell in her. Just as it had a few weeks ago, when Carola was washing her in the shower and she was thinking about Matthes.

Matthes. Malyutka Malysch.

Malyutka Malysch. Matthes.

If she was moving between two poles of equal strength, each repelling the other, then what was the state of her own charge?

Maybe, she thinks, it was being in this massive electrical field that had led to the short circuit in her brain.

There's a rushing sound behind the dunes of sleep. Several long minutes pass before the sound can haul itself up and over, chase away dreams and be there in the room now, loud and clear. Helene puts the light on and grabs the TV remote: it's 2.36 a.m., according to teletext. What's making a rushing sound here? The night nurse has left the window open. There must be a serious wind blowing outside – she can hear it over the rushing now, roaring past far above her. It's the sound of the woods which fall away behind the building and down to the lake, and it seems to her as if the trees are coming closer and closer, and will at some point push their leafy boughs through the window. Still, she doesn't want to heave herself up out of bed to close it, so pulls her covers a bit higher instead. Cold is streaming in through the window, but underneath it's warm. Autumn is coming, there's no denying it. 'Autumn always brings deep melancholy...'

Matthes said this every November, shying away from a response to her autumnal attacks of sadness. Mostly he got out of the way, wanting to wait it out until they'd passed. It had worked well for almost twenty years: until the start of December, he'd sleep in another room. In the first flat, he went in with the children; in the second, the hall; in the third, the dining room. And since they'd been in the house, he'd slept in his study under the eaves. Then, last year, Malyutka Malysch had taken up her position right where Helene's gloom would usually be lounging about. You could hardly have said she was cheerful and light-hearted last autumn, but she wasn't melancholy either. She'd acted as if she was, in order to drive Matthes into his room, then on lonely nights had wrapped the duvet tightly around her and tried not to think of anything. Sometimes Lottchen had crept in with her, and Helene had held her in her arms the way you can probably only hold your youngest child: with a creeping, subliminal pain and the desire to stay in that position forever, all the while anxious not to wake them with a careless movement. Lottchen was a sure-fire distraction from the confusion Malyutka Malysch had unleashed in her. Helene had slung a scarf over the bedside lamp and in its subdued glow looked at her daughter for hours, or so it seems to her now. Long brown hair, a small scar on her extremely high forehead, narrow eyes that were almost Asian (*Mongolian princess* Matthes had called her, the first time he saw her), slightly jutting ears – Helene had always seen in her an enchanting copy of her father. During the day, however, she'd attempted to work as usual. Malyutka had started to email her – cautious at first, then more open and frank – and Helene had awaited her messages with eager anticipation. It's 2.58 by the time her laptop has finished firing up. She can hardly wait, and is getting agitated.

22.11.02

Dear Helene,

If you knew how badly I did my back in yesterday (I was taking books off the bookcase and stacking them on the floor, so I could nail down two of the shelves) then you'd definitely laugh. You laugh at me anyway, don't you, eh? How can you expect one woman not to laugh at another woman who can't make her stomach flat, or her feet smaller, and who constantly looks as if Laurel and Hardy have agreed to make a go of it in one body... Though I'm not entirely sure myself who's actually having a go in mine. Must be the devil, wanting to let his female half see something of the world – don't you reckon? (Can you really call that humour?)

The female half of the devil only lets her boobs peek halfway out of the bloke, who can't be parted from his male form...

So, I did my back in and suddenly knew that I can't preside over the choral society any more, not as conductor and even less so as a board member. You persuaded me of that, and probably as long ago as Sanssouci, when you said goodbye again right after we'd met. As the pain evaporated, relief immediately set in. They just can't feel that I'm a woman. The singers hear my voice and get annoyed all over again, even if they don't want to let it show. They accepted me as a man once, but it wasn't actually me standing in front of them! And now that I'm me (am I me?) their feelings are probably telling them I'm not me, while in their minds I'm probably being shifted to the correct place, and the two don't match. Even your feelings couldn't reconcile what's inside me and what's on the outside – mind and shape, or behaviour and build – and as I got to know you better than I ever imagined I would, I knew you weren't doing anything other than giving your feelings free reign; you weren't trying to trip me up, say, just to see what I'd look like after the fall. When the pain shot into my back it was as if someone was calling down to me from on high, saying women should only ever fix shelves when there's genuinely no man available. A woman conductor in a dress or a skirt over a finely-stockinged man's leg, with a man's voice and broad shoulders, has nothing to offer the conventional understanding of roles – an understanding no one can actually break away from, however free we think we are. And because that's the way things are, there's no place for me in the world of work in our East German backwater. I've already had to leave three firms – ushered out, half-thrown, half glad to jump; a job creation scheme just couldn't be made to 'fit'. Once, for example, I was supposed to be doing admin for an association supporting girls who'd been sexually abused, and this included initial phone contact. In a roundabout way, I was told that my voice made the girls nervous, because it was men who'd abused them... The thing is, I could see where they were coming from! The women there found it incredibly embarrassing. When they cancelled the job offer – arranged through the job centre – they even sent me a box of Belgian chocolate seashells. Well, I hate anything sweet, so that seemed to fit.

Why am I writing all this to you? No idea. Really I just wanted to thank you for the weekend. It was lovely to see you with your family, and credit to your husband for letting us have all the time in the world to just natter. Give him my best.

Affectionately – Viola Malysch

Teletext is still humming. It's 3.06: it's taken her eight minutes to read the email and now she's off on a mystery tour, hoping to find the weekend Viola was talking about.

◆ ◆ ◆

Helene has plans. Someone has made them for her. They hang above her bed and tell her what there is to be done. This week: one-to-one physiotherapy, a trial swim, occupational therapy in the basement, massage, speech therapy, individual psychological consultations, progressive muscle relaxation, a consultation with social services, psych group.

She feels sick.

Electromyographic biofeedback isn't even on the list. Matthes had brought her a leaflet about it when she was on the Stroke Unit, and she'd got excited at the thought of being able to work on the movement of her right arm. But she's already been told it's not possible in her case – yesterday, by the doctor who'd first examined her: it's out of the question with a pacemaker. She'd got a bit angry then, especially as interference between the pacemaker and the feedback didn't seem to her to be inevitable: so far nobody here had asked her what type of pacemaker she had, and you needed to know that before you could say whether biofeedback was really possible or not. Unfortunately she'd been too worked up to say all that clearly.

She can't see herself sticking to a schedule like the one she's been given. Into her wheelchair, out of her wheelchair... The nurse must've come up with it when she was half-asleep. How's it all going to work?

Someone's already been to get her dressed, and now she's

sitting in the corner, waiting to be collected for breakfast. She's feeling small and overwhelmed when the door opens, and a hefty person – someone she doesn't know yet – comes in to get her. The person doesn't say anything – not even good morning – and merely looks past or over her, taking her to the breakfast room without a word. There it is again, all the equipment: the board with spikes for her bread roll, the cup with handles, the odd-shaped cutlery, the bibs and the chair cushions. She's a tolerant girl, she says to herself. She submits to having coffee poured for her and a bread roll cut in half, all without being asked. What are all these things here for, then, if you can't do or decide anything yourself? Now the woman's even spreading the top half of her roll with jam, when she'd rather have liver sausage. She can actually see some appetising slices of it on one of the generously-laden breakfast platters... She can't help thinking of the old East. It'd been like this in the various maternity hospitals she'd been in, and she'd submitted to their systems. The worst one that pushes its way into her memory was the women's hospital where Billy was born: the babies were only brought to you every four hours to be fed briefly, and otherwise stayed in the nursery – which the mothers had no access to – whether they were screaming or not. If anyone came to visit, a father of one of the babies, for example (though no father came to see hers), a nurse might point out their child to them through the window, if they were lucky. And as for meals, the only choice back then was to eat them or not.

The remains of her rebellion die away in an audible sigh. She takes a bite of her roll and slowly drinks up her coffee.

Her blood pressure is taken.

She gets weighed.

Every day it's done all over again.

She gets collected and taken to her therapy sessions. The physiotherapist is an approachable lady. The psychologist comes across as weirdly dim. She embarks unenthusiastically on the necessary tests, sitting Helene in front of this screen, then that screen, where she has to do puzzles, work out patterns and complete numbers and words. She's worn out by the time they fetch her for lunch, and asks for a decent lunch break.

The nurse smirks.

Matthes must've arrived while she was sleeping.

Matthes is a year older than the day before yesterday. You can see it, she thinks. His eyelids look swollen again – what *is* going on there? Today she asks him.

'Hey, what's wrong with your eyes?'

He's tired, and lies his head in her lap. She strokes it.

He doesn't say anything.

She doesn't say anything else.

That's how things stay. Not a word is uttered during the visit.

Matthes gets a little stone out of his bag, and presses it into Helene's hand. Just for a few moments she's annoyed, then gives it back to him. Her gaze wobbles. He takes the stone and smiles for a moment, then becomes serious, taking Helene's right hand, opening it despite despite a mild spasm, and putting the little stone back again. This continues a few times. One of them is letting the other know just how much the little stone is capable of. The other one doesn't really know what the first one is trying to say, but they've each loaded the little stone with whatever is most burdensome to them, and now feel relieved in their silence. They're both feeling so easy that Matthes takes his jumper off for a while, and Helene lies back on her pillows as if on cotton wool – she's floating and feels no pressure, either from the mattress or from the bedcovers.

When Matthes has gone, for a moment Helene isn't sure if he was really there.

After supper she finally has some time.

At her request Matthes has brought in her pocket diary for last year. She had to explain to him where he'd find it. Matthes has never tampered with her personal things before, but all the same it still felt like a handing-over. Although, given that she kept everything under her writing desk – in the second set of drawers, third drawer down – he could access it any time anyway, if he really wanted to...

There it is: the sixteenth to the eighteenth of November – Viola Malysch. She'd joined the days together with a bracket in blue ink. On the Friday, according to the diary, Helene had also taken the car in for repair. Now she remembers that despite the garage's initial assurances, she hadn't got it back that afternoon, and had had to walk to the train station. She'd been a bit late, having also picked up Lottchen from preschool. After their meeting in Potsdam, they'd somehow agreed to have another go in different, sheltered surroundings. Helene had made an effort to find somewhere near Viola, and had declared that she'd also be happy to visit her at home – 'Of course!' – but Viola had just looked awkwardly at her feet, as if she didn't like having visitors at all. After a certain amount of wavering, which Helene read as an evasion tactic, Viola had accepted the invitation to Karlshorst. When she got off the train on the sixteenth of November, she'd stopped next to Helene, but Helene walked right past: she hadn't recognised her. The plain grey hair she'd had a week or two ago had been newly cut, coloured and waved, and was held in place at the back by a Murano glass clip. Make-up, along with plucked and tinted eyebrows, had given her face a certain stiffness. Viola was wearing a heavy black suit which must've been made to measure, because you'd surely never get anything like it in those proportions off the peg. She had a colourful pashmina round her neck, and black ankle boots on her feet, the soles of which had been so cleverly transformed into a short, tapered heel that at first you didn't notice their size. Over her right arm she was carrying a lightweight, pale-grey faux-fur coat, and she steadied herself with her left hand on the handle of a smart little leather case. Helene walked right past her. When Viola called her name, she turned round with a start. She saw pride and disappointment battling it out in Viola's expression, and looked into a face whose disconcerting symmetry was just starting to break up, with the first cracks appearing in the thick layer around her mouth. Helene recoiled at the very thought of a hug – it took a mere fraction of a second to realise that Viola's make-up would probably get even more smeared if they got too close to each other. So they left it at a handshake, as they would four weeks later, when Viola was in the process of becoming Malyutka Malysch in Helene's head.

Helene took Viola's case and carried it down the station steps. Lottchen, hanging off Helene's hand and with apparently aloof interest, snuck surreptitious glances at this strange, large person. You could see which stops were being pulled out in her head – voice, body shape, outfit – in an attempt to square everything up. By the time they'd got to the bottom of the steps she'd presumably managed to do so, because she now held out her hand to greet Viola, completely uninhibited.

Helene bought fresh bread at the bakery before they all set off down Arberstrasse. The area still showed the odd trace of the *Russian era*, over since 1994. People used to call Karlshorst *Little Moscow*. The Museum of the Surrender was very nearby, and some of the villas lived in by senior officers and their families actually still had boarded-up windows and doors. Maybe they hadn't managed to trace the beneficiaries, or else the whole lot of them couldn't decide how to proceed with their possibly unexpected inheritance. There'd been fewer of them in the last few years.

Matthes and Helene had built their house on partitioned land. The owner of the house fronting on to the street could never have afforded to return it to a habitable state had he not decided to sell the back half of his plot. Now both parties only had a bit of garden, but Helene actually liked that. Gardening didn't suit her.

As they opened the garden gate, Lissy came towards them on her bike. As of a short time ago she'd been living in her own flat, paid for with the money she got as an apprentice. She looked stoned, as she often had recently. It wasn't just her dilated pupils that led Helene to that conclusion: her eyes were red and watery, too, and she was eating more than usual. When she threw herself joyfully at Helene in greeting, Helene could see the writing on the wall. Lissy didn't just throw herself at her mother but also at Viola, who was stuck dithering between the bike and the gate. Helene merely sighed and left the confrontation for another time. Once inside, she called Matthes out of his study so she could introduce Viola. He came down in a hurry, humming quietly to himself, and ran straight to the cooker to take a cabbage casserole out of the oven. They all sat down at the table and were joined by Mareile, who'd been at her school swimming lesson. They ate and drank wine. It was Friday, no one had to be anywhere early the next day, and so the evening proceeded without excitement: Matthes went back to his study; Mareile did some guitar practice, something she really enjoyed; and Lottchen watched a video her grandparents had sent her. Helene stayed with Viola in the kitchen by herself.

That evening Viola just couldn't put etiquette aside – she remained the newly-converted vamp whose lipstick had to be reapplied hourly. It was only after many glasses of wine – resulting in ever more trips to the toilet, and Viola taking offence at the table and the bench and the chair and the cupboard – that her mascara turned into dark rings under her eyes, she came back with lipstick overshooting her lipliner, and it started to look like her make-up was crumbling from her high cheekbones.

Helene felt an impulse to pass her some baby oil, a facecloth and a towel, but wisely refrained from doing so. What they ended up talking about came within a hair's breadth of what they actually wanted to talk about. Viola talked about the weight gain that'd been bothering her for a few years now, but neglected to mention the hormonal processes also taking place in her body, which had been started before her operation and of course had to be kept up afterwards. She talked about the creams she used to control her rosacea, but not about how shaving, which she probably had to do on a daily basis, aggravated the skin further. She told of trying to earn a crust as a freelancer, writing down old people's life stories – because old folks liked to have their biographies bound as a book to give to their children, and their children's children, and were even willing to pay for it. She said nothing about some callers, male and female, getting irritated when they first spoke to her on the phone, nor did she reveal how many potential customers she then lost after those initial irritated conversations. Only when she came to talk about earlier times – her student days, her time in the army, and yes, even her marriage – did Viola say *I* loud and clear. It was as if she wasn't at all sure of her present self.

After eighteen months of national service as Viktor Malysch, she qualified as a teacher of German and Music – but she never worked as one. Instead, she stuck a research degree on to her first degree, which promoted her to Viktor Malysch PhD and seemed to suggest an academic career. Then, when she was writing up, a woman fell into her life and very quickly became hers. Viola had felt obliged to marry her when she found out she was pregnant, and the twins were born in 1983. At that point, finally, she felt love for her wife, a woman who had no idea that the father of her sons was also a woman. They'd actually had some great years together, Viola said – so great that she'd wanted to crown it all by coming out. They had two children, which was the dream for lots of lesbian couples she knew. Yes, she'd finally lead this dream life! She must've somehow blocked out the fact that her wife wasn't a lesbian, she thought; just refused to allow it. The shock had been felt on both sides. Viola's wife had thought her fancy dress was a joke at first, surely something to do with shaving off her beard. But when Viola had taken the scarf off her head, and her wife had seen her bald head, she'd completely gone to pieces, and had a screaming fit in the presence of their nearly-ten-year-old sons. In that moment the scales seemed to fall from Viola's eyes, as it dawned on her: her wife loved beards and cocks and washboard stomachs and big biceps, all the things she found sickening and now wanted to spare no effort getting rid of. The incompatibility of their ideas of Viola brought them both to the edge of what was now a marital abyss. Of course she hadn't been able to simply stop loving her wife. They'd slept together plenty of times after that, because her wife had wanted to and believed she could change Viola's mind, remodel her, and set her back on the right path. *Exit THE DREAM; Enter THE MAN*, is what Viola had called this sex in her head. But she became more and more of a stranger to herself when it happened, and in the end she couldn't get it up any more. The dream remained off-stage. The man disappeared. Her wife had tried with her for another three years, Viola said, and shown all the goodwill in the world. When the forced separation was pending, because Viola was pursuing the operation with a change in personal status, her wife had cried a lot – it seemed inconceivable to her to be losing a husband in this way. But even if Viola had foregone the operation, and just changed her name, they wouldn't have gained anything. She wouldn't have had the emotional strength to carry on wearing a suit.

Helene remembers being taken back during that long speech to the place they first met. Viola had been dressed in a, well, gender-neutral way – only on second glance, and for a mere moment, did her masculine appearance clash with her hair being in a bun. She wondered what had prompted this complete transformation.

When she falls asleep, completely shattered, she still has her glasses on.

When she wakes up, completely refreshed, she no longer has her glasses on. She's squashed them: one lens has popped out of the frame, one arm has broken off and the other is all twisted. She wants to get angry at first, then thinks better of it.

Today is another day.

Today she pulls herself together, and manages to get clean clothes out of the cupboard. She manages to pull off her stupid pressure socks. She manages to wheel herself to the bathroom and get herself in the shower. She manages to pick the soap back up when it slips out of her hand two, three times. She manages to wash and dry herself thoroughly, and lastly to clean her teeth. She manages to pull on a pair of ordinary socks, and her pants. She arranges her bra so she can get hold of the fastener on one side with her left hand, and bring it under her right arm from the back – her arm can clamp on to it like that, in a clumsy way. Then she guides the fastener forward on the other side, pulls it, and doesn't let go until it reaches the one clamped under her right arm. She manages – yes, really! – to get the little hooks into the eyes, at least two of the three anyway, and then to pull the bra another half-turn around herself. She manages to manoeuvre her right arm into the bra strap, and to slip her left arm into the other one too. She manages. She's completely done in doing the final few things: t shirt over her head, trousers up over her backside. Matthes has brought her some white Velcro trainers. She manages...

When the nurse comes to wake her, Helene is already sat at

the desk, bent over a crossword.

Writing with her left hand feels very strange, though.

On her way back from her physio, the nurse pushes her to the door of the doctors' office.

'Just wait here a moment – you're up next.'

So she waits. Actually the doctor comes a moment later to look for her, and calls her in. She doesn't come to help, so Helene wheels herself in.

She's got a really teachery expression, Helene thinks.

A really teachery voice starts talking about Helene's many good achievements. She can get dressed by herself. In that case she must be able to eat by herself too, is that right? She can wash herself, and wheel her own wheelchair: in short, there's no place for her on this ward, where no one's supposed to be able to do that.

Oh?

Helene immediately starts to panic that she's going to be thrown out of the rehab clinic. When the doctor sees her agitation, she laughs, and lays a hand on Helene's leg. There's House 2 for the more mobile patients, who can largely manage independently. That's where they're going to move her.

She calms down.

We can't guarantee you'll get your own room there too, however, says the teachery voice.

She gets her own room. Got lucky there.

Lucky? Matthes can't believe it. It would've been much nicer to have someone to talk to, exchange a few words with!

To talk to...

She brushes aside what Matthes is really getting at.

She asks him how well he can remember Viola.

Remember well...

Matthes brushes aside what she's really getting at.

They avoid each other's gaze for a moment, at a loss.

She sees that Matthes isn't just *being* quiet, he's keeping quiet about something.

'Still, it would've been much nicer to have someone to talk to!'

In the end she's the one who suggests taking the path to the lake. She hasn't been down there yet. Naturally Matthes agrees to it. Downright eager, he packs two glasses he's brought with him back into his rucksack. He washes some grapes – must've picked them up somewhere on the long journey over here – and they disappear into the rucksack too. Helene wheels herself out and waits by the lift for Matthes, holding it for him. Where's he got to?

Here he comes.

He's tripping over his own feet, she thinks. They go down in the lift. The way out goes through the cafeteria. Helene doesn't really feel like an ice cream but Matthes has already bought two cones – lemon buttermilk, her favourite. Okay, fine, but she can't wheel her wheelchair and eat an ice cream at that same time! Matthes takes over pushing and she starts to lick. Ok, now she does feel like ice cream. The very thing that gets your appetite going is eating itself. When she spots an orange birch bolete mushroom, thrusting out of the Brandenburg sand towards the light, she pulls at Matthes's sleeve in surprise. At the same time she's cross that her ability to speak completely breaks down in the presence of any kind of excitement – even if it's only a mushroom in the undergrowth. She shuts her eyes. As her stress reaches its peak, Matthes lays a hand on her shoulder. Slowly the tension ebbs away – she's aware of her arm and hand releasing themselves from their spasm and resting limply on the arm of her wheelchair. Matthes cuts the mushroom from the ground with the Swiss army knife he always has with him, leaving a little stump of stalk. He always does it like that. She's sure she's heard it's actually better to twist the mushroom out whole. It's more considerate towards the mushroom, because it doesn't get lumbered with such a big wound, and better in terms of eating – especially with really meaty mushrooms like this – because you avoid leaving a nice bit of flesh in the ground. But there's nothing to be done, and Helene refrains from saying anything. He never used to listen to her about it before. She reflects on what you do actually hear in a long-term relationship. What does she hear and not hear from him? Do the chains in their ship clank so loudly that they can yell whatever they want at each other? With the mushroom on her lap, they continue towards the lake. A meandering, wheelchair-friendly path has been laid here. At the lake there's a fire pit and a covered seating area, which has a stone bench running all the way around it. Matthes sits down with Helene facing him. She then turns her chair so she can look out over the water, his gaze at her back. There hadn't been much opportunity for swimming this summer. They'd stopped by the beginning of July, anyway, and she can't remember whether she was still swimming in June. A grape now floats into view from behind her, dangled by Matthes. Why does he keep trying to feed her! She wheels away to the side a bit, holding up her ice cream like a flaming torch.

All is quiet.

There's no one down here apart from them.

A fighter jet paints a vapour trail in the sky. It looks slow and unhurried.

It's so quiet down here, it makes her wonder how danger might sound.

She wonders what Matthes is keeping quiet about. The way she speaks isn't sophisticated enough to let her get the better of him, she thinks. Matthes is clever. Matthes twists the words in her mouth. She remembers that. He didn't always succeed, but often he did. In her current condition he'd ride roughshod right over her, without a doubt. Pointless, then, to want to somehow confront him about it. Besides, he won't let himself be *pumped for information*. That's what he calls it whenever she asks him about something he's not currently engaged in, and it'd cost him a fair amount of mental effort – and above all, time? – to change course.

'How are they at the sides? Are they pinching?'

Helene, with Matthes, has wheeled down to the optician – the only one in Heidemühlen – to be fitted for new glasses. The optician has a mirror like a three-panelled altarpiece, so she can see herself from both sides. What does she see? Hair growth on the left is still sparse – maybe a centimetre long, if that. It's completely grey. Silvery bristles protrude on both sides of her scar. She turns her head: on the other side her hair is a gleaming auburn. She imagines how it'd look if it was all the same length – the left side grey, the right side brown – and the thought starts to appeal to her. She turns her head a few times.

'So, are they pinching?'

No, they're not pinching.

She really doesn't care what glasses she gets. Matthes, on the other hand, tries to outline all the pros and cons of the different models. She only understands the odd word. Or only wants to understand the odd word. So what if they've got extendable, unbreakable arms or they're made of plastic – she just wants to be able to see with them. She wants to look at the world. The world certainly won't be looking at her any more, anyway! She's prepared to accept that, she says, if Matthes can accept her happily handing over the choice of frames to him. But her words fan the flames. Now Matthes feels obliged to protest energetically, which he does.

She must be mad! She's a beautiful woman, who turns plenty of heads – and not just men!

What did he say? Does he even know what he's just said? He's acting now as if he hasn't said anything at all. She has doubts, and investigates the echo in her ears. She grows uncertain.

...who turns plenty of heads!

That would be four words fewer – maybe she heard four words more than he actually said? She looks searchingly into his face, but he just smiles innocuously. Her uncertainty makes her start to tremble, so he takes the glasses she's just tried on (metal frames, light blue, half-moon lenses) out of her hand, and holds it tightly to reassure her. But in that moment she hates him doing it. Glancing at the faces of the people around them – the optician and two waiting customers – she sees no sign of uncertainty at what Matthes has just said, so she must have misheard. Yes, just misheard him, that's all. But now she really wants to get out of there, so agrees to the light blue metal frames – which Matthes had thought were the third-nicest – and hands over her lens prescription. No, she definitely doesn't want another eye test done now.

She's extremely glad once she's got a bit of paper in her hand with her name and a collection date on it, and she and Matthes are able to leave the shop.

What happens to Lottchen when Matthes comes to visit? She hasn't yet been to Heidemühlen, which surprises Helene. Matthes has probably asked his parents to stop by in the afternoons and check on her. Mareile has far too much on – choir, orchestra and drama rehearsals, though no sport, to her disappointment – and Lissy is unreliable. Billy lives in Karlshorst, too, but after doing a school year in Denmark he moved in with his girlfriend. They live on the other side of Treskow-allee, maybe just over a mile away. When Helene thinks of Billy her heart swells.

She's thinking of Billy now.

Her heart swells.

To cap it all, there's a knock at the door.

'Come in?'

Billy.

'Would you believe it, I was just thinking about you!'

It's a joy to see him, all suntan and long legs. He gets his good looks from his father, of course. She'd feel a bit sorry for him if he took after his mother.

With that sensitive look of his, which always gets under her skin a little bit, he hugs Helene. He gets out a doll, a little creature almost as long-legged as he is, and puts it on his mother's lap. The worry doll. He sewed it himself on Helene's old sewing machine, which had been languishing up in the loft, completely ignored. No longer, though, clearly, because Billy does a twirl: 'Look at me, I've got a whole new wardrobe!' Helene recognises fabric from old things she thought she'd thrown out. Her old reversible wraparound skirt – black with flowers on one side, and black with white dots on the other – has done for an entire shirt and flat cap! Her dark- and light-blue checked blazer, a horrible thing, has been robbed of the black jersey that was on its collar and on bits of the front edging – it's been made to look distinctly *masculine*. It's crazy, the boy can genuinely wear anything, and any which way, and still look good.

Billy tells her that he's moved back home. It's really not easy for any of them at the moment, and even Bengt is considering taking some time off from university and coming to Berlin, so he can pitch in too.

Now she knows what happens to Lottchen.

Once again, Helene is so moved that she can't say anything at all.

Helene has her meals in the big dining room now, of course. She's been assigned a place, along with a board with spikes and a two-handled cup. The cup's no good to her at all because she can't lift her right hand even a centimetre. Whatever. Helene is sitting all by herself at this table for four. She finds that odd, because all the other tables have at least two people, and most have four. Maybe the crew for this one has recently been discharged?

She gets herself some supper. Her plate rests on her lap in front of her – it's handy, having a wheelchair. Without one, it'd be difficult to keep putting her plate up on the buffet counter while filling it with her left hand. She goes up twice, though, because she also wants some quark for pudding. When she comes back there's a surprise waiting: someone sitting across from her at the table. Doesn't she know him? She ponders here and ponders there. It takes a while for the penny to drop: it's the *damaged boy* from the trauma centre! His eyes are no longer half-closed beneath the missing half of his skull, and instead are looking right at Helene.

And filling with tears.

Well, cheers – that's just great.

If she remembers correctly, though, his body's taken a beating too – an arm and a leg. Whether they really did sew his foot onto his knee the wrong way round is something she's unable to verify at the moment. He's making a huge effort to spread something on his bread. Helene feels the impulse to help him, but realises just in time that she can't do it any better than he can. It's nice to see him fully awake now, she thinks. But he doesn't seem to like it... He probably hasn't known about his condition for very long. A tear drops on to his meatloaf, running down through the parsley garnish and falling into the crumbs on his plate. His hand is trembling, as is his mouth. But she can't exactly just wheel round now to his side of the table, and lay her hand on an arm that isn't there! She couldn't touch his head, either – she can see it pulsating, and it scares her. Around his shoulders would be okay. But what would this much younger man think if a much older woman, with half-grey and half-brown hair, just came over to his side of the table and gave him a hug... They'd probably both have a good howl, never say another word to each other and just let things lie, and the drowned parsley would probably never find its way into his mouth.

No, she doesn't like that idea one bit.

Suddenly she's not hungry any more.

She leaves everything where it is and flees.

Most of all she likes to flee to Viola, but her memory snags on something. After that Friday evening last November, there's nothing – though there must have been a whole Saturday and at least half a Sunday, too!

She goes off for a mud treatment, with a massage to follow. The massage therapist helps her undo her bra. That's nice of her. In the little cubicle she has the therapeutic mud applied to her back and shoulders, and lets herself relax. One of the male massage therapists, the blind one, quietly puts some music on which is actually pretty exuberant – what is it? Vivaldi, or Donizetti? She tries to creep her body a bit higher up the massage table, hoping to be able to hear more by moving the curtain to one side. Cautiously she glances out down the corridor – left, then right – and shrinks back, startled: the female therapist is massaging the male therapist, very carefully. And kissing him. It all looks so chaste – the way she's standing in front of him, eyes closed, loosening the muscles in his back with her hands through his tunic and shirt... Helene creeps back quickly, smirking and a little bit pleased.

It *is* Vivaldi.

In fact, it's THE Vivaldi – *Le quattro Stagioni*, The Four Seasons – but it must be an unusual arrangement for woodwind. There's just no stopping this Vivaldi chap. A few years ago, she'd been to the Chiesa della Pietá, 'Vivaldi's church', in Venice. She can remember it very clearly. When she'd asked which bits of the church had existed in Vivaldi's day, because it was only finished after his death, the guide had simply muttered gruffly and brushed the question aside. She smiles.

Why is her memory so unforthcoming about Viola's visit last year?

She closes her eyes and is falling into a doze when something crashes through her calm. The female massage therapist has yanked the plastic curtain aside. Again Helene has to smirk, because the woman's bun is askew and Helene knows why. The therapist clearly hasn't realised, however. She removes the mud pack and helps Helene into her wheelchair. In the massage room she's heaved on to a massage chair, where she's able to relax completely. A very pleasant state of affairs. After that there's infrared therapy. When the lamp is turned off, for a moment she's so cold she gets goosebumps. Shame she's too clumsy to get herself dressed quickly. She wonders what happens in previously-warmed muscles when they're exposed to sudden cold – she sees them contracting, to ward off the intrusion, and investigates her own reaction. Isn't her neck in the process of the stiffening completely once again? It's just as the massage therapist describes it, before every session: rigid muscle armour, which can only be loosened with difficulty. When she finally gets the top half of her tracksuit back on, the very tracksuit Matthes gave her on his birthday, she's pleased. She jiggles herself into a more comfortable position so she can set off for the lift, and smiles conspiratorially at the massage therapist, who clearly doesn't read anything into it because Helene only gets a desultory nod in return. At that, the therapist's bun falls out completely, which she finally notices, and immediately tries to get to grips with her predicament. In doing so she lowers her head, keeping it there for several seconds while her hands are up and fumbling with her hair, and in that instant the memory of Viola combing her hair rushes in. Viola was in a similar pose – coaxing her hair into her Murano glass clasp – on that Saturday morning almost a year ago, when Helene wrenched open the bathroom door in a hurry to get to the toilet. Viola had stared in horror towards the door she'd forgotten to lock. Helene, straight out of the warm bed she'd been sharing with Lottchen, looked in equal horror at Viola standing in front of the mirror: she was fully dressed on top, in a stripy chenille jumper, but not yet wearing pants or a skirt. Helene's heart leapt so far into her mouth, she had to swallow hard to get it to stay in her body. On instinct she pulled the door closed again, and ran as quietly as she could to the other toilet at the top of the house.

'Why've you stopped there? You're blocking the way!'

Autumn is keen to arrive. The woodland going down to the lake is mixed, and the deciduous trees are starting to excel themselves with their many colours. On the way to this slope there's a copper beech standing in an exposed spot. The area all around it has been flattened, and new grass sown. With a restricted field of vision, Helene thinks now, she'd have the distinct impression of being in an English park – so even restricted fields of vision can have their advantages. A bench has been built around the beech tree. Is it beech, too? No, it looks like that trendy new bangkirai, the mahogany substitute for outdoor use. A path leads up to it, and, to spare the grass, a wide circle has also been paved around the bench. Helene wheels over to it and, after securing the brakes on her chair, dares to transfer to the bench by herself. She stands up and sits down again a few times, practising. A woman with a drooping left eyelid, and a large, fresh-looking scar on the opposite side of her head, sits down next to her.

'Well now?'

Well now indeed, how's Helene supposed to respond to that?

'Now, now!' comes unexpectedly out of her mouth.

The woman gets a fright and runs away. Helene wants to get up and call after her, but of course she doesn't even know her... She's sorry she frightened her. Can't be helped. She gets the blanket she's brought with her from the wheelchair, and wraps herself up in it as best she can. She and Viola had also taken blankets with them when they'd driven out to Krummensee last November, on a cold but exceptionally clear and sunny day. At breakfast they'd tried to act naturally, to avoid having to think about their morning encounter in any way, shape or form. They'd giggled and joked as they spooned up their hot, very soft-boiled eggs and ate toast made with the bread she'd bought on the Friday evening. One of them had drunk coffee, the other black tea. Helene had then asked, harmlessly, what Matthes was thinking of doing with Lottchen while she took her new friend out for a drive in the Brandenburg countryside. Matthes had only hesitated for a moment, then, looking over at Lottchen, murmured something about a morning showing at the cinema. Could Helene and Viola drop them there first? Of course. They'd tipped Matthes and Lottchen out, then carried on, through Marzahn and Hellersdorf to Altlandsberg, and over to Krummensee. On the outskirts of the village lay enchanted waterscapes, and trees in the marsh whose roots were above ground. They were very alone out there, and had looked up through the bare branches into a noon-blue sky pampered by little clouds, which must have been very soft. They'd sat on a fat, fallen tree trunk, wrapped in blankets. Naturally they'd avoided the subject their morning encounter. Viola's make-up had been applied more sparingly that day, so there was no danger of it cracking. She hadn't done her eyebrows, and had used a brown lip liner to just outline the actual shape of her lips, rather than filling them in. Today she was wearing trousers, not a skirt, and her little faux-fur coat really suited her. Yesterday's war paint had been necessary as self-defence, she said.

Helene never wore make-up.

She didn't dare imagine what it was like to have to actually paint your womanliness on, and so thickly, in order to even be seen as a woman at all. But the question of the right to physical integrity – if you looked like Viola did with no pants on, and had probably never wanted to – had already started to rumble quietly inside her.

The woman is there again. The drooping eyelid makes her look sleepy. Helene's actually pleased she's come back.

'Well now?' Helene asks this time.

'Now, now!' the woman answers threateningly, and laughs.

She doesn't say any more than that, though. She sits there on the bench, smiling and looking around her, and rocking back and forth.

Helene is thinking about mood enhancers.

What might the woman be thinking about?

She's looking up at the sky, at the woods, at her feet. Her hands are wedged under her bum as she rocks. Her anorak is so orange Helene can't look at it for long. It hurts her eyes.

'Been here long?'

The woman shakes her head.

Then a frantic nurse comes over, from the secure ward Helene was on before: 'Found you at last! You can't just keep running off all the time! Oh, you're such a...'

With a sigh, she feigns being motherly, taking hold of the woman's sleeve and stroking her face, which is contorted with fear. Reluctantly she goes with the nurse, who keeps her on a tight leash and doesn't stop going on at her the whole time.

Helene sighs, too.

She doesn't have to feign being motherly, thank God – all at once she's glad she has no connection to Droopy Eyelid Woman. But she does have a connection to Mareile, who she can see coming along the path towards her. She's glad to see her waving in the distance and laughing, no longer the howling Mareile they were blessed with over the summer. Helene waves back. Mareile runs the last few metres and flings her arms around Helene's neck. Helene takes pleasure in her tall, lanky daughter, who tells her that Lissy's there as well, she's just seeing to something. Then Helene sees Lissy coming too. Her joinery apprenticeship started up again at the end of August. Instinctively Helene looks at Lissy's hands: both still attached, and the right one's holding three ice creams. All three are lemon buttermilk. Well, if that's not a show of unanimity! She wants to get back into her wheelchair and have her daughters push her down to the lake. They look properly shocked when she stands up and slides herself into it. Lissy spins the chair round for joy rather too wildly, and Helene nearly tells her to dial it down a bit, but then they're off. Mareile is talking about food, as always, and the meals Matthes conjures up for them apparently tirelessly – he does fabulous Mexican food – and she wants to know about the food in 'the asylum'. Old beanpole that she is. Lissy, pushing Helene, grins at her sister. She's the same build as Matthes, lithe and slender, while Mareile has legs like Helene's and her figure is constantly changing. She can go from being a skinny wiener sausage to a fat bockwurst in the space of a few months, but still manages to revert to wiener shape just as quickly – albeit a somewhat taller wiener each time. That's what she is at the moment. A very tall one, even taller than Lissy. Her ice cream is the first to disappear.

No, the food here isn't something Helene wants to talk about.

They talk about Lissy's apprenticeship instead. With three days of teaching and two days of practical experience each week, it's twenty per cent more likely that Lissy will keep her hands than lose them. Helene knows the calculation isn't right, of course, but Lissy doesn't need to know that. She wishes her daughter luck both out loud and in secret. After all, she thinks, they're having such a happy afternoon.

They have some fruit tea together, made by Helene in the residents' kitchen, before the girls say goodbye.

Helene waves and watches them both disappear in the lift.

Still there in her thoughts, though, is Viola. All she has of her here is a memory that stays hidden, covered up, until sporadic shafts of light start to reveal it, bit by bit... Anyway, on that Saturday she and Viola had stopped off at the village pub in Krummensee, and sat next to each other at a table for four. Now she can even see the blue-and-white-checked tablecloth, with a little bunch of plastic flowers on top, and a cruet stand for oil, vinegar and salt and pepper. Viola had ordered a beer. Helene fancied a glass of wine, but didn't want to risk it because she was driving. They'd needed something to make them giggle, so they wouldn't have to admit to each other how uncertain they both felt. Out of her bag Viola pulled a notebook full of film reviews she'd done for a magazine over the last few years, and began to read aloud. Viola's man's voice had led Helene to close her eyes, and she can still hear it today: 'In his portrayal of mountaineer Heinrich Harrer, Brad Pitt's oversight is impressive.' They cracked up at this sentence. Viola admitted she'd been drawn to the ambiguity of the word 'oversight', and wanted to see if the editor would take exception to it. But the editor hadn't noticed the irony, simply reading oversight as 'command of' rather than 'negligence'. 'Or else not read it at all,' Helene had said.

They laughed.

They thought up more contronyms.

Helene: fast – running fast; stuck fast. Viola: to bolt – to secure or to run away. Helene: sanction – permission or penalty. Viola: to cleave to, or to cleave in two. Helene: 'Well, you would think of that one...'

Suddenly she feels hot.

She and Matthes aren't currently at war.

But what if they were?

Which meaning of *cleave* would apply?

She has difficulty getting to sleep: the word *cleave* clings to her damaged brain, wedged between the Saturday and Sunday of Viola's visit, and splits the weekend in two. She just can't get the thought out of her head that she and Matthes might've been at war before her aneurysm. That her aneurysm was convenient for him – made her dependent on him. Straight away she's ashamed of the thought, but Matthes is so devoted... He fulfils her desires without her having to say anything. He's so undaunted by everything when he visits that she'll have to be eternally grateful to him anyway. If it wasn't for him, no one would've thought to admit her to the Stroke Unit, even though it was obvious she'd be best off there. The rehab clinic, too, would've happened weeks later than it did. She is indeed grateful to him, damn it. Grateful like she was in the very early years, when she'd been sure he was the One. Her depressive lows had still been so severe as to get her sectioned at one point, but Matthes had just laughed, and said he'd never come to visit her in a loony bin. She'd been so shocked by that that she'd quietly thrown away the referral papers and just never showed up. From then on the depressive episodes started to last longer, but they were noticeably less intense – in the end they only registered as a moderate dip on the mood scale. As happened in the autumn, for example, when Matthes moved into his study. The Matthes who craved commitment, and yet always had to give the impression his relationships were obligations he'd fallen into, and was now condemned to uphold. He'd fallen in love with her natural tendency to selflessness, which made him feel safe, whereas she'd been fascinated by his daring. He was just himself: he didn't spend the whole time looking round to see what people might make of his actions, and was pretty much free of the guilt that had soured her own life. It was happy chance that'd brought them together, and when it came to balancing out each other's foibles they'd developed something close to real expertise. She still finds that today. She'd become less inhibited, and more self-assured, while he was able to show his emotions. She'd grown more daring; he covered her back. And so on. And so forth. Still, happy chance hadn't been able to stop her pursuing another person, with a tugging in her stomach.

Pursuing... Had Malyutka Malysch gone to ground right in front of her? Had she even had to get herself out of harm's way?

She writes a short, innocuous email, sticks it in among other innocuous emails, saves the lot on a floppy disk and plans to ask Matthes to send them.

Today she has to see the *damaged boy* when she goes for physio – he's in the big hall being exercised on the mat right next to hers – and it's painful for her. She's surprised by the amount of empathy she feels, which she wouldn't have expected. His left foot hasn't actually been reattached to his knee the wrong way round. She remembers seeing a film about a girl suffering from bone cancer. In her case, the therapy plan had been to work on the mobility of her foot, which had been reattached the wrong way round, with the aim of using the heel as the knee joint when she came to have a prosthesis fitted later on. Something like that was bound to have a promising outcome when the operations had been planned so far in advance. When she'd first seen the *damaged boy*, though, he must've had some kind of accident, because he'd been badly mutilated on one side of his body. In a case like that there must be very little possibility of substituting one body part with another in a hurry, and getting a perfect fit. Plus it was unlikely that the foot in question had been in a good enough state for anyone to have attempted it. His damaged leg, which has been amputated about fifteen centimetres below the knee, has a contraption screwed on to it with big wheels going into the bone. Presumably, Helene thinks, it's being used to achieve elongation, bone growth. The pain is increasing – she can feel it all the way down her right side, which is starting to seize up. She releases voluntarily, and her arm and leg fall down flat again on to the mat.

'Good that you can control it!'

Helene is lying on her back, and she's supposed to be trying, somehow, to raise her right arm. In the end the therapist passes her a short stick to help her. Helene takes this in her left hand, clutches on to it with her right, and lifts. The physio quickly grabs hold from the right, and with their combined strength the clutching right hand is pulled upwards. Meanwhile the *damaged boy* is crying. Helene suspects he's in pain, because his face is contorted in misery. He's supposed to lift both legs off the ground and the stump of his arm is pressing hard on to the mat – it looks very strange. His therapist seems to relent, putting an arm round the lad's shoulders, but in fact has a new plan of attack: walking exercises. With an effort they help him up. Using a crutch – which of course aren't called crutches here but 'walking aids' – and with the therapist holding him tightly by the stump of his arm, he has to walk along on one leg. Now he really starts to howl, he just doesn't want to any more – he'd have fallen down if no one was holding on to him. Finally he lets himself be coaxed on to a treadmill, which they strap him into so he can't fall off. It starts up slowly. His step rate is low but at least his tears are drying.

During all this, Helene's had her work cut out making sure her therapist doesn't notice how absent-minded she is.

She's got some post, the first that's come directly to the hospital. At home, on the other hand, the letterbox has been overflowing with friends and relatives expressing their shock and sending best wishes. Matthes regularly brings the lot in, but she just hands it back without looking at it. She's saving it for later, she says. For when exactly, she doesn't say. But she's read her first post here with excitement: Carla wants to come and see her, and has already been in touch with the clinic. If Helene has no objections, she'd come next week and stay with her for a few days, depending on how long Helene can stand it because they'll have to share a room. Carla will get an extra bed.

Stand it?

Carla is her oldest, dearest, closest friend! But she hasn't told her anything about Malyutka Malysch... Suddenly she sees this as a breach of Carla's trust. She'll have to be very careful not to fall into this open crater.

◆　◆　◆

An attempt at swimming.

The physio has changed into her swimming costume, and wants to get Helene into the water using a ceiling hoist. Helene stands holding on to the wheelchair while the physio fastens the seat pad on to her. Now they're ready. The water is lukewarm, but even so it feels cold to Helene at first. In the water the seat pad of the hoist stays looped round her body to start with, but she has a good feeling about the whole thing and lets the physio undo it. With her right arm she manages two or three movements that vaguely resemble swimming strokes, and even more with her leg. Though isn't there more resistance in the water than there is in the air? There are some mysteries that can't be solved straight away... She gets given a water sausage, as the physio calls it – a flexible roll of foam she can sit on and hold on to. It gives her a feeling of security. Her favourite thing, though, is doing the 'dead man's float', with her eyes closed. The sounds reaching her ears come from the underwater pump. Sounds that send you to sleep. But the physio has something planned for her, and it's definitely not dozing off or being lulled to sleep. Not lying on her back and floating, but on her stomach, trying to swim, with a water sausage between her legs. All right then, she'll have a go. The next time she lifts her head she sees the *damaged boy*. So he's having hydrotherapy too. They've been allowed in the pool at the same time without having to be in a group – a real privilege. He's as keen as she was on just lying there being a 'dead man', the difference being that he's allowed to. He's looking at the ceiling. It's painted sky-blue, and there are ceramic fish, starfish and aquatic plants. The lights are on, so the rippling of the water makes its own pictures on the ceiling. She hopes he's doing some proper dreaming, and wishes him a fifteen-minute voyage free of orders, with no demands to move his arm, his leg or his stumps. She's pretty sure he hasn't got much will to live, so let him be a dead man for a while – resurfacing is bad enough in the state they're in, she thinks. Could she send him some energy? She's read about it before and dismissed it as charlatan rubbish, never giving it another thought. But what if she closes her eyes, and focuses her thoughts really hard on him? Would there be a spark? Would he be able to feel a connection?

She closes her eyes.

She focuses her thoughts really hard on him.

'Are you not feeling well? Come on, we'll finish there for today...'

Before she can answer, the physio has already activated the hoist. Helene wants to protest but suddenly decides she'd rather avoid any fuss, because of the *damaged boy*. So, obediently, she lets the pad of the hoist be fastened around her, then she's lifted out.

A shame, really. She can't help thinking what Matthes would've said in this situation: 'Your Compulsive Helper Syndrome is bleeping dangerously again.'

And he'd have been right.

Her time in the water would have lasted longer with him.

◆ ◆ ◆

As Helene comes out of the lift, she can just see a tall, hefty female form with tied-back dark hair disappearing round the corner. The after-image of the corner of her black skirt seems to linger, and Helene heads towards it – but it dissolves, just like the figure itself appears to have done. Has she just seen her, or has her imagination played a Viola trick on her? Yes, her first impression had indeed been of a well-dressed Viola. Helene goes down the long corridor from House 2 to the entrance foyer of House 1, looking in the dining room and some of the therapy rooms. No Viola, of course. It was the walk that'd reminded her of Viola, although she'd only really seen the figure take one step round the corner... Viola has a heavy, bouncing, fairly slow stride. Can she even run at all? Then Helene sees her coming towards her, arms wide, like a little girl wanting to jump into her mother's arms and, laughing, be protected by her, and Helene does in fact throw her arms wide and catches her... At that point the feeling of oversized uncertainty returns – the very feeling that had overshadowed the famous weekend. Realising this, she heads to the outdoor therapy area to be alone. There's never anyone there in the afternoons, so she'll be able have some space for herself and her memories. When they left the pub in Krummensee, Viola had reeked of alcohol after only two beers. But, outside, she showed Helene the four little bottles of Kümmerling liqueur she'd emptied without anyone noticing. There were another eleven full ones still rattling around in her bag. Helene contained her astonishment within a comical expression – something she was good at, and had practised thousands of times. She took one of the bottles out of Viola's bag, put it to her lips and drank. It tasted like Boonekamp, the awful stuff her parents sometimes used to knock back after a heavy meal; she shuddered. Can she stand on one leg? No, in fact, she cannot. Second bottle. Viola was grinning, but asked who was going to drive them home now. Helene glanced casually at the time and reckoned they'd just have to sit it out somewhere here for another three hours, 'won't we?' And so they'd trudged off, Helene in her heavy brown shoes and Viola in her little black boots.

When Helene looked back she saw the pub staff at the window, grinning and gesticulating.

With the best will in the world, they didn't manage another three hours in Krummensee. It was too much like November for that. At some point Helene decided she could at least drive them to Altlandsberg, as it was only just over a mile away down a road that was hardly ever used. They could park the car and get some 'proper food', then the alcohol problem would sort itself out. Finally they ended up at the Italian restaurant – down the stairs, into the vaulted basement. Viola headed purposefully for a table right at the back and sat in the corner, facing out, with wall behind her on each side. Was that what made her feel safe? Helene thought so, because without the need for any more beer, Viola slowly got into territory she'd kept hidden until now. Her face gained colour and her lips became fuller, until – all tension released – they bulged forth so slackly it must've made speaking quite difficult, or so Helene thought. In fact she spoke slowly, but without faltering. The day she'd decided once and for all to have the operation was the day her wife gave up wanting to sleep with her. She'd sensed a sort of silent agreement to try things another way. They'd snuggled up together, spooning. Viola had stuffed her sleeping cock away between her legs and waited, and her wife had suddenly approached her with a different kind of arousal – a kind of arousal, Viola thought, that wanted to recognise her womanhood. Her wife didn't lay a finger on her cock and eventually lay on top of her, which made them both cry – for joy, so it seemed to Viola – and at that point the decision became irrevocable. What came next was *the standard procedure*.

Helene remembers holding her breath for a moment – what exactly was *standard* about a procedure like that! Until of course she'd realised that Viola wasn't the only one in this position. Up to now, Helene had marvelled at her as she would a three-legged comet that'd landed in their midst: a case apart, an exceptional singularity! But that wasn't right: she just hadn't been aware of them until she got to know one – they weren't on her radar, until one of them very clearly signalled over to her. And that was simply to get to know her in the *normal* way, as a *normal* woman – as Viola felt herself to be, but in fact wasn't. Or as she didn't feel herself to be, but in fact was? Or didn't feel and wasn't either? Or *did* feel, and actually was?

(Helene's head is spinning, she can't work it all out. She's had extreme difficulties with negatives of any kind since she's been back in the land of the living, but especially double ones. She *feels* that all those sentences could be correct, though, depending on where you're standing and where you utter them. Feeling trumps reason: a peculiar state of affairs...)

The *standard procedure*...

Viola wasn't allowed to be married, and had to become permanently incapable of reproducing. An operation, called *gender reassignment*, would on the surface commit her to being a woman. To Helene, cementing the binary concept of gender seemed like a hotchpotch of unreasonable demands. A more fitting representation of the gender ratio – the idea of a scale between two poles – went through her head: anything flitting about between the 'male' and 'female' poles wasn't re-establishing itself somewhere outside of these, but moving around *as a person* in the particular place it had found for itself. It seemed so logical to her that she was surprised it didn't exist as the general consensus in society. If someone felt their gender didn't match the body they'd been born into, then it was their business to adapt to that, even surgically, or else to find another way in their head to work around it. In no circumstances, though, should anyone *demand* of them such a serious procedure as the law did! What if complications arose that made life difficult or even impossible? Of course Viola had wanted the operation, just as she'd wanted to be a woman. And yet: Helene had got to know her as a rather genderless person, not particularly well-groomed, and definitely not dolled up in a feminine way. That evening in the Italian restaurant, Viola had talked of all the hours she'd spent doing her daily grooming in the first few years after the operation – getting dressed, doing her make-up. Her health insurance had paid for two lots of hair removal, but when her beard grew back yet again she hadn't bothered with another claim, because she was fed up with spending so much time on it. Anyway, the pleasure she got from dresses and skirts had diminished as she got older, and also because she simply didn't have the money left to buy them. Her body had changed – she'd put on weight – but she'd been chucked out of her various jobs and so was often on benefits. She'd let herself go, just as she'd have let herself go over time had she been born a woman. So it was cheap trousers, which fitted at least, rather than looking for expensive women's clothes in a plus-size shop. And it was that ancient olive-green parka, instead of a chic little made-to-measure jacket. She'd just stopped going to the hairdresser altogether, letting her hair grow and trimming her fringe herself from time to time, and for shoes she'd found a mail-order company who did reasonably-priced *unisex* designs. Because her circle of friends had shrunk drastically (though she confessed to responding oddly and oversensitively to what were really just *normal* reactions – within the Western social norms of the time – to her official *sex change*) and she was no longer holding down a paid job with regular hours, she no longer needed to shave every morning – she only did so when she had to leave the house. Her hormone therapy was the only thing she kept going with, even though she'd started to question the point of it: her tiny breasts only ever developed into flat fried eggs, and her voice stayed like a man's. By then, she said, she'd come to see herself as a woman living in a male-*tuned* body, despite the operation, and the conflict that'd tormented her life so horribly before had partially resolved itself, giving way to resignation. This sometimes gave rise to something like regret over having the operation, and burdening her male body – which had been *her* body, after all – with so much that was unnatural. She didn't go so far as to call it a complete mistake, or believe her life would've gone better if she'd stayed a man. But knowing the actual outcome of her gender reassignment, things clearly weren't as simple as the law wanted them to be. She'd even come to imagine fathering more children with a woman who could accept her as a woman – and why not? Didn't she have an advantage there over other lesbians? But at the time of the operation, she'd just accepted she'd be permanently unable to reproduce, because she hadn't known any better in the circumstances. Plus – and this couldn't be disregarded – she'd already been so forcibly separated from her two sons when the divorce happened that she just couldn't imagine enduring it all again. From the moment Viola filed for divorce, her wife had revoked all solidarity. (Her wife had well and truly reverted to a state of total frustration, in which she (so Helene thought, but not Viola) redefined her husband's disappearance as a disgrace of even physical dimensions. She came to see it as a kind of suicide, through which he'd abandoned her in a very calculating way.) She really had *died* in her wife's eyes, Viola said. Helene felt vindicated.

'Why did you tart yourself up like that, when you came yesterday?'

After a moment's silence, Viola said:

'I wanted to feel the rift it caused in you, and fall into it.'

Oh, Helene remembers the feeling of wanting to hide herself away in the body of another person. She remembers it from occasions when she'd wanted to become really small so she could slip under Matthes's arm. She'd have liked best of all to have had a kangaroo pouch in there that she could slide into whenever she felt like it, a desire invariably tied up with her wish to stay permanently invisible. (She pours herself some Yogi tea with milk and honey – Matthes brought it in, and she's been brewing it for an hour in the kitchen. The nurse carried it to her room for her. The chai tastes sweet, and she lets it run over what remains of her tonsils – she can really feel them in her throat today, as if she's got pharyngitis. The tea brings temporary relief.) But Matthes didn't have a refuge for her – he always laughed whenever she curled herself up small on his left side, pushed her head under his arm and pulled her right leg up to his stomach. At some point he'd get fed up of this and, harrumphing and usually already half asleep, he'd turn away and tuck his bottom up against her. But *she* was the one who loved being wrapped up by *him*: her bottom tucked against him, his chest against her back and his arms wrapped tightly round her.

How long ago is that?

It's not true any more, she thinks. And: it's all still true.

Such full days!

Helene's attempts at standing have turned into attempts to walk. She holds on to a long bar on the wall on her left, and the physio grabs hold of her right side. Twenty steps. For the next twenty steps, though, going back, she has to try holding on to the bar with her right hand. She's pretty much exhausted after forty steps, but also euphoric at the unexpected possibility of maybe being able to walk again one day after all. Even the physio in the Stroke Unit had predicted it with casual certainty, but naturally Helene hadn't been able to believe it. It still feels unreal – and yet even though she stumbles, she manages forty steps. But then she wants to add on another forty straight away, and another and another. The physio laughs: that's enough for today, there are other patients waiting. But she's going to speak to the ward management to see whether next week Helene might even be able to get a rollator.

A rollator, no less. A bit of grandma kit. She'd always swerved out of the way of people using them, and even remembers wondering why they didn't just get straight into a wheelchair – surely it would be safer... She's done all right out of her wheelchair, too. She'd had one made to measure when she was on the Stroke Unit. She caresses the wheels, then looks around her, immediately ashamed. She's starting to realise that such prospects really rattle her. Flapping around in her brain. Hard to process. She wants to sleep, right now, this minute, but it's time for her session with the psychologist. Reluctantly she gets on her way.

She has no problem naming objects in the pictures presented to her. But then comes the same exercise they'd given her in the Stroke Unit. Now she's supposed to quickly change direction and recite as many kinds of fruit and vegetable as she can, alternating between them, but any compound noun with the same last word doesn't count. She still gets into difficulty, just like before. But she remembers now that she used to be able to do it brilliantly. She'd done tests like this as a student, for an older university friend who was writing her thesis on creativity. If she really thinks about it, her language impairment turns into something more concrete: she can no longer stroll through long rows of words like she used to, hanging on pegs just waiting for her to take them down. Not even synonyms. Instead she has a hell of a search finding a word that fits...

She knows the memory exercises, too. At first her short-term memory seems to be suffering just as much as it was weeks ago: the story she's retelling is a mere five sentences long but she can't even make a start. The next attempt goes really well, however, and even as the stories get longer she's able to keep up. She and the psychologist decide to put her initial failure down to a lack of adaptability. As the psychologist says, though, it's only relative – other patients have much greater hurdles to overcome.

Ah, she must say that to everyone.

When the forty-five minutes is up, Helene's tiredness catches up with her after she'd given it the slip before, and she wants to go back to her room and lie down. But she nods off while still in the lift and goes all the way to the top floor of the building, where she's woken by a lady going the same way. The lady seems a bit creeped out, taking three steps away from Helene's wheelchair before cautiously coming back and peering in: can she help at all? She can, but she doesn't need to. They both laugh. The lady's clearly familiar with extreme fatigue.

In her room her laptop is lying on the bed. She can't remember leaving it there, but then of course her memory is vulnerable to interference, as she's just learnt. She lies down next to it and puts her arms round it, because she no longer has the energy to lift it off the bed and on to the bedside table.

(A knock at the door.)

She doesn't jump, exactly, but is stunned when she realises it's already four o'clock. She's missed progressive muscle relaxation (no harm done, she reckons) and forgotten that...

(Another knock at the door.)

...Carla's coming today!

Of course!

If it was any of the nurses they'd just fling open the door, and even Matthes and the children would be in the room by now. It can only be Carla.

'Come in!' she calls loudly. Her voice cracks and she's annoyed at how slow she is getting out of bed. 'Come in!'

Carla sticks her head round the door – a bit apprehensively, Helene thinks.

Helene still hasn't got into her wheelchair, and hurries to do so. But she's forgotten to lock the wheels, so it rolls away from her and she falls flat on the floor.

Oh, come on.

Horrified, Carla leaps towards her, but Helene just laughs. It'll definitely have sounded worse than it actually was, all thirteen-and-a-bit stone of her hitting the floor. Carla helps her up. Not on to her feet straight away, but high enough to finally get her into her wheelchair. First off, a hug, and resting their heads together – Helene's grey side against Carla's short, chestnut-brown hair. That feels good. Like swearing a vow of solidarity.

When they look at each other, Carla can't help howling.

Oh, come on.

Helene's at a bit of a loss – she can't think of the right words for a situation like this. She simply takes Carla's hand. Carla takes another great sniff then pulls herself together.

'Here you are, then,' says Helene.

'Here I am, then!' says Carla.

At that moment someone really does fling open the door, and one of the student nurses comes in pulling a folding bed on wheels behind her.

Burbling conversation.

At the end there's a bit of to-do: the student has put the

bedding on inside out and wants to put it right there and then, but Carla says she can do it herself. The young girl's unsure, but faced with Carla's determined grip quickly gives up and leaves.

They sit in the window. However, when Carla says she really needs a coffee after her long journey, they head off to the cafeteria. They find a table where they won't be disturbed so easily: a little one for two by the window, and in the corner to boot. For a moment Helene thinks of Viola seizing that corner table at the Italian restaurant in Altlandsberg, and immediately realises that the uncertainty she and Carla are both feeling stems from different things. Carla doesn't know what state, what condition Helene's really in. She's maybe even afraid that she's lost a friend to some irreversible defect. Who knows... And Helene herself is heavy-hearted because she hasn't told Carla about Viola, about Malyutka Malysch, and she doesn't know whether, in her new state, she'll be able to overcome the trembling she always gets when relating something deeply buried. She really wants to re-emerge from this perceived breach of trust, she feels so dishonest towards Carla. But is it right, here, now, to simply start talking about Malyutka Malysch with a just-arrived Carla, who's uneasy enough as it is? Or might Carla just take it to be a brain fart? While she's mulling all this over, Carla goes up to the serving hatch and queues for coffee. She brings them both a piece of cake back, too.

Helene doesn't want any cake.

Helene wants a large grappa, to banish all her doubts, and then another to loosen her tongue. But they don't have alcohol here.

She sighs.

She sips her coffee.

She doesn't touch her cake.

'Why haven't you touched your cake?'

At that point she quickly and determinedly screws up courage, and tells Carla everything. About Viola, Malyutka Malysch and what was probably love, though the outcome of this love is still unclear. When she's finished, she doesn't dare look Carla in the eye.

'You haven't changed a bit,' says Carla, relieved.

Matthes only rang her today, he didn't come in himself. He knew Carla was going to show up. Helene had felt something almost like longing for him, though it might just have been the memory of times with Carla putting her in a wistful mood. After all, they'd been to Masuria in Poland together six years ago, and two years ago at Easter they'd gone walking in the Elbe Sandstone Mountains. In Masuria all the children had been there too, apart from Lottchen, of course, who hadn't been born at that point. Carla had also brought her two daughters, who were now at university in the Netherlands studying physiotherapy – a course that wasn't available in Germany. On that holiday they'd all taken up quarters in a wooden house, in a secluded spot by a little lake, and there were boats, and a big orchard and vegetable garden open to anyone – they could help themselves to their heart's content.

'Can you remember...?'

Of course Carla can remember.

But there's a lot more Carla wants to know.

Again and again she comes back to Malyutka Malysch. As if

her constant questioning could get the stream of Helene's memories flowing. Now she's asking about them writing to each other. Helene shrugs her shoulders. As far as emails go, there are only three or four anyway – they stopped in December last year. Carla wants to see them for herself. As Helene goes to plug the laptop in, she bends forward and her gaze falls on the floppy disk drive. She pauses: of course, she'd removed the email exchange with Viola from her email folder, and archived it on to a floppy-disk! Once, when she was reading an email from Malyutka Malysch, Matthes had come into her study. He'd crept up on her slowly and put his arms around her, and in doing so his eyes had turned towards the screen, whether they meant to or not. Helene had taken fright and closed the file. Whether Matthes had been able to read anything, she couldn't say, but she can suddenly and very clearly remember the state *she* was in – her heart started racing, just took off. She'd quickly stood up and kissed Matthes lavishly to keep him away from the screen, though of course there was nothing left to see on it.

The racing heart is there again, and she lays a hand on her chest.

She doesn't avoid Carla's questioning look, telling her straight away what she's just remembered. Again, Carla wants to know more. For example, where Helene has deposited the archive disk. Nope, can't help there. With the best will in the world, Helene just isn't able to tell her. It might be in the second set of drawers under the desk in her study, third drawer down. Where she also keeps old diaries and notebooks. But she wouldn't want to vouch for it.

No, Matthes definitely doesn't go into her personal drawers, unless she asks him to.

Yes, the disk was marked with a dot in red felt-tip.

Yes, there are lots of disks in the drawer.

No, she doesn't actually think it'll be in there, it was too sacred to her. She's surely stored it safely in her linen cupboard, where Mareile or Lissy wouldn't look – sometimes they did just go into her drawers, on the hunt for blank floppy disks.

Yes, she finds that more likely.

Since Carla will be spared the embarrassment of going through Helene's linen cupboard at home – she's going on to Rostock the day after tomorrow, to visit her friend Tilda – they can kiss goodbye to the floppy disk.

Kiss goodbye...

Helene tells Carla about Viola's elaborate mask on the day she arrived in Berlin. How on the following day she'd put on much less make-up, and on the third day, the Sunday, she'd only worn a dark lipstick in a warm shade. Yes, Helene can see it on her now – see the way she's smiling at her, and holding her hand...

What she doesn't tell Carla: after their visit to the Italian restaurant, she and Viola had driven home in silence. Matthes had waited up for them and opened another bottle of wine, but Viola had excused herself and gone to bed – too tired, she said – so Helene and Matthes had clinked glasses, just the two of them. It was an evening that called for the emptying of the whole bottle, however, which was a lot for her. As Matthes was about to go up to his room, Helene had caught hold of his sleeve, and started tearing the clothes from his body in a sudden blaze of wild fury. He had no idea what was happening to him at first, but joined in more and more with this increasingly passionate match. They even locked their bedroom door, once Matthes had carried Lottchen back to her own bed, and pounced on each other in such fiery turmoil that Matthes, unable to believe his joy, looked at her long and searchingly, his eyes growing wide. That's how it had ebbed away, too. She could see herself reflected in his pupils and felt something almost like happiness – it was a far cry from their honeymoon, but sweet nonetheless – and when they woke up the next morning, their mouths were bruised.

But keeping quiet doesn't feel like a breach of trust this time. She smiles.

How did things end with Viola? That morning, Matthes just couldn't leave Helene alone, seeking out every opportunity to be near her. When they were having breakfast all together, he'd cracked open her boiled egg and spooned the hot, soft something into her mouth. He'd laid a hand on her arm and almost casually touched her thigh, brushed her stomach, stroked her hair from her forehead. On the previous evening Viola had probably mustered all her courage to say what she'd said: 'I wanted to feel the rift it caused in you, and fall into it.' So this lovey-dovey display must have seemed like a very clear rejection. And even though Helene had tried to stop Matthes fawning over her, she also knew that the night had pulled out its knife. For now, the cord between her and Viola had been cut. She wasn't able to explain it, and had tried to catch Viola's eye and steer it towards hers, but Viola had avoided her gaze. That morning she packed up her things and thanked Helene warmly for a lovely weekend, where she'd been back *in company* again at last.

'Take care, Helene.'

Carla doesn't fawn over her at the breakfast table. They're having their last breakfast before she leaves. Helene has to go and get her own food, because Carla's busy picking out titbits from the overflowing buffet – she hasn't changed a bit either, Helene thinks. She's grinning widely, much wider than she'd like. Even the *damaged boy* gives her a questioning look, and given his ever-present reticence, that's got to mean something. But Helene keeps grinning, there's nothing else she can do.

Yesterday Carla had wished her luck and said she felt considerably reassured: Helene was the same friend she'd always been, and even more open than before, in fact, because she wasn't constantly weighing up *this* and considering *that* before revealing anything of herself. Helena was surprised at that, because she couldn't remember always looking for reassurance before when it came to her own actions. But if Carla was saying it, then it must have been the case. Hadn't Billy also said, on his last visit, that he felt they'd entered into frank communication much quicker than before? Strange. If the brain rebuilds itself in reverse, maybe it does so without all the learnt mechanisms of fear, and anybody could catch her as a result of careless remarks. Yes, that could be right: it's true it takes her a while before she can really get into any issue, whatever it is, but she does it, and without having zigzagged between *good* and *evil* like a snake. She does it without accounting for who's in the room and who isn't. She does it without running through possible reactions to her statements. Actually, yes: whenever she opened her mouth, she always used to consider in detail who'd say what in response! And when there were people there she didn't know, she'd wait until they'd unmasked themselves – so to speak – by talking, and only then might she cautiously start speaking herself.

'You're right!' she says, astonished, when Carla comes back with a Danish pastry. Carla looks at her enquiringly, so Helene tells her somewhat longwindedly what's just been going through her head.

'Oh, right,' says Carla. 'Ok, but I know I am...'

For the first time since they've been sitting together, Helene sees the *damaged boy* smile. So he *can* understand what they're talking about, *and* can get nuance too? She's pleased about that. She'd recently found his name by looking him up on the physiotherapy schedule: Wojziech Kostrzynski. His family had come to see him last Sunday – she'd assumed it was his family, anyway – and they'd all gone down to the lake together. A woman, a man and two younger brothers. Obviously in his case you could only speculate as to whether he looked like any of them. The parents had spoken Polish to him, while the two boys favoured a clear, accent-less German. There hadn't been any kind of conversation – he didn't say anything at all, just as he didn't say anything now, or in any other contexts. Instead he scowled silently, missing nothing. The latter especially. Carla opens her handbag, which she never goes anywhere without, and gets out a pack of sweets. She even offers some to the *damaged boy*. And, after his hand recoils a few times, he does in fact take some. They all tuck in.

Helene's appreciation grows, and a radiant halo appears around Carla's head.

She went out to the bus with Carla in her wheelchair – a farewell tour, as it happens, because when she comes back she finds the rollator in her room. She wheels round it, puts the brake on her wheelchair and stands up, but then sits back down again. She doesn't dare try walking with the thing. Then the senior nurse arrives, and right on cue for once. Helene would like to get acquainted with the rollator slowly, so wants to ask the nurse whether she might give her a hand.

Actually the nurse has only come to take the wheelchair away.

A conflict of interests.

Before Helene manages to say as much, the nurse has upped and left with the wheelchair. Helene is flabbergasted. She stands. Now she's at the rollator, trembling. Then she sits down and tries to get a hold of herself – no easy undertaking, she must confess. Right now she'd like to have strong hands around her, grasping firmly, and able to react quicker than she can if she stumbles and is in danger of falling. Reflecting on this, she realises she was thinking of Malyutka Malysch. Malyutka Malysch is bigger-built than Matthes and her broad shoulders alone promise protection. Matthes promises protection too, but only on second glance, once you know he's capable of it. Matthes is a lot taller than Malyutka Malysch, but he can't offer her broad shoulders. For a moment she's so confused that Matthes appears to her with Malyutka's face, and Malyutka with Matthes's – their shapes blur and become one, then separate again. Each with the right head, thank goodness. She's breathing fast now. Suddenly she remembers a day in March when she and Viola had arranged to meet at the Pergamon Museum in central Berlin. They wanted to have a good look at the Market Gate of Miletus, because to Helene's surprise Malyutka was planning on reading a historical novel set in the sixth century BC. Now Helene remembers that Malyutka had flown to Izmir in Turkey in the January, when it was cheap, to have a look around the place where the novel was set. Her mother had given her the money for it for her birthday. She came back quite frightened, because in Muslim Turkey it'd been a dangerous game showing herself in public – even though she'd dressed in neutral clothes, cut her long hair and even bought herself a pair of tough walking boots. She'd been crudely propositioned several times in little villages, and was glad she wasn't on her own, having negotiated a price with a driver to take her wherever she wanted for three days. Hadn't the story been about Thales and Anaximander, who quarrelled over a pupil? The novel was supposed to be set in the sixth century B. C., and Helene and Malyutka had laughed til they cried when they realised that the Market Gate was built in the second century A.D.! Malyutka had shared an anecdote people used to tell about Thales. To show all those who reproached him for being poor, one winter he rented all the olive presses in Miletus with the little bit of money he had. From the position of the stars he's said to have calculated that the next harvest would be a bountiful one. So when harvest time came, he controlled all the presses, which he sublet and made good money out of. As they left the museum, Malyutka had wished she could think of an idea like Thales's, so she could boost the little bit of money she had and finally do as she pleased. She was wearing the tough walking boots she'd bought for Turkey and was thinking about her mother, who'd slipped her money not just for the trip to Turkey but for other desires, too, which of course the authorities weren't allowed to know about. At the moment she was broke, and turned her coat pockets inside out to prove it. That was why she wanted to leave before Helene asked her to go for a drink, and things got even more awkward for her. But Helene had suddenly linked arms with her and pulled her along, sensing that she did so very willingly. They ended up in a pub in Prenzlauer Berg, where they drank wine and had a bite to eat. And suddenly Malyutka had looked at her and kissed her, exactly as she had in the shadow of the seashell stage with its marching band in Zinnowitz. Here, no one was remotely interested, no one looked at them, and after paying in a hurry there was nothing left to do but stumble on and into a little hotel a couple of doors down. They asked about a room. One was available. Malyutka tried once more to remind Helene of her acute shortage of cash, but Helene had already flashed her credit card. Later she let herself sink to Malyutka's feet, and just as she wanted to start hastily pulling her clothes off her, she suddenly remembered the night with Matthes. Whether she wasn't sober enough, or whether a sudden sadness was messing with her head, she couldn't really say; at any rate, she'd moaned 'Matthes, Matthes!' And when Malyutka – who'd surely understood what she'd said, but wanted not to have – had paused for a moment and looked at her, she realised what she'd said. She'd covered Malyutka's mouth, then, as if *it* had been the one to moan the name. She wanted to make Malyutka forget what she'd heard with her own ears, yet she still wasn't able to edge Matthes out of her fragmented thoughts, which kept coming.

When they woke up the next morning next to each other, Malyutka's arm on her chest, it had been Malyutka who said that she wasn't really a better man than Matthes. She'd said it sorrowfully, and there'd been sorrow on her face – a face lodged in Helene's memory as if Malyutka had just left the room. But it was in March that she'd left the room, in that hotel, with her sorrowful announcement that she couldn't take the place of a man for Helene. And now Helene once again feels the chill this sentence brought upon her, making the little hairs on her arms stand on end. The chill had stayed with her when she later went down the stairs and paid for the hotel, and took the train back to Karlshorst and Arberstrasse. Luckily Matthes and the girls weren't there, as it was a completely ordinary weekday – a Tuesday? Or a Wednesday? – and the first thing she did was lie in the bath and let the water run hotter and hotter, on and on. But the chill stayed, and still hadn't gone when Matthes got home from work. She was coming down with something – a *nasty bout of flu,* she'd called it, though she knew very well that it wasn't. She'd lied to Matthes, telling him she'd bumped into her friend Kerstin, and they'd drunk too much wine too fast for them to notice the soporific effects of the grappa that followed. Kerstin had made up a bed for her in the kids' room. She knew Matthes would never ask Kerstin, to check whether it was true. And she was very grateful for her *nasty bout of flu*, which gave her an excuse to spend a few nights alone in her study – though she was long past her most recent supposed November depression – while Matthes waited for her to come to him in their bedroom below.

The trembling subsides as she's remembering all this. Although she still feels very much like trembling... She's still sitting on the bed, and when she gets up she's amazed at the strength she can feel in her right leg. Not flexibility, but strength. She plucks up her courage and does a few circuits of the room, before putting on her coat and scarf, opening the door and heading out, towards the lift. She wants to be elsewhere, and alone. Away from all the bustle of the ward. Down by the lake, if she can manage it.

◆ ◆ ◆

Of course she doesn't make it as far as the lake. Her reluctance to tackle the descent with the rollator – down the snaking path with its stony terraces – increases the closer she gets to it, so she turns back. It's also surprisingly cold, even when she pulls her scarf up around her mouth. This blue viscose one is the thickest she has here, so it's probably time to ask Matthes for a woolly one. She'd never been one to feel the cold, though. Out of all the family she could go the longest without socks, and would still be going around with bare arms long after the others had started wearing some sort of coat. Everything that's happened to her has obviously thrown her senses into disarray, if she's already wanting a scarf in September. She'd also like some sturdier shoes than the lightweight white trainers Matthes had bought without taking her feet along with him. They fit perfectly, but won't keep out the wind and weather now she's getting ready to walk again. Her right foot drags along the ground if she doesn't think to pick it up. She's very often thinking about other things altogether, so it drags a lot. Even on this short stretch of path to the start of the woods, her right shoe is already the worse for it. She decides for the next fifty steps to think only about picking up her foot. That does the trick. So let's have another fifty on top, please – but then a face appears that she thinks she knows. She doesn't know where from. The man looks at her, but goes past without a word. He doesn't seem to know her. He walks with a crutch and moves his left leg skilfully, despite its considerable spasticity. His gait isn't smooth but it looks confident. Where does she know him from, then?

She summons herself back to the foot lifting. Come on then,

you can manage it as far as the lift. She doesn't notice the senior nurse walking behind her.

'You be careful, there! That doesn't look good at all, it's still far too soon. Much too dangerous – you're tripping over that right foot, you know!'

That's all Helene needs... Hadn't the nurse been the very person who'd taken her wheelchair away, just like that?

She doesn't react and just carries on walking, as if she hasn't heard.

The nurse gets into the lift with Helene and gives her a piercing look, no doubt still expecting an answer, but Helene just smiles. When they arrive upstairs the nurse seems to really want to have another go – you can see her chest inflating – but Helene just goes... 'pfffffffffffttttttt!' Showing her how to let the air out.

Completely taken aback, the nurse watches her go.

Helene has spent a good deal of time thinking about whether she'd like the wheelchair back for a while. It was an easier and safer way to get about, though she's also noticed that the rollator is better at challenging her right hand. After all, it has to close tightly around the rollator's handle, otherwise she wouldn't be able to take a single step. She's surprised at how her hand behaves. Not bad at all. Though she still can't lift the arm even a little bit! Instictively, she tries it: okay, it's come up maybe six inches. Better than it was six weeks ago, anyway, or even a fortnight ago. Something like optimism threatens to break through, just when she's drilled herself so thoroughly in accepting her fate. In her current situation, she only ever thinks about getting by. But that situation is improving all the time – something she's effectively blocked out up to now. She wants to seize that optimism by the collar so it doesn't get away. Optimism doesn't have a collar, though, and instead is suddenly standing there in the room in the form of a small naked figure, which she can't help laughing at. The little figure becomes sad – its shoulders droop and it turns around, wanting to get out of there and just scarper completely. 'Stop!' she calls out, suppressing her laughter and resolving to stand by the little thing's side – to keep her eyes glued to it, take it under her wing, feed it up and turn it into a fine, proud figure. Only at this point does she realise that Optimism is male – she can see his little willy and the fine bumfluff around his mouth. Maybe when she's feeding him up she should let him have a share of her oestrogen, and turn him into a fine, proud figure of femininity... What state is her own femininity in, anyway? Last year she'd fallen pregnant again. Her sixth child had announced itself for four months, then disappeared again. Even though the baby had been an accident and unexpected, she'd taken the miscarriage really hard. Being on the wrong side of forty, she hadn't reckoned on being able to get pregnant again. And now? She hasn't actually had a period now for over two months, has she?

Oh God.

What if she's pregnant?

What if the baby's been harmed by everything it's had to put up with over all these weeks? Suddenly she's worried.

She goes looking for the senior nurse in the nurses' lounge. She'd like an appointment with a gynaecologist.

'How old are you?' asks the male gynaecologist.

'Forty-four,' she replies.

The senior nurse got her an appointment straight away. She'd even got in touch with the patient transport service, although the local women's clinic wasn't at all far from the rehab clinic.

Helene spoke of her fear that she might be pregnant.

'When was your last period?'

She thinks it was around the tenth of July – she remembers thinking she'd been bleeding when she came out of the coma. She doesn't know exactly when, she says. The doctor does a pregnancy test. It's negative. She calculates. She can hardly tell the doctor she'd had sex three or four weeks after the aneurysm, can she? When was that? Mid-August? And has enough time passed to be able to take a pregnancy test?

The doctor says that everything argues against her being pregnant. There's no livid discolouration of the vulva, her breasts are soft and not swollen, and there's no darkening of the central line of the stomach, or the areolae. To say nothing of the pregnancy test itself.

He looks at her for a long time. Then he says that while forty-four is by no means past it, she should prepare herself for the fact that she might have seen the last of her period. That's often the case after a brain aneurysm.

She's gobsmacked. It's all too fast for her. She wants to let it sink in first, because she hadn't expected anything like this. Can she really be on the far side of the menopause so quickly, in her case after only days or weeks? Interesting. The thought, when she pursues it, is immediately slightly painful. For the whole of last year, the pregnancy's unhappy outcome had swung back and forth above her like a sword of sadness, at times alarmingly close, at others high enough over her head that she could only just make it out. Whenever it came close, she wanted most of all to crawl into bed with Matthes and start trying again, an idea which was of course driven out by common sense. But it'd been good to know it wasn't all over yet, that she *still could* if that was her intention. Now she maybe *couldn't any more*...

For now, she's sad.

Matthes would be relieved.

With Malyutka Malysch, she thinks suddenly, she wouldn't have been able to have children anyway.

That night she dreams of Putin. Putin as Ded Moroz, the Russian Father Christmas, with a white beard and ice-grey fur coat shimmering blue. At his side is his granddaughter Snegurochka, the little snowflake. Ded Moroz Putin alights from his horse-drawn troika and gives out presents. Matthes gets one, as do their daughters and her sons, and the neighbours. It must be happening in the house on Arberstrasse. As Helene goes to accept her present from Putin, Snegurochka steps between them with a coaxing, expectant smile. Snegurochka suddenly looks old, the way she's standing there and grinning. She's got a hint of a beard, tinted eyebrows and rosacea, and her lipstick's gone askew. Her hair is greying visibly, and when she beckons Helene with her finger it's rather long and spotted with age. Even in the dream, Helene knows who Snegurochka reminds her of. She wants to wake up, but the dream won't be shaken off so easily. On the contrary: Snegurochka is only just getting properly started, and begins to take her clothes off very slowly, like a stripper. Finally she stands naked before Helene, except for a red angora jumper. Her grin has disappeared and she now looks tired and sad. She probably thinks it's time to leave, too.

Is Helene waking up?

For a long time she doesn't know if she's awake.

Her ears are ringing.

Her mother used to get ringing in her ears. She'd always say, 'Someone's talking about me,' then stick her index finger in and give it a good jiggle about. Is someone talking about Helene? The longer she imagines someone talking about her, the more clearly she can see Malyutka Malysch.

Who is she talking to?

No, now that can't be right. She must still be asleep. She pushes herself further into the pillow and pulls the covers up, not just over her ringing ears but over her eyes too.

The image stays with her. Malyutka Malysch is talking to Vladimir Vladimirovich Putin in her excellent Russian. Is she speaking it so fluently that Helene can't understand what they're talking about? She wants to get closer so she can catch something of what they're saying. Now she can see Malyutka has a beard and very short hair, and there are no little breasts showing underneath her shirt, and her tie is making her Adam's apple bounce, as if it's been tied too tight. Suddenly Helene knows what she's seeing: Malyutka had told her about it. There'd been no seal of secrecy on this story, which wasn't about Malyutka anyway, but a man with the same surname and a different first name – Viktor Malysch. Towards the end of his time as a research student in Dresden, the choir Viktor Malysch was in had planned a trip to the West. Viktor had felt a certain sense of excitement, but at the same time made no move to suggest he was thinking about not coming back – staying *there*. One day, it might have been six or eight weeks before the choir trip, a middle-aged man sat next to Viktor in the university canteen, and accidentally – or so Viktor thought at first – splattered him with sauce. ('Don't worry, we'll get it off you in no time!') They got talking: the man introduced himself as a passionate folk-song researcher who had an extensive collection of audio recordings. As early as the Sixties he'd been recording everything there was to record with his Tesla B4. He'd gathered material in the Erzgebirge and the Harz mountains and on the coast, but also on the Hungarian plains and in Mazovia in eastern Poland. He invited Viktor to come and have a look at his collection, and most importantly have a listen. They could even go for something to eat beforehand. He wanted to make it up to Viktor for making a mess of him earlier, so invited him to the pub – Am Thor, on Platz der Einheit – one night the following week. Viktor had a job finding someone to look after the boys. At that point it occurred to him that he actually spent every evening with them, and looked forward all morning to picking them up from nursery. His wife, who was a nurse, often worked a late shift, and if she was on earlies or nights then she'd use the time Viktor was at home to sleep. They hadn't seen much of each other lately – she was often working at the weekend, too. Next week she'd be on late shifts, so perhaps that cousin of his could help out. He hadn't asked her for so long that he had to think for a moment to remember her name. He could picture her, with her grey-green eyes and very blonde hair, but her name only came to him after he'd rummaged around for a good while: she was called Jakobine. A nice name. He'd have liked to name one of his sons Jakob, but his wife chose Tim and Tom - names he was only able to warm to after a whole day of looking at their faces over and over again. He could've objected, but his wife had obviously made the official announcement with such certainty straight after the birth that it would've amounted to an insult, which he wanted to avoid for an easier life. He still got annoyed about it today. Jakobine was delighted to be asked, and of course agreed to do it, so Viktor actually went to the pub on the agreed evening. He found the man who'd invited him sitting at a corner table. A merry band of men was gathered there already – and everyone was speaking Russian. One of them – a slight, ugly man with a gaunt, almost fleshless face – was a little more reticent than the others. 'Volodya,' was all he'd said when Viktor introduced himself. Viktor, however, who'd learnt to watch out for situations just like this, could feel the man watching him constantly. Volodya said – only when prompted, of course – that he was a student, but was evasive when asked what he was studying, saying it had to do with engineering but also philosophy. Viktor thought he'd misheard, and was going to ask again, when the reticent Volodya suddenly banged a bottle of vodka down on the table and invited everyone there to help themselves. Today was *Metalworkers' Day* in the Soviet Union, he said. (Helene had even looked it up last year, she can remember doing it: it was observed on the third Sunday in July.) Viktor hesitated – if he started, he said, he might not be able to stop. And anyway: one of those present had asked him here for a meal, so how he'd ended up in this Russian crowd was beyond him. Although they were by no means all Russians, they spoke the language at least as well as Viktor. In Sixth Form he was supposed to be a contestant in the International Russian Olympiad, and for a while even went along to the central gathering of the Olympiad squads. It had been decreed that he didn't need subjects like Chemistry and Physics, and a Russian schedule was drawn up for him which he was supposed to achieve with the help of his teacher. He'd refused to do it. Physics was his absolute favourite subject, and even though it had strangely never entered his mind to study it at university, it held a fascination for him that was stronger than his desire and willingness to speak Russian. No one could understand that, and he'd run the gauntlet once he was back at school. Even so, Viktor spoke Russian well enough to be able to quiz Volodya, who really didn't like it. Volodya went off to the toilet, and when he came back sat down in a seat opposite Viktor. It was difficult to talk to him across the table. Viktor remembered the promised meal, and set about ordering something off his own bat – he was hungry, and hadn't reckoned on sitting around for so long. What did he eat? Tiegelwurst, a kind of blood sausage, remembers Helene, with fried onions, sauerkraut and mashed potato. Volodya was repulsed by this and had to hold his nose. He was thirty-three years old. If anyone had said, that evening, that he'd one day be president of Russia, it would probably have gone very quiet for a moment. Then they'd all have started roaring with laughter, and clapping whoever had said it on the back for telling such a masterful joke.

Viktor wasn't what Putin was looking for. Putin was looking for sly characters, Viola had said, who didn't mind having fingers in various pies. Viktor hadn't known that. Viktor hadn't even known it was Putin he'd spoken to, merely wondering what kind of company he'd stumbled into. When the folk-song researcher didn't pay the bill as he said he would, and left without saying a word about his collection of folk songs, Viktor had wondered about the secret service. Then he forgot all about it again, because having to wonder about the secret service wasn't exactly an unusual occurrence. Only fourteen years later did Viola realise Viktor had been speaking to Putin. Putin hadn't stayed entirely true to himself, perhaps, but not far off...

Suddenly Helene can't remember what Viola has to do with Viktor.

Does Viola have anything to do with Viktor?

She closes her eyes again, and sees the Adam's apple going up and down above the presumably too-tight tie.

She thinks she knows, but just can't piece it all together.

Later on, she's amazed. Amazed at what her memory divulges. Does she really know so much about Viola? Matthes, for example, had never told her in such detail about his time at school – he was altogether pretty abrupt when it came to the past. Apart from that much-repeated story of the nine-year-old who got 'five black marks, and three good ones for excellent diligence' on his school report, which Matthes always brought out as an alibi when anyone asked him about school. Helene had only known Viola for a year, Matthes for twenty-six... On the other hand, she hadn't been able to find the same feeling of intimacy in her relationship with Malyutka Malysch as she shared with Matthes. Yet another thing she can't piece together so easily: the fact that intimacy with a person clearly doesn't depend on how much you know about them.

As if to prove it, at that moment Matthes moves his spine all the way along hers. She can feel his vertebrae, how they slide down hers and back up again. And although in her head they're lying turned away from each other, she can see his face, distorted with pleasure, and his arms, resting on her thighs.

'Right, we need to pick up the pace a bit here! You can't just sleep in and miss your therapy – doesn't work like that, y'know! Three times now I've been told you didn't go to psychology. Do we not want to?'

Nah, not really.

The nurse talks like a proper Berliner. When Helene moved to Berlin she still sounded like someone from Thuringia, but that quickly faded. What does she sound like now? She doesn't feel like having a discussion with the woman. Instead she looks at her schedule: psychology, as it happens. She sighs and gets up.

Okay, she's on her way.

When the lift arrives downstairs, the door to the cafeteria is just opening and she can see through to the grounds. No, she's not going to psychology.

Outside the clear air and sunshine are both going all out to woo her. She doesn't need a scarf, or a thicker coat.

Why is she refusing to see the psychologist? She feels she's been badly treated by her. Doesn't she ask people about the jobs and the life they had before they showed up here for rehab? Apparently not. She hasn't a clue that Helene herself had worked as a psychologist for a decade. Their communication has become warped and weird. Helene doesn't think she should've been the one to have to disclose it. The fact that the psychologist's not interested doesn't show her working methods in a very good light. Discussing a patient's medical history is just what you do in such situations, regardless of the circumstances you meet them in. But that hasn't happened up to now, and it doesn't look like it's on the schedule. The psychologist can shove it, then, Helene thinks to herself – and if anyone asks, she'll say so on the record. And that's that.

So now for some fresh air. It's got so warm again that she'd have liked most of all to take off her shoes and socks, and stroll barefoot along the paths and on the grass. She's venturing towards the start of the snaking path, heading in the direction of the woods, when she sees him again: the man with the crutch, and the sure but uneven gait. She thinks she's seen him somewhere before. He approaches at quite a pace – presumably he also wants to go down to the water. When he reaches Helene, she plucks up the courage to ask whether he'd walk with her, and support her if need be. He smiles indifferently and nods. He then grips her arm so forcefully that she's alarmed, but after a while it feels safe to be walking down with him. They fall silent. He still seems perfectly at ease, but Helene always finds such silences uncomfortable. She realises how unnecessary this is in the current situation, because the man looks so charming and easy-going – she really doesn't need to say anything, and can't think of anything anyway. Nonetheless she decides to act cheerful and have a try, putting on a cheery face. No, that's not going to help. It feels like her smile's being held in place by some kind of clamp. She relaxes the muscles in her face again. She probably looks *sulky*, as her mother used to say. 'You always look so sulky – can't you pick a different expression for a change?' No. And she still can't.

'Peter,' the man says suddenly.

'Preissler,' says Helene.

Of course! It's Peter Preissler, who Matthes was at school with – they'd bumped into him years ago on the train, and later seen him again at a class reunion. 'Yes, Preissler,' he repeats impassively, not at all surprised that Helene knows his name. She's so taken aback that for a moment she stops paying attention to her right foot, and stumbles. He holds on to her, catching her. He's worth it, she must say, and smirks involuntarily. Once they're at the lake he turns back without a word of farewell – or any words at all – and with the same friendly expression he was wearing as they walked down. She wants to keep him there because she's afraid of having to get back up by herself, but in the end she doesn't bother. She has a look around her instead. The firepit is showing new scorch marks. She puzzles over whether it's patients from the clinic who're messing about making fires. The grounds are fenced off on all sides, but you know how it is, people will always find a way in if they want to. She sits down and watches the ducks and the coots. Two swans start to swim towards them in the distance.

Preissler's state of mind is a puzzle. What's wrong with him? He seems to be in a little world of his own. Clearly he's happy with being Peter, and even Preissler in the second instance, if he hears someone else mention the name, but it doesn't seem to mean anything to him. He doesn't really talk, but she doesn't either. She looks sulky, he looks happy and cheerful. But she isn't sulky – so maybe he's not happy and cheerful, either? Just as people could be wrong about her face, so they could also be wrong about his, she thinks. He doesn't look injured, or as if he's recently had an operation. The first and second times she'd seen him he wasn't walking with a stick, and he had a brisk, bouncy stride. He was the life and soul of the party: at the reunion he'd kept up a constant stream of jokes. One even comes into her head now, and her sulky face brightens. His tangle of words had been so loud and carried so far across the room that she'd even asked Matthes if they could move a bit further away, rather than sitting so close. Relieved, Matthes had got up, and with Helene in tow moved down three tables to sit with Claudia, a friend from his school days – or girlfriend? There they found themselves in good company straight away – words like *adorable* and *delightful* come to mind for Claudia. Peter Preissler's resounding bass voice was turned down to an unobtrusive level, thanks to the distance. 'Peter,' he'd said today, in a thin little voice...

Helene will have to tell Matthes about him, definitely.

The sun moves over her as she sits there, taking the shadows away with it behind the woods. Soon it'll be getting dark. She'll have to get back up the hill before then, for fear of not being able to make out the path. She sets off slowly, getting a bit more confident with every step. As she rounds the last hairpin bend, the lamps lining the path come on.

Well, well, well – she hadn't even seen those until now.

Because when she walks, she's always looking down...

Four times she starts her explanation as to why she's not interested in psychological help. And four times she gets no further than the beginnings of a sentence before getting tangled up, going red and breaking off. The doctor on the ward wants to give her something to write with, until she realises that Helene is right-handed. Helene takes advantage of the momentary cluelessness to get her laptop out. It's already switched on because she was browsing old emails earlier, trying to reconstruct lost time. In perfect German she writes down what she understands by psychological help, and why such a help cannot be expected from a local psychologist like the one here. After all, Helene has spent enough time with her to build a picture of what she's like. The doctor clearly sees this as a load of snooty nonsense – she dismisses it, anyway, with a gesture of short-tempered rejection. The nurse, on the other hand, can see very well where Helene's coming from, and attempts to interpret it for the doctor again. She'd have been better off not doing that. The very thing doctors don't like is someone far below them in the hierarchy delivering something that could be construed as a lecture, thinks Helene. She sighs, then says loudly and slowly that she's done with psychology the way it's offered here at the clinic, and she's already made her decision. The doctor tries to protest, mumbling something about Helene 'not being here much longer', but then gives up. Helene is pleased with herself for staying strong. And pleased that progressive muscle relaxation is up next.

Ten of them are sitting in a small, quiet, out-of-the-way room. The rollator is parked by the wall. Helene has actually managed to move along the chairs hand over hand, until she got to an empty one, without falling over. The nurse acting as therapist here simply pushes a little tape into a slot. But for Helene, who has mastered autogenic training and practised muscle relaxation before, it always means the same journey, to Frau Holle's blooming meadow with its apple tree and oven. As soon as she relaxes, she's there. Not right in the well, but still far below the chapped, crusted moment left behind on the surface. There in the depths – where all should be dark and uncomfortable, according to the logic of things – she bathes in light and warmth with her eyes closed. She really likes doing this. Unsaddling. Relaxing. Arms heavy, legs floppy. All limbs the same, with no noticeable difference between her good side and her damaged one. Her enjoyment reaches right into her subconscious, and when it's time to resurface she does that briskly and decisively too, a long-practised habit. Although it's such a lovely state of being that she could stay in it forever.

Today is no exception.

Today is no exception: Matthes wants to come. She's on the verge of asking him if they could start leaving a day between visits. It would be good for her, and it'd definitely be an important step off the hamster wheel for him – he's been running round and round in it like a mad thing. She can hardly imagine what his days look like, spending hours on the train and bus after work to get to her. Until he gets there, she's always waiting for him. But once he's there something unspoken stands between them, large and unsettling – she can clearly perceive it, but not wrap it up in words. Does he feel it too? She doesn't know, nor does she know whether that's not even more unsettling.

In her head she's cleaning windows. She's going round their house on Arberstrasse room by room, with her blue bucket of warm water and vinegar, opening each window and washing it first on the outside, then on the inside. She polishes them dry with old terry nappies, and can't help but laugh that she's remembering what her children used to eat. She can even match some stains on the nappies to particular varieties of baby food, but most were due to illness. Bill had once had awful diarrhoea and could only eat plain carrots – they'd left their mark on the nappies for years afterwards.

Why is she cleaning windows in her head? Is she seeking the clear view she doesn't otherwise have? She can't see far from the windows of the house. There's another house in front, and a boundary wall behind. On one side of their entrance there's a door-sized pane of glass looking on to the neighbouring plot and their drive. On the other side there's the terrace with the pergola and its exuberant vine. Its grapes taste so good that her mouth starts to water on the spot. (Yesterday Matthes had brought some with him – there are a few left, which she immediately crams into her mouth.)

No, it's probably not the view she's pining for. More likely, perhaps, she's testing the water – seeing whether she can imagine herself going back there, back to her old routine... She'd sometimes wandered through her house in her head before now, from top to bottom and back again, but she'd never done more than reclaim the rooms for herself – the furniture, the books, the carpets, the pictures. But today she's cleaning windows, and that, she decides, is the first step on her journey home. And she decides something else: that she'll focus all her attention on her physiotherapy, and on being discharged the very day she no longer needs the rollator.

For weeks she'd slowly but very surely resigned herself to life in a wheelchair, and now a simple bit of equipment with wheels has immediately convinced her that so much more is possible. That she could walk again – perhaps not as fast as she was accustomed to, but still at a decent pace. Something like euphoria is sprawling loutishly across the room, and Helene is presiding over it all in her chair by the window when Matthes comes in.

Matthes looks different to yesterday. He hasn't tied up his long hair, or washed it either, but that's not it. He looks uncertain. Vulnerable, somehow. A great deal of adversity must have been encountered over time to get to that face. She knows that face, and knows how long it takes for it to change like that. Matthes comes up to her chair, and she stands up. He hugs her, a tad too roughly, but then immediately pulls back and unwraps the flowers he's brought with him. Not wildflowers – it's probably too late in the year for those anyway – but three gerberas. The flower which, twenty years ago, she claimed was her favourite. That was when cut flowers were an impossible-to-find luxury. She wouldn't think to call gerberas her favourite flower today, but she doesn't know if that's because nowadays she gets the most beautiful bunches thrown after her on every street corner. Does it just come with age, that she now has other favourite flowers? Campanulas, for example. Preferably picked by Matthes, and sprinkled with poppies. In Ikebana, Japanese flower-arranging, gerberas represent sadness. What campanulas represent, she unfortunately doesn't know.

Matthes shifts from one foot to the other.

'She's dead,' he says.

V

Reflexes

HELENE WAKES UP. Her mouth hurts. Her tongue seems swollen. Billy is with her, and smiles in his inimitably wise way. Helene wants to sit up, then sees the drip in her arm, and the bars at the sides of the bed. An attempt to remember, but there's nothing but chopped-up sequences. But they must be from years ago! That's how it seems to her, anyway... Hasn't she been here before? In the big room with four other beds? What's going on? She feels dazed, shattered. There's a buzzing in her legs like after a long bout of cramp. Her ribs hurt. Now that she wants to say something her tongue feels enormous in her mouth, like a huge, weak, wet rag that for some reason she can't wring out. A nurse stops by and announces lunch: pasta in cheese sauce. But food is the last thing she wants! Billy tries to reassure her. Why is she here? Pretty desperate now, she looks into her son's beautiful blue eyes. The nurse comes. A tray comes too. The nurse takes a spoonful of pasta, easy-to-scoop fusilli, then dips it in cheese sauce and holds it up to Helene's mouth. Helene doesn't want it. 'Open up!' the nurse's voice thunders, and Helene is so taken aback that she automatically opens her mouth. The spoon's in before she knows it, but a strong urge to gag sends the pieces of pasta tumbling out of her mouth one by one. The nurse gets cross. At this point Billy mans up, and gives her a dressing-down. You can't just treat patients like that, when they've been put here whether they like it or not! It's obvious his mother doesn't want anything to eat! Take that! And that!

The urge to gag disappears, and Helene fills with pride.

'Take that!' she says triumphantly.

The nurse waltzes off, having achieved nothing.

Can anyone tell me what I'm doing here? She just can't get the question out. It's worse than when she lost her speech after the operation! she thinks. Back then, whenever she wanted to speak, the words mostly disappeared, whereas now they're right there but not a single one can leave her mouth! She seems to be generally stuck in some kind of jelly. She can only move her limbs with extreme effort, and Billy's blue eyes are blurred.

'You had an epileptic seizure,' he says. 'A bad one, and it had everyone really worried. I wasn't worried, though – I knew you'd come through.'

She goes back to Heidemühlen a day later, this time fully (albeit soggily) conscious. Bill has told her the course of events, but since then it's as if she's lying in a Procrustean bed which she doesn't fit into at all. She's drugged up to the eyeballs on valproate, so thinking is only proceeding very slowly. On the journey she makes another attempt at getting an overview of the situation:

Matthes had visited her the day before yesterday, and while he was there she went into status epilepticus, a basically life-threatening state of continuous seizures. She'd been taken first to what is now the protestant hospital in Henrichshorst, where she'd worked almost twenty years ago. Matthes wouldn't let them send him away, and had insisted on going with her. There they'd tried to counter the grand mal seizures with a diazepam injection, but with no success. Matthes had then demanded that they take her – in the middle of the night – to the emergency hospital in Berlin. Not only were her surgical records there, they'd also be able to remember her and be better equipped to make a diagnosis. Matthes was afraid it was another aneurysm, or a secondary haemorrhage. In Berlin he never left her side. The doctors had decided to give her valproate intravenously in order to halt the seizures and prevent any further ones. They regretted not being able to do an MRI scan because of her pacemaker, and so were reliant on a CAT scan. Fortunately, though, she'd shown no signs of another rupture, so she'd been moved to the neurological ward one floor below the Stroke Unit. That's why she'd thought herself to be on familiar terrain when she woke up – it wasn't *déjà vu*! Billy had actually managed to track Matthes down over the phone. In a flap because Matthes hadn't come home, he'd rung Heidemühlen and learnt from them that Helene had been transferred to Henrichshorst. Concerned when Matthes still wasn't back around midnight, he'd rung the hospital in Henrichshorst just as the ambulance was setting off for Berlin, and finally appeared at the emergency hospital in the flesh to relieve Matthes, and sit by his mother's bedside until she woke up. Matthes had hugged him (something which not so long ago would've been unthinkable, because the distance between him and her sons had grown rather than diminished over the years – Bill had been quite emotional when he told her about it) and then gone home, utterly exhausted. She'd sent her son home in the end, too – she was completely done in and just wanted to sleep. But scarcely had she dozed off when a whole crew of people arrived. And what a crew they were. A bespectacled doctor with protruding front teeth had waved a bit of paper about, which she was expected to sign. It said that she mustn't go swimming alone in public pools, and should avoid risky activities such as climbing. She'd laughed at that. Those things were all out of the question in her condition, anyway! Using gestures, she'd indicated that she was currently having trouble speaking. That she was feeling woozy, and just wouldn't be able to manage a signature. Nor did she want to sign anything until her head was clear again, but of course she didn't say that – not that she'd have been able to, in any case. She couldn't get rid of the feeling that the doctor was annoyed, just like the lunchtime nurse. But this time the feeling didn't bear down on her stomach, instead puffing itself up into a sense of self-confidence. Deep down she thought that something sharp or pointed might come and burst it again, but on the surface she tried not to give it any thought.

She'd been given tablets, to be taken for the foreseeable future. No, she's not comfortable with that... She rummages around in her little bag and finds them. *Ergenyl chrono* is written on the packet. She reads that the dose should be increased slowly over four to six weeks. Because she's already had the infusion of valproic acid, the doctor explained, they'd started her on the permanent dose straight away. With this sustained-release preparation and in these particular circumstances, the dosage has now been halved. She didn't know exactly what to make of this, listening to it all as she would've listened to people yacking on about newly discovered comets outside our solar system. But what else could she do but leave it like that for now, and wait and see? Again she sighs aloud, and for the first time in a long time, a fat strand of spit abseils down from her mouth. She's got her tongue under slightly better control now. She'd given it a really good bite when she was having the seizures, and it hurts. Meanwhile her face seems fat and swollen, and she's got a bruise on her forehead – she must have fallen. She sneaks a glance at the patient report. There's something on there about *speech arrest* and *postictal Todd's paresis right side*. The latter she immediately decides is a load of rubbish, because that side of her body is paralysed anyway, but the arrest of the words in her head had shaken her up completely. A shock, yes – she might well say that. (She says it: 'A shock!' The paramedic travelling with her looks at her uncomprehendingly, and she smiles a barely perceptible smile...)

On the ward she'd been moved about in a wheelchair. She's been strapped into the ambulance in a wheelchair too.

She doesn't care.

Suddenly she remembers something she does care about: Viola's death. Matthes had broken it to her.

She doesn't tremble, and she doesn't have another epileptic seizure. She's almost pleased to be stuck in the jelly, because it makes the pain that's suddenly setting in almost bearable.

She is unloaded, and put into a different wheelchair belonging to the hospital. She's asked how she is. She's being looked at. Is there pity in that gaze? She can't tolerate pity, and her face curls into solid defiance.

But: she's crying.

She's wheeled to the lift and up to her room. Someone takes off her shoes, lies her on the bed and asks whether she's in need of any *refreshment* – a sandwich? A breakfast roll? Would she like some juice to drink? Or coffee? She says no, declines everything. The window is opened, the collar of her high-necked blouse loosened, her legs elevated – and now she sees it: fluid has gathered there and her lower legs are fat and elephant-like, no ankles to be seen. Calling the doctor is considered, but then it's decided that they'll wait until the afternoon. Maybe it's all just been a bit too much. 'Have you taken those tablets of yours? We're going to have to take them all the time now, aren't we?' She hates this talk, this way of talking, and she's sorry she doesn't feel like rebelling. She doesn't actually want to, it's all the same to her.

But: she's crying.

A neck bolster is fetched and pushed behind her, and a cold damp cloth is laid on her forehead. A nurse says she intends to check on her every twenty minutes, now; that should be enough. Another one says she can always look in too, whenever she's coming out of room 264, and another thing – what's going to happen about food? 'Clearly the woman can barely move – it's a real shame when you think how well she was doing before.' (The nurse said that behind her hand, to the other one standing on her left, but Helene has heard it and is flabbergasted.) 'Well, we'll get there, won't we?' the nurse now says aloud to the room, and gives a jolly smile. It looks so fake, it almost rips Helene's chest open. The nurse strokes her cheek, surreptitiously wiping her hand afterwards on her pink scrubs.

And still: Helene is crying.

They did call a doctor in the afternoon. Helene can see something, all blurry. What is it she can see there? She can see a man – that's Matthes. And another man, who puts the little packet of pills on her stomach and places her arms next to each other, then says that she's having an allergic reaction to the Ergenyl chrono. That she's on the verge of kidney failure. Did he really say that? He gets a little bottle of tiny pills out of a bag, then does something with them that she can't quite see because he turns his back to her. Finally he gives the bottle to Matthes, saying she should take the first pill this evening at around six o'clock, but then reduce the Ergenyl tablets gradually over the next week. He writes down a plan for her. When Matthes looks doubtful, the man merely says, 'Well, it's up to you to what extent you remain a patient who makes her own decisions.' No, he can't be a doctor: he's not wearing a doctor's coat, and he's got ordinary outdoor shoes on. Now he's putting on a leather jacket, and a beret angled to one side. Helene is starting to recognise him: it's the homeopath she went to last year with Mareile, when she was having unexplained pain in both forearms. She can't think what he's called at the moment, though she knows he handed back his medical licence after finishing his training, and now practises on a purely private basis. Matthes must have asked him to come – his practice is in Wallersdorf, which isn't far from Heidemühlen at all. Helene doesn't really know what to make of him. He doesn't say much, and when he does it's with total conviction. Arguing is pointless. 'You're always free to leave.' His work methods make her think of quackery, precisely because he never comments on what he's doing. And yet, after many, many unsuccessful trips to the doctor, Mareile was rid of her arm pain. That had definitely given Helene something to think about. Matthes had kept out of it, but accused the man of occult doings whenever anyone took his occasional remarks seriously. And now it was Matthes who'd dragged him here? The homeopath shakes her hand, not a trace of a smile on his face, and hot-foots it to the door.

'What was that all about?'

The question bubbles, bursting little bubbles of spit.

Matthes answers her haltingly.

Yes, he'd asked Dr. Müller this morning to do a hospital visit. Matthes doesn't believe in epilepsy as an illness. What happened two days ago was how you'd expect a previously-damaged brain to react, albeit not necessarily on this scale. After all, there'll be escaped blood from the ruptured aneurysm that almost certainly won't have been fully reabsorbed yet. The conductivity of the iron particles in the blood meant a seizure was always on standby, but the event that triggered it did so with considerable force.

Force.

The word does the rounds. She can practically see it on its trek through the folds of the cerebral cortex. It drags other words along with it, wrenching them painfully from their compartments: Firm. Flee. Fire. Force. Fog. Fight. Unpleasant words, all of them. She wants to somehow prevent them from finding Malyutka Malysch, but they're just about to disturb her rest. Another gyration or two and they've arrived, dragging Malyutka's death out of its pigeon-hole. Force strikes. Matthes stands firm. Impossible to flee. Malyuta was a fire that'd taken hold in her by force. In the fog of unconsciousness she hadn't had to think about the fight being won without her. And the outcome? Malyutka is dead. Now she's all cried out, and her mind is half-crippled, she dares to ask about it.

She asks.

Matthes answers.

A layer of wax on his face cracks into splinters as he's speaking, little bits of it crumbling off and on to the floor. He'd opened a letter, edged in black, meant for Helene. By mistake, he says. She believes him, has no cause to doubt him, especially as the senders' names hadn't triggered any associations for him. Malyutka's sons, Tim and Tom (not Malysch), had sent a death announcement. When Matthes followed this up, they'd told him that their father's address book had only contained a few addresses. The one for Helene Wesendahl had a wavy red line around it. They'd also found the email exchanges between Helene and their father Viola on her computer, and assumed from this that they'd had a close relationship – at least until May this year, when it must have been broken off suddenly. In any event, they'd thought it best to inform the few people in the address book of the death of their father, Viola Malysch.

Matthes tells her all this, and Helene can see in him both the need to tell it, and that he's barely able to do so. Nevertheless, more questions come bubbling out.

'How did she die?'

Matthes tells it as if he'd been there.

Something like this: The boys had been in contact with their father again. ('For how long?' 'Since May!') Having crossed the border into adulthood, they'd defied their mother and gone looking for Viola. No, actually gone to see him. They, too, were choked with emotion as their father was rendered speechless with excitement. Over and over again he took their heads into his arms and held them to his chest. There was a lot more chest there than they'd wanted to picture on their father, but at that moment it didn't matter any more. From then on, they kept visiting. To tell him things. There'd be moments when they were all talked out, but then another wave of narrative would always roll in, and Viola, for her part, tried to put herself back into the picture her sons were painting of their childhood. They would often sleep over at their father's. They still referred to him as Father when talking about the past, but addressed him directly as Viola – it became so natural that they didn't even notice it any more. Viola eventually gave them a key to her flat, because they'd sometimes show up quite late – when they'd been out in Potsdam, say, and weren't going to make it home. Then the boys were in France for the whole of June. When they came back, at the beginning of July, they were surprised to see the overflowing letter box as they went up the stairs to Viola's flat. They found her in the bedroom, in bed, all nicely tucked up as if she'd been cold. Tim didn't want to believe she'd gone. Tom saw things differently, like the decay which had taken over her face. Clearly he was able to smell things differently, too.

The doctor arranged a postmortem, but the search for the cause of death proved difficult. It was said that Viola seemed to have 'passed away peacefully', just like that. Heart failure was settled on as the cause, and the date of death recorded as the twenty-third of June. Viola's body was released for burial. The boys set about organising the estate, emptying the flat and writing to everyone they took to have been friends with their father. They needed six stamps.

Matthes looks at the clock.

'It's nearly six...'

He gets the bottle of tiny pills out of the bag and looks at

Helene. She doesn't ask any more questions and takes one, letting it dissolve on her tongue.

Sugar.

When it's time for her Ergenyl tablets, she takes one less.

Two hours later: the fluid has gone.

Incredible. It decamped from her legs and made her need to wee constantly, taking wobbly steps to the toilet with her rollator. This Dr. Müller is a puzzle to her, and one that's getting bigger and more colourful with every hour that passes since he popped up here. He's no longer wearing a dark leather jacket, but something coloured, Indian. No black beret but a Rasta cap in black, green and red, with a stylised, crocheted cannabis leaf on top, and bulging thanks to the enormous bundle of dreadlocks on his head. Yes, that's more like the guru she's entrusted herself to. Wait, the whole thing's spinning out of control: it's *Matthes* who's entrusted her to him – Matthes, the rational sceptic, for whom doubting everything was everything! But doubt must have lost to desperation here, she reflects. Desperation has prevailed in her at times, too. Malyutka's death is a pain that drags its feet and goes with her everywhere, whitewashing everything, foisting its colour on everything, without allowing anything to disappear behind it. That's hard to bear. Matthes must know that – she suddenly remembers his uncertain, helpless expression when he broke the news to her. It dawns on her that he might've told the story as if he'd been there because Malyutka's sons were still at the forefront of his mind. Has he visited them? Have they been to Arberstrasse? Helene is seized by anxiety, because

Matthes has something over her: he knows Malyutka's sons. For a moment she thinks how unfair this is, but then remembers her predicament. The situation she's caught up in is still unclear to her, but since that's where she is, she takes it as a good sign that Matthes wants to understand. Does Matthes understand? And if so, what? For the first time she feels she knows what they need to talk about, and for the first time she can imagine herself doing it.

A flicker of resilience.

She's going to go through with it. Swallow the Ergenyl according to the homeopath's plan. Not say anything to the rehab doctors about weaning herself off them. Stash the tablets in a bag instead of flushing them down the toilet. Better to dispose of them at the end of her stay.

As she falls asleep, she hears the Muslim call to prayer.

At least she thinks she does.

Did she ever actually ask Matthes to allow himself a day off between his exhausting visits to her? She knows she wanted to, but doesn't know whether she'd had the time. Matthes still comes every day. Yesterday he reported that he'd been to Viola's grave at the weekend, and planted a shrub. Had the pain not shuffled over to shut the curtains, dragging its feet, she'd have got angry and wanted to sue for her own right to take flowers to the grave. Getting worked up over something like that... But is he really taking everything off her? Does he really have to visit the grave of a woman he didn't know, just to act as if he'd had some kind of relationship with her? After all, he barely knew Viola beyond her one-time visit to

Arberstrasse. Or did he? Uncertainty. Something tugs at her, pulling her further into the bed than she'd like. (Although it's time to get up: her lunchtime nap is over.) Her little heart picks a faster pace – she can immediately tell when it exceeds the pacemaker's sixty beats per minute of its own accord, as it were. It's rather nice that it happens sometimes without her having to exert herself. Without physical effort. She's still alive in her body, one thing is still connected to the other, despite the growing number of metal parts in her head and chest. Without these she'd probably have *had it*, though not as *peacefully* as Viola... Helene would either not have woken up from one of her blackouts, which regularly had her on the floor before the pacemaker was put in, or she'd have gone out gasping as her brain bled. She can hardly thank fate for it, because of course fate had made the case for her kicking the bucket before her time. Or else she can expand the concept of fate by its temporal dimension: had she been alive a hundred years ago, she wouldn't have made it to forty-four. Since fate had willed it that she should live in an age of medical advancement, it had now cancelled itself out, in a way, by allowing people to counter it.

Taxing thoughts.

She gets up, gets her rollator and walks to the bathroom. Her walking is a lot better again – in the one week since her epileptic seizures, fate has once again *turned things round for the better*. She's convinced that gradually reducing the antiepileptic drugs hasn't cheated fate, but given it a leg up instead. Although thinking is still hard work, it no longer takes place in jelly, in a sticky mass, and sometimes she can even see *out into the open*. She's mostly outdoors when this happens, with the wind moving round her shoulders and legs.

It makes her feel that it could take her with it, if she wanted: the decision is hers. She holds on tight to the rollator then, as if letting go would mean flying away. In these momentary pauses, she closes her eyes and sees what she can't see when they're open. Sometimes she can see as far as India and cooking dhal with Sulagna, to go with the rice already waiting in the pot. She goes back in time, to another dimension of *the open*, and sees herself as a child: only just avoiding a fall from her bike, because her father catches her. Or she goes forward in both dimensions, into what she sees as the third dimension of *the open* – where she enters times and spaces she's never been to before, but they don't frighten her. Those are lovely moments that she no doubt yearned for when she was in the coma. She still can't distinguish between dream and reality from that time: they are one, and she imagines they'll stay that way. On the other hand, she's pretty sure Malyutka Malysch's death wasn't a horrible dream. How can she be sure, though? She tries to imagine having dreamt it, and fails miserably. Straight away the pain swells from background noise to loud roar, and she covers her ears, letting go of the rollator. She stands still. There's no time to be surprised: she takes three steps without the thing, and it works!

Joy in pain, pain in joy.

Is she to hope that, one day, she'll once again be able to tell even these two things apart?

◆ ◆ ◆

She notices she's eating less and less at mealtimes. Can't do her any harm. As the flab melts away, your tough hide does too, she thinks. She hasn't cried about Malyutka's death for several days now, although the pain, the anguish, is ever-present. Is that being thick-skinned? She thinks of when Mischa jumped in front of the train. For weeks afterwards she'd been plagued by bouts of crying which broke ground from very far below the surface. But with Mischa she'd been mourning something else at the same time. It can't have been because she herself didn't have a son with Matthes. Possibly she'd felt guilty about the boy's death. When she first got together with Matthes, Mischa had had a particularly strong and physical reaction to his parents' split, which for a little boy simply equated to being abandoned by his father. Matthes had left him, and his mother and sister, and Helene was the marriage-wrecker – not of her own marriage, but someone else's. Mischa had started to wet the bed, refused to eat, and suffered from rashes, diarrhoea and fainting from one minute to the next, which wasn't exactly usual for a five-year-old. Helene suspected that the suffering wife had wished scabies on her – but it was Mischa who got them, taking it all upon himself. Anything that wasn't supposed to leave the four walls of their home, in fact, he took upon himself – and if he hadn't somehow swallowed these things down they'd have stayed hanging over all of them like a nightmare, conjuring fear and dread as soon as darkness fell. Helene had never thought that the nightmare might settle in Mischa's bowels. Yes, that's probably why she felt guilty. She's doesn't feel any guilt about Malyutka's death. But should she? For a moment she becomes unsure – the last few months before her aneurysm are obscured behind floaty, gossamer-like curtains. Sometimes the wind manages to push them to one side in places, but she can't yet catch hold of anything but the slightest tail-end of an idea of what might have happened. And when she does hold one of these in her hand, something usually appears that looks like the next tail-end of an idea – but when she opens her hand to snatch it up, the first one disappears again. In her irritation over this she lets the second one fade away. That's how it happens over and over again. Maybe as her flab melts away it'll at least bring increased mobility, which could really help her there. Her mind will get more supple too, she imagines, though she also reckons a bit of lard might be good for greasing between her thoughts. It all comes down to the right measure, as with everything. So she will in fact take that second slice of bread.

She's not sitting with the *damaged boy* any more. Two days of absence was all it took for her to be dropped from the programme, and for another crew to be found to man the table. At first when she got back she wanted to insist on her rights, but then that seemed ridiculous. So now she sits in the middle of a silent band of nibbling old men, who are clearly in the process of forgetting they even exist. They already seem to have forgotten everything else. She gets on fine with them, though she wonders what reason there might have been to allocate her, of all people, to this particular table. Other tables have been assembled according to age, gender or personal acquaintance, but the system hasn't worked in her case. Granted, she doesn't have any personal acquaintances here, but it's not as if she can be described as ageless and genderless. Although the side of her head with short grey hair probably doesn't fit her face, people have always said she looks *particularly feminine*: she's got wide hips and a narrow waist, a proper pear-shape. On her face it's her full lips that stand out. Whenever Matthes has had a couple of glasses of wine, he always reckons he wanted to bite them from the very first moment. What did Malyutka Malysch look like? In normal circumstances, such as when they'd met, quite obviously masculine. In exceptional circumstances she achieved the impression of a man dolled-up as a woman. Yes, it was the traces of violence which were unsettling. The violence of shaving with extreme thoroughness, and sealing your pores with a layer of make-up so any hair regrowth wouldn't be seen. The violence of jamming your feet into dainty-looking boots, and keeping your stride short. (She had such great legs, though.) The violence of maintaining a bust-out, stomach-in pose while prancing along as nimbly as possible, and sweeping your hair from your face in one expert move. The violence of heaving your own voice up an octave or so, albeit without success. On that Friday last November, Helene had felt sorry for Malyutka Malysch, submitting herself to this orgy of violence, and definitely felt relieved when it was abandoned the next day. Malyutka hadn't felt relieved. On the Friday she'd looked young, in a try-hard sort of way, with her painted face and her dyed hair up. On the Saturday, sitting in the pub in Krummensee with a tired, lined face and almost no make-up on, she'd aged again. But by the evening, and that Italian restaurant in Altlandsberg, it no longer mattered how old she was. In the presence of Malyutka's lips – which were growing fuller and redder, and naturally this time – Helene no longer saw her age. Malyutka had talked. Just let her guard down, renouncing all violence. For one evening, she was herself – before clearing out hurriedly and without ceremony the next day. As if she'd felt it was something she had to apologise for.

One of the aged nibblers lays his head on her shoulder. She jumps, puts her cup down and chokes on her tea. It takes a while for the suffocating feeling to subside. One of the serving girls banged her on the back a few times. Tears are running down her face but she laughs through them, so much so that the oldies join in. Now she's no longer sitting in silence, but at the merriest table in the dining room.

◆ ◆ ◆

How do you work out who to believe?

The situation at home is easing, if she's to believe Billy. If Matthes is to be believed, though, things are still as hard and stressful as before. Matthes doesn't say this. In fact he doesn't say anything different to Billy, and yet his face tells a different story.

Billy told her: after a family meeting, they've agreed with Bengt that it's better if he doesn't take time off university. Things are running smoothly, and if Helene comes home in the foreseeable future then the house could get crowded – she needs peace and quiet, and Bengt's practising will probably disturb her. (She protests loudly: 'Never!') Billy's expression is relaxed, unburdened.

Matthes told her: there was a family meeting, finally convened after much confusion among the participants as to the date and time. After lengthy discussions with Bengt an agreement was reached that he'll continue with his studies, otherwise things will get too crowded in the house. (No idea how to protest against that.) Matthes's expression is forbearing, covering up the fact that he's worried.

There's really no question *who* she'd rather believe. It's just, *how*?

◆ ◆ ◆

She's practising lifting her arm. The physio has laid her on the floor and turned her on her back. She has the baton in her left hand again, and clings on to it with her right as tightly as she can. Then the physio takes hold of it from the right, helping Helene's left hand lift the baton high above her head. Her right arm goes along with it. But would it by itself? After ten goes it's going to attempt it. It's still a stranger to her, doesn't seem to belong to her body. She strains so hard issuing orders to it that she goes completely red in the face, and the physio, alarmed, calls things to a halt. Maybe she's afraid the resulting pressure will cause the aneurysm to rupture again? Helene wants to reassure her that this can't happen – it's been clipped! – but her body is trembling at the very thought of another haemorrhage, so speech is out of the question. The therapist probably thinks she's trembling from the exertion, but that's not it. She helps Helene up – 'Now let's have a go at walking, to get over the fright!' – and leaves the rollator to one side.

???

'That's right, we're trying without it today!' That's all she bothers to say. The physio puts her left arm around Helene's hips. Her right arm twitches every time Helene puts down her right foot, but stays where it is on Helene's right upper arm. Helene has to laugh, thinking of Pietro, her actor friend. When the children were little, one of his skits they loved the most was Wind-up Elli. Pietro would walk in a straight line and one leg would very suddenly give way, recovering just before he fell over – only to give way again when he took another step. On balmy summer evenings, sitting under the magnificent chestnut trees in front of his little house near Anklam, they'd be in stitches as the children tried to imitate his walk. 'Wind-up Elli,' she says, laughing, and the physio bursts out laughing, too. After twenty metres there and twenty metres back, Helene is once again allowed to lie on the mat for one last try. She sends the command to her arm with all her strength and attempts to keep the strain away from her head, directing all the tension to her arm. All of it. Go on. Go on! Very, very slowly, it rises up and straightens out. It's doing it, it's actually doing it!

Well, almost.

They'd often holidayed in that little village near Anklam, not far from the Baltic coast. Certain things about the lake here remind her of back then, like the tall trees with fire pits underneath, and the stillness by the water – you can hear all the nonsense in your own head just getting up and leaving. The lake is a great field being furrowed by an underground plough, row by row. She wonders what will germinate there – potatoes? Winter barley? She sees the lake, green and billowing, and all at once feels deep joy at still being alive, and able to imagine something that lets reality roll on in an almost delightful way, letting her rock back and forth into the dream though still awake – in, out, in again. Fortune is so much more than seven simple letters of the Latin alphabet, and it's smiling on her. Back then, too, she'd basked in the summery certainty that fortune had come their way. They'd often driven up there in July and August with the four children, spending the day making pilgrimages from the mainland out to the island, Usedom, to swim and sunbathe. For a few weeks everything was relaxed and simple. Then in the summer of '89 they'd sat in front of the telly every day and watched the news. The holiday mood was over: something was going to happen. What they hadn't reckoned on was being asked so quickly to *take over the shop*, as they put it, and they found themselves in a state of feverishness and ruffled nerves. Mareile was still in nappies and the other three were demanding swimming trips, so they split it: one of them always stayed with Mareile in the house while the others went to the coast. Had they known everything would be flattened a year or two later, without them ever getting close to actually *taking over the shop*, they could've kept a lid on their excitement and stuck to their normal routine.

Summers were different after that. The village co-op closed. You needed a car to go shopping. Initially Pietro bought an old VW. In Ducherow supermarkets were opening one after the other, and everyone spent much more time doing their shopping, which now meant organising a proper excursion. Village life was rapidly slipping away. The farming collective closed down, and an investor tried to set up a commercial farm in its place – which had twelve employees, whereas before virtually all sixty families had lived off the farming collective. Andreas, who kept an eye on Pietro's house when he was away, had been the general hand on the farm, filling in wherever he was needed in the line of duty – and yes, he'd been important. From one day to the next, he became unimportant. He was helpless in the face of the changes and let himself be lured by a building firm from Lübeck, picked up by the minibus at some unearthly hour on a Monday and brought back late on a Friday. He slogged away for far less than the standard rate of pay, which he didn't even know existed. When he became unemployed, however, and remained so for over a year, he virtuously declared the 10,000 Deutschmarks he had in savings. He was told he'd have to use up a large part of that before his dole money kicked in. So he used it to drink himself to death. Just couldn't understand the world any more. In the late nineties they'd been to his grave a few times, taking daisies or violets to put on it. He was born the same year as Helene. She'd looked in horror at the number of graves for her contemporaries (she counted: ten!) – people born in the fifties, more men than women. It was as if a whole generation had just wanted to leave. Boozing became rife, and the pub in the village was still doing good trade. There weren't many children any more. The few there were, were all cross-eyed. Helene couldn't help but think of the word *incest* and wanted to box her own ears for it. The days unfolded in a different way to those of the eighties. Any men not nursing a beer would be exchanging something like words with a neighbour over the garden fence, looking as though they'd all agreed to move their mouths as slowly as they moved their bodies. They shuffled and loitered, as if any unprofitable movement would cause them unnecessary upset. They no longer engaged in long conversations – as though they were all aware of some sort of ending, and paralysed by the fear of saying it aloud. Since the nineties she and Matthes had gone up there less and less, telling themselves it was because the kids were getting older, and that they themselves were interested in different holidays and new destinations (Italy! Portugal!). But really it was because they wanted to distance themselves from the village and its ghostly atmosphere. Like the villagers, and their paralysis in the face of an ending they could all sense, Helene and Matthes no longer wanted to see up close how everything there was simply petering out. How a village was drinking its life away, Andreas leading the way, in the middle of a wonderfully thriving landscape – rape fields, potato fields, meadow and pasture, which no longer needed people in order to flourish. Those living there were simple people. The world went on and off in their conversations like images in an TV screen. Those who saved up had just enough for the one big holiday, a coach trip to Lake Garda, but when they came back they couldn't just be glad, and immediately went back to their shuffling. Helene can feel the same sadness now that she felt in the nineties whenever she thought about the village, which was always just 'the village' to them and had been for decades. Right after the Wall came down, the road in this isolated backwater was finally resurfaced. Farm vehicles hardly ever used it now, preferring to take shortcuts over the fields, and sometimes she'd seen women on bikes, hunched over and laden with shopping. The bus only did the loop into town every other day, meaning that if these women wanted to shop in between, they had to bike to the main road, which was maybe four kilometres; lock up their bikes there and catch the bus to Ducherow, returning later on; then head home on their bikes. Helene had reasoned that they couldn't afford a driving licence, and couldn't afford a car. Or else their husbands had cars in the backyard but were too drunk to drive them. The women still living here were all over forty: the young ones had almost all left and weren't coming back. Sooner or later the village would die out. Andreas's father had outlived his son by six months. Andreas's sister had inherited everything and went to great lengths to find a buyer, with no success. She herself lived with her family in Anklam, where she worked as a local government clerk. She only came to the village at weekends to check everything was in order and to have a walk round the garden, pulling up weeds and harvesting anything there was to be harvested. She'd paid the neighbour on the left to cut the grass, and he'd done it often – too often. She'd then asked the neighbour on the right to do it, and this time made sure to have a schedule in place. She often called in on Pietro and offered him the house as accommodation for his guests. Everyone in the village could remember the old days, when Pietro's garden and the fields around it had been besieged by tents. That was a long, long time ago.

In the meantime Pietro's house was more than adequate for the increasingly few old friends who came to stay. None of them could imagine living there, in this idyll. Directly opposite Pietro's 'Katzberg' was a house that'd been bought up and extended by a young family in the early nineties. It had its own pond, and was surrounded by woods and fields. Even this lovely place had been standing empty for years. The family had gone, broken up perhaps, and one person by themselves probably wouldn't manage to get the children to school and nursery – which in any case would mean you'd never be able to work, the village being so far from anywhere. When they were there last year, they'd ventured on to the property – which was open and unfenced – for a wander around. The décor and fittings weren't to their taste at all: the ceilings were spoiled by polystyrene tiles and the floors had been laid with cheap carpet. But it had been structurally sound before it'd gone to rack and ruin, before the windows were smashed and every room used as a toilet. Helene had wondered who in the village could've been roused to such vandalism. No one came to mind.

It's nice to feel this old sadness again, she thinks now – a sadness which has nothing to do with her new sadness about Malyutka. To be in two lots of sadness at the same time is no bad thing. You lie on one and wrap yourself up in the other, and when you look out you can suddenly imagine that you're only feeling them because their opposites truly exist.

Pleasure.

Ardour.

Both of them overflowing.

She wants to start writing. Not for work! Oh no. Whether she'll be able to do that again one day, it's impossible to tell. Matthes has told her that she received an enquiry from artists wanting to showcase short poems in a residential building in Berlin. Commissioned pieces, to be let into the walls and the stone floors of the building, and installed on the windows. Would she be ready for a commission like this? The thought of it horrifies her. She knows all too well that between her and any potential poem yawns a very black hole. Naturally she reads the list of other artists being asked – not bad, she'd be honoured to take part. She considers it. Eventually says no. Too scared. She won't be able to do it. What is a poem anyway? She remembers in the past having physical feelings on reading or hearing a good poem, together with mental states she can no longer recall. She'd be fired up, inspired – the words themselves triggering an avalanche in her head, so that all she needed to do was write down whatever came to mind. A wonderful state, and one she can't reproduce at present. Matthes has brought in her favourite poetry collections.

Seamus Heaney, for example – a discovery from the last few years. Nothing stirs in her now when she reads him. It's nothing to do with her *understanding* of the poems, that was never important to her anyway. Perception, reception – they were different qualities altogether. But these *qualities* are gone and can't be found, either in mind or in body, as it were. She makes a real effort. She reads two, three, four times the text that – yes! – she can remember, and that unleashed incredible things inside her. But what were they?

[From] Lightenings
VI

Once, as a child, out in a field of sheep,
Thomas Hardy pretended to be dead
And lay down flat among their dainty shins.

In that sniffed-at, bleated-into, grassy space
He experimented with infinity.
His small cool brow was like an anvil waiting

For sky to make it sing the prefect pitch
Of his dumb being, and that stir he caused
In the fleece-hustle was the original

Of a ripple that would travel eighty years
Outward from there, to be the same ripple
Inside him at its last circumference.

Nothing. Instead there's the question of who Thomas Hardy might be... That definitely wouldn't have bothered her in the past. But she can absolutely remember how fired up she'd been the first time she read the poem!

Slowly.

Picking out the key lines.

A boy – small and determined is how she imagines him, with freckles, and bare feet – is experimenting with infinity. How exactly does one experiment with infinity? He lies on his back, his head among the sheep's mouths, fervently hoping that the heavens might touch the anvil on his brow and let the pure ring of silence soar above the animals' bleating and snuffling and jumping. He lies still, but the stirring around him grows to a ripple that will spread out not just in space but in time, and even after eighty years – that is, eighty years from the moment described in the poem – the ripple would be carried further and further, and beyond him, even, when he died... Yes, that was it: space and time slamming into each other on a child's brow, remembered from afar! To deal with such an existential theme in twelve lines, with no apparent effort and such extraordinary logic, had seemed nothing short of sensational to Helene, and had played utter havoc with her insides, no less: suddenly she'd felt sick, her stomach had started grumbling and her bowels began to gurgle. A sudden drop in her blood pressure made her knees give way. Once she'd recovered, Mareile sat down close to her and asked in alarm what had happened. Helene had had to laugh and read her the poem, and when Matthes came home later he'd found mother and daughter lounging on the wide bed, deep in philosophical and poetic contemplation. When Mareile finally left the room he'd snuggled up to Helene, but she hadn't been in the mood.

She's exhausted.

She sits down quietly in the chair by the window.

The resulting state of emptiness is something she's coming to know all too well. It's as though conscious brain activity has effectively ground to a halt – she feels herself unable to think of anything, and can't evoke anything either. This sadness comes quickly now. It's the third kind – all-encompassing, impossible to see beyond. Even the view from the window brings nothing. She doesn't really apprehend what's going on down there, although she can see it in great detail: a juxtaposition of people and things and trees and hedges and stones and walls. She's unable to relate them to each other in any way whatsoever. It's a strange, disintegrating state of perception – it wasn't something she knew before, but she knows it now.

Before she can feel like crying, the social worker comes into the room. 'Hello, Frau Wesendahl, how're you?'

The social worker has reams and reams of paper in her arms. Helene's perception starts to refocus: everything centres on the papers the woman has brought with her. The question of her pension. Of home help. Now that she's no longer signed off sick through her insurer, but instead is on a rehabilitation programme paid for by her pension provider, she can book someone to come and help her at home.

'That wouldn't be too bad, would it?'

That wouldn't be too bad at all, actually. The social worker fills in the forms and Helene signs them. Her writing is awful, all spidery and often shooting off upwards, but the woman makes no comment. And the question of her pension? No, it's too soon for that, she wants to talk to her husband about it. It's a question she's never yet asked herself. Can she even do it, as a freelancer? Yes, she can: she's in the right age group, and it's allowed from a state insurance point of view. Aha. But we'd rather wait and see on that – we're not going to decide that now, not yet. Anyway, her second novel has just come out, delivered to bookshops today! Of course, the book fair! But it's all getting too much for her now: the home help, the novel, the question of her pension, the book fair. Matthes has told her there were TV crews wanting to visit her at home. Now she also remembers that she had readings scheduled in October and November, in Freiburg, Schwerin, Regensburg, Leipzig – lots of them. She absolutely must talk to Matthes about it, not to this social worker. When will she be finished? What's she even talking about at the moment?

'Hello, can you hear me?'

Yes. Helene can hear her. She asks to postpone the paperwork for now. She's exhausted. Though she's happy with the home help. All the rest will sort itself out.

Well, if that's what she wants?

That's what she wants.

No sooner has the woman gone, Helene dares to pick up the phone. For the first time. She dials their own number without having to think about it, and waits. It rings. Finally the answer machine kicks in.

'Hello?' It's Matthes. When she starts to speak, he cuts in: 'Yep, you've got it, there's no one at home... But feel free to say why you're calling, and we'll get back to you soon.' Matthes had said all that in a deep, sonorous voice she'd never heard before. There's a beep. Helene hangs up, afraid of being recorded speaking with all her flustered mistakes, enforced breaks and garbled consonants. No, Matthes mustn't hear those. And the children shouldn't have to hear them if they come into the kitchen and play the answerphone messages.

Shame. Of course, it's morning, so Matthes is at work, the children are at school and Lottchen is at pre-school.

Nothing to be done.

Pietro's here! It's so lovely to see him. It's as if he'd sensed that she'd been thinking about him often in the past few days, and of the village, and Andreas... Couldn't Matthes at least have let her know Pietro was planning to come? Then she wouldn't still have been lying around in bed in the middle of the day, totally unkempt and waiting for no one but Matthes... But now Pietro's there, and she means to jump up out of bed and 'just pop and pretty myself up a bit'. But of course she doesn't jump up out of bed, and instead gets up fairly laboriously and very slowly. Nor does she *just pop and pretty herself up a bit*, but creeps very slowly to the bathroom with her rollator. Whenever she gets up, she always needs to wait until her joints are greased and her muscles warmed up, and that takes a while. In the bathroom she rummages around in her washbag for a perfume tester she's suddenly remembered about, which she'd brought back from India and never used. It must still be in one of the little side pockets... Her fingers feel a longish shape she doesn't recognise, or at any rate can't remember, so she pulls it out. It's Malyutka Malysch's hair clasp made of Murano glass – mottled gold and brown with flecks of red. How did that get into her bag? It burns in her hand. She wants to savour the pain and squeezes it harder, but then it starts to cool down. On the spur of the moment she shoves her remaining hair into the clasp, pulling the ends over her scar. Now the back of her head is burning, but she knows it'll cool down. A flush makes its presence felt, climbing up from the neckline of her blouse and making splotches all over her face. She runs ice-cold water into her hands and flings it on her cheeks repeatedly, then rubs herself dry with a towel. Now the red splotches have given way to an all-over flush and she can let Pietro see her. She's forgotten about the perfume.

Pietro currently commutes between Berlin, Anklam and the village. He works in Anklam, at the theatre, and lives in the village. As of fairly recently he's also had a girlfriend in Berlin, which is hard. They don't see each other very often. Who is she? She's a pharmacist - he met her a few weeks ago when he was in Berlin visiting his son Moritz. Moritz was in bed with flu, and his mum sent Pietro to the pharmacy. If she'd had any idea what the outcome of that would be, Pietro says, she'd have avoided sending him at all costs. Helene ignores this, because she likes Moritz's mum just as much as she likes Pietro. Shame they split up years ago.

Is the new girlfriend pretty? She's the most beautiful woman for miles around! Pietro is buzzing. As he is with every new romance. Helene smiles. 'I wish you wouldn't do that wise smile of yours – it's like you can see right through me!' Pietro says. Oh, so her smile is *wise*... She's pleased about that. It wouldn't have occurred to her that someone might read wisdom in her smile, not with the episodes of emptiness afflicting her. Emptiness that, lately, she's sought out herself, just to make sure it's still there. In order to fill it, perhaps? Of course not – that's stupid. She wants to be in Pietro's company. How does that work, again? Engaging with him? It's nice being in the company of men when the relationship is untarnished by love, or what they think is love. She doesn't know why she's thinking that now, but it's clear and memorable. (It sticks in her mind and she sees it clearly before her.) Pietro has never been in love with her, so maybe that's the only reason she can be so certain of his attention, respect and goodwill. She starts to feels warm, basking in Pietro's talk. 'Wind-up Elli,' she says suddenly, and Pietro bends straight away. He goes back and forth across the room being Elli, making her laugh. Oh Pietro, if only you knew...

Pietro does know a fair bit. For example, he's told her that Matthes won't be coming today – two visitors might've been too much for her, so he'd let Pietro have priority. Shame. Now she can't ask Matthes about the book, which should be being delivered today if she's not mistaken. Why hasn't this come up at all until now? Hadn't she... ? Yes, she had! On the morning of the day she had her aneurysm, she'd done two indentations in the manuscript, ready for typesetting! And then, beaming with joy, had declared to Matthes that every last thing for the new novel was now finalized, and she'd be able to deliver it by the deadline! Now she gets agitated – she can't tell Pietro about it anywhere near that quickly, and he probably wouldn't know what she was talking about, anyway... But to crown it all, and with all the gesturing of a great magician – one hand on his chest, half-covered by his jacket – Pietro pulls something out of his pocket, and lays it on the table before Helene with a flourish he can mimic at least as well as a certain Wind-up Elli. *The Representative*, in fact: this is it, her new novel. It looks so familiar, even though she's holding the finished article in her hands for the first time. Matthes gave it to Pietro to take with him – yesterday a whole box of them had arrived in the post. Helene looks at it, reads the cover blurb, and everything that'd gone now comes back to her. How she wrote it, how she wrestled with the theme when it threatened to get too unwieldy. How, time and time again, she'd jumped up from the computer in a rage that spread in her like rubbery polenta, and could barely be scraped off her thoughts. How on some days she'd boasted of having done 'twenty pages!' On those evenings she'd be in a good mood, and would spend an extra-long time reading to Lottchen at bedtime. And Lottchen wouldn't be the only one in for a treat – sometimes Helene had got straight into bed, after leaving Lottchen in hers, and waited for Matthes. She was waiting to see whether she wanted sex: in the last few years she just couldn't seem to tell unless Matthes was near her. Now her memories pass the baton, and she starts to feel scared: She sees herself hunkered down in her study with a bowl of semolina, a spoonful for every three sentences; cutting her toenails at the computer because she can't just get up and go to the bathroom when she's in the zone. The children come up, but she's locked the door and won't open it, ignoring their tentative questions. When the questions stop being tentative and start to get annoyed and urgent, she does open the door, all ready to give them a good bollocking. But faced with the assembled band on the other side, the row's over before it's even begun – Helene can't help but screw her face up into a grin and, relenting, join then downstairs. She takes a pan off the heat just before it starts to burn – Mareile had wanted to fry herself some eggs. Helene has already cooked, though! The soup she made is on the balcony because the pan's too big for the fridge, and it's cold enough out there. Why does she forget about everything else when she's writing? She could at least have left the children a note saying lunch was ready, and just needed to be warmed up. Mind you, it's...

'Helene?'

Pietro is looking up at her enquiringly.

Ah yes, Pietro is sitting opposite her. She appeals to the prankster in the corners of his eyes: give me a break, it's really not all that funny in here. Are you acquainted with heartache? The grief of the soul? They've both put my time through the wringer and taken root deep within me, but I can't tell you all about it right now, ok? All I can do is ask you to give me a break... Give me a break.

Mr Prankster clearly hears this secret appeal because he disappears from Pietro's eyes. She looks at him gratefully – her eyes are swimming a bit now, eh? It's a good day, though, a lovely day. She holds her book in her hands: she's remembered who *The Representative* is, and how he helped her write this novel...

Pietro is now telling her that his position at the theatre in Anklam is shaky, to say the least. He no longer has the stomach for constant subordination in matters where – yes, it has to be said – he knows more than the director. Contracts are temporary. Because the summer season in Zinnowitz and Heringsdorf demands a full programme, lots of people now take planned unemployment in the autumn when the theatres close, with a view to being rehired afterwards. Pietro reckons that, this year, his time in Anklam is up. He's also come up with something else: he wants to perform *Lenz*, in its entirety, accompanied by a percussionist. *Lenz*! Such a great text! So knowing, clever and ahead of its time! It's been close to his heart for thirty years – the story of the man who swept over Romanticism in a whirl of *Sturm und Drang*, and then couldn't decipher the world he found at the end of his journey! (Mr Prankster has now gone from Pietro's eyes, replaced by Mrs Heartthrob. Just wait: soon he'll turn his gaze towards Lenz's madness...)

He breaks off and goes quiet. Then, hesitatingly, he asks whether Helene would write an introduction for him – something that could be handed out before the performance. For most people *Lenz* is just a total blank, they don't know anything about it, so it'd be best to introduce it in some way. Just a short text; she's done something similar for him before. Might she be able to...?

Now Helene goes quiet. Oh Pietro, I've lost my ability to speak – first I have to see how much I can get back! She doesn't say that, of course, but after a few seconds' wavering, raises her stubborn head: 'Okay, but give me some time.'

Pietro doesn't understand what's happened to her, she thinks. Can it even be understood at all? She accompanies him to the lift and they go down together. Wind-up Elli bids her farewell. She laughs until he disappears from view, because something else has caught up with her.

For the last two hours, she's known exactly how Malyutka's glass clasp got into her bag.

Last spring. She hadn't seen Malyutka for a good while. It was maybe two months since her parting shot to Helene: that she wasn't really a better man than Matthes. In almost daily emails, Helene had tried to explain how things were going for her. That she was confused and all over the place. That she felt a tugging in her stomach whenever she thought of Malyutka, but her stomach belonged to her alone – yes indeed! – and it was precisely because of this tugging that she was thinking more often, more strongly and more intensely of Matthes. That she and Matthes had become enmeshed and entangled in so many different ways that she couldn't just pick out a thread and pull at it: she was afraid of nakedness, and of being on her own, and had thrown her life and Matthes's into one pot, never finding an opportunity – or looking for one either, she had to confess – to talk about being in love with other people after he'd come back to her from her friend Heidrun. But that was sixteen years ago now – long enough for old relationships to have gone by like the years, and for new ones begin. They wouldn't have planned it that way when they first got together, though. She'd been able to sense on an almost daily basis how important she was for Matthes, while unfortunately it hadn't been the case the other way round. That wasn't nice for him or for her, because she couldn't bring herself to end things with him. Sometimes Helene used to wish Matthes had another woman. Not a secret love, but out in the open, a real person, someone who could give him what he didn't get with her – but sadly that was inconceivable. And sometimes she'd longed for Matthes, it's true! She'd happily admit that here, and on the record (that was one of her defiant phases). She doesn't know why, but that's how it was: sex with him was habit, and once they started it was all right – no, it was delightful; enthralling, even! (That was a particularly defiant phase.) It's just that she generally had no desire to for it to start at all... Her emails to Malyutka Malysch held back even as they rushed forward. She hadn't wanted to see it at the time, but it becomes clear to her as she remembers. 'Clear as mud,' she says quietly, because nothing is really clear at all here, neither in her behaviour towards Matthes nor in her behaviour towards Malyutka. It's as if she'd wanted to be suspended like a cable car in a state of limbo, just high enough for them both to have to see her and be consumed by it. Maybe she'd finally hoped to defeat them both this way, without having to take too much of the blame?

That fits. That strikes home.

Malyutka had sent her the clasp one day in May, along with a photo of her in a shirt and jacket, with three-day stubble and all her hair chopped off. On the back, in pencil, she'd written, 'Perfect, don't you think?'

There's rustling and a disturbance around her: Matthes has brought Lottchen and Lissy with him today. It's Saturday, even in Heidemühlen. Helene has lost all sense of what day it is, and is taken by surprise every morning when she reads it on the front of the paper. (Sometimes she buys a paper. Mostly, though, she knows she won't have enough time to read it because of all the therapy sessions she has.)

It's not yet ten o'clock, an unusual time for a visit. Has Matthes brought someone else with them? Yes, actually: standing behind the door is Fips, their neighbour from when they lived in their first flat together, on Feldberger Ring. A fair few flats lay between that one and the house on Arberstrasse... Where on earth has Matthes managed to get hold of Fips? Matthes says he ran into him while out shopping, and that he's built a house not far from them, on Zwieseler Strasse, 'you know, where the railway line is – right where we were thinking of building, before we found our plot!' Aha. So Fips their old neighbour is now Fips their new neighbour. Matthes says he's come with them to pick her up, if she can and wants to, of course. It was Fips's idea, totally on the spur of the moment, when he'd heard what was currently going on in the Wesendahl family.

Does Helene want to? Not really. Really she'd rather stay here. She's afraid of going home. Afraid of Matthes's lust for her. Afraid of getting into a position to hunt around in the wardrobe for the floppy disk with the Malyutka emails on it. Afraid of being aware of her study upstairs and not being able to go up to it. Afraid of being obliged by Matthes's ministrations to put on a spotlessly clean vest of affection, like a clean slate – but it doesn't fit her anyway, this straitjacket. Afraid of being subjected to a normal-seeming day. Afraid of being swaddled in too much cotton wool, and suffocating...

But now she's been thinking so long about being afraid that Matthes is looking disappointed – 'You don't have to, of course.' No, she doesn't have to. On the other hand, though, it wouldn't be at all bad to have Billy and Mareile around her, and to talk to Bengt on the phone, with Billy's help. And to show the children how she can peel a potato, which is bound to make them laugh. She's already had a go at this in occupational therapy: the potato was skewered on a special board and she had to do it with her left hand. She's already bought a similar board, with a scraper and grater built in. Maybe a chance would materialise for her and Matthes to have half an hour or so in the kitchen together, just the two of them, drinking tea – neither of them would need to say anything much, though by prodding the passing time they might be able to bring out one word after another from beneath the surface. She can remember occasions like this from previous years, and they'd always done them both good...

'Come on then, let's go!'

She says it more or less decisively, though her face shows

that her doubts still have the upper hand. But she will have to ask first, because weekend leave is supposed to be requested and approved in advance, and who knows if things are as lax here as they were on the Stroke Unit. So they set off, with the kids in tow. There's no one in the nurse's room – where can she find someone to ask? They go up and down the corridor on the ward until finally one of the nurses appears, coming out of a room whose occupant has obviously been discharged and which needs to be got ready again. She seems visibly annoyed by Helene being there and even barges into her as if by accident, her arms full of dirty bed linen. Helene starts to stammer, which doesn't often happen any more, but she has to get her request out, no matter what. Now the nurse doesn't seem at all unwilling, and even rather pleased at the prospect of having one less patient to look after today. (Though Helene wonders what difference her absence would make – after all, she does everything herself!) When should she be back? No later than quarter to six this evening, just so we're clear about that! Helene would've liked to salute, but doesn't dare let go of the rollator. She notices the jerk darting upwards through her body, though, like a hook on a fishing line – now stretching her spine along its whole length. She stands up nice and tall before the nurse – 'Yes, ma'am!' – as the hook emerges through one of the holes in the top of her skull, pulling the line with it. Her stance relaxes again as the nurse turns away from her to shove the bed linen into the waiting bin – she's been holding it tenderly in her arms the whole time, as if it were the limp form of a bridegroom. Helene guides the girls back. Lottchen jumps on to the shelf of the rollator and lets herself be pushed. This amuses her, though she reckons the wheelchair was 'much better'.

Whine, bleat, moan.

She doesn't want to take anything with her except the little handbag Matthes brought in for her on her first day in hospital. It's got all her important documents in it, as well as her purse. But this has to be got out of the safe, which is a difficult undertaking if there's no one on Reception. Ah, forget it, what would she need documents for anyway? The bag can stay where it is.

And then they're in the car. Fips is visibly uncertain, not knowing quite what shape she's in and what he can ask without causing offence, but Mareile and Lottchen leap into the breach by having a full-on row. As usual it's not clear what it's about. Matthes probably wouldn't mind dealing firmly with Lottchen but doesn't dare, and instead goes on at her not to start *that* again. But what? The girls can sort it out themselves back there, as far as Helene's concerned. What she doesn't know can't hurt her. Her rollator is in the boot clanking loudly and almost rhythmically. She moves her left hand in time to the rattling clatter and gets the sense that the right one is moving with it, but looking at it takes care of that impression. *Exit: THE DREAM* once again – she's actually starting to get used to it. She asks Fips about his wife and children, and, relieved, he tells her. She looks at him with apparent interest, but without really listening – clearly something she can still do. Her mental capacity is quickly exhausted, she knows that, so conversational tactics like this give her a welcome chance to not be too abrupt with people. And Fips likes to talk: one hand on the steering wheel, the other accentuating what he's saying. While he's doing this she loses herself in a state of emptiness, and in the end is astonished when the car stops on Arberstrasse. Fips doesn't want to come in. He gets the rollator out of the boot.

Old Frau Wierbel approaches from next door, and guess what's she's walking with? A rollator, of course. She stops short when she sees Helene then quickly looks away. She's the type who avoids contact like her own cat avoids water. Last spring Helene frequently had to chase him off because he was messing with the borders she'd laid out so painstakingly and reluctantly (and which she'd only really done to let the neighbours have their way). It was probably Helene's anger at having been goaded into doing it that contributed to the Anti-Cat Campaign, because she actually liked cats. As a child she'd overruled her mother's reservations and given her youngest sister a kitten for her birthday, with a huge light-blue bow round its neck – she'd known her father would be all for it, which emboldened her. She'd always been fearfully cautious not to tell her own children the story – after all, until they'd moved to Arberstrasse they'd lived in rented new-build flats. Anyway, Frau Wierbel is the only person who loves her cat. Helene watches after her as she slowly disappears in the direction of the supermarket.

Actually, a rollator wouldn't be a bad idea at all for shopping – you could fit loads in the basket. As if to prove it, Fips puts a big carrier bag of apples in hers and a box of Mon Chéri liqueur chocolates on top. Later, in the kitchen, Matthes tells her that the apples are from Fips's own garden. He'd requested a special permit to be able to keep their apple tree. Every house had to have a clearance of five metres from the street, so the tree would've had to come down. Only after a staff change at the planning office were the Fips' given permission to build their house eight metres back from the road. They'd definitely been lucky, too, of course: their plot was the last on the street and would stay that way, because beyond it was the railway line. This time she hadn't put on an interested face to duck out of having to listen, and hot on the heels of this information comes a question: does she want to know all this? No, she doesn't. She decides to wait for an opportunity to discuss with Matthes the issue of her capacity.

Yes, capacity. That's exactly it.

Oh, Billy... He comes down from his room and greets Helene with such overflowing joy that she feels very good indeed. When you grow particularly fond of a child, you don't immediately feel guilt towards the others, but it definitely comes later. Given the time and the opportunity to reflect on it, the five children seem as different to her as her love for each of them. The boys she treats much more... respectfully? Yes. She feels she can't identify with their experience the way she can with her daughters. This barrier doesn't exist between her and the girls, and her conflicts with them since they'd hit puberty have also been much more sharp-edged, really taking it out of her. Since getting married, often enough she'd given in to the boys instead of smacking them. But the temptation was often there, and had been ever since Bengt was four years old. He was a stubborn child who knew his own mind, and firmly and quietly tried to get his own way. When Helene had started working in Henrichshorst, as a single mother she'd been completely on her own. Matthes had been claiming he loved her for years by that point, but again and again kept deferring anything like a separation from his wife. Helene had no idea at the time that he'd finally move in with her not many months after that. It was a time when she was trying to help her sons survive with a desolate mother. One day, at lunchtime, when she'd believed Bengt to be at kindergarten as

- 278 -

usual, he'd been brought to her clinic by the wife of one of the doctors living at the medical centre. For the third day running, now, this woman had watched him playing for hours in the sandpit outside her window – was this entirely appropriate? Now and then he'd have something to eat from his lunch box, then carry on building enormous runs for his marbles. The third day running! Helene had gone completely numb. Lost for words, she'd tried to control herself. Because she had to get Billy to the childminder by bike, she always kissed Bengt goodbye on the corner of the street his kindergarten was on, then carried on her way. Clearly, Bengt – who'd never complained of an aversion to kindergarten – had waited until Helene was out of sight then happily set off in the direction of home. He'd sat himself in the sandpit outside the medical centre, which wasn't visible from where Helene worked, and waited until the other children started coming back from kindergarten – some alone; some holding hands with mum or dad. Then he, too, would come running up to Helene, who'd arranged with the kindergarten that Bengt could walk home by himself because she had to go and pick up Billy again in the afternoons. Nothing had given him away, though she had been briefly surprised that he had so much to tell her about his day. She'd even been pleased that the boy finally seemed to be finding his feet. Christ, she has to laugh when she thinks about it now, but at the time she hadn't been in the mood for any kind of joking around. When Bengt hadn't wanted to provide any information about his doings, she'd got hold of him and given him a good shake, and if the doctor's good lady wife hadn't been waiting around in the doorway to see what Helene was going to do, he'd have *got a good hiding*. She'd been livid. When she thinks about it, though, she was angry with herself for trying to amuse the children with clownish jokes in the few hours between work and bedtime. Hubris. She might have been a psychologist by profession, but *sadness* gnawed away at her as much as it did any other woman. She'd snatched up her child and marched over to the kindergarten. There she deposited him, and not without commenting that when a child was absent with no explanation for three days in a row, it might be a good idea to follow it up. Even more so given that she was there often enough – whether to sit in on classes, talk to one of the teachers or for parent-and-child days. She hadn't even looked at Bengt when she left again, after withdrawing permission for him to go home by himself in the afternoons. From then on, he was the last child to be collected every day: Helene couldn't manage to bike down and back up the hill twice, with both children, so she'd go and get Billy first.

Poor Bengt.

Involuntary forays into the past were happening to her more and more often.

Now Matthes is trying to shield her from the children, asking her to go for a walk round the garden with him. The girls are given instructions to start getting lunch ready, and take themselves off into the house, grumbling. Helene goes with Matthes across the patio and into the garden. She's left the rollator in the house, so she asks Matthes to support her. He's not fearful as such, but overcautious – so much so that she asks him to stride out a bit more boldly. How's the quince? They've had a bumper crop this year – the cellar's full of quince compote and quince jelly. The things Matthes made time for... Whenever he has something to mull over, when he's working on lectures or preparing articles, he always does something with his hands. Papier-mâché, ironing, baking. It often happens that he'll walk off in the middle of whatever he's doing – several times Helene has had to turn the iron off, or take burnt cakes out of the oven. That means he's had a thought that needs to be written down without delay. What had he been thinking about when he did the quinces? She doesn't ask – he can't handle questions. When you've been married for so many years you don't make all the mistakes it's possible to make. There are enough of them happening day after day regardless. It bothers her, trotting along next to Matthes in silence. An absence of discord doesn't necessarily mean there's harmony, just that two people might be journeying alone despite their linked arms and clasped hands. They'd often caught her eye – in Venice two years ago, for example, when she'd squatted on the Rialto Bridge, waiting for Matthes to finish faffing about taking photos: couples, arm in arm, who looked right past each other with empty eyes, despite the gondolas and palaces reflected in them. Their faces were often alike – masks of indifference, behind which you could sense a certain apathy. At the time she'd sought refuge in Matthes's arms and attempted to look right at him, but he'd been busy with his camera – he took a picture with the flash on and dazzled her. *Downright manic* was how she described his way of taking photos – but every now and then, some incredible pictures would come out of it, and Venice was no exception. She'd framed one of them and hung it in her study. She looks up at her study window, her gaze climbing with the Virginia creeper over the side door of the living room and up the wall, right up to the little dormer where her desk is. Unlike her gaze, she probably won't be able to climb up there herself. She sighs. She's come to a stop, of course, because she can't walk and look up at the same time. Matthes follows her gaze and says the gutters need cleaning. Now he sighs, and she smiles. Their sighing could be a first step away from indifference and towards harmony.

But her fear of not measuring up to Matthes's intellect in any way, shape or form is already making its presence felt, a rhythmically rising and falling tone in their communication with each other. And this communication isn't just the few words they exchange. It's also Matthes's immediate increase in pressure on her hand and arm at even the slightest unsteadiness from Helene that might be a stumble; his efforts to match her pace; the careful gauging of any desire to change direction. Shouldn't the fact that she immediately and unquestionably grasps all these things wrestle her fear to the floor? It doesn't, though, no. When Matthes speaks, she flounders in the attempt to understand three or four sentences in a row. It quickly becomes too much, and she resurfaces less and less often until she's well and truly drowned. Since she seems to have worked this out, she decides to pay very close attention after the first sentence or two, and not lose the connection to the fifth or sixth sentences. But something inside her makes her head roar – making her blood pressure rise, perhaps? – so she's unable to do anything but thrash about wildly, and then give up after all. Damn. So it's good if Matthes doesn't say much, like now. Hadn't she just been thinking about her capacity issue?

She suddenly has the feeling he's understood an awful lot.

The girls have done meat, potatoes and celeriac, and taken a vanilla pudding out of the fridge. Helene tries hard to keep her mouth closed as she eats. She mustn't let a single string of spit abseil out of it, or a single crumb fall. The strain makes her right hand seize up – she's trying to keep it under the table, but it keeps slowly coming back up. The fact that she can't cut up her own meat or mash the potatoes is making her angry, isn't it? Yes, it's anger. She needs to control herself. After all, she wouldn't like to be sat here with her stupid cutting board either. Gradually she realises that spit's rushing into her mouth, that she can't move her face to chew any more because it's distorted with crying, and her mouth is coming open. Tears roll down her cheeks. Good grief, why does this have to keep happening to her! And she can't just get up and run out! Gradually the others seem to move further and further away, and she withdraws into herself completely until she ends up right in the corner, between Billy and the wall. Where all is lost, a lost child, *enfant perdu*, defenceless – as if she's been stripped of her thick hide. She keeps her head right down. Spit-drenched sludge has long since been raining down from its big flesh-red hole – on to her blouse, her trousers, her shoes – and she's filled with shame. In her shame the sense of being utterly lost becomes greater and greater, until in the end she feels she's no longer there among the very people she used to call 'my loves' in letters to her parents (when she could still write letters), and she'd meant it too. Each one had been a great love. Is it possible to hold your own in the presence of your great loves when you're drooling spit, when you're helpless, when you have no control over your face and you lose all your composure? Suddenly Mareile hugs her, apparently not bothered by the slobber. Mind your jumper! Helene wants to call out, but nothing more comes out of her mouth. Instead her left arm suddenly flies up and around Mareile's shoulder, and her head tucks into the crook of Mareile's neck, and now she's sitting there, leaning on her daughter, feeling that her tears have probably – finally – run their course. Thank God. Later, when Helene releases herself, she sees bits of mushed-up meat on her chest and potato gloop in her waistband.

Poor girl.

Now she's smiling again.

Now the others aren't smiling at all.

Please smile now, she thinks, trying to say it with the look she's sending from one to the other. Is it an imploring look? She has no idea how you graft an imploring look on to your face, but she wants to try. Her attempts must look comical because one by one they all burst out laughing, and laugh so hard that in the end they're almost falling off their chairs.

That's how close laughing and crying are to each other.

She doesn't want a sleep after lunch, no. But she can't keep her eyes open long enough to prove it. Matthes ushers her into the bedroom, but she counters that by saying she'll only stay there if he withdraws to his study. As she's saying this – and, stupidly, she can't stop herself grinning as she does, though that's the last thing she feels like doing – a sudden memory flashes through her mind that she wants to hold on to. She closes her eyes and looks into the distance after this memory, and she's actually able to grab a tiny corner of it before it disappears – for now – into the irretrievable. Now she's pulling, tugging, trying to untangle it. In the spring – she can see the cherry trees in blossom outside her window, at any rate – Matthes had moved into his study with his whole kit and caboodle. He'd even sanded down and oiled the old wardrobe – the one Frau Wierbel had given them years ago, when they'd moved in – so it could be moved upstairs. It had been living in the cellar, where they'd stored winter gear in it in the summer, and summer clothes and short-sleeved shirts in the winter. Moving the wardrobe had been a major undertaking. It wouldn't fit up the stairs, so to avoid dismantling it they'd taken it up over the balcony. Had she not been in Matthes's study since then? She can't picture the wardrobe in there, so clearly she has no idea which corner of the room he'd put it in.

'Helene?'

Matthes is looking up into her eyes, which she's now opened again after her short trip to What Has Been.

'Matthes?'

She tries to manoeuvre a knowing look into her eyes, to blow it from the back of her skull and out through her optic nerves. It makes her think of blowing eggs: the knowingness might splash out like egg yolk mixed with white, just splash right out! But she wants to quickly take it back again, this knowingness, and acts as if butter wouldn't melt. She can do that, she realises – it's fun, even. But she doesn't allow herself this moment of fun. Just as it's about to ignite a twinkle in her eye, she thinks of Malyutka Malysch. She can't comprehend how, again and again, flimsy little episodes of fun come and try to make her forget the grief she can't yet navigate. On the other hand, everyone here has experienced grief and dread that she *hasn't* – because of her, basically – and they're not exactly going around with their misery on show. But then, of course, things have turned out all right for her. They turned out badly for Malyutka Malysch, though, the poor, lovely thing – Helene's so fond of her! And the fact that that's all over, and the most she can say now is that she *was* fond of her – she won't believe it, it can't be true!

But it is.

What's also true is that she can't share this grief with anyone here, not even Billy. That hits home, and hurts, and strips her of her power – so much so that in the next moment, Matthes is giving her a hand and getting her into bed. As requested, and with no arguments, he then leaves the room.

Where sleep is hiding, she has no idea. After a little while she gets up, and gropes her way to the wardrobe. She opens it and starts to hunt around for the floppy disk. Not an easy task with one hand. In the end she decides just to pull everything out on to the floor. Nothing in the top drawer, or the next one down. Then, in the third one, she pulls out a securely-sealed envelope from under the pyjamas, and immediately recognises the object of her search. She tears it open with her teeth, finally holding between them a black-grey plastic square which she takes in her hand. The felt-tip dot on the white label looks at her like the red eye of an angora rabbit. Yes, that's it: the aforementioned floppy disk. She stuffs it in her knickers, not wanting to hear any questions about it or answer any either. She manages to get everything back into the wardrobe, albeit no longer folded and in piles. It doesn't matter, Matthes won't see it – when it comes to tidiness he never notices anything anyway, just letting everything fall where he stands. (She's learnt to smile about it over the years. Only sometimes, at tense moments which don't arise very often, does an episode of rage threaten to boil over. Nine times out of ten, though, she can quickly put a lid on it.) When she's lying down again she notices her heart beating faster and louder, as if protesting against the pressure of her ribs. Her skin is getting hot where the bit of plastic is touching it. She shoves her hand in under the waistband of her pants, and lays it on the floppy disk.

'My darling,' she says quietly.

There's a knock, and Matthes pops his head round the door. 'Time to get going.'

What, has she been asleep that long? And not spent the afternoon with the children? They'd probably have played a memory game with Lottchen, and with five of them Monopoly would've been on the agenda. Helene would've wriggled out of it all. She'd have had to make the children understand that she can't follow games like these any more, or manage to sit through them yet. It would've been hard – they perceive her limitations much more as physical afflictions... Fips is already there, standing in the hall, and he waves at Helene. Whether she likes it or not, she has to get up. As she steps into the hall, Claudia looks round the corner – a bit apprehensive, as if she doesn't quite know what to expect. Claudia is Fips's wife and taller than him, as well as broader. They greet each other warmly. Claudia was the *Hotzen* queen. To think Helene's thought of that word! She'd leap for joy if she could. *Hotzen* is what her father had called babysitting little children. She remembers evenings of non-stop cackling, when her father would take that book off the shelf –*Traditions and Customs of Thuringia*, wasn't it called? – and read out sayings and expressions. Nobody used them any more, even back then, but they unleashed the same guffaws of laughter from her sisters and mother as they did from her. Claudia's children must've long since stopped needing a babysitter. She's still got her gaze lowered, looking up cautiously, and only a poke in the side and a cheery, encouraging laugh from Helene breaks the ice of her anxiety. Out from under it emerges the old Claudia, with the loud voice befitting her large and resonant chest, and Helene takes a startled step back when this voice, sounding relieved, finally starts to clatter and clang. Yes, that's the good old Claudia she knows. Maybe it'll be nice to have her living nearby.

Matthes has fetched two glasses of black grape juice from the cellar – one for the driver, the other for Helene. Made from their own grapes, of course. As well as this he hands Helene a bulging bag. He doesn't want to say anything about it now, but she's to take it with her. They roll out to the car. This time getting in is no major effort, because Claudia clearly knows exactly how to go about it. When Matthes says goodbye to her, she's completely taken aback to feel his tongue in her mouth. She hadn't expected that. She can't even remember the last time anyone had kissed her like that. The last time *she* kissed someone like that, though, comes back to her straight away, and she goes red. Malyutka hadn't kissed her back but had shrunk away from her, and they'd broken apart in silence and confusion. Yes, that'd been in April – they'd met one more time to analyse the March disaster. Malyutka Malysch had wanted to forget all about it, while Helene was – was thinking about pulling back! The Matthes-ship was too important for her just to abandon it and then take on a whole new Malyutka-ship, she'd said. She'd wanted to question herself closely, or at least scrutinise her relationship with Matthes as thoroughly as possible, without having a clue where to begin. She'd turned down the wine – a bottle of Rioja – that Malyutka had ordered in anticipation. Where had that been?

Her thoughts have strayed so far into last spring that Billy just can't get through to her with his 'take care, see you next time,' and the bundle of worry dolls he's made. It's only when Lottchen's little hand runs over her face, with its patina of ketchup, mud and play-doh from the whole blessed day, that she's brought back to the moment, which is one of parting. She puts Matthes's bag between her legs. Claudia sits in the back, and both women wave as the car starts up. Helene looks directly at Matthes. It almost looks like he's going to cry, and at that moment she suddenly feels properly sorry for him. She hasn't felt any sympathy for anyone in the last few of months, she feels certain of that. It pulls at her in a different way to love – not in her stomach, more in her chest and her head – but it makes her heart beat faster just the same. Her sympathy diminishes as Matthes gets smaller and smaller, his eyes now just two tiny dark dots, and by the time the car turns the corner it's disappeared completely. Her heart is beating in time with the pacemaker. It's a strange emotion, Helene thinks – only revealing itself at moments when you really *see* what other people are going through.

Claudia gives her a brief outline of what her children have been doing over the past twelve years. There it is again, her 'capacity' issue. It occurs to her that she never did discuss it with Matthes. What else can she do but put on an interested face, and look in Claudia's direction every now and then? Nothing, and she knows it, and when they arrive in Heidemühlen a good three-quarters of an hour later, Claudia actually says in all seriousness that nothing has changed: Helene is still the great listener she's always been.

Whatever, Helene thinks, and says goodbye to them both. For a moment she almost congratulates herself for her cunning ability to convey this impression, when it's actually just saving her from having to absorb information she used to be able to process effortlessly...

Today was hard work. This wouldn't actually have occurred to her, despite her long lunchtime nap, if she hadn't suddenly been assaulted by an immense tiredness, which she can't fight and which even stops her from going to see the old men's club in the dining room. No, now she just wants to go to bed.

She's forgotten all about the floppy disk.

On the way to their rendezvous, Helene had had to keep visualising Malyutka with short hair – she was afraid she wouldn't recognise her straight away. Maybe she'd turn up in a pointedly masculine outfit, too? Helene had been quivering with anxiety, the shivers shooting from her head down into her legs and making her stumble. It was mid-April – she can see herself landing in a bed of tulips in some square in the centre of Berlin... Yes, that's right, they'd agreed to meet at a café near the station in Charlottenburg, which was about halfway between them. As it turned out only two tables in the place were occupied, perhaps because it was so early in the day, so her fears proved unfounded. Despite the short hair, Malyutka instantly looked more feminine than she had done when they last met – the style really suited her. She'd matched the shade to her natural hair colour, replacing the grey in her ash blonde with glittering highlights. It looked really nicely done, you had to hand it to her. Helene didn't go to half as much trouble over her appearance as Malyutka must have done to turn up sporting this look. At first glance her clothes were unremarkable, but a second look revealed the checked short-sleeve shirt to be a blouse, and that the trousers were in fact flared ladies' jeans. She'd got more slender over the past month, and Helene couldn't help but imagine her small breasts, like two fried eggs. She looked really attractive – a lot more attractive than Helene remembered. Straight away there was a tugging in her stomach, and Helene had the distinct feeling it wasn't the man in Viola she was thinking about. He was definitely still in there, Helene thought, and would never be gone completely. But she had to consciously remind herself of him: he didn't reveal himself of his own accord. This was new, and immediately prompted a mumbled 'Late, but not too late, thank goodness,' from Helene, which Malyutka Malysch acknowledged with a glance at her (dainty! gold! ladies'!) watch, generously forgiving her the three minutes. Malyutka shook out her lower arm conspicuously, and the little watch slid a bit lower down so that it played loosely about her wrist like a bracelet. Helene smiled and asked whether 'this thing' was a new purchase. A fleeting look of pride smoothed out Malyutka's face but her brow immediately furrowed again. With particular sharpness, Helene then perceived the whispering on the next table, and the waiter signalling to the woman at the bar. And even though it wasn't clear what they were whispering and signalling about, she knew Malyutka would take it all personally. Probably with good reason. Helene hung her coat on the coat rack and sat down, ordering a black tea and a piece of cherry cake. Malyutka tossed back her first glass of red wine. She'd ordered a bottle ages ago, but waited until Helene got there to start drinking it. When she heard she'd have to finish the bottle by herself, she immediately refilled her glass.

They fell silent.

They stayed silent for a long time, and all that could be heard was the scratching of the cake fork on the plate, Malyutka's throaty swallowing sound as she drank, and from time to time the tea glass being set down on its saucer. Finally Malyutka cleared her throat and asked after Lissy, who she'd found so *striking* on her first and last visit to Helene's home. 'Not an ounce of fat on her, and yet she's somehow so strong and sinewy,' she said, and a flicker of uncertainty appeared in her eyes. Helene used the question as a chance to get the better of the awkwardness they were both feeling. She launched into progress reports for all five children over the last six months, and when she broke off, pretty well exhausted, they looked at each other and couldn't help laughing. Relieved, Malyutka said that of course she could understand how important Matthes was for Helene. That she had no right to get involved. But she'd believed herself incapable of falling in love again, and that's where Helene had well and truly upset her clearly premature plans. She wasn't remotely ashamed, though. Not of the blokey photoshoot, or of the addle-brained state she kept getting herself into: without Helene and yet very much with her, *on top of the world one minute and in the depths of despair the next*, making demands then giving in again, back and forth. That's just the way it was – she was out of practice when it came to love. Recently she'd even come to think that love between women actually happened outside the main arena, posing no threat to anything or anyone. And if Helene

- 292 -

was able to see that too, then they'd never have to tell anyone what was going on between them, would they? One day a week would be enough. Oh, what was she saying – once a month! Every two months, even! She could wait, and *would* wait, and wouldn't want to take anything away from anyone – on the contrary, she'd want to *give* something to Helene! As Malyutka spoke, she shrank under Helene's incredulous gaze, returning it with wide, puppy-dog eyes. And Helene didn't want to believe it was Malyutka Malysch who'd spoken – that it was Malyutka Malysch who thought she had no right to get involved in Helene's relationship, when in fact Helene had herself stuck Malyutka right in the middle of things, giving her a halo and letting her soar over everything that God had let happen in the last six months. No, Malyutka. You absolutely have the right to *have that right*. Helene had wanted to tell her that, today, for the first time, she'd seen her as a woman straight away, and not as a genderless person or castrated man, as had always been the case before. She hadn't been able to do anything about that: she's pretty sure it would've been pointless to do anything other than sit tight and wait for something to change. But in the same moment it immediately became too much for Helene to explain it all to Malyutka, knowing it would strengthen the very hope she'd wanted to take away: the whole way there, on the long S-Bahn journey, she'd been planning a farewell speech, searching for the *right* words to make it sound plausible. A provisional, tentative goodbye, with caveats. Something temporary, experimental, improvised; a stopgap. Goodbye until further notice, on a trial basis, subject to cancellation – a bye-for-now. The little door left slightly ajar and firmly in view. This goodbye was supposed to keep such a door open – she didn't necessarily want to have her foot in there, but could at least leave a shoe. Though she was already asking herself what, in their case, there was to say goodbye to. The daily, sometimes several times daily, exchange of emails? The days and nights they *didn't* spend together? How long had they gone now without seeing each other? The last time had been their night in March, and afterwards it was Malyutka who'd said goodbye to *her*. At least that's how it'd looked at first, until the emails started to come and go again daily, and everything snapped back to an earlier state of love declared but not lived. For Helene this threatened to turn into a life without love, if she didn't somehow put a stop to it. Didn't attempt to organise things that resisted being put in order – the Matthes arrangement she'd practised for decades but never really questioned. Yes, she was confused, and this submissive, kowtowing Malyutka was the last thing she needed. Now she realised it was precisely Malyutka's spiky, contrary nature that had *excited* her so mercilessly, rather than her hard-to-conceal masculinity or the broad stride she fell into when she wasn't thinking. Helene herself had never been contrary and spiky, but she'd only half-heartedly outgrown the model of dutiful little woman. True, she knew how to stand up for her rights – when it came to work or politics, for example: she'd learned that early on, and was nobody's fool. But in private, if harmony hung in the balance and a sacrifice could save it, she'd quickly pull her feelers in and retreat into her shell.

A servile Malyutka was unthinkable, inconceivable. She wasn't supposed to come running with her tongue out whenever Helene deigned to whistle – what, a few times a year, maybe? That was never part of the deal. It had shaken Helene, and she began to shiver. A wave of loathing broke over her gaze, which had been clear up to now, and if Malyutka, alarmed, hadn't laid a hand on her arm, the whole thing might have descended into a severe case of the shakes...

Helene has to smile thinking about it, and the smiling has a placatory effect. Even on her feelings towards what people call 'fate'? She maybe wouldn't go that far. But dawn is just now creeping towards her, painting red streaks into the black and grey, and she doesn't feel she needs to be quite so hard on today as she was on yesterday.

She turns on to her side and even manages to go back to sleep, but not before she's fished a hard, bulky bit of plastic out of her knickers. She puts it under her pillow.

That morning, Malyutka's angular face – now half-framed in ash-blonde; narrow nose powdered to get rid of shine – accompanies Helene in the hospital wherever she goes. In occupational therapy she tries doggedly to get to grips with a coordination exercise. She knows the occupational therapist – she's married to a doctor, and she and her husband and son used to live at the medical centre in Henrichshorst. Helene can clearly remember the son. His name was Ben, and he had violin lessons at the music school – he'd started in the last year of kindergarten. He was at kindergarten with Bengt and they'd been friends. When had they moved from Henrichshorst? Seventeen years ago. Years in which Helene must've changed a lot, because the therapist doesn't recognise her, and yet, to her, Helene had once been one of the *qualified staff*. It's strange, sitting here knowing so much more than this woman, and attempting to get these blasted little pegs into the pegboard one by one. Sometimes Helene manages to get hold of one firmly enough for it not to fall out of her hand. Once or twice, with the utmost effort, her right arm can be made to slide a little way across the table, but the therapist has to guide it to do the actual inserting into the board because it won't go any further by itself. Should she force the woman into a conversation about old times? It'd definitely be fun to see the penny drop. On the other hand, it's also no bad thing to know something about a person, and for that person to have no idea. Malyutka, what do you think? When she closes her eyes Malyutka winks at her downright conspiratorially, with all the brazenness at her disposal that Helene so admired.

'Oh, are you not feeling too well? Shall we call it a day?'

The voice of the doctor's wife (*Trautenau*, Helene reads on the ID badge on the woman's uniform – so her name's the same as it was, she hasn't remarried) makes her open her eyes again. 'No, no,' she says hurriedly, 'everything's fine.' She thinks about it and waits a moment.

'Actually, yes, maybe we could call it a day...'

Frau Trautenau is a snooty person. Seventeen years ago she hadn't worked, which was strange and unusual for a woman with a child of kindergarten age. Now she does. Does she have to? It's much more common now for self-styled doctors' wives not to work, even when there haven't been any children around for a long time, small or otherwise. Has her husband upped and left her? And what's become of her son? Is he still an only child? Helene remembers how the woman had boasted about her son's violin-playing in front of the assembled kindergarten parents, and she'd had him perform at parents' evening: a pale, anxious-looking little student with no hint of a smile, even after he'd finished his woefully scratchy little piece. Helene had felt so sorry for him and immediately started clapping the loudest, even shouting 'Bravo!' ...

'Do we know each other?' she hears Frau Trautenau saying. 'You're looking at me in such a funny way.'

'We'll have to see.' Helene's startled by this meaningless response, which just slips out.

Only a good while after she's left the room, and is sitting in the changing cubicle for the pool, does Malyutka whisper to her that, actually, it wasn't a meaningless response at all.

Or does she imagine that bit?

Swimming is lovely. As always.

That's to say, of course, that she's nowhere near actually being able to swim – her right leg can now imitate the necessary moves a bit, but her right arm won't join in. She'd go under straight away without her water sausage. Today, though, she's allowed to float on her back as much as she likes. Besides her, there's a group of three people in the water, none of them with mobility issues, doing some kind of water aerobics. The music is too loud, blasting out and spoiling her enjoyment of playing dead. Malyutka grimaces in disgust, too. So, one-legged and holding on under the water, Helene tries to copy what the lady on the poolside is demonstrating. Star jumps. She stands chest-deep in the water, with her right hand on the bar at the edge of the pool, and tries to jump while sticking her left leg out and throwing her left hand up into the air. Then the hand comes back down to the seam of her non-existent trousers, and the leg goes back to the starting position. Not bad at all, a sort of one-legged disabled star jump. After five jumps, though, she's short of breath and her heart is beating like mad. It was too much. Strange that she seems unable to gauge how much physical effort is required. She'd never have thought a little thing like that would leave her out of breath. She stops, pausing for a moment. Her one-to-one therapist is nowhere to be seen. She recalls having to press those little springs after waking up from the coma, and having to blow into that funny device to make a ball fly up in the air. She hadn't managed it at all.

That was only three months ago.

'Can't you see, not even the ducks don't want to come any closer!'

This sentence – spoken by a mother down by the lake, when her child, parked in its buggy, was screaming loudly – has been bothering her all afternoon. Quite apart from the fact that the child had been far too young to know the sentence was even about them, Helene is in despair because her attempts at understanding are a categoric failure. The double, even triple negative is beyond her, she simply can't follow it. 'Can't you see?' Yes, actually, she can see perfectly well. But the 'not even the ducks don't want to come any closer' won't reveal itself to her at all. What is there in her damn skull that's blocking all logic? She remembers being able to just unpick such sentences in reverse, and – in every case! – finally arrive at a result. The negative, whether double or even triple, would either make sense, not make sense, or be else be a bit too clever for its own good. But what does it signify here? The ducks don't want to come any closer? But in fact they don't want to *not* come any closer! What does that mean – don't not? There's confusion in her head and she's become anxious and agitated. She gets so worked up about having to accept and deal with these deficiencies in her knowledge. But if she shyly disclosed this to anyone here, they'd just laugh and say it was trivial. That they themselves have trouble with double negatives, and it's really not worth getting worked up about. What was it Matthes had said, when she'd brought up the linguistic deficiencies she kept noticing in herself? 'Oh, Helene, you've just finally turned into a normal person at last...' On the one hand, this sentence presumably revealed his high regard for her linguistic abilities. On the other hand, she felt strangely threatened by it, without being able to say exactly why. The sense of danger emanating from this little sentence is clear and present whenever she calls it up, she just can't pinpoint where it is. Mulling it over doesn't get her anywhere. It turns into liquid, which she imagines seeping into the grooves between the ridges of her brain, and sinking in before she can get hold of it. A similar thing happens with these double negatives, which really do her head in. And her head really did get done in, having that big bit of skull taken out – though luckily they put it straight back again, and it's healed fine. They'll probably have stored it in a freezer during the operation. When she washes her hair there's a good part of the left side of her skull where she can't feel the temperature of the water. She finds that strange, frankly, because after all they only folded her skin back – it still has its thermal receptors, which can't have been switched off during the operation. Should she be blaming the frozen bone, which might not have recovered from the shock and could be blocking the receptors on her skin? She smacks herself on the side of the head with her left hand. She can feel that, at least.

More and more often she's having attacks of despair. Since

the epileptic seizure, if she remembers correctly. She still hasn't confessed to the doctors here that she's no longer taking her anti-epileptic drugs. She's surprised there's no blood test due, as that alone would get the message across to them. 'We're going to have to check whether that dosage is correct!' She'd only own up to it if explicitly questioned, she decides. They're so sloppy about things like that here...

With all this going on, she's almost got her despair over with already. Maybe having each thought run straight into the next, strung together like houses on an endless street (you take note of them as you're moving, then instantly forget them), is one way – or at least, her way – of coping with attacks like this.

Still another fifteen minutes until supper. She's bought herself a paper today and opens it. Plastered on the local news page for Berlin is a photo of someone she knows. It's the *damaged boy*, sitting in his wheelchair at a table, and dazed with curiosity she tries to read. She has to keep pausing, breaking off and going back to the beginning, over and over again, until she can understand it.

Wojziech K., it says, was the victim of an 'U-Bahn shover': in broad daylight, his violin on his back, someone had pushed him in front of an incoming underground train. He'd been a talented violinist who devoted his time to music and computer science, though he hadn't yet decided which one his future would involve. That decision's been taken away from him now, at any rate, Helene thinks, and is immediately ashamed of the cynicism spreading inside her. It's a dispirited, instinctive cynicism, mixed with deep regret, and it has an enormous wave of pity in tow – she's thinking of Bengt, the budding musician, and how unbelievable it was for someone to be robbed of their life in this way, and yet have to keep on living. She reads the article again and again. The perpetrator is appearing in court. They've got a photo of Wojziech K. as the victim, but there isn't one of the perpetrator. Was that okay with Wojziech? Helene thought. Did anyone ask him before taking the photo? He's wearing a baseball cap, so you can only guess that part of his skull is missing. His legs are hidden under the table, and he's wearing a dark leather jacket with one sleeve tucked into the pocket. Clearly he was able to speak out about what happened. The perpetrator was found not guilty on the grounds of diminished responsibility, and admitted to a secure psychiatric hospital, it says. He'd heard voices commanding him to harm people so the world would be free of them. Wojziech looked so composed – no, *meek* and *mild* are better words: as if he'd be able to forgive the mentally-ill perpetrator everything he'd brought upon him. When she thinks about it, she hasn't actually seen him in Heidemühlen for a few days. Not that she's looked for him and not found him, just that she's now become aware of his absence. He might have been discharged or moved while the court case was happening, to keep the stress to a minimum. She'll keep an eye out for him turning up again, she tells herself. She'll use the left-hand door of the dining room every mealtime, which will take her past the table she used to sit at, and then she can switch to the right-hand side of the room and her old men's club. She'll gladly take on the detour. She considers talking to Wojziech. But if she's never done so before, then the court case is hardly a good reason to finally make contact.

She's now completely lost her appetite, having been sat here for a full hour reading the paper, red in the face. Supper will be nearly over, anyway. Instead she's overcome by a craving for chocolate. The serotonin levels in her brain must be too low, she thinks – it's evening and getting dark earlier, and the brain needs light and tryptophan to produce it. She'd read that somewhere – strange that she's retained it. So she flicks on the main light, not just the little reading lamp, and rummages in her locker – yesterday Matthes had given her some of her favourite chocolate, milk with nuts and raisins. She almost wants to see if she can taste the tryptophan the chocolate's supposed to have in it. She wants to handle her brain gently and tenderly, giving it everything she can, and once she's eaten the whole big bar of chocolate she sits at the window and waits for happiness to come. And come it does, as a sudden lightbulb moment: '...not even the ducks don't want to come any closer' is actually a load of rubbish! The woman just said it completely wrong! It would mean the ducks had all pushed and jostled their way towards the child, when in fact they'd stayed well away!

'Can't you see, even the ducks don't want to come any closer!'

If at first you don't succeed, try, try again.

The things you can achieve with chocolate...

VI

You. And You

IT'S ACTUALLY NICE TO BE LEFT ALONE BY THE STAFF. It doesn't matter that there's too few of them. Today no one's been to look in on her since the afternoon. After her chocolate she went to the little kitchen and made a big pot of Rooibos tea, which she then asked her neighbour to carry back to her room for her. He showed signs of wanting to stay a while, and she'd given in, grumbling inwardly. When he finally left, thank goodness, she hadn't said much. Ultimately she's had a fair amount of practice at driving people away with her oppressive silences – something she likes doing, it has to be said.

Opening the drawer of her bedside table, she takes out Malyutka's Murano glass hair clasp. Underneath it is the floppy disk. She'd much rather put the clasp into the laptop... What are you on about! she calls out to herself – this is something you should totally want to do! Here she is, with the chance to plunge right into the middle of the Malyutka Sea and luxuriate in the warm Viola-water! What's holding her back? She shuts the drawer in alarm – it was as if the floppy disk had moved, coming towards her with a sharp hiss. Didn't she just hear a sharp hiss?

She pauses. Looks all around. Pauses again.

She opens the drawer again slowly. The floppy disk lies there unchanged. Strangely that's no relief. With a quick, now decisive movement she takes the thing in her left hand – the laptop is waiting and swallows it up, snatching it from her fingers with a snapping sound. She's astonished: there are only three emails, and she thought there was a whole archive of them on there! It's out of the question that Matthes might've had anything to do with it. She must either have picked some out herself and deleted them, or else something's gone wrong. She doesn't find any emails at all written by her, only three from Malyutka...

04.05.2002.   01:43

My lovely little Heart-Sac-Heliotrope-Helene

Still: it's you. Your hours are my hours. The distance amounts to around fifty kilometres, maybe a hundred and seventy light-milliseconds, and what's that between your life and mine. From a cosmic perspective, we live in exactly the same place – we just need to be standing on Mars to see it. Actually, seeing things from a cosmic perspective, seeing my existence dwindle to nothing, never fails to be a comfort to me. It's rather lovely when the pain subsides, as my old ma always used to say. She was right.

I've decided to paint my flat. I started on the living room yesterday. Clearing out the books and the enormous computer gobbled up half the day. The black chap who moved into our building three weeks ago helped me stack the sofa and armchair on the bed. We'll have to see where I'm going to sleep tonight. I moved the bookcases away from the wall – just a bit at first, so I could get in between – then pushed off slowly from the wall with my hands and manoeuvred the heavy things into the middle of the room. Do you know what's curled around them, as it were? The old oak table, which I've laid on its side – three bookcases fit between its legs. I wouldn't have been able to get it through the door by myself anyway, I'd've had to ask the black chap again. (Christ, why don't I know his name?) Basically, there's not a single bit of space left in the whole flat where I could've parked it, so I'm really proud of my idea of lying it down. I've covered the windows and frames with plastic sheeting – the last time I did a job like this I couldn't have cared less about all that stuff – and I've also put masking tape on the skirting boards, laid newspaper on the floor and sheeted over the furniture too. The actual painting was a minor task after all that. White for the ceiling, and a warm orange shade for the walls – 'terracotta', the stuff's called. I wasn't watching the time at all and got a shock when Mrs Tauber from downstairs rang the doorbell in a fury shortly after midnight, to complain about all the noise – she hadn't been able to get a wink of sleep because of it. Ha, noise! I hadn't done anything apart from get paint on the roller and run it up and down the wall! Though I suppose acoustics might work differently in an empty room with no carpet. But to be honest I was glad to be reminded of the time. After that I had a bath – luckily I'd wisely taken the bookcases out first and moved them to under the kitchen table. I even vaguely considered using the bath to sleep in... Anyway, I'm now all fresh and clean and sitting at my temporarily plugged-back-in computer, writing to the woman who, one way or another, won't let me sleep. Once again, I'm almost surprised by the fact that, throughout my life, I've always loved women.

Take care!

Your munching MumbaiMalyutka

Munching MumbaiMalyutka! They'd inflicted hideous alliterative names on each other – it had been a secret competition between them. Helene only had 'H' to offer, while Malyutka Malysch also accepted the 'V' for Viola. So Helene had a lot more options.

Now she remembers laughing when she got this email,

because redecorating was the order of the day at Arberstrasse too. That very same day Helene had started stripping the woodchip wallpaper in her study. This proved hopeless, because the plasterboard clearly hadn't been treated with a sealer before the paper was put on. After half a day of repeated attempts – soaking the wall with water, using a spiked roller, steaming it with the iron – she'd given up, advertised the new wallpaper for sale secondhand and gone to get some paint from the DIY store. Terracotta... In the end she'd only done one wall with it, the sloping one, as she was already finding the colour overwhelming. She'd been annoyed, not wanting to admit the project hadn't been a success. At least her monster of a cupboard fit perfectly under the slope of the roof. She'd seen the top part of a sideboard dumped on the roadside when a nearby house was gutted, and with Lissy and Mareile had hauled it into the cellar. She'd then rung a book collector she knew who restored furniture as a hobby, and he'd come over straight away for such a decent piece. He stained it a darker colour and French polished it, fitted ball feet, and put shelves into the wide middle section that was open at the bottom, so you couldn't tell it had once been the top part of anything. He hadn't wanted any money for it, but asked Helene for a handwritten dedication to go in a collectors' edition of her poetry, published two or three years earlier. (It had felt good doing business like that, and she'd trawled the internet afterwards looking for bartering groups.)

Later, she'd looked through her folder of artwork, but then decided to stick drawings by the children on the sloping wall to take the edge off the garish orange paint. She hadn't been in her study for three months by that point. Matthes had almost certainly turned the heating off up there, so the room was cold. The more she potters about it in her mind, the more her left hand goes up and down nervily – to her face, her clothes, even her feet – and she feels the impulse in the right to do the same. Where has this restlessness come from? This fluttering impatience, directed at who knows what?

05.05.2002   22:47

My dearest little haggard herring-haul-Helene,

Still: it's you. If I imagine not living past today, a strangely sweet and almost rapturous feeling comes over me – that you exist, that you're there, and I don't have to have anything to do with you in order to be blissfully happy. That feeling is new and it comforts me no end. I've never been this calm while painting before, and dealing with the aftermath has never been this easy, either: this morning I simply removed the sheeting and the paper, and everything was spick and span – completely clean! Last time I had to spend another half a day dealing with the mess. The paint had long since dried, of course, and to get the window clean I even had to go at it with a ceramic hob-scraper. All I've done today is clean the window with newspaper and vinegar solution, and if you were to walk in here you'd probably stagger backwards a bit, dazzled by the light coming in. I'd hold you, so you didn't fall. I've wanted to do that since the first time I saw you. We'd sit down in the lovely terracotta living room – I've treated all the cabinets with furniture polish, tightened up any screws that were loose and had the carpet cleaned. So we'd sit, and if you had anything to say then that would be nice. If you didn't have anything to say, then that would be just as nice. The new, unfamiliar order in my room gives me a sort of security. We'll see how long that lasts. As yet I'm still meticulously clearing away all the tell-tale traces of my lifestyle –

so no orange peel, no beer bottle tops. Even newspapers go into a cardboard box which I've decorated collage-style, and which sits on the left under my computer table. True, it's only Day 1 post-redecoration, and I should say that I only finished all the putting away and tidying up just under an hour ago (the black chap was here again – and I know his name now!), but I've noticed I'm holding on to the order in this room as if it was a walking stick I'd carved myself. It's still not completely finished, though, because the stuff in the one and only display cabinet – knick-knacks, as my mother calls them – is really confusing me. I'll probably have to chuck out all the vases and little cups and boxes and figurines. Together they all feel like a foreign body. I'm still savouring this feeling at the moment. It's a totally new experience for me to mingle with the orderly things in my room, and to have something there that's such a complete contrast. You can see much more clearly how compatible you are with other things when there's something there that disturbs the harmony. In my mind you're always here too, I don't just see you when I close my eyes. You fit so well in this reclaimed room that you don't even have to come here to prove it. I'm in the process of setting myself up here with you, without you. Thank you for the order you've given my life.

Your melancholic mobile mum's-the-word-Malyutka

Helene looks around her plain, functionally decorated room. The walls and the carpet are mint green, the chairs stained a reddish-brown with green upholstered seats, and there are beige-coloured cupboards, bed and table. Until now she'd only been able to see everything individually, with no appreciation left over for the whole. Suddenly she feels as if she herself is the foreign body in this honest, straight-lined set-up, just like the knick-knacks in the terracotta room Malyutka had described. She hasn't brushed her hair, she's wearing baggy tracksuit bottoms and an ugly green jumper with a red print, her slippers have seen better days, and she could really do with someone cutting her nails, she thinks, because it's a long time since they were last done. Her toenails especially. She even takes her right shoe off now to have a look, and they're very long and splitting in places. Good job she's not wearing thin tights – she's got some thick socks on that she knitted herself. She often knitted socks *before* – it was what she did when the news was on, and even on the rare evenings in front of the telly she'd sometimes reached for her needles if there was no ironing to be done. For Malyutka, hadn't she even...? Yes! She'd sent her a parcel of wool socks. It must have been before the redecorating project, because it was during the preparations for it that she'd cleared out her supply of men's socks. They were all size 9, made for her father, father-in-law, friends – there'd been thirteen pairs in all! She can see herself packaging everything up. There was a large venison salami, which Malyutka was so fond of, from the organic farm in Krummensee, along with a jar of grape jelly which, not having a sweet tooth, she probably didn't like so much. And – she'd packed a floppy disk in the parcel, too. It had been one of the real angora rabbit disks with the red dot. She'd needed so much parcel tape that even now her arms grow heavy thinking about it: she'd tirelessly unwound roll after roll, as if she wanted to pack up absolutely everything to do with Malyutka so tightly that it could never get out again. It had made her feel really quite lightheaded, and when the parcel had been handed over at the post office she'd had to stop outside the door for a moment to inhale deeply and catch her breath. She'd then gone to Matthes's work – something she'd hardly ever done in the past ten years, and then only when expressly invited or arranged in advance. She'd wanted to see him, to see what he looked like when he wasn't expecting her. Matthes wasn't there – he was gadding about having some meeting or other, followed by a home visit – and she'd thought back almost wistfully to the time when they'd still tell each other every morning what they had on that day, what was on the agenda. In the past few years, and especially since living on Arberstrasse, this communication had gradually slowed to a trickle, until it had completely dried up like milk from an ageing udder. Yes, she'd been seeking to resuscitate something, wanting to drag the Matthes-ship out of the mud, without being hampered by Malyutka in the process. With Malyutka everything was so new, so vibrant, so unentrenched, that Helene could only think wistfully of how ravishing Matthes had been all that time ago, and how entrancing, beguiling, blissful, bewitching, spell-binding had been almost every moment they spent together. After that March night with Malyutka, as she increasingly sought to surrender herself completely and unconditionally to Matthes all over again, the further he'd moved away from her, in thrall to doubt. He'd drifted so far from her that in mid-April, two days before a couple of females met in that Charlottenburg café, he'd moved into his study and heaved Frau Wierbel's cupboard up via the balcony. Remembering this now, the crying comes back to her too – at the time it'd felt like it would never stop, and led to her shutting herself away in her room. It's no clearer to her today than it was then whether she was crying over the Matthes-ship apparently going down in the quagmire of time, or over the distance between her and Malyutka despite them only living thirty miles apart. Two days later she'd gone to

Charlottenburg with a steely resolve she wouldn't be able to get back now. Yes: she'd wanted to put her relationship with Malyutka on hold, in order to possibly relaunch her relationship with Matthes, but she hadn't been able to find the right words to do it. The fact that this had happened to her *then* actually creates an island of reassurance *now* in her flustered thinking. Everything there that might have turned into a thought is flapping around like a swarm of bats at dusk, but there she stands in the middle of it all, almost stoical, and amazed that words had sometimes failed her before. She who never ran out of words. Who'd bathed in words like Matthes had in work. That's so comforting... She'd never before found herself in such a state of... mental disintegration? that was capable of defying a significant part of her. What's God up to, sticking the unfathomable so close to the obvious that you can hardly tell them apart?

06.05.2002   17:50

My dearest heart heedless little halberd Helene,

Still: it's you. You must have eaten a big bowlful of codswallop when you said you wanted me to forget the things you yourself would like to forget. Believe me, I think you'll find that's completely unnecessary. It's May, the month of love, when legend has it that it's rutting season for the boys and all the girls run around with their breasts on show. When I look out of my building here all I can see are high-necked, pastel-coloured lady pensioners – 'older people', as they're called now – and only a few have a young man in tow. That's down to the area I'm in, I know – I was shipped out here by the housing office when I got my council flat. But I feel older here than I actually am, and that's a good thing. I think about the end more often. But a nice one! As if to confirm all this, I had a visit this morning – from my sons... For their eighteenth birthday I sent them their very first shoes, which I'd always kept with me, and invited them to go out to a play, concert or pub of their choice with me. And lo and behold, they turned up at my door. Oh, it was lovely! They were shy at first, but then opened up to me quicker than I ever could have hoped, even in my wildest dreams. They talked and talked and talked, as if they feel the need to reinvent their childhood now that they're adults. They're two handsome lads: tall and slim, with chin-length curly hair and glasses. Tim is long-sighted and Tom short-sighted. Isn't that strange? When they're as alike as two peas in a pod? Can you imagine how surprised and almost reverential they were when they saw my freshly-painted, neat and tidy living room! Maybe they thought it always looks like that, haha! Naturally I didn't tell them the truth – my love as a father doesn't go that far. A father's love... Oh dear, I probably wouldn't be able to say the words out loud, and can only write them with great difficulty, but in this case they're more fitting than the motherly kind, aren't they? No idea... Motherly love... Motherly love... I doubt I'd even be able to utter those words, either, in relation to myself. Isn't there a singular, sexless form – parental love? On the other hand, I'm not a singular sexless thing! Even if I act like one often enough, as well you know, so that the whispering and funny looks don't get to me too much... Since I'm living in the here and now, I've decided simply to be a mother with a father's love. Everything else is behind me, and that's that. They refer to me as Viola, but call me Father when addressing me directly, and actually that somehow makes sense to me too. Oh Helene, I'm completely drunk – and not a drop of alcohol in sight! – on the prospect of having my sons around me into my old age, and being able to spoil them a bit! My legs are like jelly and my heart's a-flutter! This past year has really been good to me – it's as if you had my sons in tow when I met you. Do you think I'd have sent them the shoes if you hadn't encouraged me to? My last memento, the thing I never wanted to give away but now might actually get back a thousand times over if I don't cock it all up. It's you, Helene, and it's my sons – and I'd even trust myself to be able to let go of you now, because you've immortalised yourself in me and will never get out again anyway. It's a lovely feeling: I imagine you crouched inside me, above my stomach, and so – as I rediscover the boys, taking their heads to my breast – I know you can feel them too, and can relieve me of this father-mother-love thing, just like that, and deduce from my heartbeat how happy I am. And now I'm going to open a bottle of wine, I should have some cheap red left somewhere. As to the rest, you know now what you've set in motion, and I'll give you your peace as you gave me mine.

Your may-you-be-happy-Malyutka

It's coming, it's coming.

'Still, it's you!'

The shout echoes in her ears. Malyutka had bellowed it after Helene as she left, and not just once, oh no: she'd gone berserk, standing up, flinging her arm around in the air and shouting over and over again. On that morning it was something Helene really hadn't wanted to hear at all. She'd considered it an unsuccessful morning, because she'd ditched Malyutka after a vigorous dispute. What a spectacle they must've made! Spiky Malyutka, hopping mad, had insisted on banging her fist on the table several times. This had been like running the gauntlet for the good-natured Helene, for all that there were only a few people in the café. She'd wanted to say to Malyutka that they should finally stop their correspondence until Helene had found a solution, whether with or without Matthes. From Malyutka's direction, more scornful than necessary, rang out 'Helene! Helene! Helene! Only ever Helene! Helene! Goodness knows what old pile of crazy they dragged you out of! I'm not as stupid as Isaac's black pig!' She'd flown into such a rage that she hadn't noticed how much her words contradicted her earlier plea for Helene's mercy, Helene's goodwill, Helene's generous donations of time, when all she'd wanted was to make herself small and wait in the undergrowth for her benefactress to show up every once in a while. Alarmed, Helene had gathered up her shrunken, crumbled courage and held Malyutka's hands tightly. She'd wanted to look into her eyes, which were flickering with a feverish brightness. Like kindling, she'd thought, and had made increasingly ambitious attempts to calm Malyutka down. They'd ended up almost wrapped around each other, to the point that the staff were wavering on the verge of intervening, when Helene finally got up and left. She snatched up her bag and coat, jumped up and ran off – and now she remembers what Malyutka's shout of defiance, the 'Still, it's you!', referred to. Helene had wanted to say to her that she wasn't a *good catch* at all, given the state she was in. That she wasn't getting anywhere with Matthes, but couldn't get anything done without him either; that he was retreating further and further from her the more she flew madly towards him. That she couldn't say why she clung to Matthes, while also hankering after Malyutka... Malyutka had tantalized her. Excited her. She'd let herself be tantalized. Excited. Helene in turn had beguiled Malyutka, bewitched her. Temptation rained down from cloudless skies whenever they met, as Helene knew only too well.

Yet she'd always considered herself to be secured by double, even triple ropes, whenever the sky was so clear: Malyutka had broad shoulders, and Matthes's height and long arms covered the second and third safety points. She'd revelled in his particular kind of protection until it'd grown around her like a shell. But she could no longer move about freely in it. She'd probably been thrashing about in the shell for a long time, unable to break free. To do so she had to break herself down and then leak out, taking all her particles with her.

For a moment it almost seems as if she's actually found herself in this laborious reconstruction phase. The idea is just starting to fascinate her when it, too, is dismantled, bringing her back to Malyutka.

No, she wasn't at all the lady Malyutka had dressed her up as in her head. Maybe during their prolonged email exchange, in that virtual space, they'd proceeded to pin on each other all the qualities they were so eager to perceive. Helene had prescribed Malyutka everything she lacked in the Matthes-ship, and Malyutka hadn't had a solid relationship for so long that it was a simple matter for her to endow Helene with every conceivable feature of someone passionately loved. But she was missing arrogance, patience, generosity, stoicism, fore- and hindsight, and Malyutka's threat of saintly patience, stinking of servility, had really got to her... Temptation had had to serve for long enough as a trial-run for dealing with Matthes! Now she wanted to pass this test, and how she'd emerge from it was a secondary issue.

It *wasn't* her, she'd thought, as she'd fled to the S-Bahn with her tongue hanging out.

No, not her.

◆ ◆ ◆

A blood test, after all. The nurse can't find a vein so jabs the canula into the crook of her arm at random. Although Helene has specified 'right in the middle' as the place she'd probably have most success, the woman pokes around at either side. It's painful, and she nearly faints. In the end the nurse gives up and fetches a young junior doctor, who gets to work with great calmness and composure. The veins are actually widening of their own accord for him, Helene thinks, and for a second believes she's sent an impulse through her body making them do just that. At that moment he does in fact find the right place, and it's exactly where Helene had indicated. Satisfaction for her as much as for the doctor. While the thick blood flows into the little tube, she suddenly informs him in an off-hand way that she's stopped taking the Ergenyl chrono, reducing it gradually. She smiles at him. It's clear from his questioning that he knows nothing about it, of course.

'Ergenyl chrono?'

It's not just his look that's questioning, his voice is too.

She needs to think how best to explain it to him. She's terrified of talking for any longer: she knows she can only see one or two sentences ahead, before inevitably coming to a standstill so she can consciously anticipate one or two sentences again. If she had better control over her speech tempo and could speak more slowly, it's possible no one would notice, she thinks. But she still wants to chatter away freely like she used to, so she ends up stumbling heavily, and not just in the physical act of speaking. It's true that she'd also, on occasion, been considered a woman of very few words. On those occasions she'd always found it difficult speaking in bigger groups, if what she had to say seemed to her to be repetition of well-trodden facts at best, and would only start to speak if a thought she deemed fresh and new appeared in her head. On top of that, she was thought of as a harmoniser in group interactions, and good at summarising and clarifying, and she'd often been flummoxed by how frequently other members of the group would repeat themselves, clearly without realising. Over the years, she'd realised that *her* perception of the way other people spoke was different to their own: she would structure their speech, her unconscious placing it in bigger contexts, and so stay silent until a junction revealed itself and something new became possible.

But there'd also been very intimate, private moments too, when she'd really let rip. Then it had been a breeze for her to speak in impromptu rhymes that scanned perfectly, or deliver a non-stop stream of jokes, and in her head she could "read aloud" words and whole sentences back to front: *dekil ehs sa ynam sa*. This had won her admiration, and at first she couldn't work out why – being able to do it had just seemed so natural to her.

She couldn't do any of those things now.

(She sometimes reassured herself in a whisper that a brain like hers first had to get over the shock of being cut up, and only much, much later would she find out what functions were hiding among the essential ones, which it's definitely ready to resume. And one fine day these functions might stretch lazily, and come to the fore...)

The doctor seems to sense her thoughts moving through this obstacle course, and offers up:

'Do you have epilepsy? Ergenyl is tolerated pretty well in most cases – what are you taking instead?'

'Nothing,' she replies gratefully and straight out, without thinking. The doctor has understood and doesn't say anything. Is it possible he thinks she's not compos mentis? She can see the cogs turning in his head. She's allowed to open her hand and he undoes the tourniquet and pulls out the canula, but says nothing more.

In the afternoon she's asked to go and see the ward managers. Three doctors and two nurses have assembled. The conversation is as loaded as the one that took place when she'd opted out of psychology. She Can't Just Do That. It's Not Allowed. What's Prescribed Is Prescribed. They Had All Thought It Through. She Must Step Back. *They* Bear The Responsibility. Not Helene.

'What, I don't bear any responsibility?'

They're taken aback by that, by the angry surge in tone from the – until now – pathetically silent Helene. Feeling the worry homing in on her, she wonders whether the doctors saw the spit bubbles forming around her mouth while she was saying this one sentence. She looks at them, but nothing on their faces indicates that they did. It's possible the bubbles burst so quickly that no one noticed. How would she feel, if someone she was talking to had spit bubbles round their mouth? She probably wouldn't even notice them either. The worry now clears as quickly as it appeared. That's new. She'd like to learn more about how she appears to other people. Do they perceive her to be mentally impaired? Disabled? She wouldn't be surprised, because she so often can't control her initial reactions, and still gets excessively annoyed by all her spontaneous grins, smiles and grimaces, and the yesyes-ing and nono-ing...

And straight away the worry is back.

Helene realises she hasn't been listening to the doctors' responses at all. The worry is instantly redoubled. She's a cart that's come unhitched, unable to find its way without the horse. Even the "wheels" can't seem to agree on a course: she feels as if her arms and legs are in constant conflict. The worry increases threefold.

'Have you thought about having the healthcare proxy assessment, Frau Wesendahl? Your husband could be appointed your carer, for example, then you wouldn't have to worry about anything else...'

Now what are they on about! She's no longer listening to any of it – it's getting too much for her now. Capacity, she thinks – she'd wanted to talk to Matthes about her mental capacity, and not about a... healthcare proxy assessment? She doesn't want to know, and shoves the topic into a waiting drawer for now. Drawer closed. Done.

The mood suddenly changes. They're turning friendly, the whole lot of them! Where's that coming from, then? Her doubting expression turns to one of distrust. Watch out, says her gut: there's something starting to stir in the bushes. Something you can't see, but that'll give you bad stomach pains if you're not careful. What is it, though?

There was smoked fish for supper today. Now Helene's got bad stomach pains. She can mostly feel them higher up – a familiar tightness that hasn't bothered her since she was pregnant with Lottchen. Her gall bladder. Nice to know *it's* still there too, she thinks scornfully, then grimaces in pain. Damn. As if everything her body's been through in the past few months somehow isn't enough for her gall bladder! She presses on it, massaging the area, but the pain literally flees to inaccessible areas before her very fingers, and gets stronger. Now it's busying itself in her back.

But hasn't the gall bladder had enough? It's certainly had enough of the fish – it's reacted to it, and is now in the process of developing colic!

What kind of word is *enough*?

As if it isn't enough? But it's had enough?

She questions whether she's dealing with one and the same word here. Her understanding is tying itself in knots, wanting to reject such assaults on it. It's just like with the double negatives, thinks Helene. And it's awful! She really can't prise them apart! Her gall bladder has had enough of the fish, she understands that bit, but *what's not* enough for it? Nice and slowly. One more time. And again. What has happened to her body in the past few months somehow isn't enough for her gall bladder – it has to stick its oar in too. But why *as if* it's not enough? No, it's getting to be too much for her. She doesn't want to deal with it and pushes it away. And just as she's packing it into one drawer, another drawer next to it pops open a tiny bit.

Healthcare proxy assessment.

She freezes.

When they were still living on Feldberger Ring, an old lady next-door to them had started a similar process, at her own request. Dementia was breathing down her neck and she was forgetting so much. She'd had such lovely lucid moments that Helene would gladly go and have an afternoon coffee in the kitchen with her. The distant past was deeply ingrained, yet she often couldn't remember which of her three doors led to the toilet, or where she'd put the milk, or that she hadn't put any stockings on even though it was hardly warm. In one of these moments she'd talked to Helene about wanting to have herself *incapacitated* so that she wouldn't get up to any mischief when the light left her, and she'd asked Helene to help her begin the necessary steps. In unified Germany, though, this process hadn't existed since the early nineties. It had been replaced by the care proxy order, which was established through a legal process. Because it was being done at Frau Schwörer's own request, a statement from her family doctor was all that was needed. If it had been someone else wanting to initiate the process, however, then she'd have undergone a thorough assessment. Helene unfreezes a little – if she was assessed by experts, she's pretty sure it wouldn't result in a care proxy order. That would be no different to actual *incapacitation* for her, frankly. But even so, it's made her uncertain. She's trembling, but that's probably the pain. So she rings for the nurse – she really needs something for this colic now before she's steamrollered by it.

Biliary colic? It could of course be any number of things, reckons the nurse. Helene knows these attacks, though! She knows what they feel like! Straight away she becomes despondent. Maybe she's been *incapacitated* for a long time without realising it. The nurses' behaviour sometimes seems to imply as much, anyway. No, she's going to insist on getting a suppository for her colic, but the nurse just says it's pretty reckless of someone not to take medication that's been prescribed to them, then demand something else. It's not self-service here, you know! Nothing gets issued here without a doctor having a look first! The door clicks shut and she's gone.

Helene has been lying there in a pain trance for a long time when a doctor finally appears and wants to examine her, but she doesn't understand exactly what he's saying or what he's asking. At least he's not one of the ones who gave her a hard time this afternoon over the antiepileptics. Maybe he's come from elsewhere, and is only on emergency call here? In the end he gives her an injection, and a few minutes later Helene feels liberating relief. Now she'd be willing and able to answer his questions – but of course he's long gone.

She turns on to her side, feeling weakened.

They've actually talked to Matthes about a possible care proxy assessment! She can't understand it. She's still a woman in control of all her senses! She can see, hear, taste, feel, smell! She's still in the fight! Emerging from the coma-cocoon cost her most of her strength, she reckons, and there's everything that lies ahead to overcome. But it must be overcome! Whenever somebody wants to reach out a hand to help her, she's overly sensitive, attempting everything herself and flying into a rage if she has to admit she can't do this or that, and perhaps never will again. Playing the piano, for example. Is that why she's pretty much tuned out music? Apart from Bengt's oboe, she hasn't let near her any of the stuff that Matthes and the kids have brought in – CDs and a portable CD player, cassettes and an ancient Walkman. Piano music? It used to be her favourite accompaniment whenever she needed some background noise – whether she was driving, or hanging out washing, or getting ready to write,. Now she prefers quiet in her head. It's a relief. A consolation, and yet oddly no comfort. What's the difference between comfort and consolation, anyway? A consolation, she reflects, is for her a momentary thing, whereas a comfort is lasting. Yes, something like that. She has to make sure of words over and over again, but whether what she thinks is correct, she just can't be sure. Or not sure enough, she thinks. That makes her hopping mad, too. On top of this she finds that she's watching people more closely than before, and often enough succumbs to the paranoid-seeming idea that everything they point to, or say, or think, is about her. Her condition. Her disability. She finds it downright *neurotic*. Not that she can think of a definition for neurosis, but the word can be used without a definition, too. She needs to rediscover some certainty when using words, and not stop herself from doing so just because their meaning suddenly seems unclear when she's about to say them out loud. And to be able to speak again without having to think about it! Granted, she can't do that, but it's not as if her perception of things is up for discussion. She can still form opinions, even if she needs a lot longer to do that, too, than she did before. What did Matthes say? 'You've just finally turned into a normal person at last...' If that was true, maybe she didn't actually need much longer than other people to form an opinion. But *was* it really true? All the yardsticks she usually measures by have gone down the drain, and she just can't gauge whether she thinks too slowly or fast enough. Before, she'd always known that she ran too slowly. It had been fast enough for her, even if it never got her a decent mark in PE, because she also knew that she was mostly a little way ahead of the others when it came to reasoning. *If you can run fast, you don't need to think fast (and vice versa)*. She had constantly consoled herself for her low running marks with this saying, even though she suddenly realises it actually means amazingly little – nothing at all, really. Now she'd get no marks at all for running, and it's touch and go with her reasoning. That eats away at her, so that the thought of the care proxy assessment comes back and everything else falls by the wayside. Matthes had rejected the idea, saying that *his wife* was legally competent and in full command of her mental faculties, and certainly not a candidate for a care proxy assessment. That's how he'd presented it to her, anyway, and Helene knows he's speaking the truth – she can see it in his eyes, in the wrinkles in his face, in the position of his ears. (She can't lay claim to 'full command', mind, but no one needs to know that.) He'd got really angry that they could take a stand against her in such an underhand way, as he called it, over medication she hadn't taken. No one here would think of incapacitating (yes, he'd used that word too) any other person in Helene's situation. It really was the absolute limit! *He* could see that she was very much with it! Helene had gone red first, then pale, and plastered on the biggest grin she could manage. That was yesterday afternoon. Today Matthes has a meeting and can't come.

Unusual for him.

Nice for her, Helene thinks.

It's as if there's a flower growing behind the hedge that some person can't see, but they know for a fact that it's there and stretching its petals towards the sun. She has no idea who's the flower and who's the guy on the other side of the hedge, but that doesn't matter. This idea doesn't seem to be quite so meaningless as the one about fast running and slow thinking (and vice versa). Having a thought like this makes her chest swell with just a little bit of pride.

◆ ◆ ◆

Silence intersects with darkness and out of it comes a moth, sitting in one of the curtain folds. Helene is surprised because it's not really butterfly season. The moth doesn't fly and simply stays quietly in its spot. She immediately wants to read all about moths: their classification, when they breed, what they feed on. Then she'd know more about the little creature which currently seems so strangely transplanted from summer into autumn. A belated greeting from this year's summer, which has passed her by? Maybe it's from Malyutka, she thinks. Around five times a day Helene likes to think Malyutka's looking down on her from heaven. When her great grandmother was still alive she'd talked constantly to the young Helene about residing in heaven after death. It had become so natural to Helene that, after the old woman died, she'd made a daily effort to catch a glimpse of her apron whenever she looked up at the sky. And it's stuck, because she often looks at the sky when she thinks of her still small number of dead relatives and acquaintances. In summer she regularly gets dazzled by the sun. Now it's a clear, starlit autumn night, and the stars are bothersome too, in their own way. There's no heavenly milk in which imagination lets the dead silently share in earthly developments.

She sighs.

Malyutka Malysch...

She plucks the floppy disk out of the drawer. After their last meeting in April, Malyutka had written to her precisely three more times. Helene had saved these three emails on another floppy disk with the obligatory red dot, keeping it safely in her cupboard, and now she remembers how, some days, she couldn't help drafting replies to them. She never sent them, always deleting them before she went to bed, so they'd disappeared off-stage in cyberspace. Where they belonged?

It would be too much.

It would be too little.

It would be a little too much, for example, in view of the impassioned effort she'd put into them. A hazy notion now resurfaces of the state she'd been in when writing to the Malyutka in her imagination, and this notion expands into images: her mood gauge had still been wobbly and unbalanced. It was as if the Matthes-ship was simply breaking up in some remote place that was completely inaccessible to her. Night after night she was now sleeping alone in a bed that was far too big, and night after night Matthes calmly wished her goodnight before he went up to his attic room. They didn't get nasty with each other, didn't fall out, and there were countless unspoken agreements concerning the children. Her image of Matthes became increasingly blurred, and she felt she still only knew very little about him – but then he hadn't known anything about *her* for a long time, nothing of her yearning for Malyutka, and its advances and retreats... It was as if the certainty that they held and possessed each other – a certainty that had grown imperceptibly over the long years – had turned into its opposite: they'd both withdrawn from each other, so to speak; each *decolonised* the other. But in doing so, were things disrupted by the set-up of a life still shared? Until that point they'd never seriously considered dismantling it. It wasn't laziness or lack of guts that kept them from changing or ending things. Rather, they saw themselves as somehow incapable of letting go, even for a moment, of the line they were using to lead each other, because they feared the disorientation which (undoubtedly, so they thought) would ensue. Yet the line had gone slack, and was no longer barely an arm's length as it had been in their first years together. Now, under normal conditions, it stretched from the double bed, over the stairs and up to Matthes's attic room, getting longer whenever either of them was away from the house. But they could always feel it: it was sacred to them, this shackle. It gave them a sense of security, and confidence, and was a mutual guarantee – without it, their existence could no longer be defined. Even Malyutka's fortress tower couldn't break it.

Where is it now, though, this line?

Helene pauses for a moment.

No, at the moment she can't feel it.

Could Matthes have cut it?

Had Malyutka yanked it away before she died?

Maybe it had just slipped off Helene's wrist! Her right hand always hung down so limply she must not have noticed. One day the useless paw probably just hadn't been able to bear its own uselessness any longer, and let the loop slide off. Yes, Helene decides, that's what will have happened.

She'll have to see how far she gets with that hypothesis.

October is coming to an end. Yesterday there was even a first shower of snow, but it didn't come to anything – the ground was far too warm for it to settle.

Helene has arranged to meet Matthes at the bus stop. They want to tackle the stretch to the market place and swap lunch in the cafeteria for a Chinese. She'll probably have to dig out a woolly hat, because when she opens the window the air is noticeably cooler than yesterday. She stands in front of the mirror with her rollator for a long time, looking at herself. Once again her appearance seems very strange to her, with her grey hair on the left and her swollen eyelids and fingers. She can't hide her fingers in her jacket pockets either – what a nuisance! – because of course she needs to hold on to her baby walker, as she calls it. Last week they'd started doing lymph drainage on her. For two or three hours afterwards there's an improvement and her fingers are not nearly so sausage-like. The cold seems to help, too, she finds: whenever she has spent longer outside, the swelling decreases a bit. She massages her right hand herself, lost in thought. She hasn't worn her silver ring since her operation – it's ended up in her purse, in a little bag. Quickly now, though: hat on, scarf round her neck. But she hasn't got any shoes on yet! She takes the hat off again crossly and loosens the scarf, because putting her shoes on always gets her in a sweat.

Ready at last.

She goes down in the lift – unexpectedly bumping into Peter Preissler, who looks past her stoically – and out of the clinic. She still hasn't said anything to Matthes about his former classmate. Had she not sensed any opportunity to divert his attention away from her? She doesn't pursue the thought for now.

She has to leave the clinic grounds on a marked footpath which crosses a vast carpark. She has a go at identifying makes of cars. There's a Toyota, a Renault, a Peugeot. Two Wartburgs. She thinks again of their first car, which they'd bought shortly after the Wall came down – it was in almost mint condition, and belonged to a well-to-do gentleman in Marzahn. He'd wanted to treat himself to a *Western car* in his old age. The car dealer had only offered him 700 Marks for the thing, though, so he'd chosen to sell it privately. Although the car was in very good repair and barely six months old, every time they drove to Thuringia it had conked out in the hills around Magdala. 'It's not something you get with every car, just this one!' That's what the mechanic two doors along from them had reckoned at the time, with a shrug. He actually ran a Wartburg garage, but even he couldn't do anything about the fact that the coolant would start to boil and make the engine overheat. If they let it have a rest in the carpark, which they only ever reached by the skin of their teeth, it then mostly ran fine until they got to the Thuringian Forest. She smiles at the memory.

Suddenly tyres screech and a car stops beside her, centimetres from her rollator. She's been daydreaming, and forgot or failed to notice in time that the footpath has come to an end at the road, which she has just ventured on to without looking. Her heart isn't beating any faster. It can't have been that bad, then, says a voice generator in her head – she can hear it very clearly, cutting in before her brain can engage – while the driver of the car gesticulates wildly and winds down the window to shout at her. But she carries on her way, smiling – let him think she's a bit simple and he'll give up sooner, she reckons. He does indeed wind his window back up, shaking his head, and Helene sees him turn to his female passenger, pull a face and roll his eyes. Ha, it worked! She feels happy all over. Previously, a situation like that would've put her in such a panic that she wouldn't have known where to turn first, apologising profusely and probably offering to buy the driver a coffee as compensation for the shock she'd given him. But she'd have ended up handing over some smaller amount of money – because having coffee with her was the last thing in the world he'd want to do – and all in all made quite sure he could go away feeling like the real victor. No, previously she wouldn't have been at all happy. Where has such an obvious change of heart and behaviour come from? Anyway, she's really pleased with herself.

At the bus stop there's a young teenage couple. The girl is thirteen at most, the boy a year or two older, and they're clutching each other and snogging like there's no tomorrow. In the bus shelter two thin old ladies, in their classic dusky pink coats, are talking about a bus trip they're hoping to make in the next few weeks – to Szczecin, over the border in Poland – and Helene sits down next to them on the bench. One of the women looks at her pityingly, while the other one tries not to look at all. The fact that she's still an odd spectacle for other people is something Helene forgets time and again. It can't be all that bad, because she's got the scar on her head hidden under her hat, but these two skinny old birds are probably still nimble on their feet, and can't imagine not being so. Now, though, she notices the spit that's collected round her mouth, and can better understand their reaction.

It's been eight days since Matthes refused to waste even a moment thinking about a care proxy assessment. In the meantime the ward doctor had turned to the specialist epilepsy centre in Berlin for advice, describing Helene's case to a learned professor. He couldn't exactly endorse winding down the anti-epileptics in favour of some homeopathic magic pills, but seems to have advised moderation. A consensus was put to her: that the clinic will accept that Helene is currently not taking any medication to prevent further, *highly likely* seizures, and she will agree in return to seek prompt medical treatment should the symptoms reappear. She feels so strangely certain that she'll never be troubled by such attacks again that she agreed to it straight away. Yesterday she'd also signed the form forbidding her from driving, mountain climbing and swimming unaccompanied *for the foreseeable future*. That wasn't so hard, because she can't drive one-handed anyway, she's never climbed a mountain, and the only swimming pool near Karlshorst closed early in the summer and hasn't reopened yet, according to Mareile – she has to go all the way to Mitte to go swimming. Helene pictures her daughter in a swimming costume. A year ago, three or four rolls of fat bulged around her stomach, but now, with her slender waist, she's dazzling. Her legs are still stumpy, though, and her calves merge with her feet with no noticeable thinning at the ankles. Just like Helene's legs. What slim ankles Malyutka Malysch had had, though – if only she could've brought herself to wear shorter skirts!

But what's she even thinking... Malyutka's dead, and her skirts have been *cleared out* with all the rest of her things. Her sons took care of that. They'd probably – no, definitely! – had a good sort through their fathermother's possessions in the flat before getting rid of them. Helene had never been there – Malyutka had persisted in making a secret of it. As always when thinking about Viola Malyutka Malysch, she has to wipe tears from the corners of her eyes. There was as much left unsaid between them as had been spoken aloud, she realises. The two things are equally weighted and balance each other out. Maybe it was also a question of balance that day in Charlottenburg, when she'd given Malyutka her marching orders by marching off herself? *To give someone their marching orders*... Does that mean urging them to go? Permitting it? But she'd never forbidden Malyutka from striking out! Hadn't Helene said many times in her emails that nothing would make her happier than to see Malyutka in a relationship? And with someone in a position to get closer to her than Helene ever could?

The bus pulls up and Matthes gets off. He's wearing a checked flat cap, in which he always reminds her of Sherlock Holmes. His way of seeing things is distinctly un-detective-like, however, whereas he always claimed that she had *second sight*. She could sniff out that people were related to each other merely from the way they blinked. She had an infallible eye for spotting facial similarities in people and an incredible memory for names and faces, plus she could make inferences with lightning speed, so that when it really mattered she could always orient herself much faster than Matthes, and in a different way.

Whether that's still the case, she doesn't know.

Matthes hugs her tightly.

She had an awful fall on the way to the market place. Now they're sitting in the Chinese and Matthes is rubbing her ankle, which is steadily swelling up. She went over on it more heavily than she ever has before, falling straight away and landing smack down on the gravel path. To begin with she just lay there bawling her eyes out. The pain was almost unbearable. In between she had to laugh, baring her teeth and blethering on sarcastically about the little things that happen along the way, just so Matthes wouldn't take it too seriously. But Matthes took it very seriously, as was his way, giving an explosive command to a passer-by to help him get his wife up – my God, she really is *his wife*! – and on to the seat of the rollator. Sitting like that he'd pushed her here and into the warm, where he'd taken off her right shoe and sock and asked the waitress for a cold cloth. Helene is finding it all pretty unpleasant, but she knows it's pointless trying to stop her husband – my God, he really is *her husband*! – showing off his skills as an emergency first aider.

'Hadn't we better order?'

She's hungry, and looking forward to spring rolls – she likes to get them so she can see what the cooking is like before the main course comes. When they arrive they're hot but very greasy, and only roughly cobbled together. Now she knows what to expect. Matthes doesn't have any spring rolls on his plate, of course. He only ever orders once she's ordered herself, and then it's usually only something small, even when she's ordered several courses. She calls it stinginess, he calls it *not being hungry*, though she's pretty sure he'd be tucking in with equal abandon if they were at home. He savours each morsel like a gourmet, and acts as if the tiniest taste exhausts his appetite. That's usually the point when she regrets having come out to eat with him at all. He's lanky – a weed next to her. It's not nice to expose yourself to looks from the staff, who see a fat woman and a thin man together at a table. The thin man hardly eats anything while the fat woman really sticks it away. That this exact scenario played out every time never failed to upset her all over again – though she'd only have had to activate her memory of the previous restaurant visit to see precisely this course of events coming! Today, though, it doesn't put her off stuffing herself. She sees him sip his hot and sour soup. No thought of reproach. Again, it's that change of heart and behaviour. Or is it to do with the line being cut, which they'd used to keep each other in check?

Matthes finishes eating before her, so she listens as he talks. Billy did well in an important maths exam, and Lissy has caused water damage in her flat. Is it bad that Helene's pleased about the maths exam, but equally pleased that being out here, she doesn't have to have anything to do with the water damage? She starts pondering this and stops listening to Matthes. Capacity! she thinks. She goes off down winding paths and, in doing so, gets to examine him in depth. She hears his voice as if from far away. It murmurs. It burbles.

Helene chokes on her food.

At the very moment that she regurgitates the bit of meat, she remembers something: Matthes, beside himself with anger, had shouted 'No sentimentals!' when they'd – had they actually? – split up. A roughly-cut film, shot in screaming technicolour, is being shown while she's trying to eat. In the end she can't manage another bite. Matthes pays. They trudge to the optician, with her sitting on the seat of the rollator and him pushing her along. Her glasses are ready and have been for a while, but the film apparently isn't over yet. Even when she puts on the unfamiliar *optical aid*, and should really be looking at the world through new eyes, instead of the pettiness of Heidemühlen all she can see is the film. Matthes notices something going on but refrains from asking about it. Instead he ferries her back to the clinic. By this point her foot has achieved lump-like proportions. By tomorrow it'll be dithering between red and blue, and there'll be a while to wait before it turns green, yellow and brown, and finally in shape and colour starts to look once more like the foot she'd put into her shoe that morning. That doesn't bother her.

She watches the film.

The new glasses bring things a good bit closer, making them clear again. She really hasn't been seeing properly at all, she thinks, when she's finally sitting in her room with Matthes behind her, on the sidelines, in the faraway darkness. She looks out of the window at the sky. Clouds are scudding across it, and it fascinates her that she can see the fine shading in the grey again, and the swirling and eddying of the wind. Suddenly she feels lips on her neck – 'Take care, my love,' – and hears the door closing. She hasn't said anything, didn't say goodbye. Instead she investigates his words further. Did he say it with a *capital* L or a *small* L? Is she his 'Love' or 'Helene, love'? Does it make a difference? And if so, what? His 'Love'... Earlier, in the film, she'd seen him small and filled with remorse. It was the beginning of July – she'd taken Lottchen to kindergarten and he'd taken a day off to do admin. In the few weeks beforehand, everything she'd wanted had withered in her hands. That's why she'd asked him to take some time off, just a day or two, when they could drive out into the blue yonder that awaited them in the deep, fresh greenness surrounding the city. This blue yonder was charged with her desire for Matthes to seek out and find a sunny spot in the woods, where he would undress her like he used to and they'd make love. The sweat on their skin would glisten in the sun, and she would run her fingers through it and write his name. Matthes did indeed take some time off, but the green blue yonder held no attraction for him. He came down to the kitchen from his room and sat at the table. His hands were folded in front of him and he was as taut as a violin string: she sensed he would chime at the slightest touch, though she couldn't have predicted whether the sound would be agreeable, either to him or to her. So she didn't touch him, even though both her hands twitched constantly with the desire to do so – to touch his forearms, his knotted-together hands. So she had talked about random things (she can't remember what) and watched him – how the random things started to make him angry, making his eyes flicker; how he pressed his hands together until, in the end, they went white; how his teeth seemed to be clenched together so tightly that she wondered whether they'd ever come apart again. Something like that, anyway. But all the while her rational mind was standing next to her, alert and watching them both but unable to interrupt the flow of random things coming out of her mouth. And of course Matthes saw how hard it was for her to cope with no touching, and how hard it was for him to be subjected to those random things coming out of her mouth. He probably felt like just getting down to business, ripping her clothes off and fucking her in the kitchen right there and then, until everything went black and they no longer had to be subjected to the green in the blue yonder. (Yes, that's what Helene thinks now.) But her skin had grown old and ashamed of itself, hanging down so loosely from either side of her stomach, despite the flab; and so pinched and creased from having babies, from her breasts right down to her bits. Those babies were now ravishing – as she had been, once. Matthes's back, bent with age, wouldn't be able to make a bow – but she'd be as pleased as ever to meet it, and would knead it while his penis stood stiffly on guard inside her: alert, listening. And so, completely self-absorbed, they'd passed the minutes not really aware of each other – each staring at their respective goals and totally oblivious of the fact that they were both staring at the same point: their oneness as a couple, without a line, and without either of them taking up occupancy in the other. Although probably neither of them could say what was going on in that moment, they'd definitely felt it was something that should determine their life together. The whole year, reduced to the single minute when the verdict was reached, lay doubled up between them on the table, until Matthes lifted it up and let it fall with a great 'Ohhh!' At which point she caught it, and tried to give it some air again so it could breathe. 'No sentimentals!' he'd shouted suddenly, turning around once more when he was already standing on the stairs to go back up. That for her was the 'Ohhh' becoming an 'Over'. The year couldn't be saved, and she grew sad whenever she looked at it in those few weeks she had left before her aneurysm, because it had hung like a dead thing from the hook of that day. And the days were dying, and becoming part of this unsalvageable year, which of course didn't breathe any more life into it.

They had nevertheless driven to Pietro's birthday party the following day.

Since yesterday she has had that song in her head again, the one in Thuringian dialect which talks about *sentimentals*. An ironic song. A professor comes across a hen that has a musical cluck and is all over it straight away, panting and slavering. He offers the hen's owner money, a Trabant (the song's got to be from the eighties) and whatever else might have aroused the average citizen's envy at the time. But the owner doesn't want to know, and chops the head off the *critter – no sentimentals!* – so he can have it *in his pot* come Sunday. Matthes used to use the phrase in jest if something came near him that didn't belong there. Billy, for example. Or the emotion caused by a beautiful photo which he didn't immediately dismiss as *kitsch*, but might do if someone tricked him into it. In general, he preferred to keep his views in semi-darkness – open to surmise, certainly, but always ambiguous, so that you ended up deep in speculation. Whenever someone spoke their mind loudly and unmistakeably, a dam seemed to break inside Matthes. He'd immediately get to work on the expressed view, as if he actually needed it in order to verify his own. Sometimes he'd practically demolish his opponent because of opinions voiced. As Helene got older, however, she came to know that this excessive rejection meant that he would arrive sooner or later at the very same view he'd just denigrated. In relation to herself, though, she expected – nothing. Matthes had stopped discussing things *with* her, perhaps deeming it unnecessary given the harmony between them – they'd made a big thing of it for years. When you take up residence in someone else's mind, you imagine yourself to be at home in the other person, and don't need to waste another word on the location of the door and windows, or the colour of the carpet and the sheets. But the belief that you're looking out of the window with the other person's eyes – or opening the door with their hand, or sweeping under the carpet the things you both want out of sight (to say nothing of the sheets) – is an illusion. To start with, you might be surprised that the other person keeps the door closed when you're about to open it yourself; or you feel deceived because the other person is picking at something you've just this minute managed to get under the carpet. Then later, for the sake of habit, you cease to even notice the other person, while they leap about on the line and forget how to see themselves as the centre of their own circle of activity. Its radius is determined by the other person anyway. They had both found themselves in this feigned state of certainty, and it was Malyutka who'd killed it off with the brittle charm that proved so dangerous to Helene. And her beguiling lack of definition, with a no less beguiling clarity in tow. She hadn't thrown herself eagerly into a relationship, but had in fact been taken over by it, and by Malyutka's unease – her *dilemma*, which Helene wanted to help her out of one way or another. Was that her helper syndrome? It has nothing to do with love, though, Helene thinks, and she had loved Malyutka. Not as a substitute for Matthes, but alongside him, independently of him, unconditionally. Matthes must have noticed, even if he perhaps wasn't aware of it. Had he been aware of it he could have acted decisively. *No sentimentals* had become a distress call in any situation Matthes found threatening. Threateningly unclear. And the most unsettling thing about it, Helene thinks now, is that back then she thought she had made her decision.

For the time being.

The wheelchair is back. The nurse has brought it up from the storeroom. Helene gets a brace on her right leg which should protect her from going over on it again. It's a leather sole with plastic splints coming out of it at the ankle on both sides. These end at calf-height in a white strap which is fastened round her leg. Why does she need to wear it if she's now back in the wheelchair again?

'For when you need to spend a penny,' says the nurse, and buggers off.

To piss, to wee, to pass water, to have to go. Some even call it spending a penny... Helene has to smile. Her foot isn't going to fit in a shoe, of course. It wouldn't at the moment even without the support, and later, when the swelling has hopefully gone down, she's going to have to cut open an old shoe if she wants to get anything on her feet. She'll ask Matthes to bring in her canvas pumps – she got them last year with the intention of going jogging regularly. (Matthes had laughed at the time, because unlike her he knew that no one goes jogging these days just in canvas pumps. Least of all when you're somewhat on the heavier side, because basically your weight then falls so unfavourably on the thin soles that pain is the result.)

The shoes really don't matter now, she thinks, seeing as she won't be going jogging ever again. She notes her satisfaction with this observation a moment after it appears, and is surprised that the pain fails to materialise. She's quickly got used to no longer being able to do this or that, and so matter-of-factly that she's already thinking about how to deal with things that are now useless to her.

She does things for her own satisfaction – she can't call it anything else.

She can hardly have satisfied Matthes in the last few years.

Malyutka did enough to yank Helene out of her structure.

If only I'd done enough for her, Helene thinks.

If Malyutka was happy towards the end, then she wants to be happy too. But she can only guess at how Malyutka spent her final weeks.

Can only let her rest.

And sleep.

There's a knock at the door and Raphael is standing in the room. Raphael, her good old friend! They rock in each other's arms for a while, and it's lovely. Raphael looks tanned even in autumn, though he never uses a sunbed. He puts it down to Arab ancestors he apparently has on his mother's side, many generations back. Nobody knows the exact details, but the saga has persisted. His mother's maiden name was Makaffreh, and a link to the infidel *kafirs* was quickly established. Helene actually sees a more obvious resemblance to the Irish name McCaffrey, but this had fallen on deaf ears... Raphael struggles bravely with recurring episodes of depression, and the fact that he's managed to saunter over here without a car from where he lives, an out-of-the-way location by Berlin standards, commands Helene's full respect. She says so, too.

Raphael is umming and ahing.

'Why are you umming and ahing, Raphael?'

'I'm leaving Germany, to go to Sweden.'

Raphael tells her how on his summer holiday in Sweden he'd met Lina. What comes next really reminds Helene of her story with Malyutka, which she hasn't told Raphael anything about. (Raphael is as much Matthes's friend as hers, and she won't let him be caught between conflicting loyalties.) Lina is a marine biologist and works at Lund University. She only caught his attention the third or fourth time he saw her - he'd already been there a week, holidaying in the little house next to hers with his granddaughter. But then the unthinkable happened, and with some force: he fell hopelessly in love. It's been four long months now – they've been alternating letters and weekend visits – and the whole time he's been wanting to share the news with Helene, to let her know something was brewing, but she'd done a runner. Happily she's resurfaced again, but now there's no time left to ask for her advice or support because he's simply decided to move to Lund. See how things go. He wants to keep hold of his flat for now. He's looking at Helene somewhat shyly, as if it might not be congenial to Helene – of all people – that he's out to ensnare happiness. It's extremely congenial to her, however! She really hadn't expected that at all! Raphael paired up and spoken for! It occurs to her that she'll probably never be able to dance again, but right now she would really have liked to dance with Raphael. She's a waltz girl while Raphael prefers the tango, so they'd probably have had difficulty coming to an agreement anyway, but still, it's a shame. 'Shall we go and get a coffee?'

They go. Raphael pushes Helene's wheelchair. He's already found out from Matthes that she needs it again. He's a real fusser, anyway, and it does him good to feel needed.

The cafeteria is heaving with residents and their visitors. They have difficulty finding somewhere to sit, so Raphael takes their cappuccino and hot chocolate out into the garden. Is it garden weather? Not really, but Helene has packed a rug in her wheelchair pouch, and if they lay it over their knees then it might be all right.

Raphael won't stop swooning over Lina. It doesn't occur to Helene to swoon over Malyutka.

Swoon... Why has she never thought of this warm word in relation to Malyutka?

Raphael's eyes, usually a sanctuary for never-ending weariness, are today displaying a submerged sparkle. It isn't noticeable straight away, but reveals itself whenever his gaze veers from side to side. His gaze veers from side to side quite often, as if he wants to let people share in his tale of good fortune. In fact he always speaks a little louder throughout than is good for him – Helene notices this and moves back a bit, so the high notes of the story don't jab her in the ears. Out here in the garden, though, there's little likelihood of anyone being able to partake in Raphael's joy. The wind absorbs the sound, and the few people sitting at the scattered tables are already focusing enough attention on each other. Helene lets him talk – he won't notice the odd hint of guilty conscience when she occasionally wanders off and away from the Lina swoon. Suddenly she perceives a new and unfamiliar tugging in her head – right where she believes the titanium clip to be, in fact. It makes her think of a strangely painless leg cramp which has shifted upwards, to her brain. It's getting better, she thinks soothingly; it's getting better... She imagines she might be feeling the reabsorption of residual blood that had leaked out; or the clip being noticeably covered in tissue which is fitting its shape and filling every nook and cranny. It's as if she is finally registering that this little scrap of metal belongs to her – as if she is *feeling* its existence. Common sense steps forward, saying that it's probably impossible to actually feel something like blood absorption, or a foreign body taking root. But she brushes that aside and is looking pleased when Raphael looks her right in the eye.

'Are you pleased with me?'

Of course she is. No, really. Absolutely. But doesn't he have any qualms about leaving his daughter and grandchild here, and his parents and friends? No, he doesn't. Plenty of things in Sweden remind him of the fallen GDR. You're not supposed to say that out loud but he's just going to say it anyway. Lots of things are free, like really good school meals for kids or entry to museums and zoos, and there's free provision of school books and equipment, and all children are educated together regardless of ability, and you can get professional qualifications while the government keeps paying your salary... Stop, stop, stop, Raphael. School meals in the GDR were neither good nor free, Helene wants to retort – you only stopped paying once you had three or more children. You also had to cough up for museums and zoos, even if it was nowhere near today's prices, and free provision of school books and equipment only applied in Berlin at best. All children were indeed taught together regardless of ability until they were fourteen, before being split into branches which led either to leaving school at sixteen, or on to A Levels. It wasn't always academic performance that determined who was allowed to continue, however – it was a pupil's social background, too. There had of course been qualifications you could do while working, that's true, but they never led to any career boost to speak of. Even people with money couldn't buy any more than anyone else unless they knew someone at the *Consumer Goods* source. Have you forgotten that, Raphael? But she doesn't say all this – it would be too exhausting. Besides, she doesn't want to discuss the fallen country with him anyway. Strange that her contrary, dissident friend, who'd put up with so much in the old days – being spied on, and banned from certain jobs – doesn't seem to see so clearly in retrospect what he didn't have back then. So Sweden isn't just Lina-land, it's also laden with Raphael's nostalgia for his childhood and youth.

They fall silent. Raphael's flushed cheeks look so wonderful against his brown complexion that Helene almost feels like

Lina now – that's how much she likes it.

◆ ◆ ◆

The days are faster than she is. She just can't seem to close in on a single one of them, and fall into bed feeling like she's got it over with. They always escape the moment she goes to sleep, so that when she wakes up she has to set about catching up with them. There's so much going on. Too much, she thinks – her brain is desperately chasing after its old self. It takes her a while to understand people. The comprehension gap probably only amounts to a few seconds, but she hasn't learnt to factor it in yet, and is horrified every time by the gaping void between the moment somebody speaks and the moment she's able to understand them. She'd rather panic than fall into a void like that, she thinks, but before panic can set in she has usually understood. Recently, and in secret, she has been trying to do some writing, remembering the enquiry she hadn't let become a contract. Texts destined for the walls of houses, or pavements or benches, have to be short – catching the eye of people going past with individual words, even. They also have to revolve around the *urban*, somehow becoming *urban structures* themselves. Strangely enough, she's not tempted to use the laptop. She uses her left hand, resulting in a writing pace that's in sync with the pace of her speech. Her first attempt:

the evening hovers, a quivering balloon,
over the town, in whose yards
prey rests, remembering
the enemy, sleep,

disguised as a tramp,
entangled in the jargon of the bottle...

It's not clear where all this came from, all she did was write –
it came into her head exactly like that, word for word. The
great strain of it has literally got right into her bones, which,
she realises now, are trembling uncontrollably. But as soon as
the next words come, the tension is released, and she has to
keep writing:

over the town
the cloudy barges
laden with swathes
of mist we've
abandoned

Helene thinks she can feel the taut sinew in her head again
now, and the clip securing it in place, and she gets warm, very
warm, as the cool text comes to her:

the cold silk of your lust
as it shuffles over the concrete
(the simple things in its wake:
love and snow)
is blue like the fish
that slips from my mouth

That's got nothing to do with towns or house walls now,
though. It's more of a... love poem?

She somehow hasn't noticed that someone has come into the
room. The female ward doctor looks nosily over her shoulder.

'You're managing pretty well there, aren't you, Frau Wesendahl? What are we writing, then?'

Helene doesn't answer.

She finds it impertinent, someone watching her like that.

Matthes brings the canvas pumps, and they do indeed have to cut open the right one. He gets some elastic out of his bag and sews it in so that the shoe doesn't slip off at the ankle. His care and attention once again leaves her speechless. When he pushes her down to the lake in her wheelchair, or they do a loop round the outside of the clinic, he hardly says anything, probably sensing that Helene herself doesn't want to say anything when he's walking behind her. She has no faith in her articulation if the person she's talking to can't see her mouth. But it's hard in any case to *exchange a word* with Matthes – they would first have to change the track they're travelling on. Helene tentatively suggests leaving the role of invalid behind. Matthes, though, is still as careful, as attentive, as kind as ever. Is he paternal? Yes, and at the same time that's what... *bothers* her. She can't communicate on an equal footing with a father. A father knows better than her, knows what's good for her – *Father is a tortoiseshell,* she thinks.

Sometimes, she thinks, words wash over her just like they did before.

Sometimes, she thinks, she has absolutely no idea what these words mean.

But she's thinking!

Father is notafather, she thinks. As she's pondering what this might mean, she remembers Matthes pouncing on her – the invalid! The damaged woman! – on her first visit to Arberstrasse after the aneurysm. How he'd made love to her with all the ruthlessness he had at his disposal: how he'd secured her, laid her bare and reclaimed her. Suddenly she sees what happened that day – though not the attack, the assault – in a very different light...

Things had turned frosty after the day of *sentimentals* in June. *Helene's List* hung in the kitchen, above the phone – an impossible-to-miss marker of the gulf between them. On this list she had written down what she intended to take with her when she moved out, and Matthes had continually acted as if he wasn't aware of it at all. They hadn't spoken about it, just as they were avoiding any words at all that might force them to make a move. Helene had no intention whatsoever of moving out, but she did want to bring Matthes to the brink of his sense of superiority. To have him engage with her. To have him come back. Not simply back to her, because of course he *was* there, in a way, but back to old, reciprocal ways that hadn't been hollowed out by habit and use. She hadn't really wanted to think thoughts of splitting up, but had continually provoked it with the manner of her retreat. To this end, she had set the stakes high. The Malyutka thrill had got deep into her marrow, all right, but she'd pressed it further and further into herself to keep herself firmly on the ground. Meanwhile her common sense floated up into the air and sometimes just floated off entirely. When she shopped and cooked for herself and the children, but didn't put a plate out on the table for Matthes. When she picked out his washing before putting a load in the machine. When she always felt miserable, rather than angry or resentful, about not being able to make herself understood any other way. Matthes had never commented on any of this – he would just get himself a plate out of the cupboard, and in the end started to do his own shopping. They used a joint account to pay for it, after all! He would do his own washing, but add the children's things if there was room in the machine, and he moved on to taking Lottchen for a walk round the block – or playing football with her, or doing a bit of archery – when he got in from work. It was as if he wanted to make the best possible use of the time he had left, or else, Helene sometimes thought, to win the child's heart so completely that she would want to stay with him after the split. A split that Helene wasn't aiming for at all, though! It was something she lugged around with her like an unnecessary bag, and Matthes was supposed to relieve her of it and just chuck it into the bushes. Then they would finally be able to get down to forgiving each other, while it slowly rotted away. But he didn't relieve her of the bag, which clearly seemed to disgust and repel him, so she ended up pursuing him with it and all *he* could do was run away. He was faster. He was more agile. If he wanted to he could put himself out of her reach for a very long time, even though they sat next to each other at the same table to eat. The wall that separated them on the upper floor of their house became charged with an unbearable heat, so she kept clear of it, always sitting in the corner of her room that was furthest away from it. She was often afraid that the house would catch fire from the heat of the wall and simply burn down, and then, when they were standing homeless in the street, he would think nothing of going off and getting his own flat. So there were always two buckets of water standing ready. For the flowers on the balcony, she said. For the fire, she meant. In the end she was so focused on her herself, and her existence in this house, that when standing outside on the balcony she no longer saw what the weather was like, or what season it was, or whether planes were flying or the bin lorry was there. To say nothing of the world which was happening somewhere out there far away, completely separate from their lives.

Into all of this came the blow that robbed them all of the bit of breath they needed to carry on as before. It released her into unconsciousness, but compelled Matthes to endure everything she no longer had to. She'd slept, Matthes had kept watch. She'll never really know what played out during those weeks. The fact that Matthes had to make sure of her, though – had to show her how things stood for him, and not using words he possibly had no idea were even reaching her: she's suddenly sure of that, and gets the piece of paper out of her pocket from yesterday on which she'd written the three short texts.

'The last one's for you,' she says to a silent Matthes.

The swollen foot only goes down very slowly. But it's time. Once November lowers its foggy grey curtain and takes away her view of the lake... No, she wants to go home. She can't yet manage without the wheelchair, though. The day she bids farewell to it once more will also be the day she asks to bid farewell to this place, she decides, and the thought does her good. What else? The Countdown, she thinks: fourteen days. Today we're on Fourteen, and when it gets to One she wants to be out of here. Or something like that. So, on a piece of paper, she writes down the numbers from fourteen to one in a neat column. Like an army tape measure, something Matthes has told her about. Next to the number one she writes *Lenz*

text – that will be her last test-run for leaving. Until then there are thirteen empty rows to fill. She works it out in her head.

She rings Matthes. Could he bring in her copy of *Lenz* and some secondary literature, whatever he can rustle up in a hurry. Not too much, just the most important texts. Something on Büchner's life, and on Lenz's. Something on psychosis - it doesn't matter what, all she wants is something she can have in front of her and refer to. Furthermore, she'd now only like to have visits once a week. (So only another two in total, she thinks, though Matthes doesn't know that. It's a shame, really, but she can't do anything about it. But then she calls herself to order – after all, a plan of attack doesn't have to be an act of brutality – and at least tells him that it's only for the next two weeks.)

She has to conserve her energy. She's still sleeping an awful lot, going back to bed at least three or four times during the day and never for less than an hour. She's always exhausted when she wakes up and it takes her a good while to get going again. Once she has managed that, her therapy sessions loom. Massage. Swimming. Not much time to work on her Lenz text, then. For Pietro she's writing on a new, blank sheet of paper, which she puts to one side to start with. First and foremost, she wants to write the Lenz text for herself. To force it to crawl out of the undergrowth in her head.

It has to.

It has to!

It only occurs to her on her second or third go at it that Lenz also had to contend with a blow to the brain. But then: she has it.

Ensnared.

◆ ◆ ◆

Matthes is there, and he's brought with him the little old leather-bound Lenz book, an ancient psychiatry textbook and a biography of Büchner. She would like best of all to pack him off again straight away. She would like best of all to pull him close. And he does in fact waver for a moment between her and the door, she can see it clearly. She's uncertain again because of that recent bit of writing – she has no sense of how to evaluate it. It was probably just gobbledygook, though perhaps intelligible even so. For a moment hadn't she herself taken it to be a love poem? She doesn't want to ask him about it.

'Do you want to hear what I think of your writing?'

It's true: he knows her. The paralysed right side of her face can't cancel out her expression, which he knows how to read. She doesn't say anything. She trembles.

Suddenly he's gasping for air – is he gasping? – and his eyes are leaking. Why are his eyes leaking? What's going on here? By the time she realises he's crying he's already clutching her, and squeezing her so hard she thinks her own eyes might pop out. She has only heard him cry once before. That too had sounded like he was gasping for air, and could be heard even through a concrete wall in their last flat before Arberstrasse. (The cat had eaten Bengt's budgie, which unleashed a whole tsunami of tears.) 'Good,' is all he can say, 'Good.' Then his head creeps under her top, and he cries until there are no tears left.

There's nothing left for her to do, either.

She sits tight until he has no tears left.

Oh, the two of them – what a pair they make.

She doesn't say that, though.

Afterwards he goes with her to physiotherapy. The physio

has asked her to bring a family member along, so they can be shown some tricks and tips for how things should be done.

◆ ◆ ◆

She immerses herself, becomes engrossed. She can work best at night, because that's when she has enough peace and quiet. She breaks off to sleep but then wakes up again. She is taking a risk, the outcome of which is uncertain. She doesn't want to think that she'll probably never be able to write literary texts again, but the prospect threatens. She can sense it and wants to know for sure. What she knows already is that she has difficulty reading and understanding. For every sentence of the Büchner biography she needs an endless amount of time, or so it seems to her. When she's in total despair, she calls it a day, but not without giving herself some encouragement. ('That really wasn't bad at all. It was a start, anyway. Something you weren't even thinking of two months ago. Pretty good, in fact!') Things get easier with the *Lenz* book: she knows and remembers it, so the sentences become familiar again more quickly, even though it's a very long time since she read it. Twenty years? Twenty-five? She creates files, makes notes. She goes down for meals but no longer sees what's on her plate. She gets through her therapy sessions, and always has her bag with her, with the Lenz and Büchner texts in it, wherever she goes. She reads incessantly. 'She's a phenomenon,' the male nurse says, but she doesn't hear that. She makes tea, she drinks and she reads, until she goes to sleep. She's still sleeping a lot. She wakes up, throws cold water on her face, dries it, and positions her wheelchair by the window during the day or under the lamp at night. She writes, she reads, she makes notes. She can't write fast with her left hand, even on the laptop, but she's glad about that because she can't think fast, either. She thinks. Does she think about being discharged? Less often, but definitely sometimes. Wondering when to mention it to the senior ward staff, and putting it off day after day. She wants to be sure that she can walk. When Matthes comes again, before he's even through the door she's asking him about Büchner's thesis, in which he'd written about the cranial nerves of a fish from the cyprinid family: 'Have you heard of it? What do you know?' Ultimately she finds it comforting to hear that no, Matthes doesn't know anything about it; did she think everyone knows everything? Probably. Probably she has no way of gauging what people do and don't know – she has to learn the art of *not knowing* and of being content with that, and learn where knowledge is hiding. The same old story. What's going to come out of it, she still doesn't know: she just writes, and keeps on writing – in defiance of blind fury, and the banning and breaking of words – because she'd promised Pietro. (In reality she hadn't promised him anything, merely agreeing to try – she knows that.) Her hair seems to grow quicker when she thinks a lot, she thinks - there's already two or three centimetres of grey now sprouting from her scalp. And she's getting slimmer by the day, so the brain work must require energy, too. She's pleased about that. She's having to use a firmly-knotted bit of elastic to hold her tracksuit bottoms up, and has prescribed the other pair a belt bought at the occupational therapy table-top sale. (She'll certainly never be *a slender girl*, but not being fat is a long-held dream she'd always pushed aside when faced with the realities of everyday life.)

It's time.

Time to get to work.

On the flab, on grief and sorrow, on stagnation and weakness. Best foot forward – and maybe one day it will be back in a normal shoe.

◆ ◆ ◆

C:Helo2/Ecstasy.doc

The Ecstasy Agent of the Lord

In the winter of 1835-36, Georg Büchner was in Strasbourg, working on his medical thesis on the cranial nerves of a fish from the cyprinid family. At around the same time – shortly before his death, it has to be said – he wrote a narrative that was open at both ends, and which read like an exposed nerve: dissected in minute detail, and describing with great precision everything it was possible to see. With his scientific eye, Büchner pores over a three-week-long episode in the life of Sturm und Drang *poet Jakob Michael Reinhold Lenz, who had come to the very same city a good half-century before. Lenz did not go to Strasbourg of his own free will, nor would it be correct to say he was forced. He was brought there by an altruistic pastor named Oberlin, from the latter's home in the Northern Vosges: Lenz was suffering from psychosis, and Oberlin no longer knew what to do with him. Büchner notes down very precisely everything that was recorded about those three weeks in 1778, from the twentieth of January to the eighth of February, when Lenz was residing with Oberlin in the district of Ban-de-la-Roche. No work of fiction, the tale is nonetheless one of the most progressive narratives in German literature. A long-running success. A soldering lamp whose glow melts and fuses all that was previously unwieldy and incomprehensible. Such as: a man made ill by his inability to look reality in the eye, because he is trapped inside without knowing it – in the very eyeball itself – and looking out. A man driven mad by the very clear feeling that, inside the very eyeball of reality, his life's purpose is managing just fine without a god – and yet who still seems compelled, with a gaze guided by God, to search for his purpose in life. An 'ecstasy agent' who sees the idealism of art as 'the most shameful contempt for human nature', and therefore a glorifying narcotic, but who in life never manages to grasp reality unless through self-inflicted, physical pain. Oberlin's devout Christian model of the world no longer offers him a way in, but nor has Oberlin proposed a rationalistic, realistic alternative, so that all the world turns into hieroglyphics...*

In the opening scene, Lenz walks towards the village of Waldbach in Ban-de-la-Roche: 'He kept on walking, completely indifferent. He did not care at all for the journey – uphill one moment, downhill the next. He never felt tiredness, merely that it was disagreeable at times not to be able to walk upside down.' Upside down is how the unborn child lies inside its mother. Lenz seems to yearn for this unborn state, and we, born since, should come to respect him as a man before his time. The curtain rises.

The whole thing seems completely bonkers. How on earth had she managed it? To infiltrate two centuries, and all the way from a neurology clinic! The only other time she has ever felt as comfortable as this in a state of exhaustion was after the children's births. It's a good introduction for a reading of Lenz, she reckons. She has feverishly copied it on to the floppy-disk with the Angora rabbit eye. She feels depleted, but her strength has been handed over to the prologue – she can feel it as she reads it over and over again. In between she closes her eyes and tries to recap – something she always used to be able to do with a piece of writing she had just worked her way through – but that's asking too much, she can't do it. She nearly gets angry about it, but in the end her joy is able to stifle the resentment.

Matthes is to print it out and send it to Pietro. Matthes was there again today, for the second time in these last two weeks. She has set her discharge in motion for the day after tomorrow. Matthes already knew about it – the clinic had informed him straight away. Helene is walking: the rollator has been back in her room since yesterday, and her swollen foot has gone down in its frame. Yes, it's still delicate, but she'll manage, she says to herself, especially as she's going to keep the brace fastened round her leg. Now, though, after a last wash and clean of her teeth, she unfastens it.

Sleep comes quickly, deep and dreamless.

Getting ready for the discharge meeting. Blood pressure, weight. The usual.

She is called into the consultant's office.

The expression on the faces of those standing around her (student, nurse, physio, junior doctor, consultant) is more smug than pleased about her clearly adequate efforts to find her feet in her new circumstances. It doesn't bother her – they belong at a different point in this story, she thinks. No, she will probably never be able to raise her arm again, the doctor says in response to her enquiry. His tone is cautionary, strange. Her tone is unassuming, equally strange.

They chat about the coming months. New fittings and alterations to the house (a step to help her get into the shower, grab rails next to the toilet). Sleep, which she is to allow herself as soon as it comes knocking. Her pension.

Her pension –

Helene wants to reply, but her air escapes faster than she can hold it in. Talk of pensions can wait, but she can't. She has no idea why or how she's meant to stick it out here until tomorrow – she wants to go, to get away from here. For some reason they can't seem to produce a consensus, which bothers her in a way that reminds her of before. She sometimes used to start *fluttering*, as she called it, when she was very obviously rambling on without paying attention to anyone else. Only here she's hardly saying anything, and it's the others who are rambling on and ignoring her.

When she's back outside the room again, she has no idea what else was discussed.

She remembers something and knocks again.

'Yes?'

'Yes, sorry... I've got something here for the consultant, with a personal dedication...'

The nurse has taken the book off her. Cursory smile; door shut again.

Okay, fine. *The Representative* will understand.

The last evening, and a pensive mood.

She has been thinking about Peter Preissler again, and has

silently asked him for forgiveness for not telling Matthes anything about him.

She has given out goodbyes like biscuits, and at some point the tin was empty so she hurriedly retreated to her room. She didn't go to supper – clean out of goodbyes.

She stands at the window. It's getting dark earlier every day. In the twilight she suddenly sees herself standing on the balcony at Arberstrasse, in the middle of summer, leaning on the handrail. Stubbing out her cigarette. Looking round, because she thinks someone has just fired an elastic band at her which has hit her on the head. No pain. (Not yet.) But the world is being chopped up before her eyes into diverging tableaux. A moment ago, the woman and child had been visible on the left-hand edge of the picture. Now, though, they are disappearing off to the right, and she can't say how they got there.

Her knees are giving way.

Sheer willpower gets her down the stairs.

Matthes is sitting in the living room, reading. She sits down quietly in the armchair next to his, and he looks at her enquiringly.

'I'm dying,' she says, calmly.

'You're not dying,' he says, calmly.

Naked Eye Publishing
A fresh approach

Naked Eye Publishing is an independent not-for-profit micro-press intent on publishing quality poetry and literature, including in translation. We are also developing a 'Potted Theses' series: academic theses rewritten for the general reader.

A particular focus is translation. We aim to take a midwife role in facilitating the translation of works that have until now been disregarded by English-language publishing. We will be happy if we function purely as an initial stepping-stone both for overlooked writers and first-time literary translators.

Each of us at Naked Eye is a volunteer, competent and professional in our work practice, and not intending to make a profit for the press. We see ourselves as part of the revolution in book publishing, embodying the newly levelled playing field, sidestepping the publishing establishment to produce beautiful books at an affordable price with writers gaining maximum benefit from sales.

nakedeyepublishing.co.uk

Lightning Source UK Ltd.
Milton Keynes UK
UKHW020139130321
380247UK00007B/383